Twisted Alibis

GHOST TOWN TRILOGY
BOOK ONE

VM RHEAULT

❀ Created with Vellum

About the Book

Sheppard

Mourning my bandmate's tragic death and the loss of my marriage consumes me. I have nothing to live for . . . until our manager hires a life coach to push me back into the recording studio.

From the moment I meet Olivia, I'm attracted to her, and I pray desperately she can help me.

I might be the frontman for the hottest rock band on earth, but it doesn't stop the siren from singing her sweet, deadly song, luring me to her watery hell. I've had arenas of fans screaming my name, but I can't get out of bed unless it's to pour myself another drink.

To put the past behind me once and for all, I need to find out if Derrick's death was really an accident.

Even with Olivia's love, I'm not sure I can handle what I find out.

Olivia

I didn't know what to expect moving in with Sheppard Carpenter, Ghost Town's lead singer, but it wasn't a sad, weary man trying to keep his head above water.

His depression scares me, but falling in love with him scares me more. I've already loved one man who struggled and lost, but I can't stop myself from doing it again.

He's my client, and when the summer's over and he's recording his next album, my job will be finished and I'll go home.

Sheppard's the hottest rockstar in the world, and once he's back on top, he won't have room for me.

I'll step aside.

He'll belong to his fans.

He'll never belong to me.

Chapter One

Olivia

My engagement ring sparkles in the sunlight. I don't need it anymore, but I can't bear to take it off. I twist it around my finger as I gather my thoughts. Los Angeles stretches before me, billboards and palm trees. I don't have either in my little Minnesota town, and I want to go home. I should never have let Agatha talk me into this.

My Golden Retriever, Scout, whines. She's sitting at my feet and is in tune to my feelings. It's been a rough few years, and they are far from over.

"Miss Bloom?"

I turn from the large window and meet the eyes of the man who said my name. Dalton West, Sheppard Carpenter and Ghost Town's manager, leans against a massive oak desk. I like him. More than I do a couple of the others sitting in this room.

"I don't do that anymore." I took this meeting as a courtesy. My literary agent convinced me to at least talk to Mr. West, but so far what I've heard scares me, and I want nothing to do with any of it.

"I understand, but . . ." He sighs. "Miss Bloom, Olivia, if I may, we're talking last resorts here. Shep's my best friend and I've worked with him and Ghost Town since they were singing in crappy dive bars in exchange for burger baskets. We grew up in this business together, and I can't just let him sink."

Last resorts. Yeah, that's what I am all right.

Offering her support, Scout nudges my leg with the side of her head.

"What makes you think he'll want me there?"

Dalton—apparently we're on a first name basis—scoffs. "He won't. I'm sure you've had difficult clients before."

"Yes, but they were never forced to use my services. I can't do my job if he's going to fight me every step of the way."

Dalton sets his jaw. "He has no choice. Ghost Town signed a contract with their label for another record, and they want to collect. I don't have to tell you there's a lot of money riding on cleaning him up."

I don't care about the money Ghost Town will earn in album sales and ticket and souvenir purchases when they decide to tour again, and I'm not here for the money Dalton's offering me to work with Sheppard to ensure that it happens. I'm here because I can't get the picture of the rockstar out of my head. Like my worst nightmare decided to materialize right in front of my face.

When I was a little girl, I was scared of the monsters under my bed, but my daddy would say, "What do we do to monsters, Livvy?"

He would scrape his whiskers over my cheek and I would giggle, "Love them and watch them bloom."

A play on our last name, and he would grin. "That's right, my girl."

My father was a pastor for a small Presbyterian church a few towns over from where I live now. He donated his time to an all-male prison praying with death-row inmates or counseling those who wanted a better life when they were free of their bars, until one day one of those monsters was let out on parole and shot him while he stood in the church's front yard during an outdoor service.

I was old enough to realize monsters don't hide under beds.

They're brave enough to look you in the eye.

One of them is glaring at me now, and she meets my gaze across Dalton's office. Melody Bancroft is Sheppard Carpenter's ex-wife. She's not as light and as cheerful as her name would lead you to believe. She's beautiful, as any supermodel would be, but she's lived a hard life of fame and fortune, and it shows in the unrelenting green of her eyes. I don't know why she's here, but I don't ask. She has more of a right than I do. Maybe she still loves him and she's hoping for a reconciliation. I don't know why they're divorced, and I didn't care enough to find out before flying to LA. She'll either be a help or a hindrance, which one remains to be seen.

I'm close to cracking, and Dalton knows this. "If you come out of retirement for anyone, Miss Bloom, please consider doing it for Shep."

I didn't retire voluntarily, and I'm not eager to resume my career. I didn't quite follow in my father's footsteps; I help people bloom in a different way.

Well, I helped. Past tense.

The others in the office are edgy and they fidget, waiting for me to acquiesce. Reggie Adler shares a loveseat with Miss Bancroft, and while they must be less than strangers, they act like they barely know each other. He's Ghost Town's music producer and he has a vested interest in their next album. Two other men sit in the back of Dalton's spacious office wearing ripped jeans, black t-shirts, leather wristbands, scruff, and messy hair. Eddie Conrad is Ghost Town's drummer, and

Brock Farris is the band's lead guitar. What I know of rock bands is from seeing bands like Train and Smash Mouth at the state fair when I was in college. It's not that I don't like music, but I'm from Minnesota. There's not much of a chance to meet rockstars, and from what I've seen today, I don't think I've missed much.

"I'll give you a week. If we're not compatible, I'm leaving. I won't put up with abuse, emotional or physical, and I won't tolerate violence. It doesn't matter if it's directed at me or not. If I don't feel safe, I won't stay. That simple."

Dalton exhales. "He won't hurt you."

I've been sworn at, cussed out, watched temper tantrums and meltdowns. One client threw a bottle of wine at me, and I pressed charges. Clients would be livid when I shoved a mirror into their faces and forced them to see who they are. There's always anger when someone sees what they don't want to see. I don't know what Sheppard Carpenter is hiding from at his beach house under the booze and probably drugs, but when I find out and confront him, there will be fury.

"Don't make promises he can't keep," I say, and Dalton has the grace to blush.

I glance at Melody and search for a sign her ex-husband abused her in any way, but her face is smooth, either with truth or Botox. I'm on my own, except for Scout.

"And if you can convince him to work with you, you'll stay the three months?"

"Yes."

Dalton nods. "That's all I can ask for."

"That's good, because that's all you're going to get." I don't mean to be curt, but I don't want to be here. I'm terrified, and my brittle tone gives me away. I don't want Sheppard Carpenter to be my responsibility. I'm not ready for it, and maybe I never was.

Dalton's not offended. He could admire what sounds like a take-no-bullshit attitude. Tipping his head in acknowledgement, he says, "I'll give you a ride to his house."

"That won't be necessary. I'll order a car." I shake with nerves, but I lift my chin when he opens his mouth to protest. I'm not scared to meet Sheppard Carpenter, but I have travel anxiety and I've never been to California before. Dalton picked me up at the airport and drove me across LA to his office. Sheppard's beach house is located in Malibu, wherever that is from here. The last time I saw the ocean, I visited my grandma before she passed away. She lived in a retirement community in Jacksonville, Florida. I don't think this will be a similar experience. "He does know I'm coming?"

He nods.

Good. My knocking on Sheppard's door won't be a surprise. "Then it's best if I arrive alone. If he thinks I'm scared, he won't respect me or take me seriously." That, at least, I can say with confidence. None of my previous clients would have trusted me if I didn't act like I knew what I was doing. They paid me for my experience and expertise. I was never quite so out of my element as I am now, but I can't afford to let it affect how I do my job.

Before Dalton escorts me downstairs, I approach Eddie and Brock. Maybe I would be intimidated if I'd known who they were before Agatha asked me to consider taking on Sheppard Carpenter, but until this afternoon, I could have passed them on the sidewalk and not had one glimmer of an idea as to who they were. "From what I understand, you've been friends with Mr. Carpenter most of your lives. Eventually, you'll be a part of his recovery. I hope I can count on you to help me."

Eddie shakes my hand, and so does Brock, but he grips it even after our hands stop moving through the air. He studies my face, and I study his in return, his whiskers turning grey with age, lines crowding his faded brown eyes. The expression in them is kind, though, shadowed with loss. Loss of friendship, loss of time. "He's going to make things very difficult for you, Miss Bloom."

I extract my hand, and for the first time since I boarded the plane at the Minneapolis/St. Paul airport, my heartbeat slows. "I wouldn't expect anything less."

Chapter Two

Sheppard

I don't know what time it is. Don't know what day it is. One is the same as the next, seagulls squawking, the waves kissing the shore. I should have chosen somewhere else to lay low, but if I had, I'd be dead. The massive expanse of the ocean is the only thing keeping me alive. When I wade into the blue, breathe in the salty air. The current tugs at my legs, the siren tempting me just a little farther, a little farther. She sings, luring me to my death as her song fills my empty soul, and for those moments, the sand swirling around my feet, I'm where I'm supposed to be.

It never lasts, but those seconds are what get me through the day.

I roll over and block out the sun with an arm over my eyes. It doesn't stop the flashes of the last few years from blinding me. My ex-wife, my bandmates, my brother and mother.

Those times are gone, and now there's nothing but pain and remnants of lyrics I have yet to write.

I should get up and see what time it is. Maybe fix a meal. Like the day, I don't know when I ate last, but I'm not hungry.

What I'm starving for I won't find in my kitchen.

I roll over and cover my head with a pillow. There's no reason to crawl out of bed.

I'll exist in this room on nothing, and maybe one morning, God willing, I won't wake up.

Chapter Three

Olivia

The ride to Malibu is thirty minutes, the driver said, depending on traffic, and I sit in the back of a brand new SUV with Scout next to me. The young girl wearing a pink and white San Francisco 49ers baseball cap who drives for the transportation app didn't mind when Scout climbed onto the seat, and that will earn her an extra tip.

On the sidewalk outside his office, Dalton gave me an envelope that contained a debit card for household purchases such as grocery delivery and cleaning supplies and a list of places I could order from. I'm not familiar with the area, and if I'm confined to Sheppard's beach house, I may not see much besides his four walls and the beach, either.

"You'll keep me updated?" he asked as the SUV pulled up to the curb.

"I will, but you have to give me space to do my job. You can't force Sheppard into wellness, Mr. West. All I can do is guide him and listen if he wants to talk. There may not even be anything 'wrong' with him," I said, using air quotes. "This could be the way he wants to live his life."

"You'll change your opinion when you see him," he said, helping the driver store my two suitcases into the back of the truck. "Thank you for doing this."

He shook my hand, his grip firm and warm, and I said, "Don't thank me yet. Things will get worse before they get better. If they do."

Dalton watched the truck drive away with me in it, and I lost sight of him when we turned a corner.

We drive toward Malibu, and I pull out the picture that persuaded me to say yes. When Agatha stopped by my little house, I knew what she wanted to talk to me about was serious. I don't have contact information online anymore. After I retired, I pulled it all down, and the only way a determined person can contact me now is through the publishing house that published my self-help book who will then give the inquiring person Agatha's name. Dalton jumped through a lot of hoops to get me to show up at his office.

The photo is a paparazzi shot of Sheppard standing thigh-deep in the water, his hands hanging limply by his sides. The utter despair rolling off him broke what was left of my heart, but even that wouldn't have been enough to convince me to take the job. It was the tears on his cheeks. This strong man who can hold a stadium of adoring fans in the palm of his hand, crying . . . It did me in. I knew what he was thinking at that moment; something I have felt many times in the past three years.

I rub my engagement ring, and Scout headbutts my hand. I slide my fingers over her nose instead.

After another fifteen minutes, the driver slows and pulls off the road and into a driveway of a black and white two-stall garage connected to a two-story house. The line of beach houses squished next to each other is at least a mile long, not wasting an inch of space. "Are you sure this is the place?" I ask, catching the driver's eyes in the rearview mirror.

She looks at me over her shoulder. "Yeah. Everyone knows where Sheppard Carpenter lives."

"The black and white garage?"

"Yep. Do you want help with your suitcases?"

"No, I'm okay. Thank you."

I let Scout out and she sniffs around the driveway, her tail wagging. I unload my suitcases from the back and slam the door shut. The driver lifts her hand in goodbye and merges into the sparse traffic.

There's a door to the left of the stalls that lets into the garage, and another cut into one of the concrete walls separating his property from his neighbors'. I wonder if he knows everyone who lives along this stretch of beach. A house like this must cost millions of dollars, but even without seeing the view yet, I bet it's worth every penny.

I can hear the waves from here, and the tangy scent of saltwater tickles my nose. It's cooler than I thought California would be in June, the air unexpectedly dry. I was prepared for the Floridian heat and humidity, but the mild temperature is a pleasant surprise.

"You look lost. Can I help?"

The man walking toward me seems familiar, but that could be my overactive imagination. Just because I'm in California doesn't mean there are movie stars around every corner. He's dressed in running shorts and a muscle t-shirt drenched in sweat, and he's squinting against the sun. He's tan, and his white teeth glint when he smiles.

"Is it that blatant?" I ask, trying to sound amused and not stressed out. Dalton said Sheppard is expecting me, but that could mean anything.

"We don't get too many women out here dressed the way you are with two suitcases and a cute dog. You're standing behind Sheppard Carpenter's house. Do you have business with him?"

"I do. Well, his manager, Dalton West, hired me to—"

"You're Olivia Bloom, I recognize you now," he says, holding out his hand. "I'm Jeffrey Morgan, one of Shep's neighbors. Nice to meet you. My significant other is a big fan of your work. She's read your book at least three times. She'll be thrilled to meet you."

"Oh," I say, shaking his hand. "Thank you. I didn't think my reputation made it this far west."

Jeffrey winks. "Thank Oprah."

I wince. "That was four years ago."

He nods. "We were sorry to hear you retired. That must have been a difficult decision."

His name clicks into place. "No more difficult than yours, I would imagine." Jeffrey Morgan earned his claim to fame as a child star on a popular sitcom in the late seventies to early eighties. He's Sheppard's age, and as an adult, decided he preferred sitting behind the camera not unlike Ron Howard.

"Sometimes we're lucky and figure out where we're meant to be."

"Sometimes. This is Scout. She travels with me."

Jeffrey drops to his haunches and briskly rubs Scout's neck. He lets her lick his cheek, already friends. "I'm guessing you wouldn't mind a little help? Shep know you're visiting?"

Visiting isn't the way I would describe my role in Sheppard's life, but I say, "Mr. West said he does. Whether he likes it or not is the question of the week."

"Let's find out. I was just coming back from a run, and I have a few minutes, though fireworks weren't on my agenda for today."

I stop him and grab his arm. "How is he?"

Jeffrey meets my gaze, his dark blue eyes warm and filled with concern. "Let's just say, Olivia, I'm glad you're here."

Jeffrey carries my suitcases and uses the garage door to let us inside. We walk through the cool, dark space, one stall housing a sleek convertible, and at the top of a short staircase, he pushes a door open that leads into the house. He sets my suitcases near what I assume is a coat closet and leads me into a spacious kitchen. Beer and liquor bottles cover every inch of space, and dirty dishes are piled in the sink. A table that can seat ten sits near a wall of glass that looks over the beach, the surface covered in unopened newspapers. Comfortable furniture fills the living room, and a bottle-blonde woman is sleeping on the couch.

"Dalton didn't say Sheppard is seeing someone," I murmur as the blonde rolls over. A decorative throw blanket moves with her, exposing one of her breasts.

"He's not in a relationship, if that's what you mean," he says.

"Oh." I try not to grimace. It's not for me to judge how people self-medicate, only help them see they don't have to.

Jeffrey strides across the room and swivels a matching recliner. It holds a sleeping brunette, not any more clothed than the blonde. Her long, lean leg pokes out from another fringed throw, revealing her hip and half a butt cheek. She's not wearing panties.

Curiously, Scout sniffs her foot and licks her toes.

The woman giggles in her sleep.

"Let's see if there are any more surprises." He gestures me to follow him.

I walk through the living room, my heels clicking against the hardwood floor. I want to look out the window at the water, but Jeffrey is already gone, and I need to keep up. This might be the only tour I'll get.

"Shep has his own recording studio here, though I can't remember the last time he used it," he says, pointing to a large, glassed-in room that's equipped with a drum set, guitars, several microphones, headphones, and in another closed off area, a computer and what looks to be a complicated sound and mixing system. "The band would stay and riff and brainstorm for days. Some of their best work came out of that room. Do you listen to Ghost Town?"

I smile painfully. "I'm more of a Bananarama kind of girl."

He rolls his eyes. "Crawl out of the eighties, Taylor Dayne." We walk down a hallway, and he opens a door. "You'll probably need the laundry room. You're going to live here?"

"Yeah, from what I know."

"Shep doesn't have housekeeping. Ever since he moved out here full-time, he's been very private."

"I signed an NDA in Dalton's office." I'm not offended. I've signed many a non-disclosure agreement. People don't want to admit they need help and are paying someone for that service. I don't mind.

Jeffrey rubs my arm. "That's not what I meant. He's closed himself off. He's a rockstar worth half a billion dollars, and he washes his own skivvies. He needs help, Olivia."

"Because he likes to do his own laundry?"

"Because he can go for weeks at a time without seeing a single soul."

"I find that hard to believe," I say, tipping my head in the direction of the living room. He's seen two somebodies in the past twelve hours.

"Okay then, someone who matters."

"That makes more sense. Well, if he doesn't kick me out, he's got me for three months."

Jeffrey nods. "The bedrooms are upstairs. He sleeps in the master suite, and there are two guest bedrooms. Come on."

White metal stairs cut the back of the house in half. The rooms are airy and bright, the light hardwood floors and cream walls bouncing the sunlight around. The master suite is the size of the two guest bedrooms combined.

"This is beautiful," I say, poking my head into one of the rooms. It has the same view of the beach the kitchen and the living room have, and the bedroom behind it offers a view of the highway and the rocky hills beyond. A bathroom connects the rooms. If what Jeffrey says is true and Sheppard doesn't have guests, I'll have a bathroom to myself, and that pleases me very much.

Scout noses at Sheppard's door. She wants in.

Jeffrey cracks it open and peers into the room first, I suppose to make sure I'm not going to get an eyeful. When he sees that Sheppard is appropriately dressed, he pushes it open wider, and Scout hurries in, her nails scraping against the floor.

Clothes are draped everywhere, and bottles crowd the nightstand. The room smells slightly of beer and body odor.

Sheppard's sleeping on a king bed, his arm covering his eyes. He's wearing boxers and a t-shirt and needs a shower. Tattoos cover his arms. He doesn't look like a rockstar. He looks like a man down on his luck, and I guess after you strip away the number one hit songs, the money, and the models, that's all he is.

Scout jumps onto the bed and rests her head on his chest.

"Will she be okay?" Jeffrey asks, backing away from the doorway.

"She knows a lost soul when she sees one. She's a therapy dog. She'll probably get Sheppard to open up easier and faster than I will." I follow him down the stairs and to the kitchen. There's a bathroom on the lower level that I missed, and I think, if Sheppard doesn't turn this into a living hell, I might like staying here for the next little while.

"Is there anything else I can do?" Jeffrey asks, resting his hand on the back of one of the stools at the breakfast bar. "Need help with those two in there?"

"No, I can kick them out easily enough. If you'll show me where the recycling goes and tell me when the garbage pickup is, I'd be grateful. You said there's no maid service, and part of my job is creating a clean and pleasant environment for my clients if they need it."

"Let me give you my number, too. We live next door that way," he says, pointing east. "Shep doesn't get out much, and we miss having him for dinner. My partner would also love to meet you. She was so disappointed when you took your blog down."

"Thanks, I appreciate that. Sometimes life punches you in the face and you have to reevaluate what you were doing before you can get back up. I can relate to Sheppard, in a way. It's easy to open your eyes one day and realize you have no idea where in the hell you are."

He squeezes my shoulder. "From what I know of you and your work, you're the best person for the job. Shep's lucky Dalton cares."

Jeffrey and I swap numbers and he shows me where the garbage and recycling bins are in the garage. Lifting a hand in goodbye, he lets himself out through the patio and jogs over the sand to his own house. It will be nice to know someone so close. When we said our goodbyes, Dalton was sure to remind me I could call or text if needed, but he's my boss, and what I do from this moment on isn't his business. Everything will stay between Sheppard and me unless he sees fit to share.

Reluctantly, I wake the two women sleeping in the living room, but they don't cause the scene I was expecting. In embarrassed silence, they dress and hurry into the driveway. I watch from the garage door as they wait for their ride. Once they're gone, I dig through my purse for an elastic and pull my hair into a ponytail. I need to shower and change, but I want to meet Sheppard looking like I'm here to put in some serious time. In my sheath dress, I'll appear more professional. Once I've made the impression I want, I can loosen up a bit, but for now, when Sheppard finds me washing dishes, I'm wearing my dress and humming "Love Will Lead You Back," bubbles hiding the reminder on my finger that my fiancé is never coming back to me.

Chapter Four

Sheppard

I wake up with tongue in my mouth, and that's not as enticing as it sounds. My hands grip fur and when I try to roll over, I can't go anywhere.

I groan and crack my eyes open for the second time this morning. A different sight greets me, and sad brown eyes meet mine as she licks my cheek, narrowly missing my mouth, though I don't know why she bothered. She's already been there, done that.

Something niggles in the back of my mind, something Dalt told me last week. Something that I brushed aside because I didn't think he'd be brave, or foolhardy, enough to go through with it, but it appears I was wrong.

Searching through the fog in my brain, I try to come up with what he threatened, but it's all a hazy daydream of harsh words and anger. He took the coward's way out, called instead of stopping by, and . . . and nothing. I got nothing after that because I was so furious I threw my cell against the wall and drank myself into a stupor.

It didn't have anything to do with a pretty Golden Retriever, her tongue poking from her mouth with a promise of another kiss. I think I would have remembered a dog.

I sit up and scrub my hands over my face. I need to get rid of whoever's downstairs. I don't want anyone here. I'm doing just fine on my own. I want to be alone, goddammit.

The dog jumps onto the floor and sits, waiting for me.

I crawl out of bed and snag a pair of dirty jeans off the floor. My bones creak and my muscles are tight. Too many stage theatrics, too many leaps into the mosh pit. No one tells you the stupid shit you do at thirty will haunt you for the rest of your life. I certainly didn't know that jumping off a dais on stage at a London concert during our Blood-Red Promises tour would fuck up my knees to the point that even two knee replacements wouldn't take the pain away.

Nothing does, but that's a different kind of pain.

I follow the dog downstairs, and a petite brunette woman is standing in my kitchen washing dishes. She's already cleaned the living room, kicked out the two leeches who talked their way inside when a neighbor a few houses down had a party. I watched from the patio. I would have been welcome, even if I hadn't been personally invited, but I kept to myself. The women noticed me as they walked along the beach and offered to bring the party to my house. I didn't decline.

In a spurt of anger, I trot down the rest of the stairs and through the living room. I push my body against hers, trapping her against the sink. "Just what in the hell do you think you're doing?" I growl into her ear.

The dog whines, batting my leg with her paw. She wants me to let her owner go, but the only place she's going is back to where she came from.

"My job?" she asks, her hands stilling under the sudsy water.

She's tiny, five foot two, maybe three, and I tower over her, a foot taller. My body curls around hers, and I pull her to me, my hand to her stomach, my lips brushing her neck. "You need to leave."

"We should talk first, and then if you don't want me here, you have every right to ask me to go."

I laugh and say sarcastically, "Thank you for giving me permission to kick you out of my own fucking house." I inhale. "What's that scent?"

"Fear?" she asks, her pulse throbbing under my lips.

"No," I say, frustrated. She's not scared of me, and I would know fear if I smelled it. No, what this is, I like it. Spicy, but with a hint of softness somehow. I breathe deeply, my nose near her ear. I'm treading near the pervert line, feeling up a woman when I don't even know her name, needing to know what scent is saturating her skin. I'm going out of my fucking mind.

"It's lavender, Mr. Carpenter. It's calming."

I release her, shoving her away from me, and she does nothing but rinse her hands, dry them, and turn around.

"Have a cup of coffee," she suggests, watching me.

She's beautiful, her hair the color of sand, the lightest brown, her darker eyebrows delicately arched above bluish-green eyes. Her lips are plump, and her dark pink lipstick is rubbing off. She's slim, wearing a dress the color of her hair, and she's barefoot, her toenails painted a light pink.

In arousal, the blood whooshing around my head in anger rushes to a different place, and I want nothing more than to turn her back around, yank up her dress, and find out how tight she is. What those two women wanted to give me last night is nothing compared to what fucking this little sea nymph would feel like.

She points to my coffeemaker, the carafe full of fresh coffee. A platinum ring glitters on her left hand, and like a bucket of cold water poured over my head, that chills me. I don't cheat and wouldn't fuck a woman who had no qualms about doing it.

Mimicking her, I point too, but toward my door. "Leave."

"I said I would, but we talk first."

"Fuck that."

Her eyes flick to my living room. "I think you've had enough meaningless sex for one day. Call Mr. West, I'm here on his dime. If he says I can go, I will. If he wants me here, we'll talk, and after that, if *you* don't want me here, I'll go. You're in control, Mr. Carpenter, even if you don't feel like you are."

Every sentence, every word, hits me straight in the gut. "What are you, a shrink?"

"Close, but nothing so unsavory. I'm a life coach. I'm here to help you, that's all."

"We'll see about that." I whip around and run up the stairs. Her dog follows me, and frantically, I search my bedroom for my phone. I don't see it among the beer bottles and dirty clothes. Hell, one of the women last night could have stolen it for the pictures and information I keep on it. In a panic, I run down the stairs and into the living room, the woman's dog thinking we're playing a fun game of chase. The living room is cleared of bottles and dirty clothes, but I don't see my phone anywhere.

"Are you looking for this?" she asks, holding up my black iPhone. It was sitting on the breakfast bar the entire time. "I found it under the couch while I was cleaning. You should be more careful. You never know when you'll have an emergency and need to call someone."

Violently, I rip it from her grasp and let myself onto the patio, the dog following me. I nearly trap her tail when I viciously slide the door shut, but she hurries through just in time. I sink to the wooden planks. I would never forgive myself if I was an asshole and hurt her dog. She butts her wet nose against my cheek, and I force back tears. I just want to be left alone.

She can see me, and I don't want her to watch when I talk to Dalt. I know what he's going to say, and what he says I should listen to. Dalton West has been Ghost Town's manager since day one. When we were jerks in college deciding to start a band for the hell of it, Dalt chose to manage us because he has no musical talent and can't sing worth a damn. Little did we know, he would become more important than all of us.

I stumble down the steps and into the sand. The dog follows me, and I look over my shoulder to see if the woman is watching, but she's not. She trusts me with her dog, and for some reason, I get angry over that too. I'm nothing to her, and she trusts me with her dog.

Dalt answers before the line even rings, and I can't force any words out.

"Shep," he says when I don't say anything. "I know this is about Olivia."

That's her name. It's pretty, like she is.

"I don't want her here."

Dalt sighs, the sound coming through the phone like static. "I know you don't, but come on. Look at how you've been living since—"

"Don't fucking say it."

"If you can't talk about it, how are you going to move past it? The band's okay without—"

"The band's nothing without him."

Dalt's quiet, and I suck in a breath. I didn't mean that, not the way it sounded. We'd do okay without our bass guitarist, hire someone else, add the chords during editing, whatever, we'd be okay, but that's not what I meant. The tangible meaning of the words.

"I hope you didn't say something like that to Eddie and Brock. You've all put your time in. It isn't fair to them or to the work you've done to whittle the band's existence down to one person. It doesn't work that way."

"I know, and it's not fair to you either, but it doesn't feel right anymore."

"Okay."

I swallow. "Okay what?" I look around for Olivia's dog, and she's sniffing at the surf, bounding away when the waves get too close.

"Okay, then that's it. Isn't that what you're saying? I'll tell Eddie and Brock the bad news, you'll fork over the damages when you don't deliver your next album. You can afford it, so that's not a big deal. Send Olivia home, and that's it. I'll miss you, Shep. We had a good run, but even the best things come to an end."

When I don't say anything, the phone beeps, indicating he disconnected.

I can't catch my breath, and I sink to my knees in the sand. Olivia's dog runs to me, pressing her body against mine, and I lower to the ground and hide my face in her neck. That wasn't where I was going, was it? Break up the band. We all go our separate ways, but I don't know where my way is.

The sun's setting when I stagger to my feet. Olivia's dog kept me company, and she's waiting for me when I let myself into the house.

"I wanted to tell you goodbye." She adds with a slight smile, "And I need my dog back. Mr. West called my cell while you were outside, and he gave me the okay to go. It was nice meeting you, Mr. Carpenter. I've never met a rockstar before."

"We're not so special."

She holds out her hand, and her ring flashes. "We all are.

You shouldn't waste what makes you unique, Mr. Carpenter. Good luck."

"Do you miss your fiancé?" I ask, though I don't know why. That she was willing to give me her time when she has a fiancé waiting at home is puzzling.

The saddest smile graces her lips, and though I don't know a thing about this woman, my heart cracks.

"Yeah, I do. Come on, Scout."

She didn't change, but she pulled the ponytail out of her hair and light brown waves float around her shoulders. Her heels give her a couple extra inches, but the height doesn't do anything to deter from her fragility.

Her suitcases are sitting in the hallway, and she struggles with them while opening the door that will let her out into the garage. Someone must have shown her around, probably Jeff, and the door closes behind her and her dog with a quiet click.

The kitchen is clean and still smells of the coffee she made earlier this morning, though she emptied and washed the pot. The living room is cleaner than it has been in a long time, and I trudge over the hardwood floor and up to my room. Olivia cleaned in here while I was sitting on the beach, and the bed is made and all the beer bottles are gone. My dirty clothes are in the hamper in my closet and the spicy, calming scent of lavender drifts from a plug-in air freshener near my bed.

I told her I liked it, and she gave it to me.

I sink onto the bed. My body feels like it's been hit by a truck. I don't want to move, don't want to think. I don't want to do anything but fall down a black hole and not have to deal with the emotions that gnaw through my brain like rats.

Dalt thinks she can help. He wouldn't have sought her out if she couldn't. A life coach. What does a life coach do? I don't need another person telling me what to do. I already have enough people ordering me to get my life straightened out, but if it were that simple, I would have done it. I hate feeling like I'd rather be dead than put up with these gut-wrenching emotions day after day.

She trusts me with her dog.

Maybe I can trust her to help me.

I inhale a deep breath of lavender-scented air.

I can't let her leave.

My heart slams harder than when I'm standing in front of a full stadium, and I run downstairs and through the garage. It slows to a dull thud when I see her sitting in the driveway, her legs elegantly tucked under her, trading kisses with her dog.

She meets my eyes when I step onto the concrete, and she holds out her hand.

I grasp it, my hand swallowing hers, and I help her to her feet.

"I'm glad you changed your mind, Mr. Carpenter."

"Sheppard. It's Sheppard." Staring into her eyes, I'm lucky I remember my name.

"It's nice to meet you, Sheppard. My name is Olivia Bloom, and this is Scout."

"A trial run, okay, Olivia?"

She nods, the breeze playing with her hair. "I'll stay for as long as you need me to stay."

I think her fiancé would have something to say about that, but I pick up her suitcases and walk with her toward the house.

And for the first time in over a year, it doesn't feel like a prison.

Chapter Five

Olivia

I pretend to use my phone to cancel the car I didn't order. Dalton said Sheppard was in a bad way, and I went with my instincts. I hoped Sheppard wouldn't send me home, and he didn't. Now that he's admitted he needs help, that things can be better, we'll start working on it. He's already bonded with Scout, and it's a good first step.

"What do we do first?" he asks, standing uncomfortably in the middle of his living room. Like Eddie and Brock, he exudes confidence and charm, and if I wasn't getting paid to be here, I wouldn't be able to look him in the face much less talk to him. He's bigger than life, handsome with sandy blonde hair that's turning to grey he doesn't try to hide, stubble to match, wearing a Rolling Stones t-shirt and jeans that cling to his legs in all the right places. His eyes are tired, and I bet he rarely smiles, but he hasn't lost what put him and Ghost Town on top. The man in front of me scared out of his mind came from nothing and is worth over a half a billion dollars.

"First, you need to relax. I'm not a dentist, and I'm not

going to rip your teeth out without Novocain. Second, I would really appreciate it if you could show me where I'm going to sleep so I can change. Last, it's been a long day, and a glass of wine and a meal would be very nice."

A corner of his mouth lifts up. "You're going to let me drink?" he asks, picking up my suitcases and tilting his head toward the stairs.

Scout and I follow him. "It's not a question of letting you do anything. I'm not your mom. Do you have a medical reason why you shouldn't be drinking?"

"No."

"Are you a recovering alcoholic who's fallen off the wagon?"

He chuckles. "No."

"Then I see no reason why you can't have a beer or two in the evenings. Though, I have to say, after how many bottles I threw into the recycling while you were outside, it wouldn't hurt you to ease up. Alcohol is a depressant, and if you're prone to feeling down, alcohol will make that worse even if it gives you a buzz first."

He stops in the doorway of the first bedroom, the one with the view of the ocean. The bed is a queen, covered in a gorgeous floral bedspread. Four pillows rest against an ornately carved headboard and a matching dresser sits along the opposite wall. The closet is a walk-in, but I don't have enough clothes to fill even the dresser. If Sheppard decides he wants me here, I can ask Agatha to send me more clothes, or if I'm brave enough to claim them as an expense, charge a few things to the card Dalton gave me. But that's a thought for another day. I have access to a washer and dryer and what I packed will suffice for now.

"I don't get many visitors, not any that spend the night—"

My mouth drops open in disbelief.

"Not like that. Those two women you politely sent on their way this morning isn't a usual thing for me." He leans against the doorjamb, his arms crossed over his broad chest.

"You don't have to explain," I say, kicking off my heels. My feet had a reprieve earlier, but it wasn't long enough. "We plug our holes in different ways." I wince. "That didn't come out right, but you know what I mean."

He laughs, and the sound is warm and smooth melting against my skin. "Yeah, I do. I'll let you change. Ah, I don't have any food here. Got anything in mind? I'll put in an order for takeout."

"I'm not very adventurous. Steak, chicken strips, most pasta is okay. You know."

"Okay. I can work with that."

He turns to go, but I say, "Hey, can you feed Scout for me? I packed a bag of kibble in one of my suitcases, and she needs some chow and a bowl of water. Her day has been just as long as mine."

I haul my suitcases onto the bed and unzip the tops. I find the small bag easily enough, but when I put in a grocery order, I'll add a supply that will last. I've been through Sheppard's kitchen and know he doesn't have anything to cook. That will change. I don't put a lot of stock in the new-age, woo-woo stuff, but I know from when I went through my own crisis that if you let your body break down along with your mind, it's that much harder to pick yourself up.

Holding the bag, he asks, "Why do you trust me with your dog?"

We can't start a relationship like the one we're going to need to have if I lie, and I tell him the truth. "Because she likes you. If she didn't, I would have left when you told me to."

"You said you're a life coach? Has she not liked any of your clients before?"

"A couple of them. Those were the clients I couldn't help."

He nods and trots down the stairs, Scout on his heels.

Drained, I flop onto the bed. From what Dalton told me, Sheppard rarely climbs out of his own bed and doesn't have any interest in the band. That has to be hard for him. Ghost Town's been his whole life. He needs to open up, and I think once he lets those emotions go, it won't be difficult for him to finally move forward. Getting to know Sheppard Carpenter will be interesting.

I change into denim shorts and a V-neck t-shirt and use the bathroom.

Downstairs, Scout's sleeping on the couch, and Sheppard is puttering around the kitchen. A fresh pot of coffee is dripping, and I pull a stool from under his breakfast bar and sit.

"How did Dalt find you?" Sheppard asks, leaning against the counter. He's tired, but I know from experience when you're hurting mentally no amount of physical rest is enough.

I shrug. "My agent contacted me, but she didn't say."

"You have an agent?"

"I wrote a self-help book. Dalton might have read it. I don't know. I haven't . . . practiced in a while. Retired, I guess. I wasn't sure I wanted to do this, but you changed my mind."

"Why did you retire?"

Tears fill my eyes, and behind me, Scout whines. Somehow she always knows when I'm thinking about Michael. Quickly, I wipe my cheeks. I'm the professional here—I can't cry all over my client. "Something happened, and I couldn't work anymore. I had some money in savings, and I took a couple of years off. It's nothing."

"It's not nothing if—"

A text announcing that the delivery driver is outside saves me, and reluctantly, Sheppard leaves me alone to retrieve our dinner. I'm under control when he comes back holding a large paper bag stapled at the top.

"I ordered Italian since you said pasta is okay."

I force a smile. "That's great, thanks. We'll get a food delivery sorted tomorrow and I can cook."

"Is that part of the package?" he asks, lifting plastic containers out of the bag.

"Sure. Unless you can?"

"A few things. Do you want a plate?"

"No, don't dirty anything. This is okay." Sheppard ordered me a double helping of spaghetti and meatballs, and I inhale the rich scent of oregano. He opens a separate container filled with breadsticks and sets it on the counter between us to share.

"Oh, and your wine," he says, pouring me a glass of red. I thought we'd drink coffee with our meal, since he made some, but wine definitely works and I take an appreciative sip.

"Thank you."

"You said you had a long day. Where did you fly in from? You flew?"

"I'm from Minnesota. With the time change, Dalton picked me up at nine local time. He needed a couple of hours to convince me to meet you."

"Did he tell you why he wanted to hire you?" Sheppard tenses, his fork poised above his own serving of spaghetti.

I shake parmesan cheese over my noodles. "No. I wouldn't let him. No one's hired me through a third party, I guess you can say, and clients tell me what they want me to know in their own time. I didn't want him to tell me anything you'll eventually share for yourself. All I know is he wants you to feel well enough to record another album. I said in the end that wouldn't be up to me, it would be up to you and the path you choose after I leave."

"Thank you."

"You don't want to record another album?" I ask, cutting a meatball in half.

He sighs. "I'm tired, Olivia."

I meet his eyes, and his are just as wet as mine. "I know." I brush his hand with my fingers. "I know."

We finish our meal in silence, and Sheppard offers to clean the kitchen if I want to go to bed. I gratefully accept and leave him leaning against the counter, his arms crossed over his chest, staring at the floor, leftovers sitting on the breakfast bar waiting to be put away.

Chapter Six

Sheppard

I can't remember the last time I showered (and yep, that's as fucking gross as it sounds), and I stand under the hot spray after I store our leftovers in the refrigerator. Scout stayed behind after Olivia went upstairs, but she didn't say anything. Maybe she's used to sharing her dog, but I appreciate it, no matter the explanation.

Scout helps me feel not so alone, and maybe Olivia understands that.

The scalding water feels better than it has in a long time, and I wish I would have thought to change my sheets before I stepped into the shower. My mind wanders as the heat loosens my muscles, and I think about Olivia's tight little body and the way she felt when I trapped her against the sink this morning. By some miracle, my cock starts to stiffen. I didn't touch those women last night, though I'd let them in with that intention. After they undressed, I couldn't. I watched them play with each other, the blonde (I don't remember either of their names) chewing on her lip, her eyes drilling into mine, as the brunette ate her out. I tried to let it turn me on, but I gave up and went upstairs.

Now I think of Olivia lying on my bed waiting for me, her legs spread, and for the first time since my divorce, I get myself off in the shower, the release better than guzzling twenty beers. I wait for the shame to come, and it does, but not because Dalt hired her to be my shrink. She says that's not what she is, but that's what she feels like. I can't forget she's engaged, has a man waiting for her at home. She's spoken for, and it might be okay for me to fuck her in my dreams, but that's as far as it can go.

My body's languid when I step out of the shower, but my mind is still heavy and my steps downtrodden. I breathe in the lavender, the plug-in saturating the air.

I scrub my hair dry with a towel and throw it into the hamper. I'll need to do laundry tomorrow, do a more thorough cleaning job than what Olivia managed today. Sweep, clean the bathroom downstairs. I never use the one connected to Olivia's room, and I was going to tell her no one has slept in the guest bedrooms for the past year, but she interrupted me with her look of incredulity. Well, I won't bother to correct her. Rock-stars are known for fucking anything that moves, but I haven't had a woman since Melody gave me my walking papers, and I was married to her for ten years. I didn't cheat on her, so you can do the math.

Scout hops onto my bed.

"Not so fast." I don't know much about dogs, but I do know she hasn't been outside since she sat with me on the beach. "You want out?" I ask, tugging on a pair of basketball shorts and a muscle t-shirt.

She scrambles off the bed and down the stairs.

"That's what I thought."

Olivia's door is closed but cracked, and I pause, wondering if I should ask if it's all right to let her dog outside. Scout didn't try to run away, but there could be a different reason why Olivia would rather be the one to give her dog a pee break.

Gently, I push the door open, and Olivia's sound asleep, her hair splayed across the pillow, her nightgown's hem revealing her slim legs. She's beautiful, and my cock stirs all over again. Her fiancé is one lucky son of a bitch.

I shut her door. She'll leave if she doesn't trust me, and I don't think staring at her like a perverted asshole while she's sleeping would earn me any points.

Scout's waiting by the patio door, her tail wagging, and I let her out, more careful this time when I close it behind us. She darts off, and I follow, my bare feet sinking into the sand.

The water calls to me like it always does, and keeping Scout in my sights, I wade, the current pulling at my legs. I don't know what keeps me from succumbing. It used to be fear. Those few seconds between life and death when I changed my mind but it was too late because the siren had me in her grasp and she wouldn't let me go no matter how hard I struggled. Now, since Olivia stepped into my life, I think it's missed opportunities. Not with the band or what I could have had with Melody if she would have stayed and worked it out, but life in general. I'll turn fifty-one this year and maybe I'd like to start a family. Eddie and Brock have kids—no wives, not anymore— but their children added something to their lives that I've always envied. I'd miss falling in love. Those first stirrings in my heart when I meet a woman's eyes, and we click. When I brush a piece of hair away from her face, and she shivers. I'd like to experience that again. Those feelings aren't meant to be trapped in lyrics, and since Melody and I fell out of love, that's where they've stayed.

I whistle for Scout, and she bounds across the sand.

The next time I'm on doggie duty, I'll bring a plastic bag with me. The last thing I need is to step in a pile of dog shit I should have cleaned up, but tonight I'll feign ignorance and I follow Scout to the house without remorse.

I brush the sand off my feet before stepping inside and wait while Scout gulps water as if she'll never have access to her bowl again. I enjoy her exuberance. I've found so little pleasure in anything these past few months.

Upstairs, I undress, and when I pull my comforter back, the scent of fabric softener mixes with the lavender.

While I was outside earlier, Olivia washed my sheets.

I fall into the clean bedding, and Scout jumps onto the bed and makes herself comfortable near my feet. I turn off the lamp sitting on my clean nightstand, and with a dog, a woman across the hall, and a mind full of nightmares, I fall into a restless sleep.

I wake covered in sweat, choking on bile. The dregs of a nightmare twist in my brain, and I gasp for breath. I don't remember what scared me shitless, but it had something to do with Melody, maybe Derrick. The feeling of losing those closest to me, one by one, until I'm all alone, everyone saying I wanted it that way.

Scout whines and belly-crawls up my mattress until she reaches my pillow, and I wrap my arms around her and bury my face in her neck. I count backward from one hundred, something stupid I read in an article online, but I lose count at forty and give up.

My muscles are tied up in knots, and my joints are stiff. It's a familiar feeling, one that will only go away with a couple shots of whiskey or a six-pack of my favorite beer. Olivia won't stop me if I want whiskey with my coffee, but the whole point of her being here is for me to work on not needing it for breakfast . . . or at all. Alcohol has been my crutch for longer than it should have been.

When I don't feel like I'll vomit, I sit up, Scout not moving an inch. There's a black Moleskin notebook sitting at the foot of my bed with a light pink sticky note that says "Use me" in elegant script and a black gel pen.

Olivia wants me to journal. I should have expected that. The notebook isn't unlike the ones I would scribble in brainstorming lyrics, testing notes, back when I could lose myself in a song. Back when I would spill my blood through the ink and look up hours later depleted, in need of a transfusion because what kept me alive was embedded in the words on the page. I lived and died for those songs.

Lived and died for the fans who would tell me Ghost Town's music changed their lives.

She didn't mean for me to scribble lyrics. If Olivia wanted me to write music, she would tell me. No, this notebook is for thoughts, my hopes and dreams. Maybe I'll try, maybe I won't. She doesn't seem interested in pushing me to do anything, instead, letting me draw my own conclusions. Calculated or not, it's working.

I shower the nightmares off my skin and dress in clean jeans and a Ghost Town t-shirt.

My cell rings as I'm about to head downstairs. I want to see Olivia, but Dalt's name glows, and I owe him an apology. I clear my throat before I answer. "Hey."

"Hey," he returns, surprised.

There hasn't been a morning in the past twelve months he

hasn't caught me hungover. My clear voice must have knocked him sideways.

"I'm sorry about yesterday. I didn't mean to push," he says.

I can picture him in his office, sitting behind his desk, an ankle propped on a knee. He has a penchant for suits, and as our fame grew, he stopped shopping at Sears and started spending his money at Givenchy. Shrewd, when we formed Ghost Town, he changed his major from art history to Entertainment Management with a minor in business. He knows the industry inside and out, and Ghost Town wouldn't be where we are today without him.

"You have every right to push. I had no right to push back. I'm sorry, too. I'm trying. I really am." Part of that's bullshit. I haven't tried, not in the past twelve months, but I am trying now.

"Then you're letting Olivia stay?"

"For a while. We're playing it by ear, I think. It was . . . nice to have someone here last night. I haven't let myself acknowledge how lonely I've been since Melody divorced me."

"It's been a hard year for everyone, Shep. If you need anything, call. I'd like to swing by. Eddie and Brock, we've all missed hanging out with you."

The four of us without Derrick would chew me up and spit me out. "I'm not ready for that."

"I know, and maybe Eddie and Brock aren't either, but, well. I just said I wouldn't push. You let me know."

"Thanks. Hey, ah, about Olivia."

"What's up?" he asks warily.

"She said she wrote a book. Would you mind sending me a copy?"

"Yeah, sure. It's a few years old now."

"That's okay. Thanks for calling."

Dalt disconnects without a goodbye. I'm sure he's having a

heart attack with how well the conversation went. He was always the brave one, getting in my face when everyone else would be too chickenshit to say what they wanted to say. He paid the price, too, and when my temper cooled, I'd grovel, looking for the forgiveness he was always too happy to give me because he'd gotten his way.

My stomach rumbles, and I slide my phone into my back pocket. I need to replace my liquid breakfasts with real ones, and when I start consuming calories that mean something, I'll pack on the pounds if I don't exercise. Maybe Olivia will work out with me.

Scout runs ahead and down the stairs, and I find Olivia standing at my breakfast bar sipping a cup of coffee, a notepad and pen in front of her. She's wearing a pair of black cotton shorts and a top that's too casual to be called a blouse but too dressy to be labeled a t-shirt. Her hair is pulled away from her face with a headband, and she put on makeup, her lipstick a lighter shade than yesterday's.

She looks up and smiles. "Good morning. How did you sleep?"

I should tell her the truth, but it turns out I don't have to. Her reading my mind saves me from having to admit my embarrassing night, but I don't like how she deciphers the expression on my face.

"Do you have nightmares? It's okay. I do, too."

"It must be nice having someone to sleep with," I say, referring to her fiancé.

"Scout helps a lot," she says, holding the mug of coffee to her lips.

I frown. I wouldn't expect a woman to jump right to her dog when speaking about whom she sleeps with, and if Olivia and I were engaged and Scout took precedence over me, that would end, quickly.

"What?" she asks.

"Nothing."

"Okay."

"What are you doing?" I ask to fill in the silence.

She taps the pen on the notepad. "Making a grocery list. I've written down what I like, but you'll need to add yours. Do you have an addiction to Flamin' Hot Cheetos?"

"Those . . . don't sound good." I like junk food, but nothing like that.

Smothering a laugh, she says, "No. Not one of my favorites." She pushes the pad at me.

I settle onto a stool, and she pours me a cup of coffee.

A sideways cross hangs from a silver chain around her neck, and I ask, "Are you religious?" I'm not a churchgoer, and I don't think I could be, even if Olivia wanted me to go. I wasn't brought up with religion, and the closest I come to praying is taking the Lord's name in vain.

She brushes her necklace with the tips of her fingers. "No. A cross on its side means trying to live your life in a way you'll go to Heaven after you die. I don't necessarily subscribe to that way of thinking, but I do try to live in a way my father would be proud of me. My sister bought it for me when someone close to me passed away. I think she wanted me to remember I'll see him again someday, but it doesn't bring me the peace she hoped it would."

"I'm sorry." It sounds inadequate.

"Thanks. We all experience loss." She takes a deep breath. "So, what would you do on a day like today? You don't have to entertain me."

"Lie in bed, sit around, and drink. You already said you won't let me do that, that means the day's wide open."

"I said I *hoped* you wouldn't do that. Help me order groceries and then show me around. I met Jeffrey, but I want to know about your other neighbors. I'm a hick from Minnesota. Amaze me."

For the first time in a long while, I laugh. "Honey, if I don't impress you, nobody will."

She squeezes my hand. "I see the pain in your eyes, Sheppard Carpenter. You've done nothing but impress me since the moment we met."

Chapter Seven

Olivia

Surprisingly, we have fun completing the list of groceries. Sheppard has ordered delivery several times before, and we fill the virtual cart with everything from steak to Ritz crackers and peanut butter. He's not a foodie, not like I would expect someone who's traveled the world ten times over to be, and he said he can enjoy fried chicken and potato salad just as much, if not more, than the meals I thought he would want. He has a thing for cheese, though, and he added five different kinds to the cart while I laughed.

Little by little, I'll try to draw out the man he used to be before tragedy consumed his life, and it doesn't matter to me if it involves a copious amount of gourmet cheese.

I added food for Scout to the cart, and not to be outdone, Sheppard ordered her every toy they had from the pet aisle. She'll love chasing after the balls and Frisbees, and I think it will do Sheppard a lot of good to get some air and sunshine.

The groceries won't be delivered until later, and we go for a walk while we wait.

"The houses are built on stilts," I say, surprised. I didn't see the beach yesterday and I'm excited to walk along the water. I love the ocean, but I don't get a chance to see it very often.

"Most of them are elevated because of the tide. There's Jeffrey's house. He and his girlfriend, Gina, live here full-time in the summer. They own a house in Brentwood and live there during the winter months."

"I don't know where that is."

"It's a suburb in LA. If you ever want to get out of here, we can go for a drive sometime. Eddie and Brock have homes that way."

"Sure. I doubt I'll ever have a reason to come back. It would be nice to see a few things before I go home."

"Is this your first time in California?"

I look up at him and wrinkle my nose. "Yeah. I haven't made it out of the Midwest much. My grandma lived in Florida and I visited her a few times, but she passed away."

"Maybe you can honeymoon out here," Sheppard says, and I have to swallow back the burn that suddenly fills my throat.

"Yeah, maybe," I whisper, trying to push away the melancholy. Michael and I talked about where we would honeymoon, but we didn't mention California.

He opens his mouth to say something, but a slim blonde woman standing on the deck of a house near Jeffrey's waves, and he lifts a hand, hollering a hello. "That's Isla Sommers. She owns a tech company in Silicon Valley. She stays here for a few weeks in the summer for vacation."

"Do you know everyone along the strip?"

"I can lose track, especially if we're touring or in the middle of recording an album. These places change hands more frequently than you'd think."

"I wonder what it's like, to have that much money," I murmur. The houses are glamorous, elegant, offering any amenity you could ever hope to want, packed together like sardines, and worth millions of dollars.

"Being a life coach didn't make you rich and famous?" Sheppard teases.

"Define rich and famous. I don't have to worry about money for a while, and that's a gift in its own way, but I don't think I'm famous. At the peak of my career I was like, oh, I don't know. Rachel Hollis. Do you know who she is?"

He shakes his head.

"Oh, umm, I wasn't nearly as famous as Dr. Phil. I'm sure you know who that is."

"Yeah. I think he owned one of these at one time."

"I didn't get into it to make money. I wanted to help people but still be able to support myself. It's lucky when you can do what you love and earn a living doing it."

"It is if you don't grow to hate it."

I sigh. "Yeah, that's true." I didn't hate being a life coach, but it was a blow to realize I wasn't good at it. It didn't save the one person who meant the world to me.

We walk along, Scout stopping to sniff at the water lapping at the sand. This is her first time seeing the ocean, and she explores everything. The sun is hidden under a haze of clouds, and the breeze is cool, but I'm comfortable in my shorts. Sheppard changed from his jeans into basketball shorts, and we blend in with the tourists checking out one of the most famous beaches in California.

He doesn't make conversation, every once in a while pointing out a house and whom it belongs to, but otherwise we walk silently over the packed sand, the chilly water grazing my toes. I like being with him. I like he keeps tabs on Scout. Not so I don't have to, but because it's a hint at the kind of person he is. He could have been a stuck-up asshole rockstar, but he's not.

We've walked about a half a mile when we come upon a

grouping of large rocks. I climb on top of one and gingerly move from rock to rock, their craggy surfaces digging into the soles of my feet. I pause on one and look over the water. "Do you like being a rockstar?"

He sits on a large boulder in front of me. "No."

I raise my eyebrows. "No?"

"Do I like writing songs? Yes. Do I like singing? Yes. When we started Ghost Town, a bunch of kids dicking around with guitars singing bad covers, it wasn't with the goal to be rich and famous. We wanted to make music, original tracks, good stuff we could be proud of. We were all music majors besides Dalt. He was an art history major and that amounts to about the same thing. We had that creativity that needed to come out. We would practice in Dalt's mom's garage, and there was nothing, even to this day, there was nothing like when our sound came together. The fame and the fans, the sold out stadiums and arenas, it's nice, but it's above me somehow. I don't know how to explain it. I'm not a better person because I've written twenty number one hit songs. I'm a better person because a guy snagged me at a bar and said he played one of my ballads while he proposed to his girlfriend and she said yes."

"That's sweet." Maybe he can't articulate what he's really trying to say, but I understand. Fame swept him away and now he's hanging on for dear life. "What would you need to want to make music again?"

"Are you picking my brain to report back to Dalt?"

His eyes are filled with humor and he's joking, but I answer his question seriously. "No. I'm asking more for myself. If I were to come out of retirement, not just for you. I don't know how I would have to live my life, run my business, so I don't end up back in the same place."

"Do you regret stepping away?"

I move to a different rock and curl my toes around the

jagged curve of the stone. "No. I wasn't good at it, so there was no reason to keep doing it." To know that, to have evidence of that very fact, scared me to death. I've had three years to come to terms with it, and saying it now isn't as scary as it used to be, but my future looms in front of me, a black hole that I have nothing to fill it with. I'm thirty-four years old and there are days when I feel like my life is over.

"That can't be true. Dalt wouldn't have hired you if he didn't think you could help me."

"I think you underestimate how much Dalton cares about you and the band."

"Meaning what?"

"Meaning he hired second best because he knew he could get me out here." Angrily, I step onto another rock. I'm not good enough to be here.

Sheppard stands, and I jump to another rock to get away from him. I miscalculate, the boulder looking closer than it is, and the top of my right foot scrapes the side as I miss my mark. I reach out, hoping to break my fall without hurting myself, and my heart leaps into my throat. Just before I crash against the rock, Sheppard catches me and hauls me against his chest.

My breath shudders from my lungs, and my gaze collides with his.

Scout barks, but the sound is lost in the blood pounding in my ears.

"Steady," he murmurs, holding me. "Dalt wouldn't be happy if you sued us."

"I signed an agreement saying I'm responsible for my own person."

His lips are inches away from mine, his hazel eyes glittering. "I'm sure you did. Olivia, Dalt, the band, *me*, we have the money to hire whoever the fuck we want. Your Rachel Hollis, or Dr. Phil. Dalt chose you for a reason. I don't know what that reason is. Maybe he told you when you met with him yesterday and you don't believe it, but you're here because he saw something in you. You're here because I saw it too, okay?"

I want to believe him, but there is so much evidence stacked against me. We're talking life and death, and it's not a game. "Okay."

"I'm going to put you down. Maybe it's best to stay off the rocks for a while."

I don't want him to put me down. I like the feel of his chest against mine, his strong arms holding me in place, my feet dangling above the sand. I fight the guilt I could be attracted to another man, a rockstar of all people, a man who is so far out of my league that the minute I drive away, I'll be less than nothing in his life.

I'm a nobody. I can slip into Sheppard's life, glue him back together, and slip out again and it will be as if I were never here. That's why Dalton hired me.

And I can't ever, ever forget that.

I lick my lips and nod.

He sets me down and immediately Scout presses her body against my leg. She's not protecting me from Sheppard, she's protecting me from my own thoughts.

There's more beach to explore, but we head in the direction of Sheppard's house, and it's not five minutes later when his cell chimes with a text announcing our grocery delivery is on its way.

We're quiet as we trudge across the sand. I'm hungry; Sheppard didn't have anything to fix breakfast with, and the remnants of the coffee I drank has turned to bitter acid in my stomach.

Jeffrey's leaning against the patio railing when we walk past his house, and he waves. "It's nice to see you out and about," he calls to Sheppard.

"He means sober," Sheppard mutters to me, and louder so Jeffrey can hear, "showing Olivia around a bit."

"Come over for dinner tonight. Gina knows Olivia's here and wants to meet her."

Sheppard looks at me, but I shake my head. "It's up to you. If you don't feel like socializing, decline."

"You'll make me eventually, won't you?"

"I told you, I'm not here to force you to do anything."

"Sure. What you say and what that means are two different things." He calls to Jeffrey, "That sounds good. What time?"

"Seven?"

"We'll see you then."

Pleased, Jeffrey waves again and steps inside his house.

"I hope you didn't do that for me," I say.

"Jeff's a nice guy, and you'll like his girlfriend. She's an indie documentary film director. I think that means she begs people to work for free."

"So did you, by the sounds of it."

Sheppard tugs on my hand and leads me up the stairs to his patio. "For a while."

I haven't lost the pit in my stomach or the arousal that stirred in a different part of my belly when Sheppard held me. We dance around each other in his kitchen, me fixing us sandwiches with the bread and cold cuts we ordered while he puts everything away because he knows where things go. I'm famished and I've finished half my ham and Swiss cheese sandwich by the time he shoves the last box into the cabinet.

He eats faster than I do, and we finish at the same time. I agree with Jeffrey; it's good to see him sober and eating something healthy. His eyes already look clearer, and his skin has lost the stink of stale booze.

We have plenty of time before Jeffrey expects us for dinner, and to give Sheppard time alone, I say, "I'm going to take a nap.

I don't think I'm jet-lagged, but I'm running on Central time and my body's a little confused."

Sheppard frowns in concern. "Do you feel okay?"

"Yeah. I don't need to be in your face every second, and I want to make a phone call."

"To your fiancé?"

I forget I wear my engagement ring, that I can't take it off because I don't want to lose what little time I had with him. That the stone held my whole future and now it's all I have left.

I cover it with my hand. "No. He's, ah, no. My agent, actually. Well, not my agent anymore; I don't have a book on submission. She turned into a friend and since Dalton contacted her about you, she asked me to touch base now and then." I try to smile, I really do, but I remember his arms around me, and I can't stop thinking about how good it felt. To have someone hold me again.

"Okay. I'll see you later."

"Yeah." I turn toward the stairs.

"Olivia."

"Hmmm?"

"I know I'm a stranger, and Dalt is no better, but if you need anything or want to talk, you can come to us. Okay?"

"Yeah, sure."

Scout stays behind like I knew she would, and when I reach the guest bedroom, I pull out my phone and attach my earbuds.

Agatha answers on the second ring, and her familiar voice fills my eyes with tears.

"Hey, hun, how are you doing? Did you decide to stay?"

I sit on the floor near the bed and rest my back against the wall. I try to speak, but I can't around the sobs bottled up in my throat. "I can't do this," I finally say, tears running down my cheeks.

Agatha sighs in sympathy. "Tell me what's wrong."

"I miss him so much, and I almost fell today, and Sheppard caught me, and his arms, and I can't."

I drag a pillow off the bed and bury my face in it. I can't let Sheppard hear me cry. At this point, I doubt he'd send me home because I couldn't do my job, but I don't want his pity.

"Liv, you're so lonely. Why do you hang on to him when he's gone?"

"I don't know." I do know, though.

"It's not your fault."

But it is. I didn't see it, didn't know, and I claimed to love him. It's all my fault Michael is gone.

"I know," I lie.

"Come home. You gave it a chance and you don't owe Dalton West anything. He wanted you because he knew you didn't have other obligations."

Sniffling, I ask, "Did he say that?"

"I didn't want to tell you, but yes, he did. He contacted several other coaches, and no one could spare the kind of time he wanted except you. He was desperate and begged me to reach out to you. I agreed because I hoped you getting out of Minnesota for a while would help, but it's not."

"Sheppard needs me, Agatha."

"He probably does, but how much do you have to give away? I don't want you hurting yourself helping him."

"If I can save him—"

"Olivia! He's not your redemption. You can't trade his life for Michael's. I won't let you try. If you won't fly home on your own, I'll come and get you."

"No. Let me finish the week. I told Dalton I'd wait a week and if it didn't work out, I would leave. Just the week. I can handle six more days."

"I don't like it. That's coming from your agent and your

best friend. I don't like it, and you're going to call me every day to check in, do you understand me?"

"Yeah. I appreciate you." I wipe my tears off my cheeks.

"You won't appreciate me if I call your sister and tell her what you just said to me. We're all worried about you. You haven't been living these past three years, and you can't keep going on like this."

"I don't know what else to do."

"Go on a vacation or go back to school. Anything is better than sitting in that house you and Michael bought. When you're done with this job and you get your fanny back here, sell it and find somewhere else to live. You're stuck in the past, and I'm not going to let you live backward anymore."

"You should be the life coach, not me."

"I'm not doing that great with my own life, so that's not likely, but I'm not telling you anything you don't already know. You sound exhausted. Get some sleep. Alone. The last thing you need, Olivia Bloom, is to fall in love with a rockstar. Keep your legs closed."

I huff a watery laugh. "Thanks. I'll talk to you tomorrow."

"You bet your ass you will. Bye."

I smile through my tears. "Bye."

I try to sleep, but after an hour, I give up and go downstairs. Sheppard's outside on the beach throwing a Frisbee for Scout. She loves it, her paws digging into the sand as she races to catch the flying disc. I sit and watch them, resting my chin on my arm. Sheppard might not be my redemption, but if I can somehow make up for letting Michael down, then maybe, like Agatha wants me to, I can finally move on.

"What does one wear to a former child star and his indie-documentary-making girlfriend's house?" I ask, looking through my clothes.

Sheppard is lying on my bed with Scout while I sort through the clothing I hung up in the closet. I try not to feel like it's something a couple would do, but it is, and something Michael and I did hundreds of times while we were getting ready to attend this and that. I can't tell him to leave. He would want to know why, and I haven't decided if I'm going to tell him what happened between Michael and me. This week, and beyond if I can handle it and Agatha doesn't have a conniption, is about Sheppard, not me and my grief. I'm letting him work through things at his own pace, and this is only my second day here. He hasn't told me anything about why he stopped singing and writing music, why he cut himself off from the band, or what led to his divorce. I need to be patient and let him share in his own way. There's no room for my problems.

"Do you have a casual dress? Nothing formal. A pair of dressy shorts? It's not a big deal, Liv."

I tense when the nickname flows from his mouth, but I don't know why. Michael would call me that, but so do hundreds of other people. It's a natural way to shorten my name, but hearing it come from Sheppard's lips skitters awareness over my skin.

"Okay." I don't want him in my room anymore. "Are you going to change, too?"

"Yeah. We have time."

He doesn't make one move to climb off my bed and I hold back a sigh. At least he likes me. I wouldn't be able to do my job if we rubbed each other the wrong way.

I move deeper into the closet and tug off my shorts and top. He can't see me, and I slide on a black jersey dress with ruching along the sides that stops just above my knees. It's dressy enough I'll feel good meeting Jeffrey and his partner, but casual enough I can go barefoot and still look like I'll fit in. I need to touch up my makeup, and I'm scraping my nails along my scalp and fluffing my hair when I step out of the closet. "Will this work? I think I'll pin my hair up."

Sheppard props himself onto his elbows, and the air knocks out of my lungs just like it did on the beach when he caught me. His eyes smolder, his gaze raking me from head to foot, and I try not to blush. Since Michael, I haven't had a man look at me the way Sheppard is staring at me now, and I can't let it get to me. I'm so starved for love and affection I can't let myself read what's not there.

"You look good," he says and clears his throat. "I'll change now too, then. Gina likes a wet red, and I happen to have a bottle in my cooler. We'll bring it over."

I don't have anything to say to that, and I turn toward the dresser. Watching my reflection in the attached mirror, I twist my hair into a bun near the top of my head and begin to pin it with a cache of bobby pins I brought with me.

Sheppard doesn't get up. Scout rests her head on his thigh.

Perspiration drenches my skin and I want nothing but for him to step behind me, yank my dress's hem around my waist, and bend me over the dresser. I haven't been intimate with a man since Michael, and I crave the closeness. Not physically, though that too, but emotionally, how it feels to be connected to someone.

With a shaking hand, I line my eyes with black eyeliner and dab a dark berry lipstick on my lips. By now I probably am too overdressed to sit with Jeffrey and Gina and I should have chosen a lighter shade of gloss. I won't add jewelry and hopefully it won't look like I'm trying too hard.

Sheppard stares at me, and I glance at the time on my phone. I need him to get out of here or he's going to know what

I'm thinking, and he's probably had enough of that from every woman with a pulse. "It's 6:45."

"Right." He nudges Scout off his leg and the mattress creaks as he stands from the bed.

To keep my hands busy, I pull tendrils from my bun to frame my face and mess my bangs just a little.

Sheppard pauses near the door.

"Is it too much for a simple dinner? I can change back into shorts and a blouse."

"No, ah. You're fine."

Finally, he hurries across the hall to his own room, and I blow out a sigh. I reapply my deodorant and dab on a light hint of the lavender body oil Sheppard seems to favor. I'm nervous, not only because he was eyeing me like I'm going to be dessert after our meal, but because I like Jeffrey and want him and Gina to like me, too.

I wait downstairs on the patio, the cool evening air chilling my skin, but it's warmer than anything we'd experience in Minnesota in June and the temperature would have to drop many degrees for me to get cold.

"Jeffrey and Gina won't mind if Scout tags along," Sheppard says, holding a bottle of wine. He changed into khakis and a white dress shirt he didn't tuck into his pants. He left the first two buttons undone, and a bit of blonde hair teases me. I've already been treated to a sampling of how strong his chest is, and the past year of imbibing to numb his pain didn't diminish his powerful physique.

"She needs to recharge just like us and it's better if she has some time to herself. I let her out while you were changing. She'll sleep while we're gone."

"Okay." He closes the sliding glass door, and with his free hand hovering over the small of my back, we walk across the sand to Jeffrey and Gina's house.

Their house is elevated too, and this side is comprised mostly of glass for an optimal view of the ocean. Jeffrey is waiting for us on the patio, and he offers me a hand to help me up the narrow set of steps.

"I can't tell you how thrilled Gina is, Shep," Jeffrey says, shaking his hand when I'm safely standing on the patio planks.

Sheppard winks at me. "She loves me for the wine."

Jeffrey reaches for the bottle. "You're not wrong." He opens a set of French doors and waves us inside. Gina hurries into the room from what looks to be the kitchen, her blonde hair a cascade of riotous curls down her back. She's wearing a black dress as well, and I relax. Compared to Sheppard, I *was* over-dressed, even if he didn't say so, but Gina did her makeup too and I hold out a steady hand as she rushes toward us.

"It is so great to meet you, Olivia," she gushes, going in for a hug instead of a handshake. "I was heartbroken when you took your blog down."

I pull away, my nose filled with the scent of an amber musk mixed with vanilla. "That's kind of you to say. I wasn't in a place to keep it going."

"Maybe one day you'll start it up again. By the comments, likes, and shares, you were touching thousands of lives."

"Thank you." My publisher was upset when I pulled the website down, accusing me of sabotaging my book's success. Since I'd earned out my advance and I didn't owe them anything, I didn't care. Agatha defended me, but she did warn me that if I ever wanted to write another book, selling it wouldn't be as easy as the first time. I didn't care then, but three years later, I'm wondering how many bridges I burned without meaning to.

"Come in and sit down. I'll pour you a glass of the wine Shep brought. It's delicious."

She and Jeffrey lead us through a huge living room to an

open kitchen and a dining table that seats eight. The table is already set with four place settings, and squat, chunky candles sit in a small grouping between the plates and utensils.

Shep holds out a chair for me while Gina uncorks the bottle and pours wine.

"I'm grilling steaks," Jeffrey says, "unless you're a vegetarian, Olivia. We'll have plenty of sides if you are."

"Oh, no, a steak is great. Medium rare, if you can," I say, smiling my thanks at Sheppard as I settle into the seat.

He says you're welcome with a touch of his fingers against my shoulder.

"Perfect. You're easy to please—we like all of our guests that way," Jeffrey jokes.

Gina serves me wine in a gigantic, but delicate, glass, and I carefully hold it, the stem so thin it would snap in half if I dropped it onto the floor. After placing a tray of cheese, crackers, and olives near the candles, she and Jeffrey sit. "Now, tell me why you retired," she says, leaning forward in sincere interest.

I try not to squirm in discomfort. I don't want this evening to be about me, and I lift a shoulder in faux nonchalance. "I realized I wasn't good at being a life coach, so I stopped. It's very difficult to keep doing what you're not good at."

Shep lounges in his chair next to me, one hand holding a glass of wine, the other resting on the back of my chair, his fingertips brushing my skin.

I try not to think of it.

"What made you draw that conclusion?" Gina asks.

"I'm thirty-four, and I retired three years ago. There was more than one person who said, 'How can you help someone live their life when you've barely begun your own?' At first I brushed it off—I went to college and majored in psychology and completed an extensive life coaching program. My father died when I was in high school, so I knew about grief, but I failed a . . . client, and that's when I said, they're right. I haven't lived enough, haven't experienced enough, and during a long bout of depression I don't think I really climbed out of, I quit."

Gina nods. "What have you been doing then, these past three years? How are you filling in your time?"

"I haven't been doing anything." Talking to a woman as accomplished as Gina, the truth embarrasses me and only validates those people who said I wasn't good enough to help others. I couldn't help Michael, and when the chips were down, I couldn't help myself.

"How does that feel?" she asks, nibbling on a cracker. "To go from a career woman at the top of her game to rock bottom? You wrote a New York Times bestseller, had a guest spot on Oprah, were asked to speak at hundreds of women's conventions, and had several high-profile clients. You went from that to nothing, Olivia. That had to hurt."

Gina's terminology doesn't offend me. I did hit rock bottom, and I'm still there. "It was easy. It was easy to stop living a lie."

"Liv—" Sheppard starts.

"No, I don't mind," I interrupt. "It was a relief I could stop pretending."

"Now you're here with Sheppard, doing what? Did you write out a treatment program, do you have a game plan?" Gina asks, her gaze swinging between me and Sheppard. "And why do you want her here, Shep?"

I stare at my empty plate. I didn't think of a game plan, don't have any idea how to help Sheppard except following my instincts and trying to be what he needs me to be without sacrificing what little integrity and humility I have left.

A pall falls over our table, and beside me, Sheppard stiffens, unwilling to talk about his own reasons why Dalton West summoned me here.

"You must think I'm terribly rude," Gina says, brushing my hand with hers, "but what I'm exploring opening that can of worms is how you can help me. I'm filming a documentary about women who have failed, and not failed in a black and white sense because to me you don't sound like a failure. Maybe put in a better way, women who feel like they've disappointed themselves. I'm speaking with a director who fought tooth and nail to get to where she is today, but for every step upward she slid down five. I'm interested in women who pick themselves back up."

"I haven't exactly done that," I say, surprised and humbled Gina would think of me as an interesting subject for that kind of documentary.

"On the contrary, you're here, aren't you? If you'd given up completely, you'd still be in Minnesota. Instead, you're sitting at my table with the great Sheppard Carpenter, and for the first time in the past year since I've seen him, he's sober. I don't care how big of a failure you felt before you boarded that plane, Olivia, but to me, at this very moment, you have accomplished what no one else has." She draws in a breath. "No offense, Shep. We've all been worried about you."

"None taken. I know I've been in a bad way. I'm fortunate Dalt has my back." He hitches an ankle on top of his knee and gently turns his wineglass on the table's surface, the candles' flames glittering in the reflection.

"I can't take credit for that. I've barely been here a full forty-eight hours. I was set to leave, but Sheppard changed his mind."

Gina taps her finger against her lips. "And that's interesting too. Why *did* you let her stay, Shep?"

He pauses, then meets my eyes. "Because when she's here, I don't feel so alone. I'm not sure if I could have connected with someone else like that, and I knew if I sent her away, I'd be blowing a chance to . . . I don't know. I told Dalt I didn't want to record another album, and he said if we didn't there wouldn't be a band. That hit me hard. I have a lot to work through, and I'm hoping Olivia's patient with me. I'm not used to sharing."

I force a smile. "Of course."

"Just one more question, and then I'll let Jeff throw the steaks on the grill—Olivia, what made you come out of retirement for Shep?"

"My whole life has been about giving back. It's why I wanted to be a life coach in the first place, and when I retired, I'd run out of something inside me to give to people. To be honest, I don't know why I'm here."

"Sometimes a journey is best taken with someone who can share what you're going through. Empathy, I've seen in my line of work, can be stronger than love." She straightens, and the mood around the table changes. "Talk to Shep about your daily schedule. All I'll need is a few hours of your time here and there. You're staying through the summer?"

"That depends on Sheppard, actually, and what he's going to need to get to where he wants to be. I try to let my relationships with my clients develop naturally, organically. I don't know what happened in Sheppard's life that made him need me."

Gina's eyes widen. "Shep, she doesn't know about—"

"No. I'll tell her in my own time, Gina." Sheppard's voice is sharp.

"Okay. I can respect that. Her not knowing won't affect what I want from her if she decides to work with me. I hope you'll consider it," she says, closing the conversation. Jeffrey pushes away from the table. "Now, let's have more wine and some food. After all this talk, I'm starving."

The serious topic melts into casual conversation, and I enjoy Jeffrey's and Gina's company. She shares stories about the last documentary she worked on—women who were hurt by the health care system. I admire her and the truths she's telling through her work, and as the evening winds down, I wonder about my own truths. If I'm strong enough to help Sheppard in the way that he needs, or if I was ever strong enough to help anyone.

Maybe I need to listen to Gina's observations and not look at things from such a sky-high point of view. I know on a micro-level I did help people—every comment thanking me on my blogposts was proof of that.

When does success start to mean something? When does it stop?

I know when it stopped. When I couldn't see what Michael needed. What he needed *from me*. But when did it start? Does it matter? Can listening to Sheppard, being the support Dalton hired me to be, give me a second chance? Agatha said he's not my redemption, and I know there's no salvation for not being there for Michael when he needed me most.

At the door, Gina hugs me again. "Jeff said he has your cell number. I'll text you tomorrow. It would be wonderful if you could weigh in on more than just your portion, Olivia. You've guided a lot of people through career changes and life-shattering events. I'm looking forward to this collaboration."

"Thank you. It means a lot someone still has faith in me."

We're standing on their patio, the moon and stars hidden by clouds and smog. The wind turned cooler, and I shiver.

"I think you'll find a lot of people still do. When we lose faith in ourselves, we believe other people have as well, and sometimes that's not true. Goodnight, you two."

"Goodnight," Sheppard says, shaking Jeffrey's hand. He kisses Gina's cheek. "Thank you for dinner."

"Anytime," Jeffrey says.

Sheppard holds my hand and helps me navigate the narrow

stairs from their patio onto the sand. I think he'll let me go when my feet reach the ground, but he doesn't, tangling our fingers in a way that's too comfortable and too familiar for what our relationship is. He holds on only for as long as we need to climb his stairs onto his patio, and then he releases my fingers to open the sliding glass door.

"I'm going up to bed, Liv," he says, the living room dark.

Sliding off my sandals, I ask, "Are you all right?"

"Yeah. Tired. Goodnight."

"Goodnight."

His tone holds a hint of melancholy and soon, if he doesn't begin to share, I'll reluctantly press. I want him to open up on his own. We're getting to know each other, but at some point, the work needs to start.

I wash my face and brush out my hair. I have a difficult time drifting off, dread and anticipation keeping me awake, thinking about working with Gina and what that could mean for my career and what I want it to mean if I let it.

I fall into a restless sleep, and it feels like only minutes later when Scout nudges me, her cold nose pressed into my cheek. "What is it, girl?" I ask, tilting my phone and checking the time. It's three in the morning.

Scout whines, and I slide on the robe that matches my nightgown.

She leads me downstairs and paws at the sliding glass door. I open it, thinking she needs to go to the bathroom. She races across the planks, her nails scratching at the wood, and she bounds down the stairs. I follow, scanning the beach to see what upset her. She didn't need to go potty.

Still wearing the khakis from dinner, Sheppard's standing in the water up to his thighs, so like the picture that prompted me to accept this job in the first place. The wind whips at his hair, and his shoulders are hunched, as if the entire world is resting on them. Scout looks at me, and she sits on the sand, far enough away the waves won't get her wet.

The water's freezing. I suck in a breath and wade toward him. "Sheppard. What is it? Did you have a nightmare?"

"You don't need to be sleeping to have those," he murmurs.

"No, you don't."

"Do you hear her?" he asks, his fingers tangling in my hair.

"Who?"

"The siren. She calls to me, her fingernails scratch at my skin. Just a little farther, she hisses. And sometimes, oh, God, sometimes, I want to go."

His anguished words chill me more than the freezing water lapping at my legs, drenching the hem of my nightgown. This is what brought me to tears when I spoke to Agatha this morning. Confronting this. Not his fear. Mine.

The ocean is a black expanse of nothing, and I know how easy it would be to keep walking and not look back.

"Do you ever feel like that, Livvy?" he asks, his voice rough.

I choke back the pain. I should ask him not to call me that. Liv is okay, but Livvy is what Michael would call me when he wanted to make love. When we would hide under the blankets after we were done, and he would say, "I love you, Livvy," and I would say, "I love you, too," but my love wasn't enough.

"Yes, I do."

"What stops you?"

I huff a sad laugh. "Do you really want to know?"

He looks down at me, his eyes mournful and despondent. "Yeah."

"I think, if I gave in, who would feed Scout? She belongs to me, and I can't do that to her." It's a stupid thing to say when we're talking about death. Thinking about who would feed my dog when the pain is so great it had come to that.

"She saves your life," Sheppard says.

"Every day."

We stand for a few more moments in silence, lights blinking from the houses up and down along the shore, the faint beat of a song thrumming on the breeze. I don't ask him whom he lives for because I already know he'll say no one. That's his truth, but it's my job to show him it's a lie.

"Come inside. It's cold and you need to get some sleep."

He doesn't fight me, only follows me onto the sand, his fingers still tangled in my hair. Scout whines, relieved I convinced Sheppard to go inside.

In his bedroom, he strips from his wet pants, and I tuck him in like I would a child, pulling the comforter up to his chin. Scout snuggles next to him, the side of her head pressed against his face. I smooth my hand through his hair, the tips of my fingers lingering near his jaw, and he stares at me through hooded eyes heavy with exhaustion.

"Goodnight, Sheppard."

He's already sleeping by the time I reach the door, and Scout will keep him safe for the rest of the night.

I let the tears come while I lie on my bed, all my doubts swamping me like they did earlier when I spoke with Agatha.

I wasn't enough to keep Michael with me, and I'm scared of what I'll become if I'm not enough for Sheppard, too.

Chapter Eight

The delicious scents of frying bacon and coffee wake me from a restless sleep. Scout is still lying next to me, her nose pressed into my cheek, snoring. I hadn't counted on her alerting Olivia. She said the Golden Retriever is a therapy dog, but I hadn't taken that to mean tattletale.

I'm grateful though, and I rub her neck in thanks before crawling around her and out of bed. I wouldn't have done anything last night. The siren and her song had a steel grip around my ankle, but flashes of Olivia wearing her black dress, her lips colored as deep red as the wine, they anchored me. When she approached me, wading into the water, the siren released her hold and slithered away, threatening to lure me another day.

I wish Olivia would have lain with me instead of leaving her dog, but that's nothing that will ever happen. She's Dalt's employee, and when I'm standing on steady ground, she'll leave. She has a life, friends, a fiancé waiting for her, and a broken old man isn't anything she'd stay here for.

Before going downstairs, I shower, my body losing its sluggishness in the absence of booze. The couple inches of red I nursed last night is nothing compared to what I've been drinking. The sudden sobriety shoves ice picks through my skull, but my head is clear.

I don't have anything to do today, and now that Olivia is settling in, she'll want to talk. I don't know what her plan is, and if she told Gina the truth—that she doesn't have one—she'll think of something. Dalt isn't paying her to sit around.

My mouth is watering when I trot downstairs, Scout awake and ahead of me, needing to go outside.

Olivia sets a plate on the breakfast bar just as my foot hits the living room floor.

"Good morning," she says, filling a mug with coffee. "I made breakfast. Sit down."

"You don't have to cook for me." I slide onto a stool and gulp down the scalding coffee as quickly as I dare. I may not be foggy because of booze, but I'll always need caffeine to wake up.

"Will you cook for yourself?" she asks, an eyebrow raised.

"Nope."

"Then shut up and eat." She pushes back a smile.

An enormous omelet covers the entire plate and four pieces of crisp bacon and two pieces of perfectly browned toast sit off to the side. I don't often cook for myself, even fewer meals when I was married. Melody lived on the adrenaline high of a modeling shoot and she never would have tasted, much less enjoyed, the steak and grilled potatoes Jeffrey and Gina served us last night.

Despite her interrupted sleep, Olivia's perky, dressed in denim shorts that perfectly hug her ass and a dressy shirt that molds to her body in all the right places. I had her against me yesterday when she fell, and God help me, I didn't want to let her go.

I tear my gaze away from her figure and pick up my fork. "Olivia—"

"Look," she says, turning toward me with her own cup of coffee, "I'm not a psychiatrist."

I frown.

"I mean, I can't prescribe medication. If you think you would benefit from an anti-depressant, we'll take the steps we need for you to do that, okay?" Tears fill her eyes. "Suicide is never the answer."

I swear under my breath; I didn't mean to make her cry. "I know. I'm sorry. I wasn't going to. There's something about knowing I can . . . but I wouldn't."

She dashes away the tears on her cheeks with a brisk flick of her fingers. "No matter what time it is, or what I'm doing, or if you think you're inconveniencing me—you can always talk to me, Sheppard. Or if you just need to be with someone, I can sit with you. Some things are better said without words. You're not alone. Not while I'm here."

It humiliates me to need anyone. I'm the lead singer of one of the most popular rock bands in the world. I've written twenty number one hit songs, was married to one of the hottest supermodels who ever strutted a catwalk, own property all over the world, yet I can't get out of bed without feeling like I'm walking straight into hell. Up until yesterday when Olivia fixed me a ham and cheese sandwich, I hadn't eaten a real meal in months. I had two modes of operation: drunk or hungover. I've lost friends and tore my band apart because I can't shake off something people say I should be able to walk away from.

I cut into the omelet, the eggs still warm enough cheese oozes out the side. Olivia fills my mug with more coffee and washes the frying pan soaking in soapy water in the sink. I don't mean to shut her out, but I don't have anything I can say that wouldn't make me sound like a pathetic asshole.

The empty day looms ahead of me, and sober, those twelve hours before it's time to go to bed again are scarier than fuck.

Olivia slides my empty plate into the sink. I have a dish-washer. I don't know why she's not using it.

I scramble for something to say but I catch Jeff on the beach cooling down after a run, and I latch on to anything that will fill even five minutes of my time. "I'm going to let Scout outside and thank Jeff again for dinner." This earns me a smile because I like playing with her dog and I'm voluntarily seeking out a friend's company.

"Thank him from me, too."

"I will."

Scout's excited and is already waiting by the door, her tail thumping. When I set her free, she races over the patio and down the stairs to the sand, and I feel the same, deeply inhaling the salty air. I don't know what's worse: being around her and wanting to pull her to me again just to see if she feels as good as she did yesterday or if it's all in my head, or knowing at some point she's going to sit me down and ask me to spill my guts.

"Shep," Jeff greets me, wiping sweat off his forehead with the back of his wrist. "How's it going?"

"Do you want the real answer or a lie?"

He laughs. "How about a little of both? Gina's in love with Olivia. She can't wait to start working with her. You got a thing for her too, huh?"

I rear back, my heels digging into the sand. "Why would you say that?"

"Couldn't stop touching her—"

"I wouldn't go that far."

Jeff shakes his head, not believing me. "Your hand was glued to the back of her chair all night. I lost count how often your fingers brushed her skin, or how many times you played with her dress's shoulder strap. I'm a director for fuck's sake; it's my job to zero in on the little things that create a scene, and you were all in. She's not your type, though. Gina's got a twenty you'll talk her into bed before she flies home, but nah. I took that bet and raised her fifty. Olivia might be just a little too country for you."

"Attraction doesn't need to go anywhere," I say, scanning the beach for Scout. She's sniffing around the supports of Jeff's house and lifts a leg. That's what he gets for betting on my love life. "Besides, you both must have missed her rock. She's engaged. I don't know much about her but I know she wouldn't cheat, and honestly, I wouldn't want a woman who would."

"Fair. There's not a lot of loyalty around these days. So, you hear anything more about the investigation?"

My heart starts to pound just like it always does when someone mentions Derrick. "No. It was an accident. There's nothing new to hear."

Jeff waves me toward the house, and I follow, Scout right behind us. He lets us into the living room and makes a beeline for the kitchen. He fills a glass of water and chugs it before he says, "That's not what *Buzz Kill*'s been saying."

"They print trash. They'd be talking shit about me, too, but I haven't been doing anything worth their time." *Buzz Kill* is a garbage gossip site that reports on everything from who coasts drunk through the drive through at In-N-Out Burger to who wears the same dress at the Academy Awards. They're dirty and like to stir up trouble, and it's only been in the past couple of months they've decided since I'm either passed out or hungover I'm not worth their time.

"You know as well as I do there's an ounce of truth to every hundred pounds of a lie. If *Buzz Kill* thinks someone's hiding something, then it could be worth looking into."

Scowling, I ask, "Why have you been trolling their site? There's nothing on it for you."

"Keeping my ear to the ground. No harm in it."

"There is if all you do is spread their rumors. It was an accident, plain and simple." And that's why it hurts to think about it. There's no one to blame, nowhere I can find revenge.

"Okay," he says, dropping the subject. "Why don't you start running with me in the mornings? It will loosen you up and a daily workout is probably on Olivia's list."

"Yeah, fine." I'm surly enough to agree to what will surely be a disastrous few weeks until I get my stamina back up to what it was before everything in my life went to hell. I used to work out all the time. No one has any idea how fit you need to be to jump around a stage while belting out songs at the top of your lungs. I'm goddamned lucky I'm not a smoker. I wouldn't be able to sing my way out of a paper bag.

"Gina will be home a little earlier today, and she wants to talk with Olivia. You don't have a problem with that, do you? Being she's on your payroll?"

"Nope. It'll give her something to do. I don't need her in my face all the time."

Jeff smirks. "But you want her there."

"Not in the way she wants to be."

"Three months is a long time. Maybe you'll turn it around."

"If I do what everyone wants me to do, I won't have time for that. I don't have any new material written. The guys and I are rusty. We have to try out our sound without Derrick, and that feels like way too much fucking work." The panic attack builds slowly, and there's no fucking way in hell I can record an album when even just thinking about it raises my blood pressure to the point where I feel like I'm dying. "I have to go."

I don't wait for Jeff to reply, and with a worried whine, Scout follows me out of his house and onto the sand. There isn't any privacy on the beach, and sucking a deep breath through my mouth, I bound up the stairs to the patio and run through the living room. I catch a brief glimpse of Olivia standing near the breakfast bar eating her own plate of eggs and toast, a notepad next to her. I can feel her eyes on me as I run up the stairs and I pray like Christ she doesn't follow me. I need to be alone.

The bed is a safe and poisonous haven, and without stripping, I crawl under the comforter. Scout follows, and shaking, I cry into her neck.

There's a half bottle of whiskey under my bed, and I grope over Scout's body for it. She knows before I do I can't reach, and she jumps down. I tumble after her and land on the floor in a jumble of grief and tears. The bottle didn't roll far when I dropped it the other night, and I unscrew the cap, my hand shaking. I can picture Olivia's disappointed face, and I chug faster to erase the image.

Scout noses me, and I push her away. Goddamned dog. The whiskey burns smooth down my throat, and the temporary peace fills my head.

I wipe some of the booze away that dribbles down my chin and go for a second helping, choking back a sob only long enough to swallow.

Sated, the alcohol hitting me hard, I rest my head against the nightstand.

Scout stares soulfully with her big brown eyes, and she rests her paw on my thigh.

The minutes turn to hours, and I expect Olivia to check on me, but she never does. The afternoon is drifting into evening by the time I stagger to my feet, sorrow and fear a tangle so thick in my heart I don't know how it can keep beating. Through the haze of whiskey, like she always does, the siren calls to me, and I stumble down the stairs, landing on my knees on the living room floor. I don't see anything but the ocean, don't hear anything but her song.

She wants me to go to her, and I do.

The first touch of water on my skin loosens the noose around my neck, yet at the same time tightens its hold. I need her grip around my ankle, and I wade into the water.

This is wrong, I know it is, and in a fit of misery, I kneel, tears streaming down my cheeks.

Water drenches my clothes, and I fist the sand.

I need something, but I don't know what.

I need to move on, but I don't know how.

I feel lost and alone, the water lapping at my stomach, until suddenly Olivia is kneeling in front of me, and she wraps her arms tightly around me.

The siren hisses in disappointment and retreats, sliding into the ocean's depths to wait for me another day.

I pull Olivia against my chest and tangle my hands in her hair.

Alcohol and grief churn my stomach, and bile rises in my throat. The shakes set in, but Olivia only grips me harder. I don't know how long she sits with me in the chilly water, but the tide is rising and soon it will force us to shore.

I rest my forehead against hers. "I'm sorry."

With her hands framing my face, she forces me to meet her eyes. "You will never be alone as long as I'm here. The next time she calls to you, come to me."

"You don't know what you're asking." She doesn't understand what that means. The siren's song is worse than an earworm I can't shake loose. It's worse than an addiction. Her song is a part of me, embedded in my bones, my skin, my every cell, and there's no way I can get rid of it.

The sunset is bleeding oranges and pinks into the sky, the

glimmer kissing the smile barely touching her mouth, the way I want to.

She brushes my hair out of my eyes. "That's the thing, Sheppard. I do."

Like she did the previous night, she leads me into the house, our clothes dripping, Scout trotting ahead of us. This will be a dangerous habit, and I need to break it before it starts.

We go upstairs together, and she releases my hand to go into her room and change. I do the same, trading my wet clothes for sweats and a muscle t-shirt.

She has something simmering on the stove, and my stomach queasily gurgles in hunger. Even on one of my benders, I didn't drink nearly as much as I did this morning, the empty bottle still sitting on the floor near the bed. I'm surprised Olivia didn't throw it in the garbage and look through my room for other stashes of liquor.

I hear her puttering around downstairs and once again, she has food waiting for me when I reach the bottom.

"I made soup, but the noodles might be a little squishy. Come have some." The bowl is huge and full of homemade chicken noodle, a loaf of crusty bread and a dish of butter sitting near it. Gratefully, I slide onto the stool and pick up a spoon.

She serves herself and stands opposite me. In silence, she butters a chunky piece of bread.

I ruined her day, and guiltily I ask, "Did you meet with Gina?"

"No. I don't know what you talked to Jeffrey about—"

I lean back in surprise. I thought the first thing she would do after seeing me rush in from the beach would be to find out what happened.

"I want *you* to tell me what's hurting you, not him. I'm not in California to advance my own career, I'm here to help you. I'll only talk to Gina if my time allows. Today, it didn't." She offers me a piece of buttered bread.

"I suppose now you'll make me stop drinking." I stare into my bowl, the noodles and chunks of carrot and celery floating in the broth.

"Sheppard, will you look at me?"

I meet her bluish-green eyes, framed by delicately arched eyebrows partially hidden under her wispy bangs. The sideways cross hanging from her silver necklace glitters.

"I'm not here to make you do anything. We already had this discussion. The minute I start trying to force you to do something you don't want to do, that will pit us against each other. I can't help you if you consider me an adversary. Once that happens, I might as well go home. I'm here to help you figure out what you need so you can make better choices for yourself. That's all. When you start doing that, life won't seem so hard."

I reach the bottom of my bowl before I ask, "What do you think I should do?"

"There is one simple thing, and you can do it from this very second. Instead of going for a drink, talk to me. Talk to me about the feelings in your heart, why you want to reach for a bottle. You want to numb the pain, I get that, but Sheppard, you have to start talking to me. I don't know why I'm here. Okay?"

"Okay." It seems simple enough—unload all my shit onto her and see what she can do with it. But speaking will require admitting things I've buried for the past year, and I'll have to trust Olivia to keep me from suffocating as the words leave my mouth.

She smiles sympathetically. "How do you feel?"

"Mentally or physically?"

"Either, both."

"Physically, I feel like shit. I've never drank that much before. Mentally, not much better."

"Drink some water. Take some ibuprofen. Shower, if that will rinse some of the cobwebs from your head, then sit with me on the patio. We'll have pie and coffee."

Something in the undemanding way she handles me, the tone of her voice, the look in her eyes that's compassion, not pity, it all overwhelms me, and I blink back tears. I want her to step into my arms the way she did on the beach, hold me while I pray what I'm feeling can seep into her and lift the weight that's dragging down my soul, but I caught what she didn't say. She wants me to start being responsible for my own self because one day she's going to leave. Until this very second, booze has been my crutch, but I can't replace whiskey with Olivia. While she's here, I'm supposed to learn how to live without one, and that terrifies the shit out of me.

"Sounds good. Do you want help cleaning up?"

"No, I got it."

"Thanks for dinner." I'm going to be thanking her for more than just her cooking skills by the time the summer ends.

"You're welcome."

I didn't notice the mail she stacked on my night table when I came up to change, and before I shower, I sink onto the bed to ruffle through it. Scout joins me, crowding me until I wrap my arm around her neck. After Olivia goes home, I may need to adopt a dog. I'm getting used to Scout and the way she needs to be in my space. I have no doubt she watched over me when I sat in the water and alerted Olivia, sensing I couldn't take it anymore but couldn't go inside of my own volition.

Dalt came through, and a manilla envelope is sandwiched

between a flyer for the grocery store and a booklet of coupons for local businesses. I tear it open and slide out Olivia's book. It's a paperback copy, and she's featured on the glossy cover, wearing a dress that's similar to what she wore her first day here. Her hair is shorter but the same color, and her lips are curved into a polite smile. The title says, *Reading Your Compass: A Self-Help Guide to Navigating Life's Rocky Road.* I flip through the first couple of pages and scan the Table of Contents. While I have her in the flesh, reading her book and journaling like she wanted me to may help. I need to do something—I can't repeat this afternoon.

The dedication catches my eye: *For Michael. Your light leads my way.*

Her fiancé's name is Michael. Lucky SOB. And understanding. If my fiancée had a job that required her to live with another man for months on end, I wouldn't allow it. I don't care if I sound like an asshole putting it that way. I can still feel her breasts against my chest as I held her, the water swirling around us, my fingers twisted in her hair. Yeah, my fiancée wouldn't be doing any of that shit, even though I'm thankful Olivia pushes aside her professional boundaries to give me what I need physically. I've been lonely since Melody and I divorced, (not that our relationship toward the end was that fulfilling) and I haven't been able to assuage it with sex, meaningless or not. I'm not ready to find someone to date, jumping through all those goddamned hoops to find a woman who wants to be with me and not Sheppard Carpenter, Ghost Town's frontman. Olivia's always touching me, maybe hoping to remind me I'm not alone, and Jesus Christ, do I need it. I wonder if her classes taught her that or if she's a natural hugger. It doesn't matter. I'll take it.

I pile the book and journal onto my nightstand. It looks like I have some homework to do.

The hot water does clear some of the muzziness, and I dress

in clean shorts and a t-shirt. Before I meet Olivia downstairs, I use my cell phone's flashlight to search under my bed and pull out three more bottles of whiskey, all varying in degrees of emptiness. I don't throw out good booze, and in the living room, store them in the bar. It will be a test of my willpower to do as Olivia asked and find her instead of getting drunk, but I have a feeling if I could let her be, she would be as equally intoxicating.

She's already outside with Scout, feeding her some of the treats we ordered from the grocery store. Plates of pie and cups of coffee sit in front of her on the built-in picnic table, and for the first time in a long while, I'm nervous. She's beautiful wearing a silk tank top and matching lounging pants, her hair pulled back into a messy bun. She's elegant and graceful, kind and compassionate, and I can't get attached. Letting her help me without growing to permanently need her might be harder than trying to figure out shit on my own. How can I keep emotionally distanced when she begs me to give her my broken mind to stitch back together again?

"Hey." I step onto the patio, and the siren's song drifts on the breeze.

"Hi. Do you feel better?"

"Slightly. I have a long way to go."

"Take all the time you need."

I sit and she pushes a plate and fork toward me. Upon closer inspection, I discover the pie is apple, and I cut into the flaky crust. "Do you, I mean, did you, ever . . ." I don't know how to ask without sounding like a fucking creeper. ". . . Move beyond a professional relationship with any of your clients?" My skin heats. I know what I sound like I'm asking her, and I hope she doesn't think I want to sleep with her.

She chews the inside of her cheek before she says, "I coached a woman who lived an hour away from me. She was the director of a large non-profit. I didn't move in with her, but I saw her every day and we clicked. In some ways that made it a lot easier to help her, you know? She trusted me from the second she shook my hand. We had the same taste in movies, liked the same books and music, but if we disagreed it was . . . harder somehow. There was a layer of friendship under the professional, and instead of looking at my opinion from a logical standpoint, she took my, not criticism, but feedback, I suppose you could say, personally. She blew up when I suggested her boyfriend was holding her back and she fired me. It wasn't long after they broke up and single, she understood what I meant."

"Do you still speak with her?" When she started her story, I was prepared to hear they'd fallen into a romantic, intimate, relationship. I wouldn't care if Olivia was bisexual, but in a selfish way, I'm glad that's not where she was going sharing her experience.

"She emailed me later and apologized, but by then, the damage was done. You don't want to lose people who understand you, as there are so few in this world who are willing to accept you as you are, and it hurts when it happens. I care about all my clients and their reasons why they need me. It's almost like having children and raising them to move away from home. It's the way it's supposed to be." She tangles our fingers together. "I already know it will be hard to leave, Sheppard. We don't have to hide from it."

Relieved, I stare across the water. "You're so blunt."

She squeezes before she lets go and picks up her coffee cup. "If I want you to talk to me, I need to expect to do so in kind."

"I appreciate that."

We spend the rest of the time on the patio in silence, sounds from the neighboring houses carrying to us over the sand. Jeff and Gina go for a walk, and they wave but don't stop.

After my bender this afternoon, our run tomorrow won't be easy. I'm not looking forward to picking up the pieces, but I can't keep on this way.

Olivia straightens the kitchen, and once she goes to bed, I retrieve her book and the journal from my room. Wrapped in a throw from the living room she must have washed after kicking out my two guests since it's scented distinctly with fabric softener, I sit on the patio, and for the first time in over a year, press pen to paper and begin to write.

Chapter Nine

Olivia

"You're looking tired," Gina says, letting me into her house.

"I didn't get a lot of sleep last night." I stayed up late waiting for Sheppard to come inside. He didn't, and past midnight, I succumbed and fell into a troubled sleep. Scout never came for me, and around three in the morning, I passed out. While I was waiting to see if Sheppard would need my help, Gina texted and asked if we could meet this morning. She said Jeffrey and Sheppard were going for a run and she'd have a couple hours free. I don't sleep in on the job, but having to get up and walk over to her house by eight cut into an hour I could have stayed in bed.

Gina frowns in concern. "Jeff said that Shep was on the beach most of the afternoon and that you finally went out late last night. Why did you let him sit all that time?"

She's angry with me, and since she cares about Sheppard, I let her tone slide. Sheppard will need his friends in the weeks and months to come. They'll be here after I leave. "Because sometimes you can't put something back together unless it's broken. Trust me, Gina, had he needed me, I would have been there a lot sooner. I didn't venture far from the window the entire time. When I felt he'd had enough, I went to him. He needs to heal on his terms, not mine. If he heals on my terms, what I accomplish won't last, and after I'm gone, he'll relapse."

She purses her lips together before she says, "That makes sense, and I'm sorry I called your practices into question. You know more about this than I do. Come into the kitchen. I have coffee and pastries set out for breakfast. I know it's early, but I thought this would be a good time to talk while the guys are out and before I go to my office. I have a meeting at ten."

"Thanks." I follow her willowy figure through the living room and we sit at the same table we did when they invited us for dinner. The coffee is delicious and much needed, and I down a mug before she can gather her thoughts and notes.

She smiles in amusement. "A woman after my own heart."

"I may need a nap later. I'm still settling in."

"Are you homesick?" Gina asks, stirring sugar into her mug.

"I don't think so." I'm not sure what to say. I've seen my mother, my sister, and Agatha frequently during the past three years, but none of them were social visits. My mom and sister would sit with me until their lives dragged them away, and Agatha cleaned my house, took Scout for walks, and encouraged me to shower. "Not at this point. Ask me again in a couple of months. I like Sheppard's company. That helps."

"You don't miss your fiancé?" she asks, zeroing in on my ring.

I shouldn't have worn it to California. It's causing problems I didn't anticipate, but because Sheppard thinks I'm engaged, it will keep space between us. I've relived the way he held me a million times, his hands clenched into fists in my hair, his chest heaving with sobs. We knelt in the water together for over an hour, and even with the rocks digging into my knees and how cold I was when he finally released me, I would have let him hold me for hours more. He held me the way every woman wants to be held—like the person holding her wouldn't stand a chance of surviving without her. I know in this instance it's probably true, but that's the whole reason I'm here. So Sheppard *can* live without me.

Rubbing my ring, I say, "It's not an engagement ring, per se. It's more of a promise that one day we'll be together that way. We both have things we're busy with, and he said he'd ask when the time is right." I hate lying, but the truth isn't for anyone but Michael and me. I won't be around long enough for it to matter.

"That's actually sweet. No rush, just faith it will work out."

"Something like that. What about you and Jeffrey? Do you plan to get married?"

A smile trembles on her lips. "We talked about it, but it didn't go any further than that. In fact, I'm waiting for him to meet someone he does want to marry. That's the way things go."

"Why do you stay if you don't think he loves you?" Probably for the same reason I keep my engagement ring on my finger even though I don't need it anymore.

"Oh, he loves me, just not enough to marry me. When he meets someone at a benefit or at a premier, I'll step out of the way. I love him, and we take what we can get, don't we? Don't worry about it. I made peace with it years ago."

"How long have you been together?"

She brushes a tear off her cheek. "Nine years this fall. We met at a fundraiser for one of my indie films. We got to talking about film production and one thing led to the next."

"You should tell him how you feel."

Tilting her head, she asks, "Why? So he can get angry and defensive? So he'll break it off with me all that much sooner?

We already talked about it, and he tabled the discussion. Would you beg a man to stay? Stoop to that level? You're a strong woman who teaches other women to be strong when they're at their weakest. Would you really beg a man to stay with you?"

"Not when you put it like that," I murmur, turning my mug around on the table's surface. I wouldn't beg anyone to love me, but maybe, had I been given the chance, I would have begged Michael to stay. Fallen to my knees, pressed my face into his thigh. He didn't give me that chance, and one day he was gone. There was nothing I could do but try to move on in the best way I could, and I still wear his ring on my finger. Gina lives with a man who won't marry her. Neither of us are doing a bang up job of living our lives the way an independent woman should.

"I can't be an example if I'm not willing to walk my talk," she says, "and you lead by example too."

"No, I don't. That's why I retired—because I couldn't lead by example anymore. Life ran me over, and I haven't been able to get back up."

"Then why do you think you can help Shep?"

"I don't. I told Dalton as much, and Sheppard, too. All I can do is my best, and maybe it will be enough. I hope it will. Sheppard needs someone."

"You still don't know why you're here, do you?" Gina asks, sliding a piece of coffeecake onto a small plate decorated with flowers and pushing it across the table.

"No, but Sheppard's getting closer to talking to me. Last night he stayed up to journal. When people can open up to themselves, it isn't long before they can open up to other people. I'll wait."

"It would be easy to find online. Everything that happened is on *Buzz Kill.*"

I curl my lip when she says the name of the notorious gossip website. "No thanks."

Gina laughs, the traces of melancholy talking about Jeffrey caused gone. "I like you, Olivia. Something knocked you down and took away your confidence and self-esteem, but I hope after your time in LA, you'll have proof that you're still the same person you were before and come out of retirement. I read your blog faithfully for years. You were helping people."

I lean forward. "But what if, what if you can't help the one person who means more to you than anyone else in the world? What then, Gina? From the time I was small, all I ever wanted to do was help people, and I did. I know I did. I have testimonials and fan mail to prove I did, but I failed the one person I would have given my life for, and now I'm supposed to help Sheppard? He's borderline alcoholic, depressed, has nightmares, and I think he's suicidal. How can I look past my own demons for him?"

I shouldn't be spouting off everything I think Sheppard is suffering from, but Gina is a close friend, or the girlfriend of one of his close friends, and when she nods, I have proof she already knew. I wasn't spilling any secrets and sipping my coffee, I hide my relief.

"You aren't the only one who's failed, Olivia. That's the whole point of my documentary. You fail, you pick yourself up and try again. The other women who have agreed to talk to me . . . a pediatrician failed to diagnose her own daughter until it was too late. By the time she suspected anything, her daughter's cancer was untreatable and she died not long after. Do you think she had trouble going into her practice every day to treat other children while having that hang over her head? I'm interviewing a CEO who didn't see her personal assistant was a victim of domestic violence. She didn't go in to work one day, and the woman found out later her assistant's boyfriend killed her in a rage. We *all* have let people down, and we all get up and keep going. We all struggle to figure out who we are after a tragedy."

"I'm so sorry." The words are inadequate.

She squeezes my hand. "Next week I'm meeting them for lunch. Come with me. Listen to what they have to say, tell your story. As women, we'll heal together."

"I'll think about it." I don't want to share my story. I don't want to tell anyone how I failed. Those women are stronger than me if they can admit their faults and not be afraid to be judged. No one judged me—I did plenty of that for myself—but I don't want to invite scrutiny. Like Sheppard, I need to heal on my own terms, and it won't be in California.

"Good. I think we've talked about enough sad things for one day. Tell me about Scout. Have you had her for a long time?"

I twist my ring around my finger. "We picked her up at a shelter when we decided we were committed enough to get married. Someone found her in a house up for sale. The people who owned her moved and didn't take her with them. We've— I've had her for about five years now. I trained her to be a therapy dog, and she's bonding with Sheppard. I'm glad he took her on the run with Jeffrey. She likes spending time with him." That's another thing I'll have to come to terms with in these short months before I leave. Scout misses Michael beyond description, and she's taken to Sheppard in a way I wasn't prepared for. When it's time to go, she'll want to stay with him. I lost most of my heart the day Michael left, and that small, tiny little piece remaining, that will be gone when I drive away without my dog.

We chat for another half an hour, and she closes our conversation with the promise of texting me tomorrow. I'm glad she was the one to wrap things up—I would have felt rude had I done it. I'm tired, and our talk wore me out. When I lost Michael, I should have found my own therapist, talked through his abandoning me, but I kept to myself in our little house and now I'm paying the price.

Sheppard's in the shower when I go upstairs, Scout waiting patiently by the bathroom door in his bedroom. She looks at me but doesn't move. I wave her off and leaving my door cracked, change out of the dress I wore to Gina's. I lie on the bed and I'm drifting off when Sheppard leans against the doorjamb.

"Need a nap? I could probably use one, too. I'll be lucky if I can walk later."

"Yeah, I'm tired. Gina asks hard questions."

"That she does, but her documentaries wouldn't win any awards if she didn't."

I blink sleepily. "They do?"

"Yep. The International Documentary Association loves her. She won for her documentary on teen mothers earlier this year." He chuckles and steps farther into the bedroom. "You were up waiting for me last night, weren't you?"

"Maybe."

There's a blanket folded at the end of the bed, and he covers me with it and smooths the hair away from my face. "I appreciate that. Go to sleep. I'm good for now."

"Thanks. Will you feed Scout?" I mumble, already slipping into unconsciousness.

"Sure."

I don't feel right napping when Sheppard's awake and puttering around, but my emotional exhaustion is wearing me down, and in defense, my mind pulls me under. For a couple of hours, I forget Michael is gone, and in my dreams, the siren's lethal song tempts me to join her in the water.

I wake up groggy and feeling like I didn't sleep at all. I stumble down stairs regretting I napped, dregs of a nightmare lingering, the scent of saltwater in my nose, the phantom swirling of the foam twirling around my ankles.

Sheppard's sitting on the patio, Scout lying next to his chair, and I help myself to coffee and join them, settling into a padded lounger and closing my eyes against the nausea that twists my stomach.

He's silent, the black gel pen gliding over the lined paper. I'm glad he's using the notebook I gave him. Journaling isn't for everyone, but I thought as a songwriter, pen and paper wouldn't be unfamiliar. I don't care what he's writing—lyrics, poetry, an essay, his dreams and nightmares—it's that he can form the words from his feelings that matters and will help him heal.

I think about ways to start a conversation. I haven't been here long, but it would be nice if he opened up to me, little by little. I don't want our talks to feel forced, and I don't want him to feel like I'm coercing him into revealing his secrets. So, I sit and sip, the water lapping at the sand as people walk by, tourists, hoping to see someone famous.

"Did you and Gina have a good talk?" he asks, closing the notebook over his pen.

I grimace. "I think I stepped in it a bit. I asked her if she and Jeffrey were going to get married, and she said no."

"Common law," he says. "They've been together for a long time and probably feel like they are."

"I think she wants more than that. She said she was waiting for him to find someone else, and that made me sad."

Sheppard meets my eyes over the little table that holds my

self-help book he got from somewhere, treats for Scout, and his coffee mug. "He wouldn't do that. He loves her very much."

"Then they need to talk, because she expects it to happen."

"If she believes that, marriage won't help. You can still move on even if you've signed papers and swapped rings."

"That's true, but isn't there a comfort in saying the vows?" I won't have that now, the promises shared in front of family and friends. I won't have that night when I make love with my husband for the first time. I won't ever feel cherished by a man who wants to keep me forever. Michael stole that from me, and I'm not under any illusion a different man can give it back.

"If there is, it's manufactured at best. Jeff's committed; Gina doesn't have anything to worry about."

"Why did you get a divorce? Would you ever consider a reconciliation?" I risk him shutting me out. It's a natural question given our topic, and if he asks about Michael, I'll tell him the same thing I told Gina. If I'm going to lie, I'll tell the same story to everyone.

Sheppard laughs, a bitter sound. "She doesn't want anything to do with me."

I frown. "Are you sure? She was at Dalton's office the day he hired me."

His jaw hardens. "Why?"

I lift a shoulder. "I don't know. She didn't say anything to me. To be fair, Reggie, Eddie and Brock were there, too, but I thought she was hoping for a reconciliation after . . ."

"After I'm better?" he finishes sarcastically.

"You won't ever be 'better,' Sheppard. You're dealing with trauma, and the best you can do is learn to live with it in the healthiest way possible. You can't deny you shut down and shut everyone out. Maybe I'm wrong to assume she wants a second chance after you've gotten some shit figured out. Why did you divorce?" I ask again because he didn't answer me the first time.

"For the opposite reason we married?" he asks, quirking his lips.

"How did you meet?"

Sheppard shifts and leans toward me. "At a fashion show in Paris. Chanel used our music and we were there to promote our album. Melody was one of their models, and she took my breath away when she walked down the runway. After the show, I introduced myself. I knew that day I wanted to spend the rest of my life with her, but if I knew then what I know now, a couple needs more than attraction and money to make it work. I wouldn't have asked her to marry me so quickly. We were married for a long time, but we didn't share any common interests, didn't share the same life goals. When she said she wanted a divorce, it wasn't a surprise. It hurt because divorce will always hurt, that sense of failure," he says, meeting my eyes. "We had some good times, but those good times centered around world tours, every Fashion Week known to man, parties, award shows, and booze. We were on top of the world, and we fell off."

"But you wouldn't consider giving her a second chance?"

"Maybe, but why? The life we lived and the life I want to live now aren't the same. I don't know if I can ever go back to that."

"Maybe she doesn't want that, either. She was at that meeting for a reason."

Sheppard scowls. "Are you a matchmaker, too?"

"No, but obviously, I'm invested in your treatment, progress, whatever you want to call it, and if Melody can help, then I want that for you." It's only partially a lie. I do want that for him. If a reconciliation with his ex-wife will put him on the path to recovery, I want that for him. But I remember how his fingertips lingered near my temple when he brushed my bangs away from my eyes, and just for a second, I wished there were more feelings behind the motion. Just for a second. "You said you don't want to go back to that. What kind of life do you envision for yourself?"

He sips his coffee and says, "I don't know. That's something I'm going to have to work out, either while you're here or after you leave. I'm lonely, and that's part of the reason I don't want to hop into bed with her, so to speak. If Melody and I ever got back together, it would be because we still love each other and we admitted our divorce was a mistake. I've lived most of my life in front of a camera, in some way or another, and I want the last half of my life to be slower, quieter."

"I know what you mean. Not to the degree you've lived your life, but I understand. When I was at my peak, I was booked for women's talks, keynote speeches, women's retreats, panels, and Ted Talks. I was writing my book and doing promo for that. At night, I would fall into bed, so high on adrenaline I couldn't fall asleep. But I loved it, you know? Helping people, listening to people tell me how I touched their lives. And then, one day, it just stopped. The noise made me so deaf I couldn't hear the silence. The neighbor mowing his yard. Scout's snores when she napped. A favorite song playing in the grocery store. You've lived so fast and so furiously for so long, that maybe you do need to find that calm, but you can't go from six hundred miles per hour to nothing. There's a balance we can find if we look for it, and maybe Melody wants to find it, too. Do you have children?"

"No. When we married, Melody was at the height of her career. By the time she would have considered the idea, our marriage was crumbling. Do you?"

I cover my belly with my hand. Michael and I talked children, and after he left I wished I would have let myself get pregnant. But I was glad too, that I hadn't because I didn't want them to grow up feeling how I do—that he didn't love me enough to stay. "No. Maybe one day."

"Your fiancé wants kids, doesn't he?" Sheppard asks, not understanding the quicksand he pushed me into.

Michael wanted kids, but the promise of a family didn't keep him with me. "Yeah."

"I do, too. Eddie and Brock have a few rugrats between them. Dalt said he never met the right woman. We would sit up late after a recording session and talk about it. What having children would mean for us, for the group. Eddie and Brock don't see their kids very often, and it hurts them." He blows out a sigh. "When I pulled away from everyone, I did more than break up the band. I broke up a family."

"If there's one thing I've learned through the years, it's that you can't depend on other people for your happiness. If Eddie and Brock are unhappy, they need to fix it, not lean on you. They need to open up communication with their ex-wives, create space in their schedules to spend time with their kids. You can't fill in for that, and you shouldn't feel guilty you can't replace what they need. The band isn't a replacement for you, either. I hope you use your time with me to find what you need to be whole without depending on anyone else."

Sheppard opens his notebook and scribbles. I let him be, hoping I offered some advice he can learn from.

"Are you happy when you're alone?" he asks.

I laugh, and it's weak and sad. "Oh, don't use me as a role model. I'm quite miserable."

"What would you need to find joy?"

He's not asking to test me, not in a "Doctor, heal thyself" type of way, though if he was, that would be valid too. It's part of the reason I retired. If I couldn't bounce back after Michael left using the lessons I tried to teach others, what good am I? I think, hoping my answer will guide Sheppard's path to his own healing.

"How does someone learn to be happy alone? Confidence, maybe, being comfortable in your own skin. You have to like yourself and appreciate the qualities that make you who you are, and right now, I don't. I don't think I have anything to offer anyone, though Gina, and you and Dalton, say that's not true. Evidence of that truth? I'm not sure. Maybe spending more time with family. I have a mother and sister I used to be close to, but I pulled away after I retired. Search for meaning in the little things. We're only grains of sand on a beach. Use that to find perspective."

Sheppard nods and settles into his lounger, thoughtfully rubbing his fingers over his scruff.

Seagulls fly overhead, and a breeze dances across the beach. People walk by, flicking us curious glances. They must know who Sheppard is, but they're polite and don't stop to ask for an autograph or a selfie. I wonder if that relieves him, or if because he's used to the spotlight, he's disappointed.

He checks his phone and sends a text. When he receives a reply, he asks, "Would you be all right if I ran an errand?"

"Yeah, sure," I say, a little surprised he has somewhere to go, and wants to, for that matter, but I never accepted this job thinking we would be here twenty-four hours a day, seven days a week, for the next three months. I may not have anywhere to go so long as I can order food and supplies for Scout if she needs them, but Sheppard is still the lead singer of one of the most famous rock bands of all time, and he wouldn't be able to walk away from his responsibilities as easily as I did when I retired.

"I shouldn't be gone long. I want to talk to Dalt, and he's still at his office. I'll be home for dinner."

"Take your time. If you decide to grab a bite with him, let me know, and I'll eat leftovers."

He brushes my cheek with his thumb. "I'd rather eat dinner with you. I'll be back soon."

"Okay."

Scout knows she's not invited to go along and watches him open the sliding glass door with an unhappy whine. Rubbing my cheek, I empathize. He didn't have to tell me where he was going, but I appreciate that he did. Maybe my time here will be shorter than I thought it would be and he's already planning on getting Ghost Town back together. I hope that's true. It breaks my heart to see him so defeated and obviously missing something so much.

After I know he's gone, I do some cleaning. I put our sheets in the wash as we were both covered in saltwater from our time in the ocean last night, and I sweep the floors. The domesticity brings tears to my eyes. On the days when I didn't have a commitment or an obligation, I would clean and cook dinner while I waited for Michael to come home from teaching. It's what I feel like now, puttering around in a beautiful house that Sheppard more than likely shared with Melody, washing windows and going over the furniture with the vacuum wand.

A beef roast with carrots and potatoes is cooking in the oven, and I'm sitting on the sand with Scout when Sheppard finds me. I'm trying my best not to cry, guilty as all hell because Michael is slipping away from me, and in Sheppard's house, I don't know if I should try to stop it.

Chapter Ten

Sheppard

I'm royally pissed off, and I speed on the way to Dalt's office. It's a thirty minute drive from Malibu to Santa Monica, and I seethe all the way there. The sunny sky does nothing to ease my temper, nor does the light traffic quell my anger as I park my BMW in the parking garage.

Thanks to Olivia, I haven't had a drink today, and Dalt's fucking lucky I'm clear-headed as I stand in the elevator and it carries me to the sixteenth floor.

Along with his suits from Sears, Dalt managed us from wherever he could charge a laptop and hook up to free internet. When we were small-time punks, we'd play any dive we could, and he'd keep track of our gigs on an Excel spreadsheet. His cushy office and pretty secretary are quite a few steps up.

We all grew up in California, and I know Los Angeles like the back of my hand, but what I've needed has always been close by.

I was surprised after the divorce Melody didn't move to New York, and she still lives in the house we purchased in

Pacific Palisades. I gave it to her and kept the beach house in Malibu. That huge fucking mansion we bought when we married was never home. It was only a place to sleep between flights, concerts, and fashion shows. Impersonal with its pool, tennis court, marble floors, and a maid who cleaned and land-scapers who wouldn't let one weed grow. I'm glad Melody is happy there because I sure as hell wasn't.

To be fair, I'm not happy in Malibu either, the only time I feel any sick peace is when I'm standing in the water, the siren singing her sweet song. The power I have knowing I can end it, just like that.

Dalt's in his office when I stride in without knocking, and I glance around before I speak. My drive gave him time to call Eddie and Brock, and I'm glad he didn't. We're hashing this out alone.

"Why was Melody at your meeting with Olivia?" I ask angrily, standing in front of his desk.

I catch the faint notes of her perfume, the cloying, heavy sent of Poison, an Alice Cooper song, incidentally, we covered back when the band started and we weren't writing our own music yet.

He swallows and rises from his chair. "What do you mean? We were all here because we're concerned about you. She's not any different."

"Did she say why?"

"Only that she wants what's best for you." He studies me, his posture stiff. Since when has the subject of my ex-wife been a topic of disagreement?

I laugh. "Really? Because I don't seem to recall her asking if divorcing was what was best for me. Especially then, when I needed her. She's half the reason I've spent the past year drunk off my ass, and I hope you realize that. You inviting her to a meeting, a meeting that didn't need Reggie, Eddie, and Brock there, if you want to know the fucking truth, is an invasion of my privacy. When people divorce that means they're no longer connected. We don't have kids. She has no rights in my life anymore, Dalt. I mean it."

He raises his hands, palms toward me. "Okay. I'm sorry. I thought having all the people you can in your corner would help, but it appears I was wrong."

"She's not in my corner and I'm not sure when the last time she was. Does she think our divorce was a mistake?"

Dalt pales. "She didn't say that."

"I didn't think so. She checked out a long time ago. In fact, I'm willing to bet she was cheating on me for at least a year before she finally served me papers. I don't know why she waited so long."

I walk around Dalt's office, Santa Monica stretched out before me. What was Olivia thinking when she stood here and listened to Dalt tell her how fucked my life was? What was she thinking when Melody sat and stared holes through her, in that haughty, snobby way she has? And Reggie? Did he have anything to say? Brock and Eddie might have spoken with her, told her a little bit about the past year, my withdrawal from the band and our friendships. Not anything more because she said she doesn't know about Derrick and I believe her. She's a life coach, and maybe my situation isn't that strange to her, but what did she think when Dalton West, manager of the hottest rock band in the world, told her its lead singer couldn't crawl out of bed because he's too drunk and depressed off his ass to shower?

I picture her here, in the dress she wore the day I met her in my kitchen, tired from her flight, leaning against the window, the sunshine highlighting her hair, as Dalt made his demands. I hear her soft voice decline, say she's retired and she met with him out of curiosity and courtesy, only for him to beg her because he's not stupid and could see the qualities in her I can that sobered me up for the first time in a year.

I understand why he met with everyone behind my back. I would have exploded like the goddamned Fourth of July if he'd had the audacity to summon me to his office to talk about my sobriety and the future of the band. He called and said something rushed and incoherent and mixing that with my inebriated state, he was able to sneak Olivia into my house and into my life where I'm already looking at her departure like I'm staring down the barrel of a gun. Four days in, and I need her.

"What makes you think she was cheating? Shep, we were just coming off a world tour. You barely saw her."

"That's exactly why I think she was cheating. She traveled with us, yet I never saw her, and she would never explain where she was. The tour felt wrong, something was off. Eddie and Brock said they didn't notice and it was business as usual, but Derrick wouldn't talk to me, went out of his way to avoid me. Do you know anything? Did he tell you anything? Was he getting tired of this life, because I sure as hell wouldn't have blamed him."

Dalt sighs and leans against his desk. "He didn't say anything like that to me. You know I was riding him hard to check into rehab after the tour. He avoided me just as much as he was avoiding you because like you, he didn't want to hear it. Do you know how difficult it is to get one single word in edgewise when you've been drinking? The only thing that would have made you listen is what I did. I knew you wouldn't hurt Olivia. You're a lot of things, Shep, but you don't raise a hand to anybody, I don't care how mad you get. I've always admired that about you."

No, I didn't raise a hand to her, but I pulled her close, threatening her, and instead of scaring her, I created a need I don't know if I'll ever be able to shake.

Well, I damned well better. She can't be mine.

All the fight drains out of me, and I drop into a chair in front of his desk. I rub my face, disoriented. I've rarely left the beach house in the past year, and I want to go back to what I know, the feelings I know.

"Is that all you wanted?" Dalt asks.

"Yeah. Don't involve Melody in my life. She doesn't belong there anymore, and that was her choice."

"Okay. I'm sorry."

Silence hangs in the air. I should have more to say but I don't. I stand to go.

"Shep."

I turn from his office door, my only thought to finding an escape.

"Even if it was to bitch me out, it's good to see you. I know it took a lot for you to drudge up the energy."

I nod. "Yeah. Thanks for sending me Olivia's book."

"Whatever you need, all you have to do is ask. He was my friend, too."

I think about that on the way back to the house. Didn't consider what Dalt, Eddie, and Brock are going through. They always acted like it didn't hit them as hard as it did me, but maybe it did. Maybe it did.

The kitchen is filled with the mouth-watering scent of a beef roast in the oven, and for once, I don't give in to the desire to go upstairs, crawl into bed, and pull the covers over my head as darkness fills my mind and soul.

Olivia cleaned while I was gone, and I bet anything I'll sleep in fresh sheets tonight, too.

The house already feels empty when she's not in it, and I look over the beach. She's not chained to the house, and if she grows close to Gina, often there will be times I'll find her in Gina and Jeff's kitchen instead of mine, but now she's sitting on the sand with Scout, her knees tucked into a large sweatshirt, her head resting on her arms, looking over the water.

I sit next to her, and she turns her head and peers at me with one eye. "Are you okay?" she asks.

A piece of her hair falls across the bridge of her nose, and I push it behind her ear. "I'm getting there."

Olivia usually stands at the breakfast bar while we eat our meals, but tonight we sit at the dining room table.

After I bought the place from a country singer who was going through his third divorce, I didn't do much renovating. I appreciated the house already had a recording studio in it, and if it wouldn't have had one, I would have put one in. Since my life has fallen apart, two guest rooms are more than I need, but I didn't have the energy or the want to do anything with them. I'm thankful now or else Olivia wouldn't have had a place to sleep. The living room is a decent size for as little time I spend there. I don't have a viewing room like Jeff and Gina, which makes sense for them, as they both watch unedited scenes from their projects. I'm only thinking about this while beef melts in my mouth because we're sitting at this large fucking table, and it doesn't feel right. Not when the others used to camp out here during hardcore brainstorming sessions. Before Brock and Eddie divorced, their wives would come out, and their kids would crawl around the house. I can still see a highchair set up for Eddie's daughter, Abby, and she'd bang her hands on the tray. We'd joke she'd be our next drummer, and he'd act all affronted. Those were good times.

Olivia's quiet, and I wonder if she made any phone calls while I was gone. To her fiancé, no doubt, to her agent, I suppose, to check in.

It's surreal Dalt hired this stranger I'm supposed to bare my soul to, and it's more surreal I want her to stay. We're strangers, but after four days, I know more about her than I know about some of my friends.

"Do you think this is odd?" I don't elaborate. I'm learning Olivia will always understand what I'm talking about.

She pushes back a smile. "I try not to think about it or I'll get self-conscious."

"So you feel it."

"I'm living in your house and I barely know you. What do you think?"

"Do you want to stay in a hotel instead? You don't have to live here," I reluctantly offer. There's a huge amount of trust on her part that I won't hurt her. She doesn't know me like Dalt does.

She cuts more roast and serves herself another slice before she says, "I think that would break Scout's heart, but more importantly, after what I've seen of you in the middle of the night, I should stay here. I don't want to think about how you've been by yourself this past year."

"I'd be fine," I say, but I'm already dependent on her and I wouldn't be fine.

"It's my job to be here for you, and I can't be if I spend half my time at a hotel. It's kind and I thank you for offering, but you're experiencing the same thing. It can't be pleasant having a stranger in your house. Someone pushed on you, for that matter."

"I resented you for about ten minutes. It was the lavender plug-in that turned it around." I'm only half joking.

She smiles around a mouthful of potatoes. "See? Then we're past the hard part. You don't have to entertain me, you can do whatever you want."

"I'm still finding my footing with that," I admit, going in for a second helping of the potatoes and carrots soaking in beef broth. I'll need to hire a housekeeper after Olivia leaves. I'm getting used to eating real food. "But you don't have to entertain me, either. You can read a book or watch something. If you didn't notice, there's a TV built into the wall in your room. Slide the wooden panels back and you can watch while you're in bed. I'm subscribed to all the streaming services."

"Thanks. Maybe. I don't watch much TV. I have a laptop and I brought a tablet with me. I have plenty of books on it, so once we find more of a routine, that will keep me occupied. How did you like journaling last night?"

"Good," I say, and I don't feel odd answering her question, not like she's poking at me to see if I've made progress with anything. It's just a question because she wants to know the answer, no hidden agenda. "Do you journal?"

"My blog was kind of a journal, and I poured a lot of my feelings into that. Writing is more of a professional stepping stone than a hobby I do in my spare time, and I would need a mind shift to write for pleasure."

"Maybe start up your blog again," I say, jabbing at a potato with my fork.

She tilts her head in thought. "Why?"

I appreciate she doesn't ask in a disgusted tone, like I mentioned something filthy. She's curious why I would suggest it. What I like best about talking to Olivia is that she treats me like an equal. She might have the psychology degree, but she's never made me feel stupid because I need her.

I bare my teeth in a grimace. "Because if I'm supposed to be making professional advances, why can't you? You're already working with Gina, and you keep assuring me I have free time, which means you, also, have free time. Make it work for you."

"I can't just dust off my website and start writing." Her hand trembles as she raises a bite of beef to her mouth. "That would be like me asking you to write a song in the morning. You wouldn't be able to do it, and it would be cruel to ask."

The thought of sitting down and hammering out some music and lyrics scares the shit out of me, but at some point it will be expected, a goal to be reached. "Then how about you figure out what you need, and I'll figure out what I need, and we learn to walk together?"

"This isn't about me." She sounds relieved, but I'm not going to let her off the hook that easily.

"Oh, but honey, if I'm going to be terrified, you can be too."

Olivia sighs and stares down at her plate, but I know I've got her.

"Baby steps," she says.

I don't know where the words come from, but I say, "Don't worry. If you trip, I'll catch you."

She swallows hard, and Scout whines. "I trust you. You've already caught me once."

We finish the rest of the meal in silence.

I help her clean up after we're done eating. The refrigerator is full of leftovers, and I suggest we eat through them before she cooks another full meal.

"Maybe you can return Jeff and Gina's invitation and we can have them over," she says.

I emotionally withdraw from the idea of having guests, people invading the safe haven I've created for myself, but asking them over for dinner would ease me into a social life if Olivia wants me to start doing that kind of thing. Besides her, I haven't had someone in my house since the day I came back from Derrick's funeral and didn't leave again. Well, that's not true, but I don't count the two women Olivia kicked out as guests. I was drunk, and they'd been unwanted and unwelcome, but it's easier to have strangers here than people who matter to me.

She senses my hesitation and squeezes my forearm, understanding glimmering in her eyes. "When you're ready."

"Okay," I say, relieved I don't have to explain.

"I'm going to let Scout run outside. Do you want to come with me?"

She would turn our walk on the beach into an opportunity to talk, maybe ask about my conversation with Dalt, and I don't feel like getting into it now. "No, thanks. I'm going up to my room. I'll see you in the morning."

A frown creases her forehead. It's a little early to say goodnight, and we've started spending time together in the evenings. I want to think she's disappointed but she whispers, "Goodnight," and simply calls for Scout. The dog is torn between needing to go outside and going upstairs with me, but in the end her bladder wins and she follows Olivia onto the patio.

Alone in the house, I almost run after her, but I force myself to stay behind and trudge up the stairs. The quiet is eerie—I'm already used to Olivia puttering around in the kitchen, Scout's nails scratching against the floor, and her gentle panting. I think of Olivia's comment she made last night about being too deaf to enjoy the silence. I stand in my bedroom and listen. The waves break along the beach, the siren calling to me, always. There's traffic on the street behind the house I've always tuned out, and a helicopter flies overhead. Olivia left her cell phone behind and it chimes with a text in her bedroom. After years of listening to the roar of the crowds, music blasting in our ears, the fans' screams, I understand what she meant. I can be scared of it, or I can learn to enjoy it.

I came up to look around online, do a little digging since I haven't been able to get Jeff's speculations out of my head, but the conversation I had with Dalt weighs on me, the expectations crush me, and instead of booting up my laptop, I turn out the light, succumbing to the heaviness and crawling into bed. I bury my face in a pillow and push back a sob.

I'm so tired, and no one seems to understand that, or if they do, they think I should be able to carry on despite it.

The sliding glass door opens and closes, and I listen to Olivia get ready for bed. Scout noses at my door, but I shut it completely and I don't get up to let her in.

It's after midnight when I know Olivia will be sleeping and I slide out of bed. I desperately need a drink, and all my booze is downstairs. My mouth waters, anticipating the burn, and the siren calls to me, luring me to her. Whiskey and the sand.

The house is quiet, and I gently open my door. I don't want Olivia to know I'm giving in, don't want her to catch me. I don't want to disappoint her. I don't need the extra guilt, but I need a drink more than I want her approval.

Pausing at the top of the staircase, I feel her sorrow in my bones rather than hear her. I backtrack a few steps and stand outside her bedroom. The lamp sitting on her nightstand glows, and her door's cracked. Through the slit, I see her sitting on the floor near the bed, her head hidden in her arms. She's sobbing into her knees, keening, and the craving for a drink dries in my throat.

She's so fragile curled against the wall, and I want to go to her, but I don't. I wouldn't appreciate her barging in on me, and I don't do that to her.

I let her be and continue down the stairs. When I reach the living room, I do the hardest thing I've ever done. I turn toward the kitchen instead of the bar and start a pot of coffee. I grip the counter while it drips, my knuckles white, my stomach churning. When it's done, I fix a mug how Olivia likes it and carry it to her room. Her door is still cracked, and I push it open. She's not crying anymore but she's still on the floor.

Settling next to her, I offer her the mug.

Silently, she holds it between her palms, and with my thumbs, I wipe the tears from her cheeks. Her skin is soft, and her eyes glitter in the dim light. Her lavender scent mingles with the earthy notes of the coffee, and my cock stiffens in desire. I want her, and I push it back. I release her face and look away, and she holds the mug to her lips.

I stay with her until she's done, steadying her hands when she almost spills the hot liquid down her pajama top, and then tuck her into bed. Scout climbs in with her, and brushing the hair away from her face, I pull the comforter up to her shoulder. She burrows into a pillow, exhausted, and sitting on the edge of the mattress, I linger until she falls asleep.

We didn't say one word aloud, but we spoke more tonight than we have since the day I found her in my kitchen.

I pour a cup of coffee and sit on the patio with my journal. The light shining from the living room is enough to see by, and as my pen glides against the smooth paper, Olivia's sobs echo in my heart.

Chapter Eleven

Olivia

I'm so terribly embarrassed. I'm embarrassed Sheppard found me crying, and I'm embarrassed he comforted me and tucked me into bed on top of it. I don't know how I'm supposed to help him when I can't help myself. Well, I think, sipping coffee the next morning, I already knew that. Regardless if I help Sheppard back into the recording studio or not, Dalton will pay me for my time. Not that the money matters. I told him I couldn't do this—I won't feel bad cashing his check at the end of the summer and I've proven myself right.

Sheppard was already gone when I woke up and showered. The morning runs with Jeffrey get him out of the house and Scout loves the exercise. She didn't stay with me long last night, either, the traitor. The second Sheppard left and kept my door cracked open, she was bounding off the bed following behind him.

Oatmeal is bubbling on the stove when Sheppard lets himself inside after stretching on the sand with Jeffrey. My cheeks flush, and I turn my gaze toward my laptop instead of meeting his piercing stare. I feel like a fool, and a hot and bothered one, at that. I've relived the way he held my face in his hands a million times, and every time I do, I buckle under my betrayal.

"Hey," he says, sliding the patio door closed behind him and Scout. "I was hoping you'd sleep in. You had a late night last night."

"No later than you if you were up to hear me cry. I'm sorry about that."

His skin glistens with sweat, and his muscle shirt sticks to his chest. He runs his fingers through his damp hair and tentatively walks toward me, his tennis shoes covered in sand. "I'm not." He flushes under his scruff and says, "You saved me from, umm, going for a drink. You said I could come to you if I needed you, and I did. I'm sorry if I disturbed you."

"No, it's okay. I'm embarrassed because I don't want you to see me vulnerable, but that's silly because we all are. We're human. I'm glad I was able to be there for you, even if you were there more for me. What did you do after I fell asleep?"

"Sat outside and journaled a bit. It was good. Sitting with you was better than a drink, even if you were lousy company," he teases, coaxing a reluctant smile from me. "What are you doing?" He nods at my laptop.

"I can't expect you to give without giving a little, too. I'm looking at the backend of my website. Skimming my last blogposts, that kind of thing. The only problem is, I don't know what to say. My followers will want to know why I dropped off the earth, and I don't want to share what happened. I can write about this," I say, holding out my hand and gesturing around his house, "but I didn't accept this job to come out of retirement, and it's not appropriate to say where I am."

It was difficult to read those last blogposts. The one before Michael when life had been perfect, and the one after when my world collapsed. Thousands of comments are attached to the very last one, and I didn't read any of them. Not one. Pulled it all down and that's the way it has stayed. I had a hell of a time getting in, too, because I didn't remember my password to the site or the password to the email address where the site sent my reset password link.

Sheppard closes my laptop with a quiet click. "I think if we're taking baby steps, you've done enough for today. What do you have over there?" He juts his chin toward the stovetop.

"Oatmeal."

"As . . . delicious as that sounds, let's get out of here. Sound good?"

I push back a smile. "Oatmeal is good for you." It does sound good, going somewhere else, not the oatmeal, and participating in an activity, even walking the beach, will help encourage conversation. Sheppard needs to start talking to me, or no matter how great we get along or how much I enjoy living here and spending time with him, I might as well leave. I'm not a scammer, and I'm not going to let Dalton pay me to putter around Sheppard's house. I'm not a housekeeper, and maid service would be a lot cheaper than what I'm charging Ghost Town for three months. The end result will be the same, but I need to earn that paycheck. Or try to.

"Hmm. So are a lot of other things. There's a basket in the laundry room. I'll shower, and you can fix some roast beef sandwiches from our leftovers last night. We'll make a day of it, okay?"

"Okay."

He looks as if he wants to say something else, but he doesn't, only turns and trots up the stairs, my dog behind him.

The basket isn't large, and we'll have an easy time carrying it, no matter how far we go. It helps that I don't pack any alcohol. If he wanted a drink last night, abstinence may be best. I don't know him well enough to guess if he needs AA, but I'll recommend it if I think he could benefit from it. Sparkling water will be fine, and I put together thick sandwiches and squish an unopened bag of sour cream and onion potato chips into the basket, too. There's apple pie left over from a few nights ago, and I pack that with plates and forks. I find ice packs in the freezer, and I add two to keep our food cold. I don't know how long we'll be gone, but if he said we'll make a day out of it, maybe we won't be back until dinner. There's leftover chicken noodle soup we can heat up tonight, and after that's gone, I can cook something new for dinner tomorrow.

There's just enough room in the basket to add what Scout will need to be gone for the day; she needs fresh water and lunch like we do. I change into more comfortable shorts and a t-shirt and tie a sweatshirt around my waist. With clouds hiding the sun, it can grow cool, and I want to be prepared.

Sheppard trots downstairs carrying a blanket, and I'm waiting by the door, the picnic basket at my feet. Scout's on his heels, excited for an adventure. It tugs at my heart she won't miss me.

"What did you do with the oatmeal?" he asks.

"I put it away. We can eat it tomorrow for breakfast."

He grimaces. "Great."

Smothering a laugh, I say, "I thought you'd like that."

"The lead singer of Ghost Town doesn't eat oatmeal. I didn't want to have to tell you, but you gave me no choice," he says, reaching for the basket when we step onto the sand. "Here, trade." He stuffs the blanket at me.

"Is that what you are?" Maybe it was a heartless question, callous, but I'm curious what he thinks. "Is that how you still describe yourself?"

He's quiet, his eyes on Scout as she races ahead. Two

teenagers walking the beach stop to pet her, and she revels in the attention.

We walk for about three quarters of a mile, passing the rocks I almost fell on when he says, "Have you ever been something for so long, it's not *what* you are but *who* you are?"

I think about that for a while because identity is important, especially to a woman. We've had to fight for every inch given to us, and we always have been and always will be, more than the daughter we are when we're born, the wife we become if we marry, and the mothers we turn into when we have our own children. "No, and that's hard for me to admit. It means I haven't done anything with my life."

"You're lucky," he says, tugging a tennis ball out of his shorts pocket. He throws it down the beach and Scout chases after the bright yellow sphere.

"Why do you say that?" I don't feel like I am, being no one.

"Because you can choose to be whatever you want to be. I've been lead singer of Ghost Town for longer than I haven't. It's part of me. So, if I choose not to be that anymore, who am I?"

"Rockstars don't sing forever. Sometimes they can't."

"True, but then that's not my choice, if my voice goes. I've been fortunate to avoid vocal damage, but if I say right here, today, that I'm no longer Ghost Town's lead singer, that's my choice."

We walk for a while, Sheppard throwing the ball to Scout, who is only too happy to retrieve it.

He isn't done and asks, "You told Gina when we were at their house for dinner you haven't done anything since you retired. Who have you been for the past three years, Liv?"

I stop and meet his eyes. "Nobody."

"That's not true. You're a fiancée." He grabs my hand and

twists the engagement ring on my finger. "Is that what you've done for the past three years? Wait to be a wife?"

I understand his anger now, the grief. I don't know what happened a year ago that forced Sheppard to cut ties with the band, and I don't know what happened between him and Melody that caused their divorce, but I do know they happened months apart. Not only is he grappling with not being Ghost Town's lead singer, he's also struggling to come to terms with the idea he's no longer a husband, and with his divorce, may not ever be a father.

Sheppard and I are a lot alike, and maybe underneath it all I knew that and that's why I didn't want this job.

"Would that be so terrible?" I ask, turning away. I keep walking, and a group of tourists, if their phones flashing a mile a minute are anything to go by, trudge past us in the sand, their eyes on Sheppard. He doesn't look like a rockstar, not in the black cotton shorts and generic muscle t-shirt he's wearing for our walk, throwing a ball for a dog, and the group pauses, unsure if they're seeing a celebrity or not. They don't know me, and they decide it's a Sheppard Carpenter lookalike and continue on, taking pictures of the glamorous houses instead.

"Your husband should want more for you than that."

Wouldn't Sheppard be shocked to learn my future husband didn't want me at all.

He slogs through the sand, his footsteps heavy. "We can stop here," he says when we reach a grouping of large boulders. We cleared most of the houses, and because there's nothing to look at, we're alone besides seagulls gliding through the air, searching for a stray bite to eat.

Scout sniffs around the sand, perhaps picking up the scent of a different dog, and I lay out the blanket. Sheppard hides the basket in the shade of a large rock and sits next to me.

"What scares you more, not being the lead singer of the

most popular band in the world, or not being a husband?" I lie on my back and squint into the sky. I don't have sunglasses, and the mid-morning sun burned through the mist, surprisingly bright and warm.

He rests his arms on his knees. "You want to know the truth?"

"Yeah."

"When Melody divorced me, that hit me hard. Maybe you understand . . . people want to be close to you, hoping your fame rubs off on them. It's difficult to get to know people because you don't know if they want you for you or what you can give them."

I dig through what he didn't say. "You're scared you won't be able to meet someone new."

"More than that, if you want to strip away the bullshit. I'm afraid I won't meet anyone who wants to stay forever. I'm fifty years old, been divorced once, which is probably a Guinness World Record for a rockstar, right? I don't want to go through that again. I want to meet someone who will stick with me for the rest of my life."

"What made Melody different? What made you think it would work with her?"

He blows out a tired sigh. "I wasn't thinking about that then, but I think it helped we were on the same playing field. She understood my professional demands, and I understood hers. It was in between the bouts of chaos we got to know each other. Long flights to Europe, sharing a laugh at an awards show. Since she divorced me, I stitched together what made our marriage, and all I came away with was a piece of fabric. I want more, but meeting someone, dating. It's not a surprise Brock and Eddie haven't remarried. It's too much work."

I prop myself onto my elbows. "If you had to choose between keeping Ghost Town together or finding a woman who would love you and spend the rest of her life with you, which would you choose?"

"Love. Hands down. There's nothing more important in life than falling in love. I want to find that again, when I look into a woman's eyes, and I would give it all up just to hear her say she loves me."

"Then you'll have to start going out, Sheppard. You're not going to find her in your house."

"I think, Liv, I'm not going to find her anywhere."

We doze, the water brushing the sand, the sun warming our skin. I've always liked living in Minnesota, but I could get used to this.

"Do you want to talk about it?" he asks.

I open my eyelids into slits. "Not really. Do you?"

He rolls onto his side and holds his head in his hand. His other hand plays with the hem of my t-shirt, the backs of his fingers brushing my skin. He looks down at me, his hazel eyes tired, scruff covering his jaw. "Not any more than you do, I suspect, but it's what you're here for. Sometimes it gets to be too much. The years gone by . . . did they mean anything? The records and the concerts, my marriage. I think about the next fifty years, and they're so empty, but there's so much expectation."

"You're too hard on yourself. First of all, a marriage takes two people. If you think you failed, you only failed by half. As for the rest, you don't believe it, any more than I believed Gina when she said I was helping people with my blog and my book and all my speaking engagements, but you said so yourself. What matters is when someone says your music saw them through a rough time, or the guy who played one of your songs while he proposed. Your band is your family, Brock and Eddie." I frown. "Didn't you play with someone else? I'm sorry, I should know this. But without the relationships you have with them and Dalton, you wouldn't have had Ghost Town at all. I think you need to get back to basics."

Sheppard searches my face. "What do you mean?"

"I mean, you're taking all of this too personally. When you pulled away from the group, you'd just finished a world tour. How many countries? How many cities? How many boobs did you sign?" He smiles in truthful amusement, and I grip his arm, relieved a tiny bit of sadness melted from his expression. "When was the last time you wrote a song for yourself, not with the intent of recording it? When was the last time you hung out with Brock and Eddie, just to hang out, not to talk about anything important like planning the next practice session? When was the last time you played a dive bar? When did you lose your joy, Sheppard?"

His fingers slide back and forth against my skin as he muses. I want to wiggle away, but I don't think he realizes he's even doing it and I don't want to draw attention to it if that's the case. He's lonely, and I recognize that in him as well as in myself. People need touch, a connection, and as long as it doesn't go too far, it's harmless.

"I think you might be right," he agrees slowly.

"Start small and rebuild those connections, one by one if you have to. You talked to Dalton yesterday. How did that feel? Is that part of the reason you needed a drink last night?"

"Maybe. Maybe confronting him was too much pressure."

"You don't think he hired me only to coerce you into recording another album, do you? I hope you give him more credit than that. When I spoke with him, it was obvious he cares about you and your friendship. It wasn't a complete act of selfishness."

"No, you're right. We've been friends for too long to accuse him of that. We talked about the tour. Something was off, it didn't feel right. He was always hiding in a hotel room, said he was on the phone, sorting out all the shit that pops up, but I don't know. Maybe he had a thing with one of the assistants, but he could have said something. No one would have cared."

"Maybe he was waiting for you to ask," I suggest mildly.

He lies next to me, and our arms brush. "Maybe. Tours like that, every second is accounted for to get the most mileage out of it. Radio station interviews, charity benefits. I didn't have time to ask."

"Well, you do now. Maybe he's still seeing her."

"Yeah," he says in surprise. "Maybe."

I turn my head and he turns his. Our lips nearly brush, he's lying so close to me.

"What does your fiancé think of you living with me?" he asks. "Michael? That's his name? You dedicated your book to him."

My heart stutters. I haven't heard Michael's name spoken aloud in a long time. Even Agatha knows if she refers to him I can't bear to hear it. "He doesn't think anything. He knows I'm doing my job."

"I wouldn't let you, if you were engaged to me."

I quirk an eyebrow. "You wouldn't let me do my job? I'm sure Melody had men eyeing her all the time. Did that create strain between you two?"

"Being in the public eye is different. We both understood it's an occupational hazard."

"So how am I different?"

"There are other ways you can still do your job without living with a man you don't know."

"Then I suppose it's lucky for you I was willing to move in with you for the summer."

"Why did you take this job? You moved halfway across the country to a state you've never been to before, leaving a fiancé and your family behind. It wasn't the money. I know you well enough, even after just a few days, to know it wasn't the money Dalt offered you."

I roll onto my side and rest my head on my arm. "When Agatha told me Dalton contacted her, she brought a file over to my house. I didn't care what was in it, all I knew was that I was going to say no. That didn't have anything to do with Michael or leaving my family for a few months. It had everything to do with me not doing this kind of work anymore. I was angry she approached me about it. I shoved the file across the table, and it landed on the floor. She'd printed a paparazzi shot of you, and it slid out. You were standing in the water, and you looked so sad, so hopeless. You looked how I feel, all the time. That's why I took this job. Because no one should feel like that."

He brushes my bangs out of my eyes. "Why were you crying last night, Liv?"

"I don't want to talk about it. Besides, this isn't about me."

With his thumb rubbing my cheek the same way he wiped the tears off my face last night, he says, "I think it is. Maybe you don't want to admit it, but I think it is."

We spend the rest of the day throwing Scout the ball Sheppard brought with us. He's smiling as we walk across the sand toward his house, but his footsteps grow heavier the nearer we get. He's quiet when we brush the sand off our sandals.

"I'm going upstairs for a bit," he murmurs, and he doesn't wait for me to respond.

I dropped a lot of weighty ideas on him today, and if he's

anything like me, he needs time and space to process them. I leave him alone and Scout follows him upstairs.

Talking to Sheppard about his future dumped a lot of heavy ideas onto myself, too, and painfully, I sift through them. I can't be retired forever. Retirement can only last for as long as you have money. I'd been able to set aside a decent nest egg, but eventually it'll run out. I'm not sure if I want to go back to coaching, but I don't know what I would do if I didn't. I have the funds to go back to school, but I was doing the only thing I wanted to do. I was lucky my relationship with my dad led me on that path, and I didn't panic about what I was going to do after high school. I immediately enrolled at university to earn my psychology degree, and when I graduated, completed my coaching certificate. My father was my role model, and I followed in his footsteps, though without the religious aspects. I don't think that's why I'm floundering now—I can believe in God and live a life He would be proud of me for without going to church or working for a church in some way. No, my faith in my ability was shaken when Michael left, and Sheppard may not be my redemption, but helping him figure out his way would be a good place to begin figuring out mine.

I think about Gina's offer of lunch with the women who failed someone important in their lives, and against my will, my curiosity is piqued. How do you keep going amidst such personal failure and tragedy?

I unpack the picnic basket and start a fresh pot of coffee. While it drips, I stand at the breakfast bar, open the backend of my website again, and brush my fingers over the laptop's keys. Where would I begin? I have to know where I'm going before I can set out. All those who wander are not lost, but I can't blog just to blog. That's not my way, and my readers deserve more. I need a goal; I need a plan. If I blog, if I post, then I'm promising something to the people who still want to hear from me, and I don't want to break any more promises.

It's close to seven in the evening when I heat up the rest of the chicken noodle soup and set out a griddle to make grilled ham and cheese sandwiches. I haven't heard Sheppard move around, and if he was taking a nap, it's past time for him to be awake again.

Concerned, I check on him, pushing the door to his room open. He's lying in bed in the dark, his head pushed into a pillow, Scout at his feet. His shoulders are shaking, and his cries are muffled.

Against all my better judgment, I cross the room and crawl into bed with him. His pain tears me to pieces and I wish with everything in my heart, body, and soul for it to stop. I wrap my arms around him, and he moves his head from the pillow to my stomach. With my fingers laced through his hair, he sobs into my t-shirt, and I'm ripped to shreds by the time he finally quiets.

"Have you always had depression?" I ask, smoothing my fingers over his forehead and down his sticky cheek.

He's reluctant, but he leans away and rests his head on his pillow. "Not really, kind of. I've always felt . . . down, not entirely happy, if that makes sense."

"Yeah," I say, because in the dark, he wouldn't be able to see me nod.

"I could usually ignore it, layer happiness over it, but the past year's been rough and there's no happiness to hide it."

"When did it start? Do you remember?"

"I've felt like this all my life. My mother said I was sensitive, not understanding how I really felt inside my head. It's always just been there, a sadness I can't shake."

"It's important to remember that depression lies. Your siren lies to you, and you can't believe what she says. She'll tell you

you're not worthy of love, that you don't deserve to be here, that people would be better off without you around, and it's not true." I wiggle closer, and he wraps his arms around me.

We lie in the dark, my cheek resting against his chest, his strong hands splayed across my back. I know what it's like to need touch. When Michael left, my mom held me for hours while I cried, the same way I held her after an ex-con killed her husband. Though it's inappropriate, I know what Sheppard needs after a year of living alone, and I let him hold me as the tension drains from his body.

"I know. I *used* to know," he says, his chin brushing the top of my head. "I would think about the band, about Melody, like you think about Scout. What would the band do without me? What would Melody do? But those reasons are gone, and sometimes I struggle."

"Just because the band isn't together right now doesn't mean it's gone. Brock and Eddie are still around, and they miss you. Dalton cares about you or I wouldn't be here. Like we said on the beach earlier, drill down, and appreciate each relationship that you have. The band is too big and too much responsibility to think about, but your friendships are smaller and closer to your heart."

His hand finds its way inside my shirt, and his palm is warm against my bare skin. I press my face into his chest, the cotton shirt scented with ocean, sand, and dog, and the air changes around us. Desire builds in my belly, and I push it away. I haven't been with a man since Michael, haven't wanted to be with a man since he left. This is not a good time, and I sure as hell didn't pick the right man to succumb to my loneliness.

Michael and I had something real, and I'm not going to tarnish it with a romp with a rockstar, no matter how much I need to feel loved. His memory deserves more than that, and I do, too. I'm willing to give Sheppard what he needs to heal as long as it's not at my own expense.

I pull away and roll off the bed. The second I do, I miss his arms around me. "Come downstairs. I have leftover soup on the stove, and I'm making grilled cheese sandwiches to go with it. Does the lead singer of Ghost Town eat grilled cheese sandwiches?"

Sheppard sits up. "Is that who I am?"

I rest my palm on his cheek. "It's who you've been. The rest is up to you."

Chapter Twelve

I feel lighter than I have in a while, and I follow Olivia downstairs, Scout at our heels. Sitting on a stool at the breakfast bar, I watch her grill sandwiches, and she serves me like she always does, ladling the last of the soup into bowls and plating the still-sizzling grilled cheese with a handful of chips. She stands across from me, and while we eat, talk of mundane things. I find out her sister is a social worker, specializing in placing kids in foster care. Her mother is a retired Kindergarten teacher, but she's still active in her church and is the director of a girls' youth group for underprivileged kids, helping them toward better futures.

"Your family was called into service," I comment, spooning up my soup.

"My mom was a Kindergarten teacher before she met my dad, but mostly it's because of him. Before he passed away, he was a pastor for a small church not far from where I live. He donated a lot of time to men who are incarcerated. He was always living his life for other people, but somehow he still had enough for us at the end of the day. I think that was part of my problem," she says, adding seconds to her bowl. "I didn't have anything left at the end of the day. I gave everything I had to the people I helped, and in the long run, that hurt me."

"I understand. I've felt like that too. After a concert, especially after a tour. Drained. But as our fame grew, so did the demands, and you just go along with it because you don't want the momentum to stop. You're afraid if you take a break, people will forget about you."

"Are you scared of that now?"

I lob the question back at her. "Are you?"

She considers my question, and that's another reason I like talking to Olivia. She doesn't try to placate me, doesn't try to bullshit me. "I'm not sure. I don't think so. Social media is funny. Post enough and your audience comes back, or you just put in the work and build a new one. Bands don't completely lose their audience, not as easily as I could if I stopped doing this for good. Your music will live on forever, but bookstores will stop stocking my book, a new self-help guru will come onto the scene, though strangely enough, that hasn't happened yet. I've been retired for three years, but I think, if I wanted to right at this minute, I could bounce back rather quickly. Isn't it customary to take time off after a tour?"

I grimace. "Not really. The second you're done, you're in the recording studio working on a new album. That's the main reason Dalt called you out here, though he *does* have my well-being in mind. We finished that tour a year ago, Melody left me not long after that, and I've been hiding here. I should be writing music, playing with the guys, getting another album ready to drop. We don't do a world tour every year, but if we were on schedule, we'd be thinking of a US tour, a small one, to promote the new album."

"Did that kind of schedule wear you out?"

"Yeah. The only reprieves we've gotten are when Brock and Eddie had their kids and when I married Melody. I insisted on a decent honeymoon, but even our honeymoon was full of commitments and obligations. I didn't argue because they were mostly hers, and I wanted to be supportive."

"It's difficult to be at your best when you're burnt out."

"Don't you teach other people how not to burn out?" I take a bite of my sandwich before it gets cold and the cheese congeals.

She smothers a smile, knowing I'm joking, but she also knows I understand finding balance is hard, no matter who you are. "Yeah. Well, I did. Until I burnt out. Could you talk to Dalton about your schedule? You and Ghost Town have been at it non-stop for what? Thirty years? No one is going to expect you to keep up that pace, and one day you *will* want to retire, especially if you find what you're looking for and marry again, maybe have some kids. It's best to be prepared for that sooner rather than later."

I scrub my face with my hands. "I'm going to have to start talking to people, aren't I?"

"Sadly, it's the only way they know what you're thinking."

Meeting her eyes, I say, "You seem to know what I'm thinking without me having to say a single word."

"It's not so amazing when we both speak the same language."

We finish our dinner in silence, and I help her clean up the kitchen. We still don't have an evening routine down. It feels natural after spending the day together to part ways and do personal things like write an email, make a phone call, or read a book. I don't want her to get tired of me, thinking she has to be "on" to help me all the time, especially since she invited me to seek her out whenever I need to talk. I'm not scared to be alone, but I don't want to be, either, and I'm reluctant to offer to let her do her own thing.

"Do you want to watch a movie?" I ask as she's drying her hands. She still washes all the dishes in the sink, and our soup bowls sit in the strainer I never use.

She blinks in surprise, but not refusal. "Sure. We ordered ice cream, and speaking of that, we're getting low on groceries."

"We'll write a new list in the morning," I say, thankful she was so quick to say yes.

I pull the carton of chocolate chip cookie dough out of the freezer and she slides two dry bowls out of the cabinet, standing on her tiptoes to reach them. Her muscles tighten, her ass firm and perky.

I've tried not to think about her in my bed, the way she molded herself to me, giving me one hundred and ten percent of herself in support. I'm fucking relieved I didn't get hard. There would have been no quicker way to ruin what she was trying to do. Somehow, she can sense I need human contact, and from the very first day she was here, when I pulled her to me as she stood at the sink, she's been generous that way. I don't want it to stop because she thinks I want to sleep with her, even if I do.

"Come on, I have a TV back here," I say, leading her toward the rear of the house. The realtor called it a den, and I haven't done much with it since the decorator outfitted it with furniture, my Steinway piano I took from the house I gave Melody in the divorce, and a huge flat screen TV.

The room is hidden by a door that looks like a bookshelf, and I push it open, the hinges well-oiled and gliding without resistance.

"Jeffrey didn't show me this room," Olivia says, looking around and holding our bowls of ice cream.

"He might not know about it. I haven't exactly been a present or hospitable neighbor."

"Do you play?" She tilts her head toward my piano.

"Sure. I play a little bit of everything." I step over to the couch and grab the remote from the coffee table.

"What do you mean?"

"What I said. I can play the piano, guitar, flute, trumpet, trombone, sax, clarinet, oboe, if I have to. My band teacher called me a prodigy, and when she had to take a day off, instead of hiring a sub, I taught class and gave lessons. For the talent show during my senior year in high school, I sang 'Right Here Waiting' by Richard Marx. Happened to be on the hottest top ten. I won, too."

"I bet you did. How does it feel to be so talented?"

I settle onto the couch and gesture for her to join me. When I answer Olivia's questions, I always feel like I can tell her the truth. "Sometimes I feel like I'm on top of the world, and sometimes I feel like I'm on top of the world all by myself."

She sits with her legs crossed on the middle cushion next to me and sets my bowl on the coffee table. Bumping my shoulder with hers, she says, "I think it's great."

I choose the HBO Max app on the TV and navigate to the home screen. "What's your secret talent?" I ask and start scrolling. I feel like I'm getting to know her, but she could be a closet horror fan and I would have no idea.

"Nothing. I can't do anything." She speaks to her ice cream.

"I don't believe that. You wrote a book, unless you're going to shock me and tell me you had a ghostwriter do it."

Lifting her head, she smiles, traces of melancholy gone. "No, but you write songs, too, so being a writer isn't that amazing."

"I've never written a book."

Around a spoonful of ice cream, she says, "Maybe you should. You've got a lot of history to share. That one."

I stop on 2012, and I lean back, pleased. The movie's two hours and thirty-eight minutes long. We'll be here for a while, and right at this moment, there's no place else I'd rather be.

Halfway through the movie, she stretches out, and I put her feet in my lap. I press my thumb to the bottom of one of her arches, and she jerks away, laughing. "I'm way too ticklish for that," she says, but she leaves her feet resting on my thigh. I encircle her delicate ankle in my hand, much like I envision the siren would do to me if I let her.

She falls asleep toward the end, and the credits highlight her face as they scroll by. There's something that nudges my heart, something I haven't felt for a very long time. If I told anyone, they would call me crazy, or worse, dependent, and I wouldn't be able to argue. What she's doing for me, the time she's giving me, Dalt may have found the only person on earth who would sacrifice so much for a stranger. Olivia's engaged, missing her fiancé and probably homesick, but she was willing to move in with me all because of empathy.

She's what I want in a future relationship. Empathy, sympathy, understanding, and time. I think that was one of the worst things about my marriage to Melody. We didn't have any time. We never slowed, even for a moment, and it's not her fault. I didn't know what I needed, and I wouldn't have been able to articulate it even if I had. I need quiet afternoons on the beach, I need evenings watching TV and eating ice cream. I need shared common interests. I need a dog at my feet wanting to go outside for a potty break. I need to wake up with someone and want to bring her coffee in bed. Olivia said I needed to get back to basics. She was talking about my professional life, but I need it in my personal life too. Small, tiny, incremental things, like a touch of her hand, a glimmer of a smile over an inside joke, wiping tears off her cheeks.

The sick part is, I'm starting to want those things with her, and admitting that to myself . . . I should send her home before this gets too far out of hand. If I kissed her now and she kissed me back, I would hate her. I can't put her, or myself, in that situation.

Gently, I smooth my hand up and down her calf. She's wearing cotton shorts and a U of M sweatshirt, the neck cut out, exposing a bare shoulder. She's only thirty-four; I doubt she'd feel anything toward me even if she were free to do so. I'm sixteen years older than she is; she wouldn't see anything in me.

Scout whines when I stand. I'll see to one girl, then to the other. I pick Olivia up, one arm under her knees, the other behind her back. Her head lolls until I cuddle her against my chest. She doesn't wake, and carefully, I carry her to bed. I can't pull the comforter down, and I lay her on top instead and drape the blanket folded at the end of the bed over her. If she wakes up in the middle of the night to go to the bathroom, she can crawl into bed on her own. I brush the hair away from her face, missing the quiet intimacy between two people.

Six months ago, I wouldn't have given one thought to finding someone to be with. Olivia's opening me up, and in retaliation and fear, I want a drink to calm my nerves. My mouth waters with it, tasting the phantom whiskey on my tongue, but instead, I grab my laptop and earbuds from my room and let Scout outside. When she's done, we sit on the patio. The siren calls to me like she always does, but I hear Olivia's words over her song. I have people who care about me, and she does too, just not in the way I'm growing to want her to.

The beach is quiet, not many passersby, though a house six

down is having a small get together on their patio, and the sounds of their guests chatting and laughing carry to me on the breeze. It's something I miss, yet something I also fear. I didn't mind sitting at Jeff and Gina's, letting them get to know Olivia, but when she mentioned having them over, I recoiled. I don't know why. Having them over for dinner, a bottle of wine, and light conversation shouldn't be scary, yet it is, somehow. Not that conversation with Gina would be light, but my conversations with Olivia aren't a walk in the park either, so it's not an excuse I can hide behind.

I boot up my laptop and adjust the earbuds in my ears. This is what I've been avoiding— speculation about Derrick's death. I need to talk to Olivia about it—the real reason why I pulled away from the band. Melody and her alleged cheating is only half the story, but I want more details before I do.

Buzz Kill's graphics are black and red and lightning strikes, wanting to elicit shock as the overall effect. It works, the harsh color scheme in sync with the news they scream. I don't know why Jeff would scroll this site unless he truly was just trolling for the hell of it. I type in the search bar, *Derrick Pavleck.* He's been a member of the group since day one, and pages of hits fill my screen. I scroll by two weeks' worth of articles to find the one Jeff mentioned that led to my bender.

I think of Olivia upstairs, how disappointed she would be if I gave in to my need for a drink, and I skim the blog article, hoping to get it over with as quickly as possible and still glean what I want to know. A reporter of some kind speaking into a microphone accompanies the post, the Chicago arena where we played our last gig looming behind him, but even though I have my earbuds in, I don't turn on the sound.

The headline has its desired effect: my heart drops and my stomach does a sick roll.

Was Derrick Pavleck's Death an Accident?

Insiders say Derrick Pavleck, bass guitarist for the rock band Ghost Town, didn't accidentally fall from the scaffolding the night of their last concert in Chicago, Illinois. Friends close to the guitarist say he's always had a love of sitting above the stage after a show, watching stagehands breakdown the equipment, but that proved fatal when some say he was pushed from the scaffolding. The only questions we want answers for is who, and why.

It would be easy to dismiss the rumors as just that: rumors. Anyone can pretend to be an anonymous insider who has a lie to tell hoping to make a couple bucks off someone else's pain, but the story, now that the alcohol haze has lifted and I can think clearly, could have an element of truth. There were quite a few people still on stage and in the arena after the concert. There were even some fans still lingering on the floor hoping to get a glimpse of us or sneak backstage for an autograph. If someone was there and saw what happened, I'd need to reconstruct that night, find out where everyone was. Melody had been with us, looking forward to going home as Chicago was part of the last leg of the tour. I couldn't find her, and fed up, I went back to our hotel alone. News of Derrick's fall didn't reach me until the next morning when I woke up and Dalt was sitting in my suite, drinking coffee with a shaking hand. He'd wanted to give me the news in person. Derrick fell from the scaffolding, dropping hundreds of feet, breaking his back and neck and fracturing his skull. He died on impact.

I switch over to a social media video sharing site and search Derrick's name. Videos with the most views were the ones filmed after Derrick's fall, when the stage crew and production manager surrounded him, hysterical cries calling for help and to dial 911. We were held in Chicago for days afterward. The Chicago PD launched an investigation that came up with no suspects, no guilty party, and later the case was closed,

Derrick's death deemed an accident. His autopsy report indicated he had enough alcohol in his system to intoxicate an elephant, but that was normal and one of the reasons Dalt wanted him to go to rehab. A tragedy, and unfortunately, not an uncommon one.

Did someone really see something? Does someone know the truth?

I don't know if I'm ready to jump head first into something like this, but to put it away, it might be what I have to do.

Heartsick, I let Scout into the house. The lure of whiskey is just as strong as the siren's call, but I think of Olivia and her offer to be there whenever I need her. I brush my teeth, change into clean shorts and a t-shirt, and shuffle quietly into her room. She's still lying on top of the comforter, the blanket tucked around her shoulders. I'm crossing a line, but I can't help it. It's her or a drink, both dangerous, both toxic, and I have to choose because I can't go without either.

I spoon her from behind and wrap my arms around her. Scout jumps onto the bed and settles at our feet, snoring seconds later.

She smells of lavender and I breathe deeply, my face tucked into the curve of her shoulder.

"Are you okay?" she mumbles, turning slightly, half on her back.

"No," I say, tears lodged in my throat.

Wiggling into my chest, she says, "Nighttime is always the hardest. Stay and get some rest."

I relax and listen to Scout's snores. Olivia falls back to sleep, and I close my eyes.

I don't wake up until late morning, and when I do, Olivia's side of the bed is empty.

Despite waking up alone, I slept better than I have in months, and clearheaded, I shower and dress in clean clothes. I'll have to put in a load of laundry today. I have more clothes than I need, but my hamper is overflowing and I don't want to ruin the work Olivia's done in the house.

I find her downstairs sipping coffee and writing on a notepad. Besides ordering groceries, we don't have anything planned, and I think if I'm going to try to put Derrick's death behind me, today is as good a day as any to start.

I sit at the breakfast bar wondering if she's going to mention the fact I slept with her last night, but all she does is serve me a bowl of hot oatmeal with half and half and brown sugar on the side. I pull a face, hoping to see her smile, and she rewards me appropriately, tamping down a laugh. She pours me a cup of coffee and turns to the list, her cursive feminine and full of loops.

"You said your sister bought you that necklace when someone close to you passed away. Did you ever get over it?" I ask, reluctantly picking up my spoon. I don't want to waste food, even if it is oatmeal.

She stares at the notepad and when she meets my eyes, a tear is running down her cheek. "You don't ever get over losing someone close to you. If that's what you're struggling with, it's best to understand that right now. He or she left a hole in your life that can never be filled because that person was irreplaceable and gave you something you won't find in anyone else. The best you can do is remember the good times, and thank God you had those."

"Have they been gone a long time?" I know I can't put my

healing on a timetable, but it would be nice to know the pain lessens as the years go on.

She dashes any hope of that when she says, "A few years now, but it feels like yesterday. Is that what you're dealing with? You lost someone close to you?"

I blow out a breath. "Yeah." I'm not ready to tell her all of it. I'm still processing what I found out last night and deciding how I'm going to look into Derrick's death . . . if I am.

"There's no right way to grieve. People will tell you you're doing it wrong, but we all have our ways of coping with pain. Sometimes it isn't healthy—like drinking too much, or cutting yourself off from the people who care about you—but you have to reconcile that loss on your own terms. I didn't get the help I should have, and I dealt with a lot of pain alone. You don't have to do that. I'm not a grief counselor, and if you're interested, I can find someone you can talk to, or if you think I'm good enough, I'll listen. There are stages of grief, and we can talk about that if you want."

"That would be good. How did you feel?"

She scribbles on the pad as she decides what to say. "I blamed him for abandoning me. I was angry, and I hated him for leaving, though in my heart I knew it wasn't his fault. Then I blamed myself for not being enough for him to stay. I prayed all the time, trading my career success if he would come back, promised I would live a perfect life if God gave us a second chance. That didn't happen, obviously. It was just hard to accept I was never going to see him again. We would never share another joke or sit across from each other at dinner. All the things I looked forward to, the years of planning our life together were gone, a future I built for us was gone." She rubs her engagement ring, tears running down her cheeks. "I'd never get to tell him I love him, never feel his arms wrapped around me. That was the hardest part."

That's what I'm grappling with, too. The band without Derrick, future albums without his stamp on them. How could we keep creating music if he wasn't going to be a part of it? Maybe it was right to break up the band, but Derrick wouldn't want that. He wouldn't want to be the cause of something like that, even after his death. "How did you keep going?"

She touches my hand. "I didn't. Just like you're not."

I can't argue with that. I haven't been living for this past year, only drowning in alcohol and counting the minutes until a new day started and I could do it all over again.

"I'm sorry I bothered you last night."

"You didn't bother me. But," she pauses and meets my eyes, "be careful. I can't be your recovery. I'm only here to help you get there."

"I know, but, Liv—" I start, needing to, I don't know. I can't tell her I'm starting to feel things for her. She's not available and the minute I tell her, she'll be responsible for how I feel, and that's not her place.

She steps back. "Sheppard."

Her eyes are haunted, tear tracks glittering on her cheeks. Her warning does nothing to cool the burning in my heart when I look at her. Heat crackles between us, and I can't tear my gaze away from hers. She swallows.

Jeff chooses that moment to knock on the glass and open the patio door. "Are you not running with me today?" he asks, looking between us. "Did I interrupt something?"

I clear my throat, and it slices through the tension. "No. I mean, yes. I'm running. We stayed up to watch a movie and I overslept. Let me grab my tennis shoes and I'll meet you out back."

"Okay," Jeff says carefully, his eyes on Olivia. "Are you okay?" he asks her.

She forces a smile. "Yeah. Just some hard conversation this morning, for both of us, I think."

"If you're in the mood for more, Gina said she's ready to film part of your interview."

"Today?"

"Sooner the better," he says.

Olivia flicks a glance at me. "I'll check with Sheppard, see when I'll have some free time."

Jeff looks between us again and says, "I'll let her know."

"Thanks."

He retreats onto the patio and Scout follows him, knowing the drill.

"I better go. I shouldn't blow him off," I say, the tension and heat returning in full force now that Jeff's gone and we're alone.

"Okay. When you get back, we'll, umm," she stumbles.

I hate that I put us in this position. "Order food."

"Yeah, sounds good."

I escape with my shoes, and when I look over my shoulder through the glass, Olivia is where I left her, standing at the breakfast bar and staring into space.

Jeff's smirking when I meet him on the street. "Did I call it or what?"

I sit on the concrete, brush the little rocks off the bottoms of my feet, and shove on my shoes. "You interrupted her telling me she's not available."

"It's only been a week. What did you want her to say? That she'd be willing to be friends with benefits while she's here? You said you wouldn't have any respect for her if she did that, so I don't know what you expected her to do."

"I shouldn't have said anything, but I had a rough night last night, and I slept with her so I wouldn't be alone."

"Any particular reason?"

Jeff knows I'm rusty, and he's been taking it easy on me. We start off at a slow trot along the path that borders the highway.

Scout shoots ahead, relishing the freedom. She doesn't run away and I don't put a leash on her. I'm not sure Olivia even has one.

"Been thinking about what you said. Last night, I looked up that piece on *Buzz Kill*, and I don't know who saw what. I wasn't there when it happened. I'd already gone back to the hotel."

"Then what are you thinking?"

"Talk to the production manager, talk to Eddie and Brock. Dalt was still at the arena, too. Try to find some answers, and if I can't, let it go."

"Will you be able to do that?"

"I won't have a choice. Sometimes there's no explanation. Shit happens. I think you're right, though. This is the closure I need to put it behind me, finish grieving, and pick up the pieces."

We've been running three miles, sometimes four, and Jeff urges me to add another mile. Running is getting easier without being hungover or having whiskey for blood, and I go along, enjoying the sun and fresh air.

"You're getting better at this," he says when we're back at the house.

"Thanks to Olivia."

We let ourselves onto the beach through Jeff's fence and stretch on the sand. Scout plops next to me, panting.

"She warn you off her?" he asks, leaning over to touch his toes.

"Not in so many words. I think she's more concerned about me growing dependent on her, and it's something I need to keep in the back of my mind. If I get too needy, I'll send her home. I don't want to be dependent on her, either." I rest my arms on my knees. "How are you and Gina?"

He shrugs. "Fine, I guess. She's busy with her documentary. Why?"

"No reason. Why don't you get married?"

"What's the point? We're fine how we are. You know the Hollywood types. The second you sign on the dotted line, it all goes to hell."

"What if she wanted to?"

Jeff narrows his eyes. "Did Gina say something to Olivia?"

"Not that I'm aware," I lie. "Though, if she and Olivia talked about Olivia's fiancé, the topic probably came up."

"We talked about it a while back. We decided we're good."

"You both decided, or *you* decided?"

He sets his jaw. "I think you need to pay attention to your own love life."

I grin. "I don't have one. That's why I'm meddling in yours."

"Meddle in Eddie's and Brock's. They need your help. I don't."

"Yeah. I plan on talking with them, today, maybe, if they're free."

Jeff slaps my arm and staggers to his feet. "You're doing a difficult thing. Don't be too hard on yourself. Lean on Olivia—that's what she's here for. And if you really have feelings for her, check it or tell her. You can't dance around each other for the next three months."

"Yeah. I'll see you later. Thanks for the run."

"It's good to see you feeling better."

"Thanks."

Scout follows me into the house, and the kitchen's empty, the dreaded oatmeal gone. Olivia wouldn't save it again, so I think I'm off the hook there, but not how I feel about her.

That's never going to go away. The only thing I can do is figure out what to do with it.

Upstairs, Olivia's door is closed, and she's speaking to someone on the phone. I don't disturb her. After slapping me back, she's probably talking to her fiancé. If she tells him, I bet he asks her to go home. Can't blame the guy. I told her the truth when we were talking on the beach. If she were engaged to me, I wouldn't have let her do something like this in the first place.

I shower, my heart slamming like I'm having a heart attack. I can't put off texting Brock and Eddie. I won't invite Dalt, not this time. I'm not strong enough to have the three of them here without Derrick, even if Olivia is here to support me. She would tell me to do what I need to do to heal on my own terms, and for now I'm going with that. I'm not any calmer when I shut the water off and dress.

I'm a weak son of a bitch, and I can't text Brock and Eddie without her. She's in the kitchen sitting on a stool and sipping on coffee with her laptop in front of her. I cuddle her from behind, wrapping my arms under her breasts. She stiffens for only a moment, and then she melts into my embrace. With her head resting against my shoulder, I pull out my phone.

Chapter Thirteen

Olivia

After I eat mine for breakfast, I throw the remaining oatmeal into the garbage. Sheppard managed to worm his way out of having any, and if he detests it that much, I won't cook it again. Jeffrey and their run was a convenient excuse, but I won't complain. It's good to see him spend time with a friend, and the physical exertion will give him a healthier high than drinking.

After I clean the kitchen, I go upstairs and plug my earbuds into my phone. Agatha has sent me a couple of texts here and there, asking if I'm okay, but she never followed through with her threat to call me every day. I don't mind. She's too busy for that, and I'm too old to need a babysitter.

"Hey, hun," she says, answering her cell. I can picture her sitting behind her messy desk in her office at her literary agency in Minneapolis, manuscripts towering behind her on a filing cabinet, her intern scrolling through her email and book-marking promising pitches. When I sent her a proposal for my book, she contacted me the next day. I'd already had great success with my blog, public speaking engagements, and coaching clients. A book would just be another feather in my cap, and she quickly signed me and sold it by the end of the month in a lucrative deal. "How's it going? You didn't sound so hot the last time I talked to you."

"It's going okay. He's sober, which is more than I can say for him when I first got here. He still hasn't told me the reason Dalton hired me, but at breakfast he said he lost someone close to him. I think he's dealing with a lot of loss, and once he gets back on his feet, he won't need me anymore."

"That's your job," Agatha says, "so why do you sound miserable?"

"I'm not."

"Liv, I've worked with you for a long time, and I've been your friend since the day we met. I don't need to be a life coach or a psychologist to hear you're unhappy."

"He's depressed, and I'm having a difficult time dealing with that. He's so much like Michael, but I didn't see it, not then, not the way I should have, and it scares me now."

"Is Sheppard talking to you?" she asks.

"Yeah. We actually talk a lot." I'm surprised to find it's true. While I don't know the real reason he needs me here, the event, besides his divorce, that caused him to spiral, he does talk to me, never brushes me off. He listens when I speak, too, and I like the back and forth. "I think it helps that I'm going through what he is. Trying to find my path, where I want to go, what I want to do."

"Good. Are you thinking about coming out of retirement?"

"Yeah, I am," I say slowly. "I looked around my website yesterday. I'm still paying for my domain name because I didn't want anyone to steal it, and all my blogposts are still there. The website could use an update, and I would need to tell everyone the real reason I retired. I couldn't expect my followers to welcome me back with open arms if I can't tell them the truth. I'm not ready for that, but I'm closer than when I was in Minnesota."

"Talking with Sheppard has done you a lot of good. I'm happy for you. So, tell me about him. What's he like?"

I sit on the bed and her question brings me back to lying in his arms. I felt him crawl into bed with me last night, the mattress dipping under his weight. I didn't know he carried me upstairs until he roused me awake spooning me from behind. I missed the end of the movie, so content to be with him that I'd fallen asleep on the couch as he idly ran his fingers up and down my leg. Michael and I would do that, my head in his lap. He'd smooth my hair away from my face, his fingers lingering along my jaw and tracing the shape of my lips. We'd make love there, during the credits, and he'd tell me he never loved anyone as much as he loved me.

"Liv?" Agatha asks when I don't answer.

"Sad, tired. I think he misses the life he used to have, but at the same time, he's glad he doesn't have to live that hard anymore. It's thrown him off track, and we talk a lot about what he wants to do. He's lonely, and he said he'd like to get married again, maybe have a couple of kids. He doesn't act like a rockstar—he dresses in shorts and t-shirts. I've never heard him play his guitar, but he has a huge piano in his living room. He misses the music, and once he finds his way back to that, things will fall into place for him."

"He's a nice guy?" She's not impressed with his superstar status, caring more about his personality than his fame. Agatha's worked with a lot of high-profile celebrities who approach her about selling memoirs, cookbooks, travel adventures, and more. If Sheppard ever does want to write a memoir or a history of the band, Agatha would be a good match for his project.

"He's very sweet. He likes to be touched, needs it, at this point. Scout took a liking to him. She'll want to stay here when I go."

"Liv," she says softly. "You don't have to let him keep your dog."

"I know, but she'll be happier with him, and it will be easier to move home knowing she's with him."

"You've slept with him, haven't you? After I told you not to." She's always blunt. Sheppard said he appreciated that about me—he'd love Agatha.

I chew on my bottom lip before answering her. "Define sleep."

"Sex, Liv. You were engaged to a man and was living with him. You know what it is. When he puts his—"

"All right. We've shared a bed, if that's what you want to know. Nighttime is hard. You know it is." No one knows that better than I do, or her, for that matter. Her past couple of years haven't been as rocky as mine, but she's had her share of trouble and I wasn't there for her the way she was for me. Someone else was. Someone who shouldn't have been.

"You're falling for him. I can hear it in your voice, but you need to be careful. From what you've told me, you were hard and fast with Michael, too. Why do you need to rush? Why can't you slow down and enjoy the process?"

"What process?" I twist the earbud cord around my finger.

"Falling in love. Because that's what you're telling me, aren't you? Under all the excuses? That you're falling in love with him?"

"Co-dependency isn't an excuse, it's a perfectly valid reason why I should keep my distance. Even you said so. The last thing I need is to fall in love with a rockstar. He can have anyone he wants. He isn't going to choose a girl who doesn't know what the fuck she's doing. He's sixteen years older than me and can do a helluva lot better than that. Besides, he thinks I'm engaged. It's better that way."

"Your ring and your lies are a flimsy shield at best. It's a little hypocritical that you're asking him to spill his guts all the time, yet you aren't willing to come clean about your own tragedies."

"This isn't about me."

She scoffs. "I hope you don't say stupid shit like that to him. If he's crawling into bed with you, he knows damned well you're hurting just as much as he is, and he's going to want to know why."

"It's none of his business."

"No, it's not, but—" She cuts off and sighs. "You're allowed to fall in love again. You shouldn't feel guilty if Sheppard Carpenter is giving you something you need. Michael could have talked to you, found a therapist, went on medication. All of the above. He could have done a hundred things other than what he did. He was selfish."

"Agatha." I never accused Michael of being selfish. Never did because I always blamed myself for not being there, for not being enough to save him.

"I won't apologize. Someone needs to say it."

"That may be true, but it's all the more reason why I can't get involved with Sheppard. I've seen the picture you showed me come to life, and I can't be here, be in a relationship, be *in love with him*, always worried, always waiting for him to walk into the ocean and not come out. I couldn't live through it, I couldn't."

"Well, there's one very big difference between you, Michael, and Sheppard."

"What?"

"Michael never asked for help, and neither did you. Maybe Sheppard didn't ask for help, but he didn't send you away, did he? To me, he's already miles ahead of where you are and where Michael was. At least, in all this mess, give him credit for that. I gotta go. I have an offer call I need to make. If you don't want anything with him, come home, and if you're not willing to do that, lock your door at night. You're leading him on. Bye."

Agatha isn't one for drawn-out goodbyes, and I can barely say my own before my phone beeps.

I'm not leading him on. His needing physical comfort and me wanting to give it isn't leading him on. Humans need touch; we can literally die from loneliness and isolation. But I need to be honest with myself. Am I letting him touch me for his recovery or for mine?

I twist the ring on my finger. There's no reason for me to wear it anymore, and I should have taken it off a long time ago. If I took it off now, met Sheppard downstairs without it on my finger, he would want to know why and I wouldn't know what to say. I don't know what he wanted to tell me this morning before I stopped him. Was he going to ask me to do more than just share a bed with him while I'm here? Was he going to tell me he's starting to have feelings for me? I've never been a liar—only to myself, not to anyone else—and if he admitted something like that to me, I would have no choice but to do the same. My ring may be a flimsy shield, but it's all I have and I'm not so eager to throw it away.

Leaving my ring on, I throw some laundry into the wash. Sheppard came home while I was talking to Agatha and he's in the shower when I settle in the kitchen with a cup of coffee and my laptop. I don't plan on blogging, but Sheppard's question made me consider what my first steps would be if I were to come out of retirement.

I don't hear him walk up behind me until he's wrapped his arms around me. I shouldn't let him. I should pull away and tell him he's my client and what he's doing, what *we're* doing, is inappropriate, but his skin's scented with a woodsy bodywash, still damp from his shower, his arms strong around my ribs as he holds me close. Unbidden, I melt into his embrace and smother a sigh when he pulls away.

"I'm going to text Brock and Eddie and ask them to stop by," he says, pulling his phone from the back pocket of his pants.

He's wearing crisp jeans, a white button down shirt, and socks. My eyes hungrily roam his body, unaccustomed to anything but his usual attire of cotton shorts and a muscle t-shirt. He didn't shave, but he combed his sandy blonde hair away from his face. His eyes are haunted by the idea of speaking to his bandmates, but they're clear and there isn't a hint of alcohol on his breath. That he can invite them here for conversation without needing liquid courage is a good sign, and I squeeze his arm in encouragement. "That's great. Are you comfortable telling me why?"

He smooths a hand down the back of my head. "Thanks for phrasing it that way. When they leave, we'll talk, okay?"

"All right. No pressure. That you feel strong enough to ask them over is good enough for me."

"Liv, this morning—"

"I'm living under your roof, and we've been talking about some difficult subjects. It's made us feel close, that's all." I congratulate myself on coming up with an explanation that not only sounds true, but could be for anyone but me. I know what I'm feeling, and it's not because we've had some deep conversations.

Sheppard steps away. "Right. If you ever feel this is over your head, tell me. I don't want you to be here if it's not what you want."

I link my fingers with his. I can't stop touching him, and if it consoles both of us, then I don't see a reason to stop if we understand the boundaries. "I've only been here for a week. I told Dalton if we took to each other I would stay all summer, and I'm not backing out on that. It's up to you, Sheppard. This is your house and your life. It's all up to you."

"Yeah. Okay." He pulls his hand away, and I lean against the stool's backrest in disappointment until I realize he needs both hands to send his text. It isn't seconds later he receives a reply. Smiling wryly, he says, "They're both free and can be here in an hour. I think they would have made time even if they would've had other things going on."

"Do you want me to fix lunch? I can serve it when they get here."

"If you don't mind. You're not a housekeeper."

"No, but I'm here to help, and I want to."

He's nervous and tense, and I nudge him onto a stool. He's agitated, and I think in the next grocery order we put in I should order decaf coffee. He stopped drinking and that will go a long way, but we're always making a pot of coffee and a caffeine break would do him good too. Despite the caffeine, I pour him a cup, and to keep his mind off of Eddie and Brock, I ask about his run with Jeffrey and if he wouldn't mind running with me for exercise. This leads us into a conversation about workouts and how I let mine fall to the wayside after I retired.

By the time someone knocks on the back door, Sheppard's relaxed. He leads Eddie and Brock into the kitchen, but I don't get more than a second to lift my hand in hello before Sheppard herds them into the hidden room where we watched our movie last night. I get to work on lunch—club sandwiches—and when I serve them later, I'm not sure what I'm walking into. I can only hope that Sheppard is finding what he needs in his friendships with the people who are closest to him.

Sheppard will have a full life when he's able to fight his way through what happened, and I have to remember that I'm not going to be a part of that life.

I shouldn't want to be.

But I do.

Chapter Fourteen

Brock and Eddie look the same, though it hasn't been that long since I've seen them last—at Derrick's funeral. After the Chicago PD released his body, his wife arranged a funeral and burial in a cemetery not far from his mother's old house where he grew up. Clarissa asked Brock, Eddie, Dalt, and me to act as pallbearers, and unless someone stopped by the beach house, since that day, I haven't sought anyone out.

They don't look as tired as I do, but I'm glad they haven't been living it up in the thirteen months since Derrick's death. I don't know what they've been doing with their time; I've been too checked out to ask.

I clear my throat, pissed I'm awkward around friends I've had since high school.

Brock wanders around a room he hasn't stepped foot in since our tour, trailing his fingers over the keys of my piano. The perfectly tuned notes hang in the air before they fall and dissolve into nothing. "How have you been, Shep?"

"Not well," I say honestly, and there's no sense in lying. If

I'd been okay all these months, Olivia wouldn't be here, the band would be working on another album, and things wouldn't feel so fucked up. "How are you guys? What have you been up to?"

Eddie sighs and sits down hard on the sofa—the one where Olivia fell asleep. He props his booted foot onto the edge of the coffee table. "Nothing. I don't have much going on besides catching a date here and there, hanging with Brock, drinking beer, and playing Madden. Shelly still won't let me see Abby, but I'm used to that." He tips his head back, but he's not going to cry. He's not a crier, not like I am, and he's had years of dealing with this.

"I'm sorry. Is there anything I can do?" I ask lamely, hating that I've been so wrapped up in my own shit I haven't been there for him.

His lips twist. "Turn the clock back ten years?"

"Not sure that would be helpful."

He laughs, but it's full of bitterness. "You're probably right. Shelly hasn't wanted anything to do with me since the day our divorce was final. I *still*, to this second, have no fucking idea what I did. When I try to see Abby, she won't talk to me, can barely look me in the face. I stopped going over there. I hate making her uncomfortable. It's fucked up."

Brock settles on the piano bench and taps out a one-handed "Chopsticks." Don't know why he bothers. He can play Mozart's entire library from memory.

"How about you? You seeing anyone?" I ask him.

He clears his throat and scratches at the back of his neck. "Nah. Eddie disappears, and he can leave me out of it." He pauses, pecks out a few more notes. "I'm in the same situation as he is with Abby. I'm a stranger to my own kids. Brianna doesn't let me see them, not that they care about seeing me. I saw Layla's post on social media she passed her driving test.

She never bothered to let me know, and I have no idea what Lexi's into these days. I haven't been doing much of anything except sitting around the house waiting to hear if we're going to do another album. Dalt's been just as much of a stranger as you, and it hasn't felt right to do anything else."

"Is that what you called us out here for?" Eddie asks, tapping his thumbs against his thighs and bobbing his head to the silent beat. "Talk about a new album?"

Sweat runs down my back and I wish Olivia was here, in the room with me, not just somewhere in the house. Eventually, we'll have a conversation about a new album, but not today. Whether we will or not isn't something I've decided, and I feel a long way from being able to talk about it much less plan one and write music for it.

I swallow hard.

I need a drink, and there's a bar in here, a few feet away from where I'm standing. I could have a glass of whiskey in my hand in under sixty seconds, but I wouldn't do that to Olivia . . . and she wouldn't want me to do that to myself. I stand rooted to the floor, and I dig my toes into the hardwood, my socks an unfamiliar feeling on my feet.

"No. I wanted to, ah—" I stop as panic grips me. Anxiety gathers in my chest, the pressure nothing short of a heart attack. I don't know how I'm going to sound, how I'm going to come across. If they think I'm delusional or crazy, I'm not sure how I'm going to react. I was counting on their support to hash this out. "I wanted to, ah, talk to you about the night Derrick died."

Eddie raises his eyebrows. "What about it?"

"There're rumors he was pushed." I'm not going to say where I heard them. Admitting I'm reading *Buzz Kill* is the fastest way to discredit myself.

The piano is positioned behind the couch and Brock meets my eyes over Eddie's shoulder. "We've . . . heard them."

My breath whooshes out of me. "Do you think there's any truth to it?"

Resting his arm against the back of the couch, Eddie twists sideways on the cushion and talks to both of us. "It's doubtful. The Chicago PD didn't find anything. They talked to everybody who was still in the arena when it happened. I think they would have found out who did it, don't you? Derrick was drunk like he usually was. Honestly, I'm surprised it didn't happen sooner."

Now that I can think clearly and I'm not consumed with grief and booze, Eddie's comment doesn't hurt as much as it could have.

"Did the cops get everyone's alibis?" The word sticks in my throat.

Shrugging uneasily, he says, "I don't think they looked that hard. No one had a motive. Who would want to kill Derrick? He was just a drunk who didn't want to play anymore because Clarissa was unhappy and he didn't want her to leave."

I look at him in surprise. "I didn't know that. They weren't married long."

He scowls.

I frown. "What? What am I missing?"

"Nothing."

Brock flicks a glance at Eddie. He didn't know about Derrick and Clarissa, either. I'm glad I'm not the only one who was in the dark, but I understand. You don't know what living this lifestyle is like until you're living this lifestyle. Clarissa having second thoughts so soon into their marriage is common, and our tour only months after their wedding wouldn't have made things any easier on her.

"Where were you two? Was Dalt with you?" I try not to sound accusatory. I'm not blaming them for anything.

Brock shifts on the bench and says, "After you and Derrick

disappeared, Eddie and I hung back and worked the tail end of that PR thing. We were signing autographs and shoving people out the door because we wanted to leave too. A kid reporter from the University of Illinois was brave enough to ask if he could interview whoever would talk to him for the college newspaper, and we chatted him up for a minute, snapped a picture for the article. Dalt wasn't with us, and we assumed he went back to the hotel with you and Melody."

I shake my head and lean my ass against the edge of the entertainment center. "Melody wasn't with me. I went to the hotel alone. I told the detective that when they questioned me the next morning, and the limo driver confirmed it. Was Dalt seeing anyone? A groupie or one of the assistants?"

"I don't know. He's been just as lonely as we all have, but if he's seeing someone, he didn't tell either of us," Eddie says, gesturing between Brock and himself. "Melody must have gotten tired of waiting around and left before we finished schmoozing. Was she in your room when you got there?"

"No. I took another shower and went to bed. I thought I left her behind at the arena."

"She could have been drinking and playing Scrabble with Dalt somewhere."

I wave that off. Melody and Dalt hung out a lot, played Scrabble and Cribbage when the rest of us were busy. Out of anyone in the band, Melody got along with Dalt best. I never cared and was never jealous, only grateful she liked other people in the group and was willing to travel with us when we went on tour.

"What about the stagehands? The production manager? The arena's manager was still there, wasn't she?" I straddle the coffee table and rub my sweaty palms over my jeans. I should know all this, and I've waited too long to find out.

"I don't know, Shep. Nobody was taking attendance,"

Eddie says, leaning forward. "We were in shock, and the PD took care of all that. You'd have to call them and find out what they know. Derrick was a fucking monkey, always climbing on all that shit. Do I really think someone followed him up there? Why? What would have been the point?"

"When I spoke to Dalt a couple of days ago, he said Derrick was avoiding him."

Eddie glares, angry I met with Dalt behind their backs. Anything we've ever done, *everything* we've ever done, has always been a group effort, including, much to my humiliation, hiring Olivia. "He was avoiding *everybody*. Dalt wanted him to go to rehab, and it pissed him off. I overheard them arguing when we were in Indianapolis. Derrick was already drunk before we even hit the arena."

Fuck. I didn't know it had gotten that bad, but I was too busy—

"You should have been in his face, too, Shep. Why weren't you?"

"I think Melody was cheating on me and I was preoccupied."

Brock asks in surprise, "Really?"

"Yeah, but that's over and done, and it doesn't matter if she was or not. I can't let go of how he died. It's almost as if they saw the opportunity because I wasn't at the arena anymore."

Eddie thoughtfully rubs his lips and then asks, "Who knew you went back to the hotel?"

I lift a shoulder. "Everybody? Nobody? I said thank you and goodbye to a few people while I looked for Melody so we could ride together, but I didn't see her and took off. I didn't want to leave her, but I wanted to get the hell out of there."

I remember that night as if I were trying to drudge up a dream, wisps of memory, details, featureless faces. No one wants a night like that to end, and groupies hung out in the hallways where the public was permitted, bored arena security keeping them out of places they weren't, inventive fans figuring out how to sneak past them to ask for an autograph or a selfie. Even the arena's lobby was still swarming with people, the vendors who sold souvenirs packing their remains and staff who worked the food carts and beer kiosks cleaning up. Dust Bunnies, the all-female rock group who opened for us and warmed up the crowd were long gone, hopping on a bus the second we took to the stage for our next stop which was supposed to have been in Des Moines, Iowa. We never saw them again.

"That was a long time ago now," Brock says, swinging his gaze to the door as Olivia pushes it open with our lunch.

"I refuse to believe someone didn't see something. There were people all over the stage breaking it down while he watched," I say, striding across the den, relief shooting through me she's here. I steal a second and brush her bangs out of her eyes, my fingers lingering, as they always do, near her temple. Reluctantly, I pull my hand away and relieve her of the large tray laden with club sandwiches, chips and dip, and a small pitcher of what looks like strawberry or raspberry lemonade. I didn't eat breakfast and I'm eager to dig into the thick sandwiches, my stomach rumbling. The rich scent of bacon wafts from the tray.

She smiles and pauses for a moment, but I want to keep her to myself and don't ask her to sit with us or even offer to reintroduce her.

"Thanks, Olivia," Brock and Eddie say over each other, filling in the silence, and she backs away and closes the door. I doubt I hurt her feelings, but she probably expected more than that.

I carry the tray to a table near the windows. When they were smaller, Brock's and Eddie's kids colored while we jammed. I've had this place for a long time. Maybe I'll sell it and find something else.

We help ourselves to the platter of club sandwiches, chips, and lemonade.

"How's it going with her? You seem pretty cozy already," Eddie says around a mouthful of toast and cold cuts. "Is she going to stay?" He doesn't miss a thing, and he'll be asking me if I'm sleeping with her by the time we finish eating.

"Yeah. She's getting me to think about a lot of things. I can't say when, but I know we need to talk about the band and what we're going to do."

"Well, you look good, and if it's because of Olivia, all the power to her." Brock lifts a glass of lemonade in toast. "It's been a long year."

"Yeah, it has." As hungry as I am, my appetite dies. I didn't find out anything new talking to Eddie and Brock, and I'm back to where I was before I forced myself to invite them over. I can't say it was for nothing, it's good seeing them, but I'm not any nearer to finding the closure I suddenly want to move on.

They carry the bulk of the conversation, and the hole Derrick left behind rips me to shreds, his ghost sitting in an empty chair at the table. Eddie doesn't ask what I spoke to Dalt about and I'm glad. I don't want to get into my fight with him about Melody and why she was at the meeting when he hired Olivia. I'm still pissed about it, still curious why she cared to be there when she could have told Dalt to fuck off because she didn't love me anymore, what I'm going through is no longer her business, and she doesn't want it to be.

After we finish eating, the guys linger, and my nerves are stretched thin to the point of breaking by the time they reluctantly say goodbye. They don't ask when we'll get together next, and I don't offer. Dalt gave Olivia three months, gave me three months to figure my shit out, and I'm taking them.

She isn't in the house when I search for her, and I find her on the beach, throwing a stick for Scout. She's wearing jean shorts and a lacy white tank top, and the front part of her hair is pulled back and secured with a small clip. What she said to me before Brock and Eddie arrived was pure bullshit. We aren't close because we're talking. We're close because when I see her, when I'm with her, all I can think about is how in the hell I can get closer. My heart doesn't give one fuck she's engaged—he deserves it for letting her be here.

I need her, in every way a man can need a woman. I want to sink into her as she pants my name, I want our clothes tangled together on the floor. I need to be able to reach for her in the middle of the night and find her there. I need to be able to talk to her about the band, and I need to know her thoughts and opinions because I need her future to be my future. I need all that, and you can tell me I'm a dumbass for thinking I need it only a week after we met. Maybe you'd be right, but she gives me something I've been missing since Derrick passed away. When I'm with her, I can almost believe things will be okay.

I'm desperate for her, and I can't stop it.

I tug the socks from my feet, and without taking my eyes off her for one second, I open the glass door and hurry over the sand. She's laughing at Scout's enthusiasm for the game, and I twirl her around with an aggressive grip on her arm, her goddamned ring glittering in the meagre sun.

"Sheppard—" she starts, but not in objection, only concern, and my eyes flash in anger that she would have the stupidity to come here engaged.

"I don't care," I snap, hauling her to me. I cover her lips with mine, tangling my fingers in her hair, jerking her head as our mouths fit perfectly together. This does nothing to sate my need, and I shove my tongue into her mouth, tasting bacon and her.

She struggles, but I pin her to me, her heart slamming against mine. The more I take the more I want, and I swallow her cries, devouring her. She pushes against my shoulders, but I'm stronger than she is and it does little good. I only release her when she tries to pull in a breath, and her wet cheeks brush against my face.

I drop her to the ground, and she staggers backward, sucking in air.

Scout watches us with deep brown eyes, but she knows I won't hurt Olivia and only sits, waiting for the game to resume.

I'm hard, and I want to drag her into the house and into my bed. I want to drown her the way I think about drowning myself, until there's nothing left of her but us. "I don't give a fuck if you're engaged, and I'm not going to apologize. I need you. I need you, Liv." I shake her, begging her to say something, anything.

Tears stream down her cheeks, and she says the last thing I expected her to say.

"I'm not engaged."

I can barely understand the words over the sobbing. She's holding her middle as if all of her guts would spill onto the sand if she moved her hands away.

"What the fuck do you mean?" I ask, grappling.

Her face is white when she meets my eyes. "Michael committed suicide. I still wear his ring because I can't take it off." She turns toward the water, and the siren has never been louder, her song never purer in its agony and temptation. I know why Olivia can hear her now, and the truth shreds my soul.

She wades into the cold water, her intent clear. She won't stop when she reaches her thighs, not like I do, resisting the pull even while it's everything I want.

Faster than I am, the water is to her waist when I catch up, and I jerk her to me, my arms tight around her. "I'm sorry," I say against her ear. "I am so sorry."

She gives up then, the water's buoyancy and my arms the only things keeping her from sinking, and she keens in grief. Every note, every pitch of her cry, is what's been in my heart since Dalt told me Derrick fell to his death. I loved Derrick like a brother, and to lose him so unexpectedly was a shock I knew from which I could never recover.

I've never heard a cry so saturated in anguish unless I count my own days after Derrick's funeral. I understand who Olivia was referring to now, before Jeff interrupted us. She was talking about her fiancé.

I curl my body around hers, my face pressed into her neck while she wails. I hold her as the minutes turn to what is certainly hours, people watching us, taking our photo. We'll be all over social media by the time we go inside, but I don't care. More than likely Dalt will see the pictures and want to know what's going on, but none of that matters as Olivia dumps her pain into my heart.

When her sobbing turns to hiccups, I pick her up, water dripping from her feet, and she trembles against my chest.

"I've got you," I murmur against the top of her head. "I've got you."

Scout follows us into the house, and I pause. Olivia's freezing, but if she showered to warm up, I'd want to be there. Not to take advantage, but I don't want to leave her alone while she feels like this. I carry her into the den and push the door closed. I don't want anyone interrupting us, not Jeff because he saw what happened, or Eddie or Brock coming back because they forgot to mention something. There's a large fleece blanket folded on the back of the couch, and I sit and cover us both. She's shivering, her face pressed into my shirt. The scent of bacon still hangs in the air as does the talk of Derrick's death, perhaps his murder, but for once, I'm not bogged down with my own pain.

When she lifts her head, the clock is crawling toward dinnertime. Her eyes are bloodshot, her skin blotchy. Her hair is a tangle, and she's so tired. I never would have suspected she carried something so heavy when she spoke to me, always quick with a laugh or a smile, an offer to listen. That she sacrificed so much to take this job will never not bring me to my knees.

"I'm sorry," she whispers, voice raspy from crying.

I don't know what to say, and I gather her close and cover her lips with mine, praying she doesn't push me away.

Chapter Fifteen

Olivia

His lips are firm, but soft, like he is. I haven't kissed a man since Michael, didn't get drunk one night and go home with a guy to rinse his taste from my mouth. Sheppard's mouth fits differently over mine and I fit differently in his lap, too. Michael taught at a community college and donated his time to local literacy programs. He didn't exercise much, saying the mental workout teaching and grading papers was enough, and Sheppard's hard muscles as he holds me feel unfamiliar, but not in a bad way.

My clothes are soaked, and so are his, but the blanket and his arms keep me warm.

I lean away long before I want to, but Sheppard deserves an explanation, and he might send me home for telling lies.

He cups my cheek, forcing me to look at him. "How long has he been gone?" he asks, his thumb brushing over my skin. He doesn't seem angry now, but that doesn't mean he won't be later.

"Three years." I can't move my head, but to avoid his probing stare, I talk to the top button of his shirt.

"That's why you retired, isn't it?"

"Yeah. I didn't see it. I didn't know how bad he felt. I was so busy with my clients and speaking engagements, I didn't know." I start to cry again, desolation creeping over me the way it always does when I remember the last few days before Michael's death, when life seemed normal.

Sheppard holds me, and it's everything I missed, everything I need to feel like maybe I might live through what Michael did. I burrow into his embrace, grateful that for now he's not angry I kept this from him. "Can you tell me what happened?" His voice is low and soothing, and I swallow back the sobs the floodgates opened.

"I was out of town for a speaking gig, just a couple of days," I say, the scene coming back to me, and I almost lose the lunch I ate while Sheppard was talking with Brock and Eddie. "I drove myself to the airport and left my car overnight in their long-term parking. Michael offered to give me a ride because he knew I have travel anxiety, but the night I flew home, he had an evening class. He taught English and Creative Writing and I didn't want him to cancel for me, even though he would have." I can picture our quiet street, the car rumbling under my butt, the steering wheel steady under my hands. Nothing was wrong. I was looking forward to seeing him. Catching up after making love. Those were always the best times, when he said he missed me so much all he could think about while I was gone was when I would come back. "Everything was fine. He'd called earlier, told me to have a safe flight, mentioned a late dinner. He picked up my favorite bottle of wine."

I press my mouth against Sheppard's shoulder, and tears leak down my cheeks.

"Shh," he says rubbing my back. "Shh. Don't say any more."

Shaking my head, I say, "I have to do this now, or I won't be able to tell you."

He kisses my forehead. "Take your time, then, Liv."

I remember the night so clearly. The sun setting, the kids playing in their yard across the street. The relief I was home again. "A couple of years earlier, we bought our house and adopted Scout. I was so happy when I pulled into our driveway. My life was everything I wanted it to be. I had a career I could grow into, I was engaged to a man who loved me, I had friends and family who cared about me. I never thought . . . I used the garage door opener, and as it lifted so I could park, he was hanging—" I can't get the rest of the words out, and I sob into his chest.

"Jesus Christ," he mutters, pulling me closer, but I don't know how that's possible because I can barely breathe as it is.

Sheppard gives me plenty of time to cry, and I'm so tired and rung out when I finally lift my head and wipe my cheeks. "I called 911, and the fire department cut him down. I didn't know what to do, so I did the only thing I could. I unpublished my website, canceled all my speaking events. I stopped coaching. I couldn't pretend to help anyone when I couldn't help Michael, not even see that he needed me. I couldn't get out of bed for months, and that made things worse—the bed where we would plan our lives together, the bed where he showed me he loved me. It was all a lie."

"He wanted those things," Sheppard says. "He did."

"I wasn't enough."

"Nothing is enough when you feel that way. Did he leave a note?"

"Yeah. He bought me flowers, and a card was sitting by the vase. It was blank, and all he wrote on the inside was, 'I'm sorry.' Don't buy me flowers, Sheppard." I try to turn it into a joke, but I look into his eyes and it's more of a plea. "Please don't." I don't know what I'm asking now. Please don't buy me flowers, please don't try to kiss me again, please don't say you love me. Anything, nothing, I don't know, but Sheppard seems to understand and he nods. He tangles his fingers in my hair and nudges my head down to rest against his shoulder.

I'm uncomfortable in my wet shorts, the saltwater scratching my skin. He can't feel any better, his jeans soaked, dried sand flaking off his feet, but all he does is hold me and rub my back. Scout whines from her place on the floor. She needs to go out and have something to eat.

"I'll understand if you don't want me here because I lied," I say, wiggling on his thighs. My butt is getting numb, and I have to go to the bathroom.

"You didn't lie. You could accuse me of assuming. Just because it's a diamond on your left hand doesn't necessarily mean you're engaged. But, Liv, you never took it off. You still live in the same house? That must be incredibly hard for you."

I try to smile. "What have you done this past year? Multiply that by three. If Dalton wouldn't have called me out here, maybe that's what you would have done too." I pause. "I know what loss is, and I hope you know you can talk to me about anything."

"What I want with you doesn't involve words," he says. "Not that kind."

There's no use denying it's what I want too, but—"I haven't been with anyone since him."

"And you're not ready. I know. But if you can tell me you're open to it, I'll wait. I'm starting to care about you very much, Liv, and if you can't handle that, you should go home."

I stare at my hands laying in my lap, my ring sparkling on my finger. I should have thrown it into the ocean but I was too busy crying, too relieved to have Sheppard's support while I broke down. I'm starting to care about him too, but I can't see the line between wanting him because I do or needing him because now he knows the truth and he's offering something I should have sought out on my own years ago.

I won't know if I leave, but it would be safer for my heart if I did.

Twisting my ring, I'm on the verge of telling him I should go pack when he says, "Don't go," and with his hands gripping the sides of my face, he claims my mouth. I moan under his lips, and for the first time since I've been with him, I feel him harden under my leg.

"I can't be with you like that tonight," I say, breaking the kiss. I don't want to lead him on. This is what Agatha thought we were doing, and we weren't then, but we are now.

"I know. I won't pressure you, but you're sexy, kind, and you're beautiful. I'm going to respond to that. I can't help it, and wouldn't if I could. I didn't sleep with those two women you found in my living room. I haven't been with anyone since Melody left me. I don't play around, and I take physical intimacy very seriously. I don't have an STD, never have, and I didn't sleep around before I married Melody, either. You can blame it on my depression, maybe, or just the kind of person I am, but I will respect every inch of you—your heart and your body."

"Okay." I lick my lips, and his eyes follow the movement, smoldering. I'm playing with fire not going home. He says he won't pressure me, but there's no way we can ignore the sexual tension now that we've acknowledged its existence.

"I'm sorry about Michael," he says, rubbing at my bottom lip with his thumb.

"I am, too. I have a lot of unresolved feelings when I think about him, when I try to decide where to go from here."

"I can help you, if you let me," he says.

Something inside me lightens. For all the years I've felt alone, sitting in his lap this very second I don't, and the relief fills my eyes with tears. "I would like that."

"Good. Are you hungry? You're tired. Do you want to shower? I don't like the idea of you being alone right now."

I don't like the idea either, and I say, "Will you kiss me? Just a little?"

He smooths the hair away from my face, and his eyes sparkle with humor. Maybe he feels a little lighter too. "Yeah." He lowers his head and brushes my lips with his. "Ah, Liv."

Scout whines, and reluctantly, I crawl off his lap. We let Scout out onto the beach to pee, and Sheppard doesn't leave my side for one second. I'm grateful, and I lean into him.

I fumble when we're standing in his kitchen. He doesn't want to leave me alone, and I don't want to be left. I can't start what could be a relationship with Sheppard wearing another man's ring, and as he watches, I slide it off my finger and set it on the breakfast bar.

He swallows and offers me his hand, linking my ringless fingers with his when I accept. True to his word, he doesn't leave me alone all night, and when I get up the next morning to make coffee, the ring is gone.

Sheppard held me all night, and I wake up, tucked against him, his cock pressed against my ass. I roll over onto my back, and in his sleep, he kisses my cheek. I rub my fingers through his scuff, and he cracks his eyes open.

"I like this," he mumbles.

I like it too, and it scares me. I don't know how to be in a relationship. I failed so dreadfully in my last one, how can I know what Sheppard needs to be happy?

"What do you want to do today?" I ask, tucking my arm under my head.

"I think we should stay in, order groceries, and make out until they're delivered."

He said it so seriously, and I push back a smile even though his eyes drifted shut and he can't see it. "Does that mean you don't want to run with Jeffrey this morning?"

"I texted him last night while you were brushing your teeth and said I'd be busy. You dropped a bomb on me yesterday, and I just want to hang out, take it easy. Okay?"

"You didn't have to do that," I say, though I'm grateful he did. A day with Sheppard while I find equilibrium without Michael's ring on my finger sounds like just what I need.

He brushes my bangs out of my eyes, a gesture I'm becoming familiar with. "Yes, I did. What you need will always come first, before anything. The band, Dalt, Jeff. Anything. All you have to do is ask, and I will do whatever it takes to get it for you."

I pull away. "You've known me a week. You can't possibly mean that."

He snakes his arm around my stomach and nuzzles my ear with his lips. "Okay, maybe not completely. I owe the band a lot, I owe Dalt more than that and a lot of time. I've broken promises in the past year, contracts, reneged on PR events, but I didn't ask you to stay only to be halfway in a relationship. I fully intend on giving you my entire summer to see where it leads."

My heart sinks.

That's what I was afraid of . . . that's what was lurking in the depths of my heart while he held me against his chest all night. That this will be over in three months. I can't forget I have a job, *Sheppard* is my job, and once he tells me what threw him off, once he opens his mind to making music again, he won't need me anymore. I want to stay because I'm falling in love with him, but I want more than anything in the world to watch him pick up his guitar, step onto the stage, and do what he was meant to do. I'll do it because I care about him, and I'll fly back to Minnesota at the end of August because he's Sheppard Carpenter, Ghost Town's lead singer, and the only thing I'll be to him is a life coach, someone he worked with, someone he used to know.

I turn my head so he can't see me cry. He'll think it's over Michael, and I don't need that, either. Rolling off the bed and out of his arms, I say, "I'm going to make coffee. I started a grocery list but I didn't finish it."

My voice sounds far away and hard to my own ears, and Sheppard eyes me, his head resting on a folded-up pillow. "What did I say?"

"Nothing."

He knows it's not nothing but doesn't come after me.

Downstairs, I let Scout outside. Runners trot along the beach, their tennis shoes sinking into the sand. I watch for a moment, envious of their lives. I don't remember what it's like to feel like nothing is bothering me, like something isn't pushed beneath the surface, festering. I got used to Michael's death, the constant ache, said goodbye to him and his family the best I could. His mother was heartbroken he was gone and wouldn't have me for a daughter-in-law. I still speak to her, sometimes. Meet her for lunch now and then. I haven't talked to Sheppard about his family, I don't know if his mother and father are still alive.

He traps me between his body and the counter, much like he did when we first met. I'm measuring coffee grounds into his coffeemaker, and he kisses my cheek. "Tell me what I said."

I drop the little scoop into the canister, turn around, and plaster a smile onto my face. "Nothing. We have the summer. I know that."

"Liv," he sighs my name, and just for a second the old Sheppard comes back, the one who needs a drink, the one who hasn't seen another living soul for weeks. "How can I ask you to stay when you know what I am? You are so much more than me."

I rest my head against his chest. I was thinking the same thing only in reverse.

"I have to take it slow, or I'll scare you off. Please, don't do this."

"I'll give you the summer," I say, throwing his words back at him.

"Then if you want to leave, I'll let you go." He picks me up and sets me onto the counter. Caressing the nape of my neck with his warm palm, he tentatively, and oh so gently, brushes my lips with his. I spread my legs and he steps closer, his other hand pressed between my shoulder blades. "Touch me," he murmurs.

I draw back, my heart thrumming. I want to be closer, want the intimacy, but I'm scared of going too fast, too soon. If we're already talking about saying goodbye, how can I give myself to him without breaking my heart? "Where?"

"Anywhere."

He kisses me again, and my head thumps against the cabinet. I brush my fingers over his shoulders and down his chest. He shudders but follows my cues, moving his hands under my pajama tank top and rubbing the sides of my breasts with his thumbs. When I don't stop him, he takes more, lazily gliding his thumbs over my nipples. Sensation shoots right to my core, and I gasp against his mouth. He chuckles, warm and smooth, and I do the same to him, scraping my fingernails over his nipples where they harden into tiny pebbles.

"You're not rusty," he says, teasing, and kisses the tip of my nose.

"Maybe not, just—"

"Skittish. I know. I said I wouldn't push, and that's exactly what I'm doing. Finish making coffee. I'm going upstairs to shower. Are you okay?" he asks, settling me onto the floor so I don't have to jump.

"Yeah. This is all new to me."

"Trust me, Liv. I was married for ten years and barely dated before that. You might not be rusty, but I am."

With that, he trots up the stairs, Scout on his heels now that she's had a potty break and breakfast.

I finish making coffee and carry a cup with me to the bathroom I've been using and shower. Gina texts as I'm drying my hair, asking when we can get together. Now that Sheppard knows the truth, I'm going to have to come clean with her. I don't know how it will affect what she wants from me or what I want to give her. Coming out of retirement is just as frightening as what Sheppard and I started, but I have to tread carefully and savor every second of both. The relaunch of my career will be the only thing I have left after the summer's over.

Sheppard's sitting on a stool at the breakfast bar sipping coffee while he waits for me. I don't know what we're doing today short of ordering more food, and I'm wearing jean shorts and a casual tank top.

He swivels, the grocery list in front of him, and spreads his thighs into a V like I did for him when I was sitting on the counter. I step between them, and experimenting, smear a kiss along his scruffy jaw and down his neck. He blows out a sigh, tangling his fingers in my hair. "Definitely not rusty. Let's order, and after we get everything put away, let's go for a walk. You shared, and now it's my turn."

I step back and blink. "Are you ready for that?"

"I may never be ready, Liv. Sometimes you just have to jump. You didn't have to tell me about Michael. You could have used him to keep distance between us, but you took a chance. Besides, I said I would tell you about what Brock, Eddie, and I talked about. I'm not going to lie or you won't trust me."

I force a smile. "I don't think you would have cared one way or the other if I had truly been engaged."

"I don't cheat, Olivia," he says, his voice hard, "but I would have tried my damnedest to lure you away."

"Well, then, I guess it's lucky you don't have to try so hard."

"Damned straight," he says, nudging me closer, the woodsy scent of his bodywash mingling with my lavender oil. "Now I can put all my energy into convincing you to let me make love to you, and I'm going to start right now." He buries his face in the curve of my neck and growls playfully.

Laughing, I persuade him to let us order groceries first, and true to his word, we make out until they're delivered.

Chapter Sixteen

Olivia walks ahead with the blanket, and I carry the picnic basket, Scout never leaving my side. I told her I wanted a minute to check out her ass in her shorts, and she shook her head and rolled her eyes, but what I really needed was time to sort through my feelings.

When I kissed her yesterday, the last thing on earth I expected her to say was what she did. I thought she would push me away, staunchly defend her engagement, tell me to fuck off. I need her, falling desperately in love with her, and I question who I am needing her this much that I didn't care she promised herself to another man. All I can say to console myself is that if Olivia would have told me she was in love with her fiancé and I didn't have a chance, I would have given up. To my greatest relief, I'll never have to find out what I really would have done. I don't like my answer.

She's single, and that brings on a whole new set of issues. The way Michael died and what I'm struggling with is too close, much too close, and maybe Olivia doesn't realize it yet or maybe she does, but my depression is going to be an obstacle, not so easily maneuvered.

She stops where we sat a few days ago and looks over her shoulder in question. She brushes her hair out of her eyes, and with the sun highlighting her skin, she's the prettiest thing I've seen in a long time. I nod, liking the spot. We're alone but near a public access and portable outhouses. I want to spend the day here, and it's convenient having a place to go to the bathroom.

The wind gives her a bit of trouble as she shakes out our blanket, but I help her after I drop the basket behind a rock for shade. When we put in our grocery order, we chose premade subs from the deli and packed them with bottles of water and chips. I thought I would miss drinking, but I don't, spending time with Liv a better buzz than anything I could find in a bottle of booze. Which is just another hurdle I'll have to face down the racetrack. I haven't forgotten the whole reason Liv's here is to help me stand on my own two feet without a crutch. Trading whiskey for Liv probably wasn't what Dalt had in mind when he hired her, even if I'm healthier and happier for it.

I settle on the blanket, Scout next to me, and Liv tucks her body between my legs. I wrap one of my arms around her and with my other hand, ask her to look at me. I search her bluish-green eyes for an objection before I lower my head and kiss her.

She sighs under my mouth, and it holds so many emotions. Sadness, uncertainty, fear. Maybe guilt. She wore a dead man's ring for three years, and I had no problem hiding it. Out of sight, out of mind, though his presence in her heart is something I'm going to have to deal with. I suspect that's why she's reluctant to let me into her bed—she'll feel like she's betraying him. After all, I bet they'd be married by now if he were still here. I need patience. I don't want her to regret what we do.

We sit for a while, enjoying the sunshine and the waves.

She doesn't pressure me to talk, and I love that about her. It's something else I need—time. Dalt and the others would tell me I've had enough of it. Maybe it's not only time, but what kind. This quiet, with Liv in my arms, this is what I need. Not the kind I've taken for myself this past year—lying in bed drunk and crying as the siren calls, using my own misery against me.

I push my hand under her tank top and splay my fingers over her ribs. She cuddles into my chest, and with my chin brushing the top of her head, I explain how Derrick fell to his death while he watched the stagehands break the equipment down. After my talk with the guys, the funeral is fresh in my mind, and I tell Liv about that too and mention he and Clarissa were headed for a divorce. I repeat *Buzz Kill*'s gossip and speculation that someone pushed him, that it's the reason I asked Brock and Eddie over to the house. The months after Derrick's death are a boozy blur, and I stumble through those weeks when Melody filed for divorce. I don't cry. Maybe it's Liv, or I'm cried out, or both, but my voice is clear, though a bit rough. "I told you I was always down, since I was a kid, always a fog in my brain. Derrick's death triggered something. I spiraled, and I've never felt so unstable, so unbalanced. For months, I could barely move. I didn't eat. The way you found me, I lived like that for almost a year. I don't think I gave Dalt enough credit when he hired you. I think you saved my life."

She looks up at me, and tears are sliding down her cheeks. "I'm sorry, Sheppard. That must have been so hard for you."

"Not any harder than what you had to go through with Michael, and you gave me a lot to think about after you told me about him. The way I was grieving wasn't healthy, like the way you grieved Michael's death. Hiding doesn't work when that loss is a part of you—it only fucks you up more because you cut yourself off from the people who care about you. But I couldn't be around Brock and Eddie, especially if Dalt was there, because Derrick wasn't with us and never would be again. Even yesterday I felt his absence, and it tore me up inside. The band will never be whole."

"That's why you don't want to record another album," she says, finally understanding the real reason behind my actions.

"It doesn't feel right, and I don't know if it ever will. Other bands have gone on to record more albums, but I don't know if that's what's right for Ghost Town."

"What do Brock and Eddie want to do?"

I shrug. "I think they'll do whatever I want—they both seemed open to recording new music. They're at loose ends, but if the band breaks up, maybe that will help them find a different path. They've lived in limbo since Derrick's death, waiting for me to decide."

She twists and sits in front of me, her legs crossed like a child's. "What do you need to move on? Not just so you'll record an album, you don't have to do that if you don't want to, right? That's just something Dalton wants you to do? What do you need to move forward in your life, personally as well as professionally?"

"You're a good start," I say, risking her disapproval, and she doesn't disappoint.

She scowls. "I told you, I can't be your recovery."

"No, but you're a part of it. You can't deny that. I'm sober for the first time in months. That's because of you."

"Fine, but you need to *stay* sober because of you."

Rubbing my face, I say, "Yeah." I get it, I really do.

"Besides me, what do you need?"

She's too far away and I cuddle her to me again. She wraps her arms around my waist and nibbles my jaw, my whiskers scratching against her lips. "I don't know. I asked Eddie and Brock if they saw anything that night, but neither of them were on the stage. I'd already left for the hotel. I couldn't find

Melody, and Dalt was tucked away in a back room, probably banging a groupie he'd never see again. We've always done our own thing after a concert except when Dalt books us a PR event. He didn't usually, unless it was important because by then we're exhausted and we just want to sleep it off. That night we had a little something, but I skipped most of it and let the other guys pick up the slack."

"If you're thinking someone pushed him, what you're saying is you want to figure out who did it."

"And why, yeah. Derrick didn't have any enemies. Why would anyone want him dead?"

Liv sighs and leans away. "Don't get mad, okay?"

I tense, already hating what she has to say. "What?"

"You said he wasn't happy, drunk all the time. His wife was lonely and was going to file for divorce. He wanted out of the band."

I open my mouth to protest, but now that Liv said it, that could be exactly what Derrick wanted. He didn't want to be part of the band anymore. He wanted to retire and try to fix his broken marriage. "Yeah."

She bites her lip and weighs if what she wants to say is worth my anger. "What if he . . . jumped?" I rear back, but she rushes on. "No, don't be like that. You're the same way, don't deny it. The way you stand in the water and listen to your siren. Is it so out of the realm of possibility Derrick heard her too, and drunk, he gave in?"

I sag and consider she could be right. Intoxicated, maybe Derrick thought it was hopeless to try to repair his relationship with Clarissa. Maybe he didn't know how to tell me he wanted out. He was avoiding me and Dalt, and I know how isolating it can feel on the road. I was fortunate I avoided a lot of that, but Melody disappearing at all hours agitated me when she should have been by my side supporting me. "If that's really what he did, he didn't leave a note. We went through all of his things before we returned them to his wife, and there wasn't anything in there that hinted that's what he did or that he was thinking about doing it. Even his notebook where he jotted down song lyrics didn't have anything like that in it."

Liv curls in on herself, drawing her legs against her chest and resting her head against her knees. She stares over the ocean, her thoughts with Michael. I hate it, but I'm going to have to share her. For a little while.

We sit like that, not speaking, while I rub her back. We skipped breakfast, and my stomach growls. "Do you want to eat?"

She turns toward me, and her eyes are dry. "Yeah, that sounds good."

I drag the picnic basket over to the blanket. Liv shares half her sandwich with Scout, and when she's done, she uses the bathroom and throws a Frisbee for the dog along the water. I watch her for a long time, wondering what I'm going to do if she doesn't stay when the summer's over.

I can't think about that—I need to focus on one thing at a time, and for right now, that's Derrick's death. I have to put it behind me in one way or another, or it won't matter if Liv stays or leaves. I won't be able to completely get on with my life if I don't know.

After tiring out Scout, she sits with me again, and I push her until she's lying on the blanket. I lie next to her and kiss her, my hand resting on her cheek. She kisses me back, the faint flavor of tomatoes and onion on her tongue, until she needs air and wiggles sideways a bit, allowing me a clear view of her face.

"If you don't think he jumped," she says, flinching when she says the word, "and you really believe he was pushed, how are you going to find out? The police investigated, didn't they?"

I'm grateful she's willing to talk about it and simply not call me crazy. "Yeah. I can talk to the detective who questioned everyone. I can speak to the stage crew who were breaking up the equipment to load into the trucks for our next concert. I don't know where Melody was. Don't know where Dalt was either—not for sure. There's a lot of snooping around I can do."

"Okay."

"Okay, what?"

"Okay, then that's what you should do. I'll support you, Sheppard. Make your phone calls, write down your thoughts. Talk to me—I can try to be an unbiased opinion."

"You don't think I should . . . let it go?"

"I think it will be okay if you ask questions, but you can't let this take over your life if you don't get the answers you want. Sometimes bad things happen and there's no one to blame."

"Yeah. I appreciate that, Liv."

"Anything I can do, just ask." She brushes a kiss over my cheek. "Do you want to head back? What do you want me to cook for dinner?"

"I don't know. You decide."

We pick up our things, and as we head back to the house, my footsteps drag. I'm glad I told Liv everything. She knows all the reasons why Dalt hired her, but even with her here, things feel like they are just too much. I set the basket on the breakfast bar—Olivia will clean it out and put it away—and I trudge up the stairs. I feel her eyes on me, but she lets me go. I'm disappointed but at the same time relieved, needing space and time alone but scared of it too, because time alone only allows me to think bad things and tonight isn't any exception.

I lie on my bed, twisted thoughts tangled in my heart. I didn't consider Derrick jumped, or at the very least, changed his mind the split second it was too late. I haven't talked to Clarissa since the funeral, and maybe she would know more about the state of his mental health. He'd avoided me for so long I don't know where his thoughts were at before he died, and if he was suicidal, I didn't have a fucking clue. Eddie had a valid point, asking me why I didn't demand Derrick sober up. The music wasn't affected—Derrick played well drunk off his ass (we all do if you want to know the truth)—and preoccupied with Melody, that's all I cared about. Now I feel like shit for not stepping up and being the friend he'd needed me to be.

I bury my face in a pillow and let the pillowcase soak up my tears. I was a shitty friend and I was a shitty husband or Melody wouldn't have left me.

Scout whines and nudges me with her nose. I hug her and cry into her neck instead. It doesn't seem so pathetic slobbering all over Olivia's dog.

I should get up, wash my face, and ask her if she needs help with dinner. We ordered a ton of groceries and she has her pick of what to cook. I just can't bring myself to care enough.

She doesn't leave me alone as long as she did the other night, and an hour later, she knocks on my door before pushing it open. The sun hasn't set yet, and the light glimmers through the window. She changed into pajamas, silk lounging pants and a tank top, her hair pulled into a messy bun at the back of her head. "Do you want dinner?"

"I want you to leave me the fuck alone." I'm hurting and I'm nasty.

"Okay," she says, but she sits on the edge of my bed.

I grab her arm, and in two seconds, I have her pinned under me, my cock hard and pressed into her cleft. She gasps and bucks, trying to wiggle out of my hold, but that only eggs me on, and I grind against her. "Is this what you want?" I ask, turning making love into some ugly thing that matches how I feel about myself. I cover her mouth with mine, our teeth gnashing together. She tries to turn her head, but I won't let her, and I force my tongue into her mouth.

The only thing that breaks through the red haze is her sob, and ashamed, I let her go. She scrambles off the bed, her chest heaving, and she wipes her mouth with the back of her hand. I don't have an apology in me, and I roll over and face the wall, Scout tucked up against me the way I slept with Olivia last night.

"Come downstairs with me," she whispers.

"No." I don't turn around to answer her.

"If I leave this room alone, I'll leave your house alone, too," she says, and her words are like hooks dredged into my back, pulling me against my will, tearing the flesh from my bones.

The siren's song calls to me, her voice soft, deadly, and I can feel the water swirling around my feet, her grip on my ankle. "Then go."

I can't be who she needs me to be. She's already been hurt once, and if I'm going to do it again, it's better I do it now than later when we're so far into it I won't be able to live without her. Well, I can't now, so there's not much difference. It might save her a little pain, though.

"I need you, Sheppard."

"That's your mistake."

"Yeah," she says softly, "I guess it is. Take care of yourself."

I don't answer, and the only thing that remains of what I had with her is the quiet click when she shuts the door.

You know I'm pretty bad off when I hurt too much to cry.

Chapter Seventeen

Olivia

I eat dinner alone, sitting at the breakfast bar with my laptop and the backend of my website staring me in the face. I pan fried chicken with mushrooms and I cubed red potatoes and baked them with salt and pepper, and after I pulled them out of the oven, slathered them with butter. Between bites, I sip a crisp white I found in Sheppard's wine drawer. I'm not drinking to get drunk, just to take the edge off a little. It's not even about what Sheppard did to me upstairs, but this blog, this career, this life.

I don't plan on leaving, despite threatening him with it. If I left, if I ordered a car and packed my bags, it would destroy him, and when he comes around, I need to explain that in a way he truly understands. When people do things, there are consequences, others left behind, people who suffer.

I clean up my dishes, store the leftovers in the fridge, and text Gina. I apologize for the inconvenience. I shouldn't meet with her tomorrow when Sheppard is feeling this way. She understands, giving me the time and date of the lunch she invited me to and offering me a ride if I can get away.

The bar in the living room is stocked, and if I feel a twinge pouring all his booze down the kitchen sink, it doesn't last long. He can afford to replace it, but I hope he never does. I do a little more straightening up, and later, Scout comes downstairs, her tail tucked between her legs. She feels like she's abandoning him, having to go outside to pee, but I murmur she's okay, and after she goes, it bolsters her spirits enough to have a bite to eat before trotting back up the stairs to resume her vigil.

I never swept in the hidden living room, and I do that now and shove the blanket Sheppard used to cover us into the wash. There's a bar in here, too, and I empty it.

It's almost midnight by the time I head to bed. Even if we talked mostly about Sheppard's issues, problems, roadblocks, however you want to label them, it's still draining. Like the woman I made friends with, when you care about someone, their troubles can weigh so much heavier on you.

I fall into an uneasy sleep, wondering what I'll find in the morning, but I don't have to wait that long. At 2 AM, a sob so gut-wrenching I almost wet the bed screams from Sheppard's room. I sit up, my heart pounding. I was waiting for this to come. For the time when Sheppard was finally so broken he could be put back together. A turning point, and now he can finally start healing.

Tentatively, I pad into his bedroom. He's crying so hard I think the neighbors might call the police. Scout's not scared. She's heard this level of grief before—from me. I sit on the edge of the bed prepared for retaliation. Dalton said he'd never hurt me, but he didn't consider Sheppard would hurt me to hurt himself. That he would let me leave is proof of that very thing.

I rest my hand on his quaking back. "Sheppard." I don't

know if he can hear me, and I rub soothing circles over the t-shirt he wore on our picnic.

His sobs quiet, and I sit for a long time waiting for him to look at me.

The sun is starting to rise, faint pink glimmering through the glass when Sheppard finally lifts his head. He's exhausted, and my heart breaks just looking at him.

"You didn't go," he rasps.

I wipe his cheeks, falling so in love warning signals flare bright. I shouldn't get involved with another man who has depression. I shouldn't because these last three years have been a nightmare, and I should steer clear of anyone who's capable of doing that to me again.

"No, I didn't. I'm never going to abandon you. I know how it feels, and I would never do that to another person."

He sits up and lifts me into his lap. Hugging me to him, his shoulders shake with sobs he won't let go. I'm surprised he has anything left, but I shouldn't be. How many months after Michael's death did I weep, never running out of pain, misery, heartache, and tears.

"Shh," I console him, my hand resting against the side of his neck. "Shh. I will always be here for you."

"I'm sorry, Livvy," he mumbles against the top of my head.

"Sheppard, you need to understand that you don't have to feel this way. You're punishing yourself for Derrick's death, and it isn't right. What happened to Derrick wasn't your fault. You have to stop punishing yourself, sweetheart. You have to stop punishing yourself."

"I'm so tired," he says, and I can still hear the sorrow in his voice, but it's clearer somehow, and I know things will start getting better.

"I know, and you won't be able to truly rest until you start moving forward. Sleep now. You're exhausted, probably hungry and dehydrated. I'll be here when you wake up and we'll start a new day."

He settles onto his pillow, and Scout jumps onto the bed and curls up at our feet. I lie next to him, and he wraps his arms around me.

"I need you, Liv," he mumbles before sleep takes him.

He needs me now, but God help me when this is over and he doesn't need me anymore.

Chapter Eighteen

Sheppard

I crack my eyes open, and they're crusted with tears. I rub at my eyelids to clear my vision, and Olivia is lying next to me, a hand curled under her chin. There is so much I have to apologize for, but apologies are empty unless there are actions to back them up. I brush my fingers over her cheek, needing to touch her, affirmation she's here, living and breathing. Her eyes flutter open, and she smiles, but not in happiness she's with me in bed. What I did last night turned our intimacy into something ugly, and I'll regret that for the rest of my life. Her smile is full of sympathy, and she rubs my cheek too, her fingertips grazing over my stubble.

"How are you feeling?" she whispers.

"Luckier than hell you're still here," I say, knowing I am.

"Things have to change. You can't keep going on this way."

I lean closer and rest my trembling hand against her cheek. "I'm sorry, Liv. What I did to you last night is inexcusable, and I'll understand if you don't feel safe here and want to go. Really go home."

"Under your pain, you didn't want to hurt me, not like that. You were lashing out because you're comfortable with our relationship, and you feel safe sharing your emotions. That's a good thing. You were also trying to scare me into leaving, but you're smart enough to understand the situation you would be in if I did."

She doesn't mean because I'm falling in love with her, though I am. Dalt hired her because she has the skills I need to figure my life out, puzzle out what I want with the band and if I decide I don't want to keep the group together, what else I would do. I'm too young to retire, and while I've never believed the adage "Idle hands are the devil's playthings," in my case, having a goal, a purpose, a reason to get up in the morning, could be the difference between finding steady ground and walking into the ocean and never coming out again.

"You're scared," she says, wiggling closer, "but you have plenty of people supporting you."

I'm terrified, and to cover it up, I ask, "Can I kiss you, Liv?" Before I did what I did, I wouldn't have asked, assumed that's what she wanted, but I ruined the fragile newness of our relationship. What we had will need to be built back up again.

She smiles, and this time it holds more happiness than before. "How about," she whispers, sliding her arm under my pillow and molding her body to mine, "I kiss you?"

Her lips are warm and soft, and her taste isn't tinted with coffee or what she ate an hour ago. It's all Liv—hopes and dreams, a future. I'm not sure what the future holds, but with Liv with me, I can stop hiding from it.

My stomach rolls queasily from hunger, and reluctantly, I pull back. She forgave me, and I can't waste it. I want to show her what happened last night won't happen ever again. "I'm going to let Scout outside and shower. Did you eat dinner last night?"

"Yeah. There are leftovers for lunch, if you're hungry."

"That sounds good." I trap her with a hand to her back before she rolls off the bed. "Thank you."

She searches my eyes, deciding on what to say. She could be glib and say that's what Dalt is paying her for, or she signed a contract and didn't want to break it. I think our relationship is more than that now, at least, I hope it is.

Instead, she says nothing at all, only kissing my cheek before scrambling off the bed and into her bedroom. A second later, the water turns on.

I let Scout outside. The beach is empty, but the siren sings from her watery hell. If I learned anything last night, it's that I can hear her calling whether I'm on the beach or not. Lying in bed, her grip was just as firm as it is when I'm standing in the ocean. I need to shake her off. Maybe not completely, as I've dealt with her lullabies all my life, but I need to quiet them or one day I'll succumb. I have too much to live for to do that. I want to say now that Liv is in my life, but that's not true. Melody had her reasons for divorcing me, and there's a lesson somewhere in Derrick's death. Liv was right in a way—I was punishing myself for what other people chose to do. I may have had a hand in both those things, but I'm not fully responsible. I have to stop acting like I am. No, if Liv left today, I would still have plenty to live for, and that's something I can never forget.

Jeff and Gina's house is dark. Olivia's putting Gina off because of me, and I want to encourage Liv to spend time with her. I think Gina could be good for Liv's comeback. She doesn't seem to have many friends and visiting with Gina will help her open up.

Scout follows me inside and attacks her bowl full of kibble. When she's finished, she waits while I take my own shower, but I'm quick and sipping coffee and doing an internet search on my laptop before Olivia trots downstairs with her hair dry, wearing denim shorts and a teal blouse. Her blue eyes seem even more blue if that's possible and she steps between my legs and offers her lips for a kiss. I'm so relieved she's not angry and won't hold what I did to her against me, I devour her mouth, my hands gripping her hair, holding her in place.

Laughing, she pulls away, and the silky strands slide through my fingers. "What are you doing?"

I decided to tackle the scariest, but most important, thing first. "I'm researching therapists. I found one I think I'll click with—he used to be a member of a boy band back in the seventies and knows about the business. I called and scheduled a consultation. I asked about medication, but he said that's a choice we could talk more about if I decide he's who I want to work with. I have a good feeling about him."

She reaches onto her tiptoes and presses her lips to mine. "I'm proud of you."

"I know you don't like hearing it, but I couldn't have done it without you. No, not couldn't. Wouldn't. I wouldn't have done it without you."

"Then I'm glad I'm here."

She rounds the breakfast bar and pours herself a cup of coffee. She looks at home in my kitchen, and I like it. "What else are you doing today?"

"After my consultation, I'm going to make a few phone calls. I found the arena manager's phone number, and I want to talk to the production manager who was in charge of our equipment. I had to find him, and he's traveling with Viola Young right now. He can ask the stagehands if they saw anything— they're employed by the same company and he works with a lot of the guys who traveled with us. I can track down the detective who was in charge of investigating Derrick's death and ask him what he knows. Eventually I'm going to have to ask Melody where she was and find out what Dalt was doing. If he's seeing someone like you suggested, I should support him. He's been alone for a long time. Ghost Town isn't a good substitute for love."

She holds the mug close to her mouth and asks carefully, "And if you do all that and don't find anything?"

I already know what I want to say. "Put it behind me and start looking to the future. I owe that to Brock, Eddie, and Dalt. If I don't think I can keep Ghost Town together, be honest about it, and if I don't want to, figure out what it is I *do* want." I slide off the stool, walk around the breakfast bar, and frame her face in my hands. "You will never know how fucking scared I was when I thought I made you leave. I never want to go through that again."

She sets her mug down, rests her forehead against my chest, and clutches my t-shirt in her little fists. "Seeing you like that scared me, too. I want you to feel better, Sheppard. Maybe you'll never feel normal, but I know you can do a helluva lot better than the way you were last night."

"Finding a therapist will be a good start. You should text Gina. While I'm gone, you can work with her. I'll be busy most of the afternoon."

"Sheppard . . ." she starts reluctantly.

"No. You've been subtle about it, but I need to go through this for me and then for the rest of the people in my life. I can get myself to Royce's office, and I can make those phone calls alone. In fact, maybe I *should* make those phone calls alone. I don't know what they're going to tell me. After Derrick's death, I checked out. The investigation, that time afterward, even Derrick's funeral, it's all a blur. Space will be a good thing, Liv. You can't prop me up, just promise to be there when I need you, because I know I will. Somehow."

"What you said—"

"I was an asshole. Maybe I shouldn't, but I'm glad you need

me too. I want you to need me, and I never want you to think it's a mistake. I don't ever want to prove to you it's a mistake. Whatever you need, I want to be able to give it to you. I meant it when I said it, and I mean it now, but I can't be there for you the way I want how I was last night. I thought I hit rock bottom a long time ago, but that was nothing compared to how I felt when I thought I was never going to see you again."

She blows out a breath and lifts her head. I brush the bangs out of her eyes, my fingers shaking.

"Okay, but you're my priority, and Gina understands that. If I can't do what she wants when she wants me to do it, then she'll have to leave me out of her documentary."

I chuckle. "You don't know Gina. Once she sets her eyes on something, she always gets it. If she wants you to be part of her documentary, then you will be, the end. Now that I know about Michael, I can help you start moving forward too. If I can pick up my guitar, you can write a blogpost."

"It's more than writing a blogpost," she says, the delicate skin between her eyebrows furrowing with an elegant frown.

"Keeping Ghost Town together is more than me picking up my guitar, too, but we have to start somewhere."

Twisting her lips, she says, "Point taken."

She reheats the dinner she made for us last night, and she texts Gina while we eat. Gina responds quickly, and I'm glad Liv will have something to occupy her time while I meet with Royce and do my digging. I want her to get her career back on track, but I also want her to make friends with Gina and other women in the area whom Gina knows. That's the selfish side of me. If she has friends here, if she finds a little niche for herself, she'll want to stay when the summer's over.

I leave while Liv's cleaning the kitchen. She'll be gone when I come back to make my phone calls, but I like knowing she'll be next door at Gina's.

Royce Porter's office building is a few streets over from Dalt's, quiet hallways and large windows that let the light shine in. Older than me by about fifteen years, he shakes my hand with a firm grip and we sit across from each other, a coffee service between us. I explain why Dalt hired Olivia, why I need her and why I need to see him. The meeting is comfortable, casual, and I'm not nervous talking to him. It helps he's been in my shoes, his boy band earning him millions and a claim to fame that will never die. He doesn't write anything down, only nodding once in a while as I unburden myself. He heard about Derrick's death, and I tell him how it triggered my depression into something deeper I'm not equipped to deal with.

He said he can work me into his schedule twice a week and go from there, and I balk. If I see Royce twice a week and run with Jeff every morning, that's time away from Olivia. But if I can work up to the point where I can tell her I love her and want her to stay here, we'll have separate careers and won't spend all day together like we do now. I want her to coach again. I want her to blog and write another book, and I want her to do those things while I write new songs about love and loss, only knowing I've found love and will never lose it again.

Reluctantly, I agree, and he's sharp, sensing my hesitation. He'll ask me about it next week at our first appointment, and I'll have to admit I'm in love with Liv. I don't know what he'll think of our relationship when she was hired to help me, but that worry will keep for another day. Olivia has a few things she still needs to work out too, and since she suggested therapy, maybe she'll come with me once in a while.

Just like I thought, the house is empty when I return, only Scout lying by the sliding glass doors waiting for me to come home. She bounds to her feet, and in excitement, her tongue lolls from her mouth. It occurs to me, like a flash of lightning, that if Olivia had really gone when I told her to go, she would have left Scout behind. I'm not sure how I feel about that except I don't want Scout without Liv. I let her outside, and I look at the beach with new eyes. Before, whenever I would step foot on the sand, I did so knowing the siren would call to me. She does, but I hear other things, and her hand around my ankle isn't so tight.

I make a fresh pot of coffee, decaf this time, and settle in the den with my laptop, phone, notebook, and a full coffee mug. I don't want to sit in the kitchen in case I'm on the phone and Olivia comes home. Comes back. This isn't her home . . . not yet.

I call the arena's manager first. She was still in the building when Derrick fell, but from what details I can remember of the investigation, she wasn't on the floor or anywhere near the stage. She won't have anything to tell me, but I want confirmation for my own notes before I write her off.

"This is Jane," she answers, her voice amused, as if she heard a joke just before she picked up the phone.

I picture a happy blonde leaning in her chair, legs crossed. I met her briefly during the sound check when she asked if there was anything we needed. I don't remember everyone I meet during a tour, and I keep to myself for the most part. I'm there to do my job and go back to the hotel, board a plane, hop on a bus. I love the fans, but over the years I've learned to protect my emotional bandwidth or they'll take all they can, and afterward, there's nothing left.

"Miss Carlson," I say, using her last name I found on the arena's site, "this is Sheppard Carpenter."

She pauses. "Mr. Carpenter, what can I do for you? Are you planning another tour? It's unusual for you to be in charge of that, isn't it?"

It is, and I've never had a hand in the touring schedule.

Dalt works with a touring company booking arenas and hotels years in advance. "I'm not calling in regard to that."

"Then what can I help you with?" she asks, her voice full of caution. She knows what I'm calling about now. During the investigation, the detective assigned to the case cleared the arena of any wrongdoing. Accidents happen, and Derrick fell from our stage equipment, nothing that was on loan from the arena.

"I'm calling about Derrick Pavleck's death. I was wondering what you could tell me about that night."

She pauses, searching her memory. "Unfortunately, not a lot. I wasn't on the floor when he fell, and I ran down from my office as soon as I heard. My assistant was sick with a summer flu, and I was doing some last minute things for the Chicago Marathon expo that was going to be set up the next morning. Some vendors were dragging their feet, but we like to have the space entirely accounted for."

That's what I expected. "You didn't hear anything, rumors, anyone talking on the side about how someone could have pushed him off that scaffolding?" I scribble in my notebook: Jane Carlson=Chicago Marathon. It will be easy enough to check the arena's calendar to see if she's lying but there's no reason why she would be when it's easily proven.

"By then, everyone was in a panic, screaming for someone to call 911. Your manager was there, but I don't remember his name. The stagehands were shaken, to say the least, and he was calming everyone down. Were you still at the arena, Mr. Carpenter?"

"No. That's why I'm calling. To ask if you happened to have seen anything or heard anything suspicious."

"I'm sorry. That night was just a blur after he fell. You have my deepest condolences. Perhaps the detective turned up something when he was questioning everyone."

"He's on my list. Thanks, Miss Carlson."

"Anytime."

She hangs up, not impressed to be talking with me, probably quite the opposite considering what tragedy is now connected with her arena.

Before I move on, I double check the Chicago Marathon expo was scheduled for the weekend after our concert, and it was. Tapping my pen against my notebook, I debate on who to call next. The production manager may be harder to track down, and I might need more time to find him. I have to call the touring company and leave a message, but a secretary calls me back the second I disconnect from the voicemail. She rattles off the production manager's name and cell number and it's seconds later he's answering his phone.

"Yeah, this is Hicks," he says gruffly, voices in the background.

"Mr. Hicks, this is Sheppard Carpenter," I say, expecting him to ask me to call back. Viola Young is playing Nashville, and I bet Hicks is knee-deep in setting up fireworks and trapezes. I don't know Hicks well. Most of what we need is already set up by the time we reach the arena for sound checks and a few practice songs before the concert.

"Shep," he says, then yells away from the phone, "I need five!" He pauses, and the noise fades. "What can I do for ya?"

I swallow back the panic attack slowly building in my chest, the knot of anxiety I have to learn to control or I'll never get to the bottom of Derrick's death. Sweat beads along my forehead and I wish Olivia were here after all, but I can't need her like that. "I was wondering if I could talk to you about Derrick's fall."

"Yeah, sure." There's a *snick* of a lighter and the puff of a cigarette.

"What do you remember that night? There've been some rumors it wasn't an accident."

Hicks grunts, and there's nothing on the line after that.

I wait him out. Derrick fell thirteen months ago, and Hicks has worked on many concerts since then.

"I don't know what to tell ya," he finally says. "He went back with you after the last encore, right?"

"Yeah, he did." I search through my memories of that night, reliving the adrenaline and the high performing always gave us. We're getting old, but we hadn't lost our touch. Every song, every chord, every note, was perfect, and the audience went ballistic. After the final song, we headed down to the locker rooms and showered off the sweat before the meet and greet Dalt arranged. Derrick was with us, almost sober since we don't drink while we play, and our concert that night lasted two and a half hours. "We had a small PR thing Dalt set up for us, but Derrick and I cut out before it was over. Brock and Eddie stayed behind and signed more autographs. Derrick couldn't decompress until he was sitting up in the scaffolding, watching you guys break down our equipment, and he took off earlier than I did."

Hicks doesn't give a shit what we did after the concert ended. All he cared about was clearing out and getting on the road. "We started to pack up as quick as we could," he says around a mouthful of cigarette smoke. "Don't pay attention to much else. You know that, Shep."

"Yeah. But you didn't see anyone who looked like they didn't belong? Did you see Melody?"

"Nope, didn't see her, but I wasn't looking for her, neither."

That's the way it was. Everyone had their own job, wanted to get to it, because by the time we left the stage it was past midnight, and the guys wouldn't be packed up and on the road to our next gig until four or five in the morning. They'd sleep on the bus all the way there and do it all over again.

"All right, thanks," I say because there's nothing else *to* say.

"Talk to a couple of the other guys. Let me give you their numbers. Place was fucking huge, maybe somebody saw something while they were fucking around."

"Yeah." I'm discouraged, but I try to push it back. I have several people to talk to and I haven't spoken with the detective who questioned everyone. No one was allowed to leave until he had, but I was already at the hotel and he didn't get to me until the next morning when Dalt woke me up and told me the news.

I chat with a few of the stagehands, the ones who could answer their phones. Viola Young is on scale with P!nk, and her stage is an elaborate set of trapezes, fireworks, and daises lifting her into the air. Everything is constructed with the utmost care and consideration, and no one would let anything distract them while setting up her stunt equipment.

They tell me the same story Hicks did. They were on stage, breaking down our sound system, our instruments, loading everything into the trucks. One kid said he saw Melody floating around the back hallways, but when I asked him what time, he said he didn't know. He was coming in from having a cigarette, and she was rushing in the other direction.

"This was before Derrick fell?" I ask, trying to piece together a timeline.

"Oh, yeah, for sure. Nobody was doing anything except screaming after that happened. Sorry, Sheppard."

"No, it's okay. I'm trying to figure out where everyone was before the accident. Did you see Dalt at all?"

"Not until after Derrick fell. I think he was with someone; he had a smear of lipstick on his neck and his pants were wrinkled. I only noticed because my girlfriend travels with me, and after my smoke break, we had our own quickie in the women's locker room. Can you not tell Hicks, though? He'll fire me for wasting company time."

I would have been amused if we weren't talking about something so serious. I don't doubt the kid has sex on his brain twenty-four/seven. "Wouldn't think of it. You're doing me a favor. You don't happen to know who he was with?"

"Nah. Didn't see anyone with him. The lipstick was sparkly—the glitter caught the stage lights—it's how I saw it at all. He looked ruffled, but by then, I would have been suspicious if he hadn't. I'll never get the image out of my mind. Is that all you got? I gotta get back."

"Yeah, thanks. Hicks gave me another name. Josh Johnson. Is he around?"

"Uh, JJ's working with the pyrotech. Leave him a voicemail and when he's done with that, he'll call you back. I'll give him a heads up you wanna talk to him."

"Thanks. Thanks for your help."

"No problem. I'm sorry about Derrick. It was a big loss." The kid disconnects.

I leave JJ a voicemail, asking him to call me when he's got a free second. I'm tired, the emotional toll of talking about Derrick and his accident for over an hour getting the better of me. I decide to phone the detective another day, and with Scout at my heels, I shuffle into the living room. Olivia's still at Gina's and I use the free time to start a load of laundry and snoop around the kitchen for a snack. I miss her when she's not here, her steady presence something I've come to rely on even after such a short time. She would be concerned if I told her that, but I doubt anyone can truly stand on their own without some kind of support. If Olivia weren't here, I would still have Dalt, Eddie, and Brock, and Jeff and Gina. We all need people in our lives and I won't apologize I added Olivia to my list.

I have a lot to think about, and after I feed Scout and let her outside to pee, we settle on the patio together. She jumps onto the lounger that Olivia usually lies on when we talk, but her soft brown eyes and her panting are a comfort in their own way. It means Olivia isn't far, that she'll be back soon.

For the first time in a long while, I'm at peace, the siren's song merely a whisper. I'm journaling and reading snippets of Olivia's self-help book when she walks across the sand from Gina's and curls up in my lap like she was always meant to be there.

I hold her as the sun sinks. I'm learning to be grateful for the little things, to find peace, like Olivia mentioned days ago, in a bird's song or the laugh of a child chasing a beach ball. I'm grateful for her, her cheek pressed against my chest, not speaking, able to simply enjoy being together.

I'm alive, I'm loved, and I'm blessed.

Chapter Nineteen

Olivia

Gina texts me just as Sheppard backs his car out of the garage and asks if I can wear the black dress I wore to their house for dinner. I don't question the request. If she's filming me today, she'll want me to look professional, yet approachable. I add a black blazer and keep my cross necklace on. I'm not a stranger to interviews, and I know to keep my makeup light and to accentuate my eyes with eyeliner. I wish she would have sent me a list of questions beforehand, but it wouldn't surprise me if she wants to film my natural reactions for a raw, guttural, gritty tone. It can't be easy for the other women to talk about their failures, either, and while failure can feel isolating, knowing you're not alone in your imperfections can be soothing, too.

"You look great," she says, meeting me at her patio door. She's wearing a sky-blue sheath dress, her wild curls pinned into a huge, messy bun. She's barefoot. I didn't know what to wear for shoes as I wasn't sure of the camera angles she planned to use, and I carry the flat sandals I wore here for dinner.

"Thanks. I haven't had to dress for an interview in a long

time," I say, stepping into their living room that's attached to the kitchen.

"I hope you're not nervous."

"I've done this too many times to be nervous."

"Well, I'm not Oprah." She holds back a smile.

Laughing, I say, "That was a fluke."

"Some fluke," she says, an eyebrow raised in question as she ushers me into the kitchen.

Sheppard and I slept through breakfast and our lunch was on the later side, but Gina has coffee going and she set a platter of finger sandwiches out for us to nibble on. I suppose she's trying to get me to loosen up before the interview. She didn't have to bother. I'm not nervous, but I'm already embarrassed because I know I'll cry. While Gina will be sympathetic, she'll be pleased, too. Real emotion is what wins awards.

"One of her assistants was reading my book on set, and Oprah happened to see her. She asked for a copy and apparently the things I said resonated with her." I shrug. "She had one of her people reach out, and a few months later I was filming a guest spot on her show."

"You're very young for that kind of success," Gina says, and I wonder if that's going to be one of her questions.

"I wasn't ready for it, and my inexperience bit me in the ass." Staring at the table, I wrap my hands around my mug.

Gina doesn't miss anything. "Your ring is missing. Did you and your fiancé have a fight? Over Sheppard?"

"No. I was wearing it under false pretenses." I explain Michael's suicide. Her eyes are wet when I finish, but I don't cry.

"What made you tell him?" she asks, knowing there's a story behind the story.

"He kissed me," I say softly. The way he trapped me against his chest, his lips covering mine in an aggressive, possessive kiss, his anger I was spoken for, his fury he didn't care, it all still takes my breath away.

"Jeff and I could tell when you were here for dinner. That something was between you. Let's talk about that in front of the camera. This will change some of the questions I want to ask you."

"All right."

She leads me into part of their house I haven't seen yet, a sitting room on the second floor that looks over the ocean. It's done in white, mint green, and a blue that matches her dress. Mirrors on the walls reflect the light shimmering in from the window. A loveseat is positioned against the middle of one wall, and a camera fastened to a tripod stands in front of it. The natural light will be flattering, and I sit on the side that's near a table decorated with a lamp, a glass bowl full of seashells, and a small, square box of tissues. The wall behind me is empty of artwork. My face and emotions will be on full display.

Gina drags an ottoman over, sits, and adjusts the tripod, positioning the lens evenly with my face. She studies the screen and nudges the tripod back just a little. "Perfect. What we say here, the questions I ask and your answers, anything you don't want included, you can tell me later. If there's anything you're not sure about, we can always re-film. Nothing we do today is set in stone, okay?"

"It's fine. Don't worry about it." I smooth my hair, lick my lips, and adjust my blazer.

She swivels and slides a notebook off the desk behind her. "I wrote up a few questions, thinking that your answers would lead to more questions, but what you told me downstairs slants this interview in a different way. If there's anything I ask, Olivia, anything at all, and you don't want to answer, just say so, and I'll edit it out. Okay?"

"Okay."

She begins the way all interviews begin, asking how I started coaching, what drew me to it. I always tell the story of how my father passed away and how I wanted to follow in his footsteps, but in a way that I was comfortable with and could make my own mark. I finger my necklace as I do, and Gina asks the significance of the piece of jewelry. I speak briefly of that too, knowing that these questions are just a foundation for the real ones she wants to ask me—the focus of the documentary.

"How did you and your fiancé meet, Olivia?" she asks, writing notes as I speak.

The question surprises me. I asked Sheppard how he and Melody met, but he never asked about Michael. Maybe he didn't want to know.

"A friend of mine asked me to talk to her class. She taught, well, she still does, teaches at a community college. It's an exploratory class for students who don't know what they want to be when they grow up. I was twenty-six at the time, younger than some of her students. She wanted me to share how I'd come to realize what I wanted to do with my life while I was so young. You know I have my father to thank for that, and I talked to her class about following your passion, creating action-able steps that will get you there. I hadn't graduated with my coaching certificate that long before she invited me to speak, and we talked a lot about finding a school, figuring out funds to pay for tuition. Speaking to her class about that topic was what I was meant to do, and I think I helped every one of those students that day." I pause and slightly shake my head. "But that wasn't your question. After class, we stopped at a campus coffee stand, and Michael was there. He taught English, was on his way to class, and she introduced us. He was older than me, some would say by a lot, but I never thought about it. He shook my hand, and his touch . . ." My voice fades off and I'm standing in the college's corridor, his thumb rubbing over my knuckles. "There was something in his eyes. Weary, tired. Like maybe he hadn't gotten enough sleep, but it was more than that too. He asked me out for coffee and it turned into kind of a joke because we were standing there already holding coffee cups. I said yes, and it wasn't long after that I said yes to a different kind of question."

"You were serious quite quickly, then," Gina comments.

"I've been accused of that, yeah." I rub my empty finger.

She catches it and uses it. "Did you know Michael was suicidal?"

My eyes fill with tears. This is what she wanted, the answers to these kinds of questions. "No. I knew he was, not sad, but, subdued, maybe? There was always a tissue buffering his emotions. I thought that was just the way he was. Not everyone is exuberant, and I thought Michael was a quiet person, like I am. We enjoyed sleeping in, long talks. In the winter, we would drive out to the state park and look at the Northern Lights. He enjoyed life in a different way, or so I thought."

She doesn't ask what happened, not the gruesome night I told Sheppard about. Maybe the details aren't needed, but she says, "Can you explain why you retired? You had a successful career coaching, including some notable figures in the Minneapolis/St. Paul area. You wrote a bestselling book, and dedicated it to Michael. Why did his suicide derail you?"

I hold out my hands, palms up. "I failed. How can I coach someone, *anyone*, to live their best life when I couldn't see the person closest to me needed my help? I didn't feel qualified, not after that. Certainly not qualified enough to charge someone for my so-called expertise. I lived with him, shared a space with him, for three years, and never once did I see he needed help."

Gina pauses, and that pause will feed tension to anyone watching. I know how valuable timing can be, but Gina's a skilled interviewer and her next question shakes me down to my core.

"Do you have survivor's guilt, Olivia? Do you feel guilty he's gone but you're still here?"

"Every day."

She pauses again. "Do you think it should have been you?"

I meet her eyes and mine are dry. "Yes."

My answer doesn't surprise her, she only smiles sympathetically—a smile people watching the documentary will never see.

"What do you think Michael would say if he heard you just now?"

He would be disappointed in me. Out of anyone in the world, Michael was my biggest supporter, my biggest fan. He sat in the audience when I was Oprah's guest and afterward, pretended to be sad she didn't give them a car. I laughed and said a copy of my book would have to suffice. He quirked his lips and shook his head like there was no way my book could be better than a car, and the second we made it to the hotel after filming, we made love.

The way he loved me before he was gone made what he did that much more heartbreaking. I wasn't enough, and deep down, I know I won't be enough for Sheppard, too.

"He would tell me it's not my fault." The way I told Sheppard last night Derrick's death wasn't his.

"Would you believe him?"

"If I did, I wouldn't be sitting here. I wouldn't be in LA. I'd still be coaching, blogging." I don't mean to sound angry, but it seeps into my tone. What Michael would or wouldn't say doesn't matter. He's not here to say anything. "Of course it's my fault. I was too busy with my career, too busy coaching other people, to pay attention to what was going on in my own life."

"If Michael wouldn't blame you, do you think he'd want

you to move on? You've been living in limbo for three years. Don't you think he'd want you to pick up the pieces? Fall in love? You're very young, Olivia, to stop living."

My stomach churns. I've already fallen in love with Sheppard, but I never once thought about what Michael would think. Would he be happy for me? Disappointed I didn't mourn longer, harder? Scoff that Sheppard's a rockstar? Would he say, "You can do better, Livvy, than a washed up drunk." No, he wouldn't say that. He'd never be cruel to anyone. If it came right down to it, Michael and Sheppard would be friends, comparing lyrics to poems, how the creation differed, how it was the same. Sipping beer and wondering what the point of life really is. Sheppard is a lot like Michael, not only in terms of living with depression. They are both very deep, passionate men and I'm fortunate I didn't know them at the same time. I don't know how I would have chosen between them.

I let too much time go by, and she'll have to edit out my pause. Or maybe she'll leave it in. God only knows the expressions that have flitted across my face. Gina knows me personally. She already knows I'm in love with Sheppard, but what I'll let myself do with it when push comes to shove is something else. What will Sheppard want to do with it? He started this whole thing kissing me on the beach.

She fills in the silence. "Do you think Michael would want you to find someone to give you what he couldn't?"

I'm getting tired of her pushing, though that's what this interview is for. "Do you think he would resent me for finding a man and giving that man something I couldn't give him?" I toss back at her.

Gina's a professional and takes my question in stride. "What could you give another man that you didn't give your fiancé? What could you give another man that your fiancé didn't accept? You can give, Olivia, give until you have absolutely nothing left of yourself, but the person you're giving to has to be able to accept it, should *want* to accept it. And more than just accept it. He should treasure it because it's a part of you."

Suddenly we're not talking about Michael and me, we're talking about Jeff and her, and how she's trapped herself in a relationship with a man who doesn't love her enough to marry her.

"I wasn't enough," I whisper.

A tear slides down her cheek. "Olivia, honey, a woman by herself never is."

Sheppard's sitting on the patio with Scout, my joke of a self-help book lying open on one thigh. When he sees me walking across the sand, my sandals dangling from my fingers, he sets the book and his journal aside and opens his arms.

I slide into his lap just as easily as I would Michael's, but I wonder now, what he was thinking when he would hold me, if he was trying to think of ways to say goodbye and in the end couldn't face me. People say committing suicide is an act of cowardice, selfishness, that they don't think of the people they're leaving behind. I think Michael was brave. He was brave until he couldn't be, and I never blamed him for what he did. Only blamed myself for not stopping him.

Turning my head, I press my face against Sheppard's chest. He changed clothes when he came back from the psychiatrist's office, and his t-shirt smells freshly laundered with fabric softener. His jeans are worn and soft against my skin, like he is. The cotton threadbare in places but the seams still strong enough to stay together. What does he think when I'm tucked into his lap like this? Thinking of what to say when the summer's over and he can go back to being Sheppard Carpenter, lead singer of Ghost Town.

"That bad, huh?" he murmurs against the top of my head.

"Do you think about what you would have told Derrick if he'd told you he didn't want to be part of the band anymore?"

He's silent, his hand warm against my back. I wish I didn't have my blazer on so I could feel his fingertips grazing my skin, but I don't want to distract him by taking it off.

"I haven't," he says thoughtfully, staring over my shoulder to the water. "Until you said it, I didn't consider that's what he really wanted to do, but, yeah, when it comes right down to it, it's what he wanted. He wanted to fix his marriage. The guys think it would have been too late for that regardless, but maybe he would have gotten her to change her mind if he would have said he was done. I'd like to think I'd have understood. We've been at this a long time. Why?"

Leaning away, I look into his face. I love his scruff and his tired eyes. "Gina was talking to me about Michael. I told her the truth and she asked me if I thought he'd want me to give up my career, if he wouldn't want me to find someone to spend my life with. Then I started thinking about Ghost Town and what Derrick would have wanted for your band. Do you think he'd want you to keep going?"

"If he wanted to leave, he probably wouldn't have cared what we did. He didn't need any more money. He wanted the time we took away from him, the time we took away from Clarissa. You can't buy time. Once it's gone, that's it. Was he looking forward to having children? He didn't have any, like me. Was he looking forward to family vacations and helping his kids with their homework? We had different kinds of experiences. Award shows and world tours. We didn't think we were giving up anything for the life we were living, but once that time is gone, you can realize your mistake. Brock and Eddie said their children are strangers to them now. There's no way to start over. You can only keep moving forward because you can't wind a clock backward."

"If Derrick were still alive, would you keep the band going without him?"

Sheppard runs his hand over the back of my head. "It wouldn't be up to me. When someone wants out, it affects all of us."

"It sounds like it's up to you now."

"Isn't there a way to keep both?"

I look over the ocean. "I don't think so. I thought I had it all. A career, a fiancé who loved me. We were talking about having a baby after we got married. When you try to have too much, something always loses. Your kids don't have enough of your time, you're not a hundred percent at your job. You don't have time for friends and you drift apart. I don't think someone can truly have it all. I tried, and I failed."

I think he's going to argue, but he says, "I said that to myself last night. If I had been more present in our marriage, maybe Melody wouldn't have wanted a divorce. If I had been a better friend, maybe Derrick would have been comfortable talking to me. I gave all I had to the band, and there was nothing left. People suffered."

"Then you understand where I'm coming from."

"Sure, but you said we can't be responsible for what people do, and that's true. Melody never told me she was unhappy. Maybe I was too busy to see it, but she should have told me, too. If Derrick jumped, that was his choice. There were a million different things he could have done. Maybe I wasn't at the arena anymore, but Brock and Eddie were. So was Dalt. He could have called Clarissa. She didn't hate him . . . the opposite, in fact. She loved him and wanted more, but he wasn't around to give it. He could have talked to a stagehand. He could have called me and asked me to go back to the arena. He could have called a crisis hotline. You can't tell me that Michael didn't have options. You blame yourself because you were on a business trip. You were working, building a career he knew you had when he asked you to marry him. He didn't do what he did because you weren't home. He did what he did because he listened to whatever siren was singing to him. She drew him in, Liv, and she didn't let go."

I rest my head against his shoulder, and he cuddles me closer. "Did you find out anything today?"

He sighs. "No. I talked to the stage producer, but he was busy breaking things down. A stagehand I talked to said the same thing. He saw Melody roaming the back hallways, but I don't know where she was when I was trying to find her. He confirmed my, our, suspicions that Dalt was seeing someone. He said Dalt had lipstick on his neck. I want to know who he was with and how long he's been seeing her—if he still is. He couldn't remember when he saw Melody and said he saw Dalt after Derrick fell, so he wasn't that helpful with the timeline I'm trying to piece together. The fact is, there are so many people around after a concert trying to do their jobs to get the hell out of there, that even if the stagehand who was too busy to talk to me today calls me back, he's not going to have any new information."

"I'm sorry." I want to comfort him but I also know the benefits of being able to handle things on your own. I can listen, but ultimately he's going to need to decide for himself what he'll do with the band.

"It's nothing I didn't expect, I was just hoping for more."

"You still have people to talk to, don't you?"

"Yeah. The stagehand who hasn't called me back, and I also need to talk to the detective on the Chicago PD. Maybe he found out where everyone was and can fill in my timeline for me. I can talk to Clarissa. She might be able to tell me where Derrick's mind was at, but in the scheme of things, I don't know how helpful it will be. After that, I'm done. I'm going to have to admit that either Derrick jumped, fell, or someone pushed him and I'll have to live with not ever knowing which one. He was drunk. The autopsy results prove it. That's the best I can do."

I sit up. "You sound like you feel better about it."

He holds my face in his hands. "Last night scared the fuck out of me. When you said you were leaving and I told you to go, I've never felt like that before. Not when Melody asked me for a divorce. Not when I heard that Derrick fell. You shut the door and I thought I would never see you again. This morning when I woke up and you were still here, I promised myself I would do whatever I needed to do to never give you another reason to leave. I know you don't like hearing that. I understand I need to put this away for me, but you are part of that reason. I *will* get past this, Olivia, just like eventually you'll put Michael's death to rest and start living your life again without him."

"Sheppard . . ." I *don't* like hearing he's doing this for me, but helping him put Derrick's death into perspective so he can move on is my *job*. When he says he's doing it for me, he's doing it because I'm here and doing my job. When this is over and he can function without me, it means I've done my job, and I can't forget that. How he feels about me or how I feel about him shouldn't be taken into consideration. In the end, all that matters is that whatever he chooses to do with Ghost Town, he's choosing with a clear mind and no regrets. "As long as you know I'm only helping you, and that nothing you're doing is actually *for me*. You're doing all this for yourself, first and foremost."

He presses his lips into a firm line and his eyes narrow. "You know I have feelings for you, Liv."

I stare down at my lap. "We can't let what we're doing get tangled up with why I'm here."

"It's too late for that. It was too late for that the second you crawled into my bed and let me cry all over you. Unless you do that for all your clients." With a finger under my chin, he asks me to look at him.

"No, I didn't do that for any of my clients. You're the first."

"And the last," he says, twisting his fingers in my hair—another gesture I'm becoming well acquainted with. "I want to kiss you."

"You don't have to keep asking. I understand why you did what you did. I even understand why you told me to leave. You were testing me because up until that point, you felt like the most important people in your life were leaving you and you wanted to add me to the list to prove to yourself that you deserved it. I will never abandon you when you need me."

He seals his trembling lips over mine, and I grip his wrists as he devours me. His tongue licks at my mouth and I open for him. Desire pools in my belly, and my heart races. If I told Sheppard I wasn't ready to make love he would back off, but how long can we circle each other? How long can I hold him at arms' length claiming . . . what? That I'm still in love with Michael? Can you be in love with a ghost? Can you be in love with the remnants someone leaves behind? There's nothing there but what could have been, and that won't keep me warm at night. I can't share my future with broken promises. I won't be sharing my future with Sheppard, either, but I can let him help me put some of the past behind me. I can open myself up to a relationship with him and start blogging with his support, and when it's time to go back to Minnesota, my loss will be different than what I was dealing with when I came here.

"Will you make love to me?" I whisper against his lips.

"Are you sure? I don't want to pressure you into anything. I'll wait for as long as you need me to wait."

I rise onto my knees and tug my blazer off. The cool breeze slips over my skin and I shiver. "I'm scared, Sheppard, but you won't hurt me."

"No, baby, I won't hurt you. But not here," he says, standing from the lounger.

Scout jumps off hers and races onto the sand.

I stand awkwardly next to Sheppard while Scout does her business. I should go after her, clean up if I need to, but asking Sheppard for a moment to pick up dog poop would break the mood. Scout doesn't need more than a minute, and she's trotting up the stairs to the patio ready to eat and go back to sleep, off the job now that Sheppard's calmed down and I'm back from Gina's. She's used to tension, but she knows the sexual kind isn't her concern.

Sheppard opens the sliding glass door, and he holds my hand and leads me up the stairs. Scout's crunching follows us as she digs into her dinner.

I thought Sheppard would walk me into his bedroom, but instead he tugs me into mine.

While I stand nervously in the middle of the room, he pulls the drawer of the nightstand open and sets a box of condoms near the lamp. "I bought these when I was out earlier today. I didn't know if you would ever feel comfortable enough for us to do this, but I wanted to be ready in case you were. I don't have anything, and while I would like kids, I don't want them to be an accident. Are you on birth control, Liv?"

Heat travels up my neck and stains my cheeks. As a life coach always encouraging people to make proper choices, I was ready to make love with Sheppard without using anything. I hadn't thought of birth control at all, certainly not condoms. I went on the Pill the day I met Michael, knowing with our chemistry we would tumble into bed quickly, and we did. I stopped taking it the day after his death, not needing it, knowing I wouldn't need it for years, maybe never again. "You're ahead of me," I admit. "I'm not on anything. I haven't needed to be. Why did you put them in my nightstand?"

"So if you found them, you would know I'm thinking about it but wanting to keep you safe, too. It's okay. Going without would be a dream for me, but we're not there yet, okay?"

I blow out a breath. "Yeah."

"You're nervous. Sit on the bed with me. If you change your mind, you can always say so."

I climb onto the mattress and sit with my legs folded under me. I'm not in that position for long. As soon as Sheppard sits, he drags me into his lap, lacing his fingers through my hair and covering my mouth with his.

The house is quiet. Scout found somewhere to sleep, giving us privacy, and there isn't a sound besides Sheppard's soft licks as he kisses me. I didn't open the blinds to my room this morning, and we're sitting in semi-darkness. I will myself to relax enough to enjoy Sheppard's kisses. I play with the hair at the nape of his neck, and he moans. If I focus on how lonely he's been this past year, maybe it will be easier to give myself to him instead of thinking about my own inexperience.

He tears his mouth away, his lips rubbing over mine. "Does it bother you I'm older than you are?" he asks, sliding a strap down my shoulder.

"What?" I ask, the question unexpected. I lift my arm out and he runs his fingers along the top of my breast. I'm wearing a strapless bra and he'll need to unhook it when he takes my dress off.

"I'm older than you. By fifteen years or so."

"Oh. Ah, no. I've always been attracted to older men. Do you mind I'm younger than you?"

He slides my other strap over my shoulder, and I pull my arm out of the loop. "You don't act younger than me. I think that's why I let you stay. When I pushed you against the sink the first day we met, if you would have blown up or started yelling at me, you would have been out on your ass. I couldn't handle behavior like that. Your maturity impressed me."

"That's not maturity. It's loss and sadness."

"Maybe, but there's a peace about you that only comes with wisdom. That's what I need." He unzips my dress and moves the bodice away from my body. "You're so beautiful, Liv," he says, brushing his fingertips over my collarbone and down my cleavage.

"Thanks."

He pulls his t-shirt over his head. "You sound like you don't believe me."

"I do, but it's been a long time since I've heard it."

"Then I'll be sure to remind you. Touch me now," he murmurs against my lips.

Lightly, I trace my fingers over his skin the way I did the other morning in the kitchen. He's not skinny, and his chest is solid under my touch. His muscles are firm, his abs taut. He might not have been working out for the past year, but his body has suffered few consequences.

He unhooks my bra and tosses it onto the floor. I whimper as he fills his palms with my breasts. He's tender and gentle, teasing my nipples with the pads of his thumbs. "That's it," he murmurs, "lift up for me."

I position myself on my knees between his legs, and he nibbles from my jaw down my neck and sucks a nipple into his mouth, his scruff deliciously scraping my skin.

My belly trembles, and I'm uncomfortably wet and swollen. It's been such a long time for me, and before Michael, I'd been with only one other guy—a man I met at the university who was in most of my psychology classes. I don't know what to do.

Sheppard skims his fingers over my skin and finds the apex of my thighs. "Can I touch you?" he asks.

"Sheppard," I say, my voice coming out in a quavering squeak.

He meets my eyes through the hazy light. "Ah, Liv. You're done with foreplay, huh? If you're too scared, we don't have to go any further."

"I want to, but . . ."

"You miss Michael," he says. "Take your dress off."

It's not that I miss Michael, exactly. I think he's been gone long enough I don't miss him the way Sheppard implied I do. I miss being intimate with someone, miss sharing kisses in the dark and connecting physically and emotionally with another person. Another person who understands you and who loves you because you're that person.

I try to be elegant but I almost fall off the bed, and he steadies me with a tight hand to my upper arm. While he watches, I shimmy out of my dress the rest of the way, his eyes smoldering with want, need, and jealousy. I tug off my black lace panties and stand in the middle of the bedroom. His eyes rake me from head to foot. If Sheppard would have met me two years ago, he would have been appalled at how skinny I was. Some people eat their grief away. I starved mine, and I became underweight and malnourished to the point I looked anorexic.

Agatha threatened me with an intervention if I didn't start taking care of myself, and over the past twenty-four months I've put on most of the weight I lost. My hips are curvier now, my belly flat. My breasts I inherited from my dad's mother, always bigger than they needed to be for my frame and height. "Am I okay?" I ask, the weight of his stare pinning me in place.

He clears his throat. "You couldn't be more beautiful, and that's the absolute truth."

I try to smile, but while I was only thinking about Michael, Sheppard said his name aloud, and like a psychic summoning a ghost from the dead, his floats around us, an unwelcome observer.

I scramble onto the bed, all sophistication lost, and I watch him as he watched me.

He undoes the button of his jeans and unzips his zipper, the rasp leaving a trail of goosebumps down my spine. When they're nothing but a heap of denim on the floor, he takes off his boxer briefs, and studying my face, he frees his cock from the material. He's huge, but I wouldn't expect a man who has Sheppard's confidence, charisma, and personality to be anything less than what he is.

My mouth dries. I'm not naïve and think that he's going to hurt me or that he won't be able to fit because of course he will, my body's made for this, but he's going to need a lot of patience to work with me and I think he lost a lot of that when he said Michael's name. All of a sudden he's in competition, and now he feels he needs to prove himself. I never asked that of him, and I wasn't thinking it, but now it's between us.

"I won't hurt you," he says, roughly grabbing the box of condoms off the nightstand and tearing the box open with more force than necessary.

"I know you won't." I draw in a shaky breath. "I don't want to disappoint you. I might be mature in some ways, but I'm not in others. You were married to a supermodel who could—"

"Liv, I've wanted *you* since the moment I saw you. Who I was married to doesn't matter one fuck right now. You miss your fiancé, I get that. If he were still alive, you'd be with him and not me. That's how things work. If I wouldn't have been a fuckup of a husband, maybe Melody wouldn't have sent me packing. But those things did happen, and somehow, God, if you believe in Him, or Karma, Fate, something pushed us together. I have never been so grateful than I was this morning and you were there in bed with me after the things I said and the things I did." He rips a packet open and with a little adjustment, rolls the condom over his cock. "Now, let me show you how much I care about you because all the songs that say we need more than words are true. I need to feel you wrapped around me in every way that means, and more than anything, I want to wrap myself around you."

Tears fill my eyes. "You're not a fuckup."

He sits on the bed, his back against the headboard. "Yeah, I am. Come here. Just like this. I want you to look at me while I fill you up."

I straddle his thighs and wrap my arms around his neck.

"I need to touch you now, and make sure you're wet enough. I didn't buy any lube."

"Okay. I haven't done this in a long time and I got nervous and—"

He doesn't let me ramble anymore. Fisting my hair, he kisses me, our teeth gnashing together with the force. With his other hand, he finds my slit and slowly, pushes one finger inside me. I gasp against his mouth and he moans, his cock hardening even more in anticipation.

"Holy fuck," he mumbles against my lips.

Slowly, he slides his finger in and out, and it feels so, so good. I forgot how it feels to have someone touch the deepest part of me. "More," I whisper.

"Like this?" he asks, adding another finger.

I move my hips, wiggling against the pressure. "Yeah."

"Look at me, Olivia," Sheppard orders.

My eyes flutter open.

"Things won't be the same between us, and I'm not going to

apologize for what happens next. I won't. I want it, and you do too, or you wouldn't let me do this. But you have to understand, sex changes things for me. I told you before, I don't fuck for fun. I won't fuck around with your body or your heart. Do you hear me?"

"Yes."

"Then lower yourself onto me. You're ready, baby."

He slides his fingers from me but holds me open, still gripping my hair, giving me no choice but to meet his eyes as I gingerly hold his cock, position the tip, and sink onto him. My skin tugs against the condom and I shift, rising up a little and then lowering back down. His eyes don't release me, demanding every ounce of my attention until he's deep inside me and his arms are wrapped tightly around my back.

It's stupid to cry, but the emotion carries me away and I press my face against the side of his neck, trying to swallow against the tears.

"Shh," he says, his lips near my ear. His rigid hold turns into a caress, and he smooths his hands up and down my back. "Shh. Everything will be okay."

Wiping my eyes, I sit up. The new position pushes him farther into me, and I need how it feels. I've felt hollow for so long, to have this man want me, my body, anyway, I need that. I need to feel loved again, even if it's make believe on my part, even if it will end when the summer's over. This will change things, but I don't believe Sheppard meant for his whole life. We'll be a couple until my job is done, and then we won't be one anymore.

Tears drip down my cheeks. I love him, and I fell in love with another man who won't need me for the rest of his life.

Sheppard wipes them away. "Liv, don't cry," he whispers. His hand moves between our bodies, and his finger finds my clit. He rubs, and my pussy clenches around him. "That's it. I want to feel you come on my cock." He pinches one of my nipples as he circles my clit with his finger, and I move, the tip of his cock hitting that one spot inside me. Rolling my hips, I sink as deeply onto him as I can, and his finger catches the tempo. "Come on, baby," he murmurs.

The orgasm builds, and I grind onto him. I press my mouth against his, needing every part of me touching every part of him. I'm sobbing when I come, the pressure building under my clit until I explode. His cock is huge, and my climax hurts, adding to the pleasure as sparks sizzle across my skin. My nipple tingles where he pinched, but I don't have a second to think about that or anything else. He changes our position with a strong hand to my back, lowering me onto the mattress without slipping out of me. With his arms braced on either side of my head, he starts to move. The delicate friction arouses me all over again, and my hips match his tender rhythm.

Growling, he holds me still with a hand to my ass, his fingers digging into my skin. Sinking into me as deeply as he possibly can, he comes, his eyes never leaving my face. His cock pulses inside me, and like the stupid female I am, I wish he wasn't wearing a condom. I want him to mark me, give me something I can remember him by when all this is over.

He lowers himself onto me and slides his hands under my head. "Don't regret this, Liv, please," he whispers, the tortured man I know floating to the surface of the calm he managed to find this afternoon.

I nudge his cheek with my nose. "I would never."

"Don't say something that could be true later."

Maybe one day I could regret this, when I'm home alone on a winter's night, the wind howling, the snow pelting against the windows. I could think back to these days, relive the feel of his arms around me, and how just for a moment after Michael's death, I felt loved again, like I mattered to someone. That a famous rockstar saw something in me that he wanted to keep, no matter how short of a time.

I rest my palm against his cheek and bring my knees up, tilting my hips. He's still hard, and he adjusts, filling my body as full as my heart. "I will never regret that I chose you after Michael's death. No matter what happens, Sheppard, you taught me I can love again, and I will always remember that."

A tortured look haunts his eyes. "Liv, I—"

"No, I'm sorry. I shouldn't have—" I said the wrong thing, took the "love" in making love too far.

He stops me with a finger to my lips. "Yeah, you should have, and I am so very, very happy you did."

We make love again, but he doesn't say the words back to me. Soft and sweet, bruising my lips with his passionate kisses, I'm sore everywhere when he finally tucks me against his chest, his hand splayed over my belly. I'm hungry and Scout will need to go out again by now, but I don't want to move.

He props himself onto an elbow, and his nose skims the shell of my ear as he curls his body around mine. He wants to say something. I always know when someone wants to say something but they're too afraid to say it. I don't want him to say whatever he's scared of saying. If he says it when he's scared of it, it won't last.

"I should let Scout outside," I say, my lips pressed against the back of his hand.

"Okay," he says, but he doesn't loosen his hold.

"That means I have to get up."

"Hmmm," he hums in agreement, his breath tickling my cheek.

"I'll come back." I try to wiggle away from him. I should get dressed. Wearing a robe anywhere than my room would be inappropriate. I doubt Sheppard wants anyone to know what our relationship has turned into, and I don't need to advertise it by walking around his house half naked.

He turns me over, and I'm tamping down a smile, already prepared to deflect a joke, but he's as serious as I have ever seen him. "You wouldn't have to come back if you don't leave."

I can't read into his words. I know the kind of life he'll lead when Ghost Town records another album and they go on tour to promote it. He won't have time for me, and with my career up and going again, it would be stupid to invite another man into my life. Sheppard can absolve me of all my sins, or try to as much as he likes, but the bottom line is, I wasn't there for Michael when he needed me. I'm better off alone when I go back to work. I pretend not to understand what he means. "It's only downstairs."

He slides his hand from my stomach. "Sure it is."

I don't want to put on the dress I wore to Gina's, and I find the shorts and tank top set I sometimes wear to bed in a pile on the floor. I scramble to dress as quickly as I can, and Sheppard watches me, fury shimmering in his eyes. I don't know what he wants from me. Well, maybe I do, but he'll only want it until he finds something he needs more, and like Gina pointed out, that's not a position women like to find themselves in.

Needing a minute alone, I lock myself in the bathroom. There's a bruise on my thigh. I don't know how Sheppard gave that one to me, but the bruise on my wrist I remember well, when he pinned my hands above my head and went at me with such a hunger I'm surprised I could sate it. Maybe I didn't.

That's my problem. I can't. He'll always hunger for more than what I can be.

When I finally come out of the bathroom, the bed is empty, and downstairs, I find Sheppard on the beach with Scout. He's standing in the water, the surface lapping at his thighs. Scout lays on the sand, ever watchful.

I sit on the patio and watch him for a long time, the siren's grip tight around my ankle.

"What will you blog about, when you put your website back up?"

Sheppard said he didn't want me to cook after wearing me out all afternoon, and we ordered pizza for a late dinner. I was surprised we liked the same toppings—pepperoni, mushrooms, and extra cheese—but Sheppard said, "I'm not," like he expected us to have several of the same things in common, if we only gave ourselves time to figure out what they are. Maybe, but we only have two and a half months, not a lifetime, and like a lot of what he says, I don't read into his words.

We're sitting on the couch in his hidden living room, and I'm leaning against an armrest with my feet in his lap, the leftover pizza sitting in the cardboard box on the coffee table. He's been playing with my toes, "This little piggy," though I don't know where he heard the children's rhyme. My father used to play that with my sister and me, and his loss weighs heavy on my heart.

"I don't know. I'll have to explain why I suddenly dropped off social media and stopped blogging. I'll have to twist it into some kind of a lesson or I'll look like a self-help expert who couldn't help herself. That's what I am, but it's not good for business."

"Did you?" he asks, his hand encircling my ankle. He doesn't know he's doing it, mimicking what the siren does to both of us.

"Did I what?"

"Learn something from Michael's death?"

"Did you learn anything from Derrick's?" I ask instead, curious of his answer since he asked me.

He slants me a look, but I lift a shoulder. We'd talk about something like this whether I was here for a job or not. Couples share this type of thing. Usually.

"I could say the normal stuff, don't take people for granted, don't drink and climb." His mouth quirks. "But I think out of anything I could say, it's learning to take responsibility for yourself. I said Michael and Derrick had choices, that they didn't have to do what they did. We don't know if Derrick jumped, but he never should have been up there as drunk as he was. I let myself fall down a rabbit hole of depression, and yeah, they had choices, but I had choices too. I should have found someone to talk to long before Dalt stepped in. I pushed a lot of my responsibilities onto other people. Melody wanted a divorce, but I didn't ask her why. I just let her have her way. I figured by then it didn't matter, but of course it does. She was unhappy, and I should know the reasons. We were married for ten years, but I just said fuck it and let her walk. Dalt's been dealing with the band alone. He's our manager, but the guys have always looked to me, and after Derrick passed away, I let them down. I learned what I do affects people, and all hiding does is create new problems."

I smile, hating hearing Melody's name on his lips. She looked so hard when I met her in Dalton's office, her face frozen in an expression that was half smile and half sneer. I have a difficult time picturing them together. Sheppard's so warm and passionate. Ten years is a long time; they must have found a happy medium between his fire and her ice.

"But I also know you can't force someone to get the help they need. If they aren't ready, they won't take it no matter how much you push. I was at that point where I knew something needed to change, but I didn't know what or how to go about it. I also know that the right person has to be the one to offer that help. Dalt cares about me, the other guys, and the band, but I don't think I would have turned around as fast as I would have with anyone but you. You make me want to be a better person, Liv, and no one else would have made me feel that way. What about you? You grieved for a lot longer than I did . . . am. I guess a person never really stops grieving a loved one who's no longer here. What did you learn from Michael's death?"

That I wasn't enough.

That I gave too much to my career.

That he didn't love me when he said he did.

That he didn't value the future we were piecing together.

That he didn't want a family with me.

Some of those are lies, and I say, "I think you're right. It wasn't what Michael's death taught me, but what you taught me that I should take away from it. He had choices, some that concerned me, some that didn't. Maybe, like you, he didn't know how to ask. I didn't know how, and I didn't want to, either. Not until I saw your picture and thought you didn't have to live that way. It didn't click *I* didn't have to live that way until I told you I wasn't engaged and I had to stop pretending I was to keep him with me." I walk on my knees toward him. "You're wrong, what you said to me upstairs. I don't miss him. Not the way you meant. I miss what we could have had, but that's not the same, is it?"

He brushes a piece of hair behind my ear. "Yeah, it is. What he could give you and what another man will aren't going to be the same. You had a little house on a quiet street in a nice neighborhood, trees in your yard, maybe a garden you planted yourself. You had faculty dinners with other professors at the college and walks in the snow with Scout. You had road trips during the summer and gave away candy when trick-ortreaters rang your doorbell. You had family holidays, and hot chocolate after watching the Christmas tree lit up in your small town's square."

I blink. "How did you know all that?"

"Because that's the life I pictured for you, and you fit in it so easily. Another man won't be able to give you those things." He kisses my forehead and sighs. "I'm going upstairs to journal for a bit. You okay?"

"Yeah. Sheppard . . ." I don't know what to say.

"It's okay. That's another thing Derrick's death taught me. People move in and out of your life. They give you what you need when you need it and when they're done, they fade away. It hurts like a son of a bitch to say goodbye, but you have to let them go because their time in your life is finished. You can't keep someone where they're not meant to be."

I nod. That's the whole basis of my career. I show up in someone's life, give them what they need, and move on. When they were strong enough they didn't need my help anymore, I signed another client, and the cycle continued. Before I retired, I stayed in touch with some, mostly through comments on my blogposts they kept reading or an email here and there asking my advice, but I was never a part of their lives like I was when they were paying me to be.

He trails his fingers down my cheek before stepping away from the couch, and Scout follows him into the living room. He leaves the wall open, maybe in invitation to follow, but I sit alone as I always have been.

Chapter Twenty

She's already thinking about leaving, and I can't stop her, not yet. Two weeks into her stay here, and I want her for the rest of my life. I should have told her when we were making love that I was falling in love with her. She gave me an opening. Maybe she didn't fling the door open, but she cracked it, and I should have barged my way through.

The problem is pacing, timing. Move too quickly, and I'll scare her off. Move too slowly, and she'll think I don't want her. I know the value of a pause, a heartbeat. How to use the silence to draw in the audience. When a song ends and there's nothing as that last note fades in the air but feeling—from us because we created it and we're immersed in the craft; from the audience because they experienced it and they don't want to let the magic go. That's what I need with Liv. I need the pause, the heartbeat, the magic, and it's only when she's holding her breath waiting for more can I give it to her. Not what she would have had with Michael, but what she can have with me.

She drifted into my life because I need her. I can't let her leave because I always will.

I stay up late journaling, wisps of lyrics bleeding from my pen as I try to piece together my feelings for Liv on paper. I never used to have a difficult time writing love songs. I could find inspiration almost anywhere, but especially from my own heart, yearning for something I never thought I would find as our celebrity grew and it became more difficult to meet women who weren't blown away by the fame.

After I met Melody, most of the songs I wrote were about her and the way she held herself apart from me. She wasn't untouchable, no, that's not the way I would describe her. Our marriage was like having sex with a condom. I could feel everything, but there was something between us, thin, barely discernible. It was there and I never was able to get through to her all the way. Liv will talk to me about anything, everything. She's an open book I eagerly devour. Melody was an open book, too, but all her pages were blank. There was always something missing, but I was too busy to do anything about it.

I free write, Liv's face, her eyes, the way she listens, the way she cried while we made love, all in the back of my mind. How I felt when I met her, how she looked kissing Scout in my driveway while waiting for her ride after I sent her away. The touch of her hand when I helped her to her feet, her smile when I asked her to stay. It's all there, a collage moving in slow motion.

The lyrics will take me a few days to parse out, turning emotions into words, something tangible, but they'll come. They always do.

What I'll do with them is another matter.

I let Scout outside, and this time I use the garage door and let her sniff around the driveway. While she pees and paws at a hedge, I text Jeff and tell him I can run in the morning. I've skipped the past couple of days, but if he's willing to be my running partner, I shouldn't waste it. Liv's reminding me it's better to have people in my life than not. Pushing people away has consequences I don't want to pay anymore.

Liv's sleeping when I bump her door open, and again, I'm overwhelmed with a sense of gratitude she's here and doesn't hate me for the things I did. Instead, she understood. Even the deeper, terrifying, reason why I tried to force her to leave that I didn't admit to myself.

She told me I don't need permission to touch her, and I don't wake her to ask if I can sleep with her. I'm wearing boxers and she's still dressed in the pajamas she wore while we ate pizza. I push my hand up her tank top and hug her to me. She rolls over and presses her face into my chest, her lips warm against my skin.

"Are you okay?" she mumbles.

"Yeah. I am now. Let me make love to you, Livvy," I beg.

She's never not given me what I need, and tonight is no exception.

"What happened to you?" Jeff asks, catching me stretching in the driveway behind the house. I was barely finding my stride before I took a break, and today's going to hurt. Jeff won't take pity on me, but I don't deserve it.

"Minor setback," I mutter, shoving sunglasses onto my face.

"Yours or hers?" he asks, bouncing on his toes.

Yep, today's going to hurt.

"Hers? What do you mean?" We start out with a slow trot, Scout running ahead of us as she normally does, happy to be outdoors and able to stretch her legs.

"Don't you go online? *Buzz Kill*'s dredged up who she is, and the picture of you holding her in the water is all over the place. Her appearance on Oprah's talk show is getting thousands of new hits on YouTube. You might want to clue her in." He pauses. "Gina told me what happened to her fiancé. That's tough."

"She didn't come back from her interview yesterday in a very good place. They talked about some heavy shit," I say, trying to sound like I'm not gasping for air.

"That's Gina," Jeff says, his footfalls steady against the pavement.

Bits of the ocean flash between the houses, and seagulls fly above us, searching for a snack. We're not the only ones enjoying the sunny day, and a woman pushing a toddler in a stroller stops and they pet Scout, the baby's hands digging into her fur. Scout stands patiently, swiping at the little girl's face with her tongue before bolting off, determined to stay ahead of us on the trail.

"You talk her down?" he asks when I don't say anything.

"Among other things."

Jeff shoots me a look, smirking. "Don't let any grass grow under your feet. She gonna stay here then?"

I stare straight ahead, but I don't see the path and fluffy white clouds in a blue sky. I see a tiny house with a postage stamp yard, and a pregnant Liv, tending a flower garden, a man who isn't me hunkered down beside her, asking if she feels okay, urging her to rest.

"I don't think so. I can't give her the life she wants."

"In LA, you mean?"

"Yeah."

"Then split your time. Buy a mansion on Lake Minnetonka and invite her family to stay with you for a couple months a year. It's not a big deal."

I scowl. "Are you an expert on Minnesota all of a sudden? How do you know so much about the place?"

"Gina dragged me up there for a documentary thing in Minneapolis one year. A producer owned an enormous house on Lake Minnetonka—hot tub, swimming pool, huge boat, the works. Some gorgeous property in that area. It's not the middle of nowhere people think it is."

"I never thought it was. We've played Minneapolis/St. Paul before."

"Yeah. You saw an airport, the arena, and a hotel, then you left. If Liv likes it there, compromise. It's not a big deal."

"So you keep saying. I don't think it's the place, necessarily. I think it's me."

"Yeah, well, there's not much you can do about that if that's the case. She doesn't like you're a famous rockstar?"

"Eventually, I think what I'll do, and what Ghost Town does, will get in the way."

Jeff shakes his head and rubs sweat away from his eyes. "I wouldn't be too sure it's *your* fame that will interfere. Olivia's famous in her own right. Not everyone lands an hour on Oprah, and now that they've got a hold of it, social media's churning her fiancé's death into something ugly. It's not a secret she's here with you, and I don't know if she had a PR person when she was coaching, but she needs to look into something. You might be more famous than she is, but it won't be long before she catches up. People are talking about her and what she's doing with you."

I stop in the middle of the trail and lift my sunglasses. "It's that bad?"

Jeff stops too, and he draws in a deep breath. "You need to take a peek out of that slice of utopia you found for yourselves and do some damage control. Maybe this wouldn't have hit her so hard if it wasn't you, but it is, and next year, when Gina's documentary drops, it will stir it all up again, whether you two are together or not."

"Thanks. I didn't know that was brewing. I'm surprised Dalt hasn't said anything."

"Are you two on speaking terms?" Jeff starts running again, catching up to Scout who stopped to sniff at a butterfly.

"Not exactly." I'm still pissed Melody was at that meeting when she was the last person who should have been there.

"Maybe he thought he should keep his nose out of your business."

"My business has always been our business, and he hired Olivia."

"If he saw the picture that's online, it's not difficult to guess what you two have been up to. Maybe he thought it best to keep his opinions to himself."

Nothing has ever stopped Dalt from sharing his opinion, and if he thought Liv and I were a bad idea, I would have heard about it. The only thing I can take away from his silence is he approves of Liv and me getting together, and while I don't care if I have his approval or not, things will be easier if we're not butting heads over it.

We jog in silence for the next two miles, which is fine by me since I was struggling to run and hold a conversation at the same time. He stops at a public access to a rocky section of the beach about three miles from our houses, flops onto the sand, and stares over the water, much like I do when I'm chewing on something and need peace to think.

Scout lies near a boulder and closes her eyes.

I wait him out, rolling a small rock between my thumb and forefinger. He didn't need the break; he wants to talk.

He doesn't look at me when he asks, "How did you know Melody wanted a divorce?"

I throw the rock toward the water, but we're so far away it

doesn't come close. "I didn't. I knew things were changing in our marriage, but that happens. I was surprised she wanted to go on tour with us, but I never saw her for the entire six months we traveled. I had suspicions she was cheating on me, a rich lover following us from city to city, but I didn't confront her. Two months after Derrick's death, she filed for divorce. I haven't given it a lot of thought because I've only been sober for the past couple of weeks thanks to Liv."

Jeff rests his arms on his knees. "I think Gina's cheating on me. She didn't come home until late last night, and she'd been drinking. She wouldn't let me touch her, and that's usually a good indication a woman's been with another man."

"Maybe she was just blowing off steam," I say uneasily. "This documentary seems different than the ones she's done in the past."

"Has Olivia said anything?"

"Not about you two. Liv said Gina asked her about Michael, and if she thought he'd want her living the way she's been because he was gone. That doesn't sound like anything Gina would relate to, does it?"

Jeff blows out a breath and says, "No, but God knows what else they talked about."

"Have you been thinking about moving on? Maybe she feels that and decided to bail first."

He frowns. "You know I can still remember the second I saw her? She was standing across the pool area at some schmuck's house in Beverly Hills. A fundraising thing. I didn't even see her face, only her back. She was wearing a black dress and her hair was pinned up. Her spine was so straight, and she held herself with such grace."

Though I've heard the story before, I let him go.

"I was in love with her before we were even introduced.

There's no one else in the world I want to be with." He rubs Scout's nose, and she whines in commiseration.

"You'll have to talk to her. When Melody kept disappearing during the tour, I should have cornered her, but I let other things get in the way. If you don't confront Gina, she'll think you don't care."

"Yeah. I was hoping maybe Olivia said something that would give me a clue."

I already broached the subject of them getting married. Gina could have decided to throw in the towel and find someone who would give her a real commitment. I don't know what caused Jeff's reluctance to put a ring on it, but he's going to lose Gina if he doesn't bend. "No, I'm sorry. I think their sessions are more about Liv than Gina."

He rubs at his face. "Let's get going. I have a conference call I need to listen in on later, and this girl needs a drink. No lakes around here."

We run back without speaking, which is just as well. I couldn't spare the breath for even one word by the time we reach our houses, and instead of saying goodbye, exhausted, I lift a hand in thanks and let Scout into the house where she promptly heads toward her water dish. It's funny I don't remember the kitchen without her bowls of water and kibble. Without Liv sitting at the breakfast bar sipping coffee with her laptop in front of her.

I crowd her from behind, and she doesn't pull away, even when I press my sweaty face against her neck to breathe in the scent of lavender.

"Did you have a good run?" she asks, tilting her head and giving me more space to kiss along the delicate curve of her shoulder.

"I don't feel like I'm dying, which is a nice surprise, but a hot shower will loosen me up. Jeff thinks Gina's cheating on him. Do you know if she is?"

"Didn't you tell me to stay out of their relationship?"

"Yeah, but I thought she might have told you something."

She pushes her laptop away, the backend of her website open and waiting for her to write. Resting her elbow on the counter, she says, "We talked about not being enough. I wasn't enough to keep Michael here, and you weren't enough to keep Melody from divorcing you. Those are lies we tell ourselves because when something bad happens, it's human nature to place blame, and it's human nature to blame ourselves. No one can be everything to someone else, but she's afraid she's not giving Jeffrey what he needs to be happy. I told you, she's waiting for him to find someone he'll love more, and if that's really what their relationship is, I don't blame her for leaving before he leaves her."

"He loves her more than anything."

She lifts her hands and spreads her fingers. "Then he needs to tell her that and be willing to show her. As Oprah likes to say, 'Love is a verb.' How do you show someone you love them? A man drops to his knees and begs her to be with him for the rest of his life because he can't live without her. If that's what she wants, and he won't do that, I don't see a compromise, do you?"

I reach out and touch her cheek. "How did Michael ask you?"

She shakes her head, and my fingers drop from her face. "How did you ask Melody?"

I grimace. "That's a discussion best left for another day."

She laughs, and I appreciate her giving us space. She could have pressed, and our conversation would have gone downhill real fast. She was already defensive of Gina's predicament. She took Gina's side, not in a "sisters stick together" type of way, but in a logical way that makes sense. You do have to show someone you love them, but it can't always be on your terms. Jeff is only willing to love Gina in his own way, and it's not enough for her. We'll talk about proposals again, but I'm glad Liv knew it wasn't the right time for us now.

Tilting her head, she offers me her lips, and lightly, I press mine to hers. "I'm going to shower, then we need to talk."

It's her turn to grimace. "Why do I think that it's about something not good."

"Because it's about something not good, and it's my fault, too." I eye her; she's still in her pajamas. "Shower with me? I'll wash your back." I made love to her this morning as the sun rose, but I will never tire of having her. I want her against the wall in the shower, her hand pressed against the glass as she comes.

"I'm not done with my coffee."

"Bring it with you."

She does, but she doesn't have time to drink it.

Olivia says she needs to shave, and reluctantly, I step out after I've had my way with her and washed off the sweat.

Steam and the scent of lavender saturate my bathroom, and I revel in the calming effect of both the fragrance and Liv's presence. I hope she's not angry with the attention she's getting online because of me.

She meets me downstairs dressed in black cotton shorts and a green tank top with a droopy neckline that I think is supposed to look like that. It's cute, showing off just a hint of her breasts, but I'd like Liv wearing anything. She's still wearing her sideways cross, and as I get to know her, the reasons become even more clear.

The hidden den has turned into our haven, and I'm waiting for her on the couch when she walks into the room with Scout. The dog curls up on the floor under the piano, and I want to take a picture and frame it.

"What did you want to talk about?" she asks.

I gesture for her to sit in my lap, and she burrows against my chest. I wrap my arms around her. I could sit like this for a million years.

"Have you been online?" I ask reluctantly.

She lifts her head and frowns. "No? What's going on?"

I wince. "Jeff said there's a lot of gossip about us. Some paparazzi took photos of us the day you told me about Michael's death. There's speculation about what you're doing here, and I hope this doesn't cause problems for you."

"Will it cause problems for you?"

"Why would it do that?"

Lifting a shoulder, she says, "People know who I am, *what* I am. They know you haven't recorded an album like you should have because of what happened to Derrick. Won't you be embarrassed people will know I'm here with you and why?"

Her question surprises me. "I've never had one thought to be ashamed. I go enough times, the paps will catch me either going to, or coming from, Royce's. If there wasn't a stigma when it comes to mental health, maybe more people would be willing to admit they need help and ask. I will *never* apologize for needing you, in any way. All my life I've been someone people looked up to. If you're brave, if you follow your dreams, look what you can achieve. If I can be that for a music student who doesn't think they have the talent to make their wishes come true, then I can be that for someone who can't crawl out of bed or sits with a gun in his hand or a bottle of pills and a gallon of booze. I can be that hope, because when the siren sang her song, you gave that to me, and there's no shame in it."

Tears trickle down her cheeks. "That was beautiful, Sheppard."

"I never thought to hide what you are to me, but I can understand if you don't want anyone to know we're in a relationship. You broke a code of ethics or something sleeping with me, didn't you?"

She sniffles. "I wasn't exactly thinking about moral conduct when I asked you to take me to bed."

"Will it fuck things up for you?" I ask, rubbing tears off her cheeks.

"More or less than a life coach who couldn't see her fiancé was so depressed he committed suicide?"

"Liv, it wasn't your fault."

"I know," she says, but her tone belies her words. "It won't cause any problems. People get attached during trauma. How many movies are there where they fall in love during a life-altering event? The romantics will eat it up, and the cynics will call me a gold-digger. It will blow over."

Gripping her chin in my hand and forcing her to meet my eyes, I say, "You think that's all this is? A traumatic event?"

She blinks, her eyes still watery. "No."

"Good, because it's not, and unless it affects you starting your coaching again, it's no one's fucking business what we're doing." I pause. "You weren't surprised."

"No. While you were running with Jeffrey, Agatha called me. She saw the picture. She knew there was something going on because I told her about you catching me when I fell jumping from that rock. All that picture did was confirm it."

"Really?" I'd felt it, holding her against me, her heart pounding against mine, but from what I thought were completely different reasons.

"Yeah. I tried to fend it off. It was difficult to confront your depression after what Michael did. It scared me, but the longer I stayed, the harder it was for me to think about leaving."

"I'm going to get a handle on it, Liv. I promise. I've lived with it all my life, and I can't say things will always be easy, but I will never do what Michael did. The siren sings, but with you here, I'm learning there's beauty in her song."

"Some of the most beautiful things in the world are deadly," she whispers.

"I know, but I have a lot to live for."

She nods, but I lost her, her gaze sliding away from my face. She wanted to be what Michael lived for, and she wasn't.

"Did Agatha say anything else?"

"That it would be a good idea to get in touch with Tammy, the woman who did PR for my book. I agree, but the best thing I can do right now is put my website back up and write a blogpost explaining what I'm doing and why I dropped off social media. Then a press release, maybe, pointing reporters in that direction. The NDA I signed for Dalton will keep me from having to answer any questions. It will be okay."

"I'm sorry."

She rests her head on my shoulder. "Don't be. The day you kissed me . . . I'd been lonely for such a long time and when you held me, I needed that. It doesn't matter people were taking our picture. It doesn't matter we're on all the gossip sites. When you put your arms around me and let me cry . . . you say I saved you, but you saved me, too."

I want to say I love her, but it's too soon, and all I do is rub her back as I hold her, Scout's gentle snores the only sound in the room.

"Do you want to see something?" I ask.

The minutes drifted by and soon we'll have to move and find something for lunch. I don't know if Liv ate breakfast, but I didn't. I've never been able to work out with food in my stomach, and it growls now, an hour past noon.

She presses her warm lips against my neck and laughs. "I've already seen it three times today."

"You're funny." She's not wrong, and if I have it my way, she'll see it again before we go to sleep. "You need to write a blogpost and I need to figure out what I'm going to do with Ghost Town. Come here." I nudge her off my lap and lead her toward the rear of the den. I use a keypad to open a locked door, and it slides open to reveal a small room that stores all my guitars. They hang on the walls—some I've used during concerts and the ones I've collected over the years that I would never touch, like the Gibson J-200 Elvis played when he filmed *G.I. Blues* in 1960 that I managed to snag at auction, or the Maton acoustic guitar Richard Marx signed and sent me to congratulate me when our first album ran away with five hit singles. Somehow he'd gotten a hold of my senior year talent show performance, and the card read, "Dream big and never settle. You got what it takes." I've carried those words with me for years. Some of these mean the world to me, like the one Dalt, Brock, Eddie, and Derrick bought me for my fortieth birthday.

"These are gorgeous," Liv says, looking around.

"Thanks. There's a lot of money in this room," I try to joke. The keypad and the locked door might have been too over the top for her.

She squeezes my hand. "There are a lot of feelings in this room."

I sigh. Trust Liv to understand. "My mom bought me this one when I was ten. It's the first guitar I ever owned. When she realized I had notes for blood and sheet music for skin, she did whatever she could to push me in the right direction. Piano lessons, voice lessons . . . after I hit puberty," I add with a laugh. "She paid an older guy in our neighborhood to teach me to play, but it was only a few months later I was teaching him new things. I'll always be thankful Mom saw my talent. I wouldn't be where I am today if she hadn't."

She found it at a thrift store, a Gibson 1942 Banner LG-2 Acoustic. The store manager didn't know what he had, and he sold it to her for ten bucks.

"Is she still alive?" Liv asks, her fingers trailing over the strings of a prop '62 Fender Stratocaster guitar that was used in the film *Eddie and the Cruisers.*

"Yeah. She lives in a retirement community in northern California near my brother."

"Are you close?"

I test the Gibson in my hands. I haven't touched a guitar since Derrick fell, and the weight is foreign and not altogether pleasant. Like this conversation is turning out to be. "No. We lost touch years ago when my life was going six hundred miles an hour and I could barely breathe. They were there when I married Melody, but our wedding was full of, I don't know. Famous people. Other models and musicians. MTV filmed the ceremony. *Rolling Stone* covered it, too, and the reporter tried to talk to her. She gave birth to the great Sheppard Carpenter, after all. She and my brother were uncomfortable, and they left before the reception ended. I tried to stop them. They knew the guys, but they didn't feel like they fit in. They sat in a corner and kept to themselves. It's difficult to explain."

"I've been awestruck. I met Oprah," Liv says wryly. "I think I get it."

"Did your family have problems with your fame?"

"I wouldn't exactly call it fame, but they didn't go to Chicago to watch my interview. They couldn't get away, and I understood. I had a huge tour the year my book came out, and my sister went to the signing at a Barnes and Noble in Minneapolis. She took a picture and said she couldn't believe a hundred people were waiting in line for my signature. She was proud of me. I'm sure your mom is, too."

I doubt it. I've won awards for my songwriting, the band has won awards, contributed to soundtracks of blockbuster movies, but I don't know what she thinks when she sees a picture of me in a magazine or on a gossip site. I don't know what she thinks about my divorce or if she saw pictures of me and Liv and wants to know who she is and what she is to me. Melody didn't care to get to know her, an older woman who lives in Crescent City, California, population 6,673, and I don't think Mom wanted to get to know her. Melody was nothing more than a nameless face she'd see on issues of *Vogue* and *Vanity Fair* while she waited in line at the grocery store.

"You should call her," Liv says when I don't say anything. "Go see her. What about your brother? What's his name?"

I position my fingertips against the strings, the chords wanting out into the air. "Princeton. He prefers Tony. He's a family practice doctor in the town where our mom lives."

She bumps my arm. "I'd like to hear how she named you two."

"Mom blamed the drugs, but Princeton is her maiden name, and I'm named after my dad's father. It's not so mysterious."

"Is your dad still alive, too?"

"Yeah, but he and Mom got a divorce years ago. Tony and I took up where he left off after he went out for smokes and didn't come back, and I haven't thought about him in a long time."

"Call her. When my dad passed away, my sister and I had a lot of regrets. It was sudden, and there was no time to apologize or make amends. That lives with you. It's a gift you have time to right a wrong, and it will stay with you if she passes away and you didn't do what you could to fix your relationship. She encouraged you to be who you are. Don't ruin it for her."

"If I go see them, would you come with me?" I know what I'm asking. What it sounds like. Meeting family.

"Sure. You don't think my fame will make her nervous?" she asks, teasing.

"Well," I drawl. "You did meet Oprah."

She laughs and tilts her head toward my guitar. "What were you going to do with that?"

"Serenade you while you blog."

She presses her forehead against my chest and says, "That might be the only way I can."

Holding my guitar in one hand and anchoring Liv against me with the other, what I want and what I need tangle inside me. What will I do if I have to give up one to keep the other?

She sits on one end of the couch, her feet propped up on the coffee table, her laptop tilting on her knees as she types while I struggle to keep my feelings in check on the other end, my guitar in my lap, my hands frozen in place. Playing is as natural as breathing, and I know what to do. I could play hundreds of songs off the top of my head, but I can't force my fingers to move. Liv grows paler and paler as the keys click, her fingers shaking. I can't watch it anymore, and relieved I have an excuse to put my own nightmare away, I set my guitar onto the floor and cover her hands with mine. It's a welcome distraction. Before Derrick's death, I could jam for hours, writing songs, rehashing covers I learned when we were just starting out, but holding my guitar and wanting to play feels like I'm betraying him and all he could have done if he were still alive. He'd been a gifted musician, and all that talent is gone.

"Take a break, babe. Let's find some lunch." My hunger pangs faded with the heavy talk, nausea a constant companion when subjects like Derrick and my family pop into conversation. Speaking with Liv is different. We talk about those things not only because that's why she's here, but because I want to share my life with her. Wanting it didn't stop the churning. In the silence, my hunger returned, my stomach reminding me I haven't eaten for the better part of the day.

"'Babe?'" she asks, an eyebrow lifted.

I close her laptop and set it on the coffee table. Hauling her into my lap, I cover her lips with mine. One day we'll become a permanent fixture on this couch, and all this talk about our futures will be pointless. "What do you like? Sweetheart? Baby? Cupcake? Sweetie?"

She laughs under my mouth, just like I wanted her to. I encouraged her to resume her career, but it will be painful to watch.

"I've never had a nickname like that. People call you Shep. Do you like it?"

"It's fine. Natural, I suppose, like people shortening your name to Liv." I want to ask what Michael called her in the early mornings when he'd wake her to make love or if he was looking for ketchup in the fridge and couldn't find it, but I quickly learned if I ask her a question like that, she turns it onto me and with her hands pulling my t-shirt out of my jeans, my ex-wife is the last person I want to talk about.

She nibbles down my neck and says, "My dad used to call my mom Val."

"Because her name is Valerie?" I ask, my cock stiffening. I'll eat lunch, but not in the kitchen.

"No, because they met on Valentine's Day at a church

luncheon, and he said the moment he saw her he fell in love and knew one day she would be his wife. He said he gave her the nickname because he could never forget the first time he looked into her eyes on that day devoted to lovers."

"That's really sweet." I reverse our positions, and when she's lying on her back, I unbutton her shorts.

"They loved each other very much," she says, lifting her ass and allowing me to tug them off her legs.

For the next little while, I try to show Liv how much I love her too.

It's two in the afternoon by the time we fix lunch, a tuna and macaroni salad Liv said her mom used to make when she and her sister were kids. I've never heard of it, but I like tuna and go along, leaning against the counter sipping on sparkling water as noodles boil and she chops an onion, pickles, and celery.

"What do you think of inviting people over tomorrow night?" I ask, trying to smooth out the tremor in my voice. The first time Liv suggested we invited Jeff and Gina to the house for dinner, I panicked. After twelve months alone in a drunken stupor, the thought of having people other than Liv in my living space scared the hell out of me. "We'll cater in some food. I don't want you to cook for a large group."

She looks at me, her cheeks pink from the steam, surprised. "Are you ready for that?"

"Nothing big. The guys. Dalt. I owe him a thank you and an apology. Jeff and Gina. We'll light a bonfire on the beach and people will drift over from the other houses. I'll tell the guys to bring their guitars. Maybe if I'm not playing by myself, it will help."

"As long as you're ready. There's no rush."

Gently, I pull the knife from her grasp and lift her onto the counter. Holding her hand, I lick pickle juice off her fingers. "I know, but the guys have been patient, and you need to hit publish on that blog."

"I didn't finish it."

"Yeah, and if I'm in a better place with my music, I can be in a better place to help you. Okay?"

She parts her lips, and I know exactly what she's going to say. That she doesn't need my help. That she shouldn't need my help. That she's fine on her own. All the bullshit I used to tell myself before she came into my life and proved me wrong.

"I can help you. Let me read over your shoulder and point out all your typos."

"I can't pass up an offer like that," she whispers, holding my face between her hands.

"The offer stands. Always." I kiss her, and her lips are soft and tinged with salt. "After lunch, we should go online and look at what people are saying. They'll ask at the party, and Dalt will want to know what's going on. When you finish your blogpost, you can address some of the rumors that are going around. Then after all the depressing bullshit, we can put on a movie and fall asleep on the couch."

"Will you call your mom in the morning?" she asks, never letting me have the easy way out.

"If you call yours."

Everything I'm going through, she is too, and I want to share every second of every difficult minute with her.

She mumbles against my lips, "Deal."

After we eat, we hole up in her bedroom with my laptop and sift through gossip sites and blogposts, watch news clips on

YouTube, and check the video of her interview on Oprah's show, comments popping up in real time, they post so fast. She shrinks in front of me, this strong, intelligent woman worn down to nothing as she reads the nasty accusations. Not all of them are. There are thousands supporting her and her decision to retire, but for every positive comment that defends her, there are several that blame her for Michael's death, and one brave soul asked, "If she couldn't save her own fiancé, what the fuck is she doing with Sheppard Carpenter?"

We can't get away from the picture of us in the water, me holding on to her so tightly as she's doubled over in pain and tears.

"I need a minute," she whispers, sliding off the bed.

"Liv, it doesn't matter what they say."

"Please."

She's hurting, my baby's hurting, and there's nothing I can do. Even Scout knows how much she's suffering and instead of staying with me, she follows Liv into the hallway and down the stairs. A moment later, the sliding glass door opens and shuts.

I last the sixty seconds she gave me, and I'm down the stairs and out the door. She's barely managed to reach the sand by the time I'm grabbing her arm and asking her to look at me.

Without a word, she shakes me off and heads toward the section of beach where we would picnic and I'd share all my dirty secrets. I keep pace with her, my bare feet sinking into the soft sand. Tourists give us curious looks, not brave enough to approach us and ask for autographs. Jeff's right. It's not me they want to speak with, but Olivia.

"It doesn't matter what they say," I repeat, willing her to listen to me.

We stop at a deserted section of beach, and the siren's silent, as if for once, she's the one listening.

"It's easy for you to say that because they aren't saying it about you." She purses her lips, not against tears but against shame, and she stares across the water, Scout headbutting her, wanting her to be okay just as desperately as I do.

"They aren't? You weren't reading the same articles I was then. What they said is exactly what I've been telling myself for the past year. It's what fueled my depression and drove me into the water night after night. What they said was what you were telling yourself for the past three, but they don't know you, they don't know me, and they sure as fuck don't know what's between us. I have never felt as good as I do when I'm with you. I haven't had a drink in days. Today, I picked up my guitar for the first time in months. I want to invite people I care about to a party because I want to spend time with them, and you did all that, Olivia. You did that."

Water swirls around her ankles, and her arms are crossed over her chest. In the breeze, the ends of her hair skim her neck and shoulders, still messy from when I made love to her on the couch. She's everything I want and everything I need rolled up into a woman who's five-three and a hundred and twenty pounds. She may be slight and she may be petite, but she's strong enough to handle anything I throw at her because she's already handled a ton of shit for herself.

"So go back in there," I continue when she doesn't respond, pointing toward the house, "and write the most heartfelt blogpost you have ever written. Lay it all out there. Don't worry about the NDA you signed. You quote me and tell those assholes that if it wasn't for you, I wouldn't be standing here. I'd be lying in bed, drunk off my ass because I believed everything they have no fucking right to say."

"You're tangling up how you feel about me and what I'm supposed to be doing for you," she says, avoiding my eyes.

"That's not true. Do you know when I knew you could give me what Dalt hired you for?"

"No."

"When you gave me a lavender air freshener plug-in for my bedroom. I asked you about it, and you gave it to me because you knew I needed it. It was that one very small simple thing that made me realize you could help me. You knew what I needed, just like you know what all your clients need. It's what made you a successful life coach. It's what made your book a bestseller. It's what made Oprah want to have you for a guest on her show. This has nothing to do with how I feel about you, and everything to do with your skills. You got me to open up when no one else could, and believe me, in the past year, Dalt and the guys tried. Your empathy and sympathy cracked me wide open. You might have been scared of it, and you probably still are, but my depression didn't chase you off, and like all your other clients you've helped over the years, I'm thankful."

I know what I'm doing, and my heart hurts. I've relegated myself to simply being one of her clients, not a boyfriend, not a fiancé, not a potential husband. She was hired to be here. I rub my face. She was hired to be here.

"Michael wasn't your client. He was your lover, your fiancé, your best friend. Your relationship was different with him, and it was supposed to be. You didn't see what was going on because you were working too hard or because you were traveling too much. Relationships work both ways and he should have told you, Liv. Relationships need faith, they need trust, and he broke yours when he didn't tell you how lost he was. How many nights would you lie in bed and plan, thinking of the future? And not even the distant future, but the next week, the next day. Where to go for lunch, what you needed at the grocery store. All it would have taken was a minute of your time. He didn't, and that's not your fault."

She sighs and moves a foot through the water. She's

listening at least, but I don't know how much she believes me. "And what are you to me, Sheppard?"

If I knew she would say yes, I would ask her to marry me, I love her so much. The thought of any kind of future without her scares me more than the siren's grip around my ankle, but the timing, it's just not there, and she would say no. She's not convinced I need her because I want her. She's not looking at me now as a man she wants to marry, she's seeing a client, a depressed, fucked up rockstar who can't get his shit together enough to record another album. Until she can see more than that, all I'll ever be is a client.

"Whatever you want me to be. I want to give you whatever will make you happy." I hold out my hand, and I don't release the sigh I've been holding since I followed her onto the beach until she places her soft hand in mine. I pull her to me, and she presses her face against my chest, my t-shirt absorbing her shuddery breath.

Scout whines, her own sense of relief palpable when she doesn't move from Liv's side.

On the way back to the house, we garner the same amount of attention as we did before, people staring at us, knowing exactly who we are and why Liv is here. This isn't only her career under a microscope, it's mine, too, and I'll need to talk to Dalt at the get-together about contacting the band's PR company and releasing my own statement. What I told Liv is the truth. I don't mind admitting I have depression, don't mind people knowing that for a brief time I was suicidal and the reasons why, and I want people to know it was Liv who showed me things could be better.

I make a fresh pot of coffee, and she sits on a stool at the breakfast bar while it drips. I can't be more than two inches from her at any given time, and I stand between the V of her legs and tangle my fingers in her hair.

Scout has a snack and some water, and knowing things are back to a shaky normal, falls asleep by the glass doors.

I fix Liv's coffee the way she likes it, and once we both have mugs of caffeine, I lead her into the den. Her laptop is right where I left it when I closed it and set it aside, and my guitar mocks me, leaning against the side of the couch.

She sits in the far corner of the sofa, but I don't sit on the opposite end. I have to be close to her, always, and sit in the middle, my guitar in my lap.

Sweat drips down my side, and my nerves are stretched as tightly as the strings on my guitar. Liv trembles next to me, and I rest my hand on her leg. "It's okay."

She nods. "Yeah, it is."

Her quiet bravery is all I need, and I start to strum, the chords a comfortable dream as well as my scariest nightmare. Her eyes flick to me as she recognizes "Right Here Waiting," and I hope she understands the message. I will always be here for her, always waiting to show her that she's not alone, and won't be, ever again.

I don't think I could have done this without her next to me, highlighting what she'd written and deleting it all, changing her mind after what we saw online and maybe our conversation on the beach. Closing my eyes, I let the music carry me away. The years I've had with Ghost Town were good years, the very best, but life goes on. Things can never stay the same and we can either accept that and look for the good in what those changes bring, or we can live in the past. My past has been amazing, but those years didn't have Liv in them, and that's what I want now.

The last note fades and her quiet, uneven clicking picks up where Richard Marx left off.

"What kind of music do you like?" I ask, surprised I don't know this about her. Before Derrick's death, music was my entire life. Now I can't remember the last time I turned on the radio.

"My mom loved eighties music. I grew up listening to a lot of that," she says, her eyes never leaving her screen. "We would dance around the kitchen while we helped her make dinner."

"Let me see what I got," I say, sifting through the songs I know without sheet music. I don't remember exactly how it goes, but I must do an okay job when she smiles as "Eternal Flame" by the Bangles floats around us. "Can you sing it?"

She laughs. "No one wants to hear that. People call an ambulance when I sing 'Happy Birthday.'"

I chuckle. "Maybe one day."

"You do what you do, and I'll do what I do," she says, pointing to my guitar and then to her laptop.

"Fair."

While she types, I think of other romantic eighties music I know by memory. It's not a wide selection, and I run out when I finish "Time After Time" by Cyndi Lauper. "That's all I got," I say, setting my guitar aside and picking up my coffee cup. The coffee's cold, but I still sip, my mouth dry.

"How did that feel?" she asks.

"Terrifying," I admit, "but under the fear there was a thin layer of hope and maybe just a tiny bit of happiness. Music has always been a part of me, and cutting myself off from it after Derrick's death hurt almost as much as losing my friend."

"You felt like you didn't deserve it in your life anymore."

"That's part of it, but after his fall, it didn't fit. There was no room for it."

"There doesn't have to be room. Your grief and your music can co-exist. Put them together," she says, clasping her hands as if she were praying.

I sit back. That's exactly what I was doing. I separated

Derrick's death and the loss of my marriage from my music when all along I should have fused them together.

"Then you do the same." I touch her skin above her heart and tap the laptop's screen. "Push your grief into your work. They aren't separate."

"You're right. I used my father's death as a way to relate to clients who were dealing with the loss of a loved one, but I never knew what losing a significant other could do to someone because I had never experienced that. Now I know, and instead of hoarding those feelings, I should share them."

Before she can turn toward her keyboard, with a hand to the back of her head, I kiss her.

She laughs under my mouth. "I need to keep going or I'll be at this all night."

Kissing her forehead, I mumble, "Okay, but I'm done for the day. I'll journal while you finish. I'm gonna go get it."

I leave my guitar where it sits leaning against the couch. I'll never lock it up again.

Olivia's typing when I come back from grabbing my journal and her self-help book from my room, and we share a quiet couple of hours as we both crawl out from our darkest pits and into the light.

I'm lost in thought when she closes her laptop.

"I'm going to let that sit for a bit. If Dalton stops by tomorrow night, I can talk to him about what I included."

"I can read it too, if you want," I say, dog-earring the page I was reading in her book. "I'll tell him I approve of whatever you need to write. We have to give you leeway to defend yourself if that's part of what you wrote." I pause. "Did you talk about us?"

"Anyone looking at that picture would know we were on

our way to bed, but no, not like that. I explained why I retired, why I came out of retirement to help you. That I didn't think, like a lot of people online, I was qualified enough to take this job, but Michael's death and grieving him actually put me in a place where I could help you better than if I hadn't had that perspective. I mentioned Derrick and why you stopped making music, and you can tell me if I overstepped. As far as I know, you never publicly explained."

"No, I didn't, but that wasn't it completely. His death triggered my depression, and Melody leaving me heaped on top of it."

"Those will be your stories to share, and what I wrote will be enough. Like you said, it's no one's business, but we chose the careers we did. Your fans and my readership and clients deserve an explanation, even if it's only partially the truth."

"How did that feel?" I ask, marveling we're going through the same thing in a completely different context.

"Terrifying," she says, pushing back a smile, "but even though what people are saying online put me on the defensive, I know it will help someone out there, and it's worth it."

"Come here," I say, and she crawls into my lap straddling my legs with her thighs. Holding her face between my hands, I brush a kiss across her lips. "You were brave today. Let's order Chinese and watch a movie."

"I'm brave because of you. I watch how you struggle, how you deal with your friend's death, and it humbles me. You're so strong, even if you don't feel like you are. I'm proud of you for picking up your guitar, and maybe just a little impressed you know so many eighties songs." She nuzzles my cheek with her nose.

"I'll learn 'em all for you, Liv." I search her eyes, looking for some kind of promise she'll always be with me, but of course, I don't see anything but fatigue, and I say lightly, "Scout needs to go outside. While we wait for the delivery, I'll text the guys and Dalt, touch base with Jeff and invite him and Gina over and double check we're running in the morning. Sound good?"

"It sounds perfect."

And perfect is what my life will be if I can keep Liv in it.

<h1 style="text-align:center">Chapter Twenty-One</h1>

We fall asleep on the couch like he said we would, but in the middle of the night, I wake up in bed, Sheppard wrapped tightly around me. He will never understand what it meant to me that he played his guitar while I wrestled with all my horrible thoughts and feelings as I wrote that blogpost. He will never truly understand the courage he gave me battling his demons while I battled mine.

Out of anything anyone has ever said to me about Michael's death, what he told me while we were on the beach eased something inside my heart, and a peace I have never felt before, not from going to church, not from spending time with my dad, not even from my most cantankerous client when he finally saw reason, filled me. Michael had never shown me even a glimmer of the depression he dealt with. He'd been happy, teaching his classes, going to lunch with colleagues, and planning a future with me, and he gave me no reason to try to look past that fake happiness. *We* were happy, and I simply didn't know. My clients will tell me what they're afraid of, what they think they need to work on, the speed bumps that have slowed them down and kept them from reaching for what they want most. Then I create a plan with actionable steps to work toward the changes they want to see in their lives.

Michael and I bought a house, adopted Scout. We were planning our wedding, and in the quiet bliss in the middle of the night when we would talk, he never said anything. I would fall asleep in his arms, thinking things were nothing but perfect.

I won't blame him for not talking to me, and it's not my fault for not listening to the words that weren't there.

Sheppard has another hour to sleep before meeting Jeffrey for their run, and I carefully slide out of bed. After we ordered Chinese, I grabbed my laptop from the den and helped him look up restaurants in the area that would cater on such short notice. I was sure any restaurant would bend over backward for Sheppard Carpenter, and I wasn't wrong. We had several promise the short notice was no problem. In the end, we chose a deli whose manager said they would be delighted to put together, deliver, and set up a massive charcuterie board along with several flavors of sparkling water. Sheppard said people would bring their own booze if they wanted something stronger and he wouldn't mind watching other people drink. All I can do is take him at his word. If he noticed his empty bars, he hasn't said anything.

Our phone calls to our mothers linger in the back of my mind, too. I let Scout out onto the beach for her morning pee, and I scribble a mental note to remind Sheppard to call his mom after his run. I plan to call mine at the same time. I want to experience that with him, like his playing and my writing. Whatever we can do together, that's what I want.

I doubt I'll ever meet his mom and brother. Sheppard's

breaking out of the cocoon he created for himself when Derrick died. I can see him slowly emerging into a stronger person and once he starts writing songs and singing with the band again, my time here will be over. It was natural for him to invite me, and it was natural for me to accept, but there's no reason for it.

Whenever I think about living without Sheppard, the siren's song is just a little louder, and I want to press my hands against my ears.

Gina waves from her patio and starts toward me while I wade in the water. She moves closer, and she looks just as miserable as I'm sure I do. Dark shadows rest underneath her eyes and she's lost weight.

"What's wrong?" I ask, clutching her arm. "Are you feeling okay?"

"I'm going to move out of the beach house and I'm looking for a place to live. It's poor timing with this documentary, but last night Jeff accused me of cheating on him. He doesn't know me at all if he thinks I would do that. He doesn't want to marry me, but he doesn't want anyone else to have me either. Don't worry, I'll finish up your part before I move out. Jeff doesn't know, so I would appreciate it if you didn't tell Shep."

"I'm sorry, but you're brave, you know, for not settling."

"I don't feel brave, just heartbroken." She drags in a deep breath through her nose and fixes a smile onto her mouth. "Jeff read Shep's text. It's a big deal he's inviting people to a party, and we'll be there. If he asked the rest of the guys and they sing, you'll be in for an experience of a lifetime. I'll see you tonight, okay?"

"Yeah," I say, but she's already turning toward her house, her shoulders hunched in defeat. She fought for a long time, but she lost.

Just like, in the end, I'm going to do.

Sheppard's still sleeping when I let Scout into the house, and I sip on a cup of coffee while I proof what I wrote yesterday, the chorus of "Eternal Flame" whispering through my mind. He knew all the love songs, and yeah, I could have sung them all, but I'm not that brave. As much as it will break my heart, I very much want to listen to Sheppard if he and the guys sing tonight.

I haven't lost my writing style and my blogpost sounds good. An even mixture of heart and professionalism, I tried to explain what happened and why I disappeared. I addressed the rumors online, why I'm here in LA, and what I plan to do next. I mentioned another book, focusing, maybe, on dealing with grief and moving on despite the guilt. I didn't say much about Sheppard, regurgitating what's already online. I don't think Dalton will have an issue with anything I've written, but since he's the band's manager, I'll ask him to skim it before I click Publish.

My thoughts go back to Gina. Maybe Jeff will stop her from leaving, but she didn't seem to think that was a possibility. Maybe it isn't. Maybe he's waiting for her to leave. I don't believe he loves her as much as Sheppard says he does. Not because I think a wedding ring is final proof of true love but because if he really wanted to keep her, he would have wanted to tell the world she belonged to him and he didn't. It's not that she's not enough, not like she thinks, or maybe not like I thought about my own relationship with Michael, it's that she isn't enough for *him* and I wasn't enough for Michael. That doesn't mean one day we both won't find a man whom we *will* be enough for, and there's a big difference between the two.

"Those are some heavy thoughts," Sheppard says from behind me, dressed for his run. "I felt them all the way upstairs."

"Not so bad. Just thinking about what you said to me on the

beach. I won't know why Michael didn't talk to me. Maybe he thought he couldn't, or he didn't want to show me he had a weakness. Maybe, like we talked about, he didn't know how to ask and thought he had to suffer alone. You said you don't know why Melody left you. Are you going to ask her one day?"

He pours a cup of coffee and stares into the black liquid. He didn't shave, and scruff covers his jaw. I like the grey streaks in his beach blonde hair. He's wearing shorts and a muscle t-shirt, and his biceps bulge. He reminds me of a worn bear, but one who would rather snuggle than attack.

"I will, but it doesn't seem as important as it once did. We were growing apart, and I felt it. In the scheme of things, for people like us, ten years is a long time. Instead of being surprised we got a divorce, maybe I should be surprised we lasted as long as we did."

"That's bleak."

He smiles wryly. "Yeah, but that's life. She met someone and fell in love. It's not like you can control something like that, but she should have owned it and told me. I don't care who the guy is, and as long as she's happy and he doesn't hurt her, what she does with him is none of my business. She should have said something, that's all. She didn't have to cheat."

"Are you sure that's what she did?"

Scowling, he says, "No, but we were on a world tour for six months, and I rarely saw her. What was she doing if she wasn't shacking up with another man? Crocheting a blanket?"

"I don't know, Sheppard, but you should be sure. It's a serious accusation and you shouldn't believe it if it's not true. You could hurt her in a way you don't mean to."

"Yeah. I'll talk to her. I want to, anyway. I'm still piecing together the night Derrick fell, and I need to ask her where she was. One of the stagehands said he thought Dalt was with a woman, and I'm going to ask him who he was with and if he's still seeing her. I'd like to meet her."

"You miss your friends." As much as it hurts me to say it, I'm glad, too. It means he's opening up and that he's healing.

He sets his mug onto the counter and rounds the breakfast bar. He kisses the tip of my nose and says, "Not as much as I'm going to miss you."

A hot ball of tears burns my throat. "Me?"

"Yeah. While I'm on my run. You wouldn't turn down another shower when I come back, would you?"

"Oh." I let out a shaky breath. "I suppose I could be persuaded."

"Good. I better get outside. I don't want Jeff to have to wait for me. Come on, Scout. I know this is your favorite part of the day. I'll see you in an hour." He pecks me quickly on the cheek and hustles Scout out the back door.

I'm going to have to get it together if I'm going to cry over innocent statements like that. One day Sheppard won't need my help anymore, and I'll go home.

My life isn't here, but it isn't in the little house Michael and I bought together.

My life isn't anywhere, and resting my head on my arms, the tears come after all.

We shower together, but Sheppard doesn't make love to me until we're done, and gently, he tugs the towel wrapped around my body and lets it drop to the floor in my bedroom. Sitting on the bed, he nuzzles my breasts, his scruff scraping against my skin.

"You're so beautiful," he whispers, finding me wet, and I suck in a breath as he slides two of his fingers inside me.

I will never get used to how he handles me, delicately, as if he were afraid to touch me but can't help himself. He's never taken me hard or aggressively, always softly, tenderly. I've had rough sex before, but Sheppard is content to hug me as he makes love to me, coming quietly, his labored breath in my ear.

He does that for me now, covering my body with his and pushing into me inch by inch while he stares into my eyes. My body has gotten used to his size, and he doesn't stop until he's as deep as he can go. "Are you okay?" he asks, his lips skimming mine.

"Yeah."

"Good. I never want to hurt you, you know that, don't you?"

"I know."

He helps me come, his fingers finding my clit between our bodies slick with sweat, and I cling to him, my face pressed into his neck, as the orgasm zaps all my nerve endings. I love coming with him inside me while he holds me so tightly I can't breathe, and he comes too, my climax subsiding and my muscles rippling around his cock.

Sheppard has never kept the "love" part of making love from our intimacy and I love him so much for knowing I need it. Until life settles down for both of us, maybe we won't have fun, playful sex, but I think I would like that, too, when our situation doesn't feel so heavy.

"Are you okay?" I ask, rubbing my thumb over his jaw. With the phone call and the party, maybe there's too much on his plate.

"I'm good. Just stealing a couple of quiet minutes with my girl," he says, kissing down my neck and licking at one of my nipples. The sensation travels right to my middle, and my muscles clench at his cock in response.

"Are you up for a little more, Miss Bloom?" he says, sliding out and then gliding back inside me.

My hips lift in eager anticipation. "You are," I tease.

"I will never get enough of you. I could make love to you every day, spend every second of the rest of my life with you, and it would never be enough. I hope you realize that."

"Sheppard," I sigh, touched.

"What? I know there are things I have no right saying because of the circumstances, and for every one thing I say, I keep a hundred to myself. I *know*, Olivia, and don't think I don't hurt."

"I don't know what to say," I murmur.

"Don't say anything. Show me how you feel."

He rolls us over the bed until I'm on top, my hair a wet tangle against my back.

Leaning over, I kiss him, and while I'm not very experienced at this type of thing, I try with all my heart to show him the things neither of us dare say.

He dresses in his room, and when I see him again, he's wearing faded, worn-out jeans and a black t-shirt. His face is pale and lines I haven't seen since my first day here hug his eyes and mouth. "Are you okay? With the party, maybe you should put off calling your mom. You can do it tomorrow morning instead. Would you feel better about it?"

I don't want to push too much on him at once. If what Gina says is true, this party will be an emotional rollercoaster for Sheppard. She would know more as she's seen him for the past year and I haven't, and I trust her judgment.

Leaning against my doorjamb, he says, "Calling her shouldn't be scary, but I don't know how she's going to react."

"Well, you've got two options. She'll either be happy, or she'll be indifferent. If she's indifferent, at least you'll know where you stand, and you can work on getting her to come around. Uncertainty is always worse than not knowing, even if it's bad news, but I think she misses you. If anything, she'll be relieved to know you're okay."

He blows out a breath. "Yeah. You nervous to talk to your mom?"

"A little. I didn't tell her I was coming to LA. My sister is a social media junkie; I'm sure she knows where I am and what's been happening. I bet she's told Mom all about it, and Mom's probably hurt I haven't told her myself. They both will be, but they knew how devastated I was after Michael passed away and they were always good about giving me the space I wanted. I just took too much. It was unhealthy, but when you push people away, they respect your wishes because they love you."

"I didn't consider it that way. Puts them in a difficult position."

"It does, and when we do that to them, then we're stuck in the difficult position of fixing it."

"That's where we are now."

I smile. "That's where we are now."

He shuffles into my room and cuddles me to him. "I don't know where I'd be without you, Liv."

I press a kiss to his chest, the soft cotton of his shirt rubbing my lips. "Ditto."

"You have no idea how happy that makes me."

"Is that one of those things you've tried not to say?" I ask, turning toward the mirror and dabbing a colored lip balm to my lips. My hands shake.

"No. I don't want you here because you're scared not to be. I want you here because you want to be here, too. You probably know a lot about co-dependency. I don't want that to be us."

My eyes widen. "That's very astute."

He grins, and a little of the tension fades. "What can I say? I'm a very astute kind of guy."

I tamp back a laugh. "I'm sure you are. Go call your mom."

"Meet me downstairs?" he asks, reluctant to go.

"I'll meet you downstairs."

He crosses the hallway and closes his door, Scout by his side. She'll watch over him. With what he's told me about his mother, I don't think he has anything to worry about. She wanted him to be exactly where he is, only no one could have predicted how fast he would get here and how brightly his star would shine.

I have to keep the timezones in mind, and I quickly run through where my own mother is now. Sheppard's run, our shower, and our long, drawn out love-making session ate up most of the morning, and it's just now a little past eleven o'clock. Saturday at 1:10 PM Central Time, Mom's just finishing a women's Bible study at our church. It's always a potluck lunch in the basement, and after everyone contributes, there's plenty to go around. I've attended a time or two, when Mom's asked because what they're studying complements some area of my expertise. She doesn't ask often. She knows I get sad when I go to church because Dad's not the pastor anymore.

I risk her chatting with some of the women and bring up her number on my phone. Settling on the bed, I plug my earbud cord into the base and adjust them in my ears. I connect her number, my heart slamming as it rings. She won't be mad at me, disappointed and concerned, maybe, but there is one good thing about growing up in a religious family. She'll tell me she gave everything to God, living with faith He'd guide me back to her, and if that helps her worry less, I'm grateful for it.

"Olivia," she says, relieved, and then to someone in the background, "I have to take this. It's my daughter. Have a good day, Lorraine," and then back to me, "Livvy, how are you? You've had me twisted in knots for months, then Becca tells me you're in California with a rockstar. She showed me that picture of you in the ocean. What is going on?"

"A lot. Do you have time to talk?"

"Of course I do, or you would have chosen a different time to call. Life hasn't changed that much. How are you? How did you come to be in California?"

I explain Agatha's part in it, the picture that slid out of the file, how in Dalton's office I almost said I wouldn't take the job.

"It's lucky you did," she says, closing a door somewhere in the background. "I'm willing to bet you saved that young man's life."

"He's not so young. He's fifty."

"That's younger than me."

I laugh. "Not by much."

"Maybe not, but when you get to be my age, every year counts. I found a quiet spot in Pastor Duncan's office, and I have an hour or so before the youth group comes in for afternoon activities."

My ears perk up. "Pastor Duncan? Is he new?"

"Pastor Reeves was called into ministry across the state to a little town that couldn't afford to support their pastor anymore. Because he lives on family money, he wanted to relocate and help out that community. Martin transferred here after his wife passed away, wanting a change. God saw what was needed and provided."

A change in pastors wasn't all God provided. "You like him."

"Would you think poorly of me, Liv? I loved your father, but he's been gone a long time. Martin and I pray for him and his wife every day. I won't ever forget him. I promise."

"Of course not. I'd be quite the hypocrite if I said I would.

You deserve to find someone who will make you happy again. As long as he treats you well, that's all that matters. How long have you been seeing him? I'm sorry I've been so checked out."

"About a year now, and I think . . . he wants to get married but he's waiting to ask. He'd like to meet you before he does. When are you coming home?" She pauses. "*Are* you coming home?" She pauses again. "Do you *want* to come home? Are you in love with him?"

My heart sinks. I don't want to hold up Mom's life because I'm in LA. "I signed a contract with Sheppard's band's manager, and I gave him until the end of August. Then, I don't know." I have to talk around a burn in my throat that seems almost permanent. "I love him, and I think, maybe, he loves me, too, but we would have to work through a lot, and I'm not sure if it's possible. *I* have a lot to work through, alone. Dad's been gone for seventeen years and you're still hesitant and wondering if moving on is the right thing to do. Michael's been gone for only three, and I was still grieving when I accepted this job."

"Martin struggles," my mom says softly. "He doesn't want me to know, but he does. It bleeds you dry when you love someone so very much that you can't picture your life without them, but you're already living that life because they're gone and they're never coming back. Your father and I had a good life, and I know you don't believe in God the way I do or your father did, but He would never do anything without a reason or a purpose. I've prayed on this a long time, honey, and it's what I truly think. If you love him, give him everything you have and don't look back."

"Then you should do the same. I can see if I can fly out sooner than August, maybe for a weekend visit, but I haven't been here long, and it's not a good time to get away. We might have turned this into a personal situation, but he's struggling with a lot of things, and it's my job to be here for him."

"I understand. Sheppard Carpenter. What's he like? Is he kind?"

"You sound like Agatha. Mom, he's the kindest, most gentlest person you will ever meet in your life. He's so patient with me, and we spend hours, *hours,* just talking about life. It's my job to listen to him, but he listens to me, too, and I think, in this one instance, you're right, and God knew what He was doing sending me here."

"I'd like to meet him. Does he go to church?"

I hold back a laugh, but it dies quickly. "No, he doesn't go to church. I don't think you'll ever get to meet him. There's a scandal online, and I'm going to put my website back up soon with a new blogpost. I hope a reporter doesn't try to talk to you or Becca. Apparently, me being here with Sheppard is a big deal. I need to call Tammy and ask her for help because this fall I'm getting my coaching business going again, and Agatha said after my time with Sheppard, she'd be able to sell another book. I'm too young to do nothing for the rest of my life."

"That doesn't sound like a future with Sheppard in it," Mom says quietly, always reading between the lines.

"No, it doesn't, but he's tied to a contract and he'll be busy with his own responsibilities."

"Are you sure, Liv? The way he's holding you in the water while you cried . . . I think if you asked, he would do whatever he needed to do to keep you there."

I sigh. It doesn't matter whom I talk to: Gina, Agatha, my mom. The story doesn't change. When Sheppard is well enough to record another album, that's it for us. I'm not Melody and I can't keep up with that lifestyle. I don't want to. Maybe she modeled around their tours and his recording sessions, the parties and award shows, but I can't accept coaching jobs based on his schedule. That's not fair to my clients or to me. "I don't want him to give up anything for me."

"He wouldn't be giving anything up if he had you in exchange."

"That's not how healthy relationships work, and you of all people should know that. I agree that both people should be willing to compromise, but when one person does it more, resentment sets in. Sheppard would be giving up a helluva lot more than I would if we tried, and that's not a position I want to put him in. I already know, Mom. Now tell me how Becca is. I can't talk about this anymore."

"Okay. I'm sorry. I would miss you if you moved to California, but promise me, Liv, after the summer is over, and you're home again, start living. You've mourned Michael, and with the way you feel about Sheppard, you'll be right back to where you started. I don't want that for you. You said you're too young not to work, but you're also too young to write yourself off as a grieving spinster. Promise me the past three years won't repeat themselves."

"They won't. I would like children someday. It just took me a long time to come to terms with the fact it wouldn't be with Michael. I already knew going into this job what Sheppard and I are doing is temporary. My heart already knows. Please, Mom," I say, my voice cracking.

"Oh, Liv. I hate seeing you hurting."

"I'm fine. I miss you."

"I miss you, too." She pauses, and I think she's going to push me into more conversation about Sheppard keeping me here, but she says, "Becca and Stephen are fostering. A home burned down on the north side of town, and the mother passed away from smoke inhalation. Apparently, she fell asleep with a cigarette still burning. She had five kids, all under the age of nine, if you can believe it. Becca couldn't find a foster family who could take all of them, and it broke her heart to separate them. She said she would, and Stephen, God bless him, jumped right in. She would never admit it, but she's happy."

"I'm sure she is. That's horrible. How did the children get out?"

"A neighbor walking his dog saw the flames in her bedroom window. Her door was shut," Mom says in disapproval, "and they were locked in a nursery. CPS visited her before, but foster families are scarce in this area, and there was nowhere for them to go."

"I remember Becca complaining about that." It's why she had her own foster care license—so she could step in when she was needed.

"They're darling, all five of them, and Martin and I are holding a fundraising raffle at the church next weekend. Becca and Stephen do well, but five children will put a strain on their finances for a while."

"I'll write her a check, too."

"I didn't tell you that to beg for money," Mom says.

I know she didn't, but even with my three year sabbatical, I'm still comfortable and can afford to help. "I'm offering. I'll match what the church brings in, and you won't even have to tell her. Is she mad at me?"

"No, sweetheart. She's concerned, and she was a little surprised to find out you were in LA, living with a rockstar, no less."

"How did she find out?"

"A woman Becca works with saw an article on social media and showed it to her during a lunch break. Becca's gone down to part time for a while to look after the kids. The closest daycare that could take them all on such short notice was in Baxter, and that's too far of a drive every day. She works

Mondays and Tuesdays and does what she can from home the rest of the week."

"That can't be much with five children. Can she hire a nanny?"

"I don't think she wants to, even if she could. Those kids have gone through so much, and adding another stranger to their routine would make things worse. The little ones are so confused and cry their days away. I spend as much time over there as I can, but the fact is, their future is up in the air."

"Hmm. Well, if anyone can help, it's Becca. I'm going to be here for the next little while, but I'll try to be home as soon as I can. That may not be soon enough to do Becca much good."

"It will ease her mind to know you're doing okay, and that will help more than you know. We love you, Liv, and hearing from you has eased my heart. I need to go, but start calling me on a regular basis, and if you can't do that, at least email me once in a while. He's not keeping you chained up in the basement, is he?"

"No. We're at his beach house in Malibu. It doesn't have a basement."

"Then he's got you chained up somewhere else. Give Scout a kiss from me."

My eyes widen. My mother made a sex joke. "I will. She's in love with Sheppard."

"I'm sure you'll agree she has good taste. Goodbye, Liv. Thank you for calling. I love you."

"I love you, too."

Ever since my dad passed away, Mom jam-packed her days to keep herself from getting lonely. Now that she spends her time with Pastor Martin Duncan at the church, she's a different kind of busy, and when she's not with him, she'll be at Becca's. I was lucky to catch her today and going forward I'll switch to email. I don't want to call her when she can't answer the phone. Knowing her, she would feel badly if she couldn't talk.

I disconnect my earbud cord from the base of my phone. Sheppard's door is still closed, but his murmuring voice carries to me. I'm glad he was able to get a hold of his mom. I didn't want him to have to go through the buildup again. It stressed him out, and now it's over and communication with her can ease into a comfortable routine.

I lie on the bed, the sunshine attempting to glimmer past the blinds I didn't open. When Michael passed away, I spent all of my time in the dark, and it's a habit I haven't broken. I'm thinking about Mom and Pastor Duncan getting married when Sheppard opens his bedroom door. We were supposed to meet in the kitchen, but he catches my eye and staggers into my room, Scout at his heels. He climbs onto the bed and wraps his arms around me. Scout jumps onto the bed too, curls into a ball, and falls asleep.

"Can we nap, Liv?" he mumbles against my hair.

"Yeah. Go to sleep."

I sit up long enough to tug the blanket from underneath Scout, much to her annoyance, and cover us. Once I'm secure in his arms again, he's asleep in seconds. Unless he tells me otherwise, I'm going to assume the call went well, and his emotional exhaustion is due to that and nothing else. If it had gone poorly, Sheppard is sensitive and comfortable enough he would have cried on me, not fallen asleep. He values his family too much not to let something like the deterioration of his relationship with his mother do anything less than destroy him.

I'm happy for him. It's one more step closer to getting his life back, and unfortunately, one step farther away from me.

Nudging his cheek with my nose, I burrow in his arms and doze. Hours later, he kisses me awake, and under the blanket, shows me his appreciation.

I'm the one who's grateful.

Sheppard's healing my heart, one kiss at a time.

For a late lunch, we heat up the left over Chinese and sit in the kitchen. I've never seen Sheppard look so relaxed and at ease. Even after sex, there was always something strung tight inside him, a tension I couldn't erase, and I realize now that was his tenuous relationship with his family.

"How is she?" I ask, scooping up a spoonful of beef fried rice.

"No, you first. I want to hear about your mom and sister."

I shrug. My family news isn't as important as his. "My mom's getting married to the new pastor of our church. He's a widower and relocated for a fresh start. She's been waiting for me to surface so she could tell me. He sounds nice and wants to meet me before he officially asks her."

Sheppard freezes. "What does that mean? You're leaving?"

I cover his hand with mine. "No. I told her I wouldn't be able to get away until the end of the summer. Maybe sooner if something works out, but it's not an emergency. It's okay. Remember the dependency thing? You would be okay if I wasn't here."

He shudders out a breath. "Right. She was okay with that?"

"Yeah. They haven't been seeing each other, that way, for long. She didn't say anything about having to wait."

"Okay. Good. How's your sister? Is she married?"

"Hmm, yeah," I say around a huge forkful of rice. I'm starving, and I was crying too hard this morning to eat breakfast. "I don't know if I told you she's older than I am, and she's been married for about six years."

"Do they have kids?" he asks around his own mouthful of eggroll.

"Not biological. She and her husband have just taken in five kids she couldn't place together."

"That's right. She's the social worker."

"Yeah. It's like Becca to do that, and why she got her own foster care license. Five kids. I can't imagine it." I would love it though, to have a houseful of children. "They lucked out when Becca took them in."

"How long is she keeping them?" he asks, offering me an eggroll that's cooling.

I gladly take it. I might need to search for something else to eat before the party. The charcuterie board is supposed to be a snack, not a meal.

"If she has it her way, forever. She can't have kids. Before she met Stephen, she had to have a hysterectomy. She suffered from severe endometriosis and fibroids. She wanted kids so badly, but she was always in pain and didn't have a choice. When Stephen asked her to marry him, she said no. She didn't want him saddled with a barren woman. Her words. It took him a long time to wear her down. The state will figure out if the kids have any other family who can take them in, so it might be a while yet before Becca can go down that path. Stephen will be on board. He's done whatever he can to make her happy."

Sheppard sits on a stool the way he normally does, and I'm standing opposite him on the other side. I like how casual we are with each other, talking around mouthfuls of food, eager to share information as well as fill our bellies. He's genuinely interested in my family, too, and it's endearing as much as it is baffling. That he would care about a family in central Minnesota he'll never meet when he has such bigger things going on in his life.

He breaks apart the last eggroll and offers me half. I lean across the breakfast bar and smack a kiss to his lips. "Thanks."

"That was messy, but worth it," he says, licking at the soy sauce I left behind. "It sounds like they need money. Do they need money?"

"Oh, well," I say, flustered. "Mom said they're going to do a fundraiser at the church, and I told her I would match that. The state will give them benefits for fostering."

He shakes his head. "We can do better than that. I'll talk to Dalt tonight. While we were napping, he and the guys texted and said they would be here. He can overnight a check. Fifty thousand? Is that enough? More?"

I hurry around the bar and wrap my arms around him. "No, Sheppard. I didn't tell you so you would offer something like that. They'll be okay. Mom's congregation is the best. They'll pull through."

"We don't need anyone to pull through. I have a ton of money. I won't live long enough to spend even a quarter of it, and I have no one to leave it to. Mom's getting up there, and my brother is older than me. He's married, but they didn't want kids, that means no grandkids, either. The buck stops with me. Please?" He leans away and holds my face in his hands.

A tear drips down my cheek, and he brushes it away with the pad of his thumb. "Thank you."

"You're welcome. I'd do anything for you, Liv."

"I know, and I said I don't want that responsibility." I don't. I don't want to be the reason he makes the choices he does regarding his family or the band. I always want him to decide for himself because I'm not always going to be here.

"I understand that, but this is a small thing. Let me do it."

"Okay. Thanks."

"Sure." He looks around the room. "What should we do now?"

He's nervous about tonight, but once people start to arrive and he remembers how much they care about him, his nerves will smooth out. For now, I say, "Let's clean up the kitchen and play with Scout on the beach. You ordered all those toys, and we haven't used half of them."

His expression softens. "You always know what I need."

I stick my tongue out at him to let him know I'm kidding. "And *that* is what you pay me for."

Cuddling me to him, he laughs.

We throw a Frisbee for Scout, and Sheppard tells me how his talk with his mom went. His phone call lasted longer than expected because he called when his brother was visiting her, and he was able to touch base with both of them. I'm very happy to hear that, as I'm not sure if he would have called his brother otherwise. He doesn't speak much about him, and while Becca was never jealous of my fame, such as it is, I don't know how Tony reacted to Sheppard's. There's always going to be a hint of sibling rivalry, but jealousy is difficult to fight against.

It's windy today, and the breeze whips at my hair and carries the Frisbee in a different direction than where Sheppard throws it. Scout doesn't mind, chasing the flying disc as if her life depends on it.

"She heard about Derrick while she was watching the news, and one of her friends in the retirement community showed her an article in a gossip magazine about my divorce."

"What did she have to say about that?" I ask curiously. Some people are against divorce and think you should work it out no matter what. We aren't Catholics, and my mom is a little more flexible when it comes to that kind of thing. She still has her religious moral code, and despite teasing me, if she and Martin want to add intimacy to their relationship, they'll do it after they get married.

"She said it didn't surprise her, and that was part of the reason she didn't feel comfortable at our wedding. She didn't like Melody and didn't think we were a good match."

I flick a glance at him. "Did you know that?"

Color seeps into his cheeks and he rubs his hand over the nape of his neck. "No. By then, my career was at its peak, and she didn't meet Melody until right before the ceremony. I should have introduced them long before that, but I didn't make the time. It's sweet your mom's boyfriend wants to meet you first. I'm not overly traditional, but I would like the next woman I marry to at least have met Mom before the wedding, and not just before she walks down the aisle. It would be great if they got along. As much as I hate thinking it, she doesn't have much longer, and now that we've reconnected, I'd like to spend more time with her."

I force a smile. Sheppard so casually mentioning his next wife shoves pins and needles into my heart. I suppose one day I'll be paging through a magazine or standing in line at the grocery store, and their wedding picture will be front page news. Another model maybe, or I don't know. There doesn't seem to be any normal people in California. They're all Jeffs and Ginas and Islas, hitting it big and striking it rich, and I'll be in Minnesota writing my little books on self-care and telling people to stop drinking soda if they want to lose weight.

We trudge through the sand, ignoring the usual gawkers. Sheppard's used to it by now, and they don't bother me. Though my life in Minnesota was small, I was still asked for the occasional autograph at Target, and I signed my share of Starbuck's cups. It will get worse when my website is online again and my blogpost goes viral. That's not me thinking I'm all that either—it will be entirely due to Sheppard and what I'm doing here.

"You're quiet all of a sudden," Sheppard says, nudging my arm while Scout runs for another throw. Sheppard's strong—that Frisbee flies forever. "Did Michael get along with your family?"

"Yeah. There weren't many people who didn't like him. You weren't far off how I lived, how we lived. Family holidays, Sunday dinners, evenings playing Rummy. He wasn't religious but he didn't mind going to church for this and that if it made Mom happy. I liked his mom, and after he passed away, I still met her for lunch every once in a while. I didn't tell her I was coming here, and she hasn't reached out. I think I remind her he's gone. When he told her we were engaged, all she could talk about was when I was going to get pregnant. She's older, near eighty, and she'll never have grandkids. Michael was an only child. How old is your mom?"

"Late seventies, too. I think she was disappointed in Melody for that same reason. She's not exactly the maternal type."

I look at him, playfully shocked, and slap my hands to my cheeks. "No way."

Sheppard presses his lips together. "You didn't like her, either."

"She seemed very cold."

"A lot of it is just an act. She opens up in private."

I don't know how we could have gotten any more private than Dalton's office with people she's known for years. "That's between you, then. I was in Dalton's office for forty-five minutes, and she didn't say one word to me and barely looked at me for that matter. Snowmen in Minnesota are warmer than she appeared to be, but you loved her and don't have to explain that to anyone. There's no reason to defend yourself."

"After Mom told me that, I started thinking about things, that's all."

"Your mom liking or disliking her had no bearing on how your marriage turned out."

"You're right, but if they had gotten along, maybe Mom and I wouldn't have drifted apart."

I shoot him a look, my BS meter off the charts. "That's on you. Not your wife."

He grabs my hand as Scout races toward us with the disc clamped between her jaws. "I didn't mean to make it sound like that."

"Then how did you want it to sound?"

He shrugs.

I stop and face him. "If your mother would have said she didn't like Melody and asked you not to marry her, would you have listened?"

Sheppard throws the Frisbee again, and Scout runs after it, perhaps a bit more slowly. I think she's finished with the game.

"No."

I sympathize and brush my hand up and down his arm. "You feel guilty over the lost time, but the quicker you see it's no one's fault but yours, the faster you can get over it. She didn't blame you, did she? She was only happy you called because she missed you. Let it go and visit her more often than you have in the past. That's all you can do. How's your brother?"

"Good. The same."

We turn around and walk back to the house. I'd like to clean up a little in the other rooms before guests start to arrive.

"Do you get along?" I ask.

"Maybe not as well as you and your sister, but yeah. We were close growing up. When the guys and I practiced in Dalt's mom's garage, sometimes he would stop by and listen. He didn't have a lot of free time while he was in med school and when our first album went crazy, we kind of drifted apart. Ghost Town has given me many, many things, but it's taken away a few things, too."

"You're in control, Sheppard, and always have been. Find a way back to the things you've lost."

He swallows and fear shoots through his eyes. "Will you help me?"

Wrapping my arms around him, I rest my cheek over his heart. "I will always give you whatever you need."

"That's good, because right at this moment, there is nothing I need more than you."

Does he mean me or my skills as a life coach? Maybe someone without my training could have gotten through to him, but maybe not. Maybe someone else would have left the night Sheppard told me to get out, especially when he turned the threat into potential physical harm. But maybe not. I accused him of tangling up how he feels about me and what I'm doing for him on a professional level, but to do anything but that would be impossible. The line has gone from thick and black to blurry and grey to nonexistent.

I'm in love with him and I should never have let it get this far.

I look up and smile. "I'm right here."

The unspoken words linger, they always linger, lyrics to the siren's song.

For now.

Walking Scout didn't relieve Sheppard's tension like I hoped it would, and with half an hour before the deli is supposed to deliver our charcuterie board and sparkling water, I lead him to my bedroom and drop to my knees.

"Liv, what are you doing?" he asks, tangling his fingers in my hair.

"Giving you a little something to loosen you up." I unbutton and unzip his jeans and free his thick, hard cock from his boxer briefs.

He stands in the middle of my room, tense, wanting me to do it, but reluctant to let me.

When he doesn't say anything, I lick his shaft from the base to the tip and sample the pre-cum. I've never tasted him before, and I enjoy the tangy, salty flavor. One of my favorite things in the world is when a man eats me out after he comes inside me, and then kisses me, our flavors mingling on his lips. Sheppard and I won't have that unless I go on birth control, but I won't be here long enough to bother.

A breath hisses out of him, and his fingers tighten in my hair.

I cover him completely with my mouth and grip his thigh with a hand, steadying myself.

He's in control and lets me suck him off at my own pace. From, umm, prior feedback, I know my blowjobs are good, and Sheppard agrees, a moan trembling from his chest. "Liv," he rasps. "If you don't want me to come in your mouth, you better stop."

I pull away for just a second to answer him. "No. I want you to. I love how you taste. Do it."

Cupping his balls, I slide him down my throat as far as I can and it's only a second later with my tongue's pressure against the side of his cock does he explode. Greedily, I lap up the thick, gooey semen, wanting part of him inside me. At the end of the summer, it would have been nice to go home pregnant, just a little something to remember him by, but Sheppard is too responsible to let that happen. Even when he wakes me in the middle of the night to have sex, he's already got a condom on, waiting for my consent. Swallowing his cum will have to be enough.

He pants, his fingers gripping my hair, burning my scalp as his cock jerks in my mouth. His thigh quivers under my palm, and when he's done and he lets go, I peer at him from my place on the floor. "Did you like?"

"Jesus Christ," he growls. "I want to know where you learned how to do that. On second thought, no way. I'm not going to think about that lucky son of a bitch right now. Yes, I liked it. Thank you." He urges me to my feet with a hand to my shoulder and covers my mouth with his.

Breaking the kiss, I say, "You don't have to worry about tonight, and if you get to a place where you need everyone to leave, let me know. I'll play the bad guy, okay?"

"You know what I need even before I do. Do you want me to return the favor?" he asks, zipping up his pants and going for the button of my shorts.

Even though I'm wet and reciprocation would be appreciated, I say, "No. We don't have time for that. I wanted to change, and the delivery people from the deli will be here soon. Would a dress be too much?"

"Change if you want, but what you have on is fine. We're going to be mostly sitting on the beach, and I'm staying in this. When Brock and Eddie get here, I'll ask them to help me set up a bonfire. We'll have everyone within a two mile radius outside in no time."

"Are you going to be okay with that?"

"With you here, I'll be just fine." His eyes twinkle, and he's fighting a smile. The blowjob I gave him worked its magic. I want him to enjoy tonight.

"Okay." I pause, not knowing how to ask, but I need to

know so I can act accordingly. "We're close, Sheppard, and I don't know if you want people to know."

He crowds me against the bed, and when I can't go any farther, I fall backward onto the mattress. He follows, lying on top of me, trapping my hands above my head.

He's furious, and his eyes snap. "You are mine, and I want everyone to know. I'm going to hug you, kiss you, and touch you whenever the fuck I want, and I don't care what people say. If you don't agree with that, you better tell me *right fucking now.*"

His chest heaves against mine, and he sounds so angry I would suggest he do anything but shove our relationship out there for everyone to see.

I'm stupid because I'm reading into his words again, but his sincerity sweeps me away. I struggle until he releases his hold on my hands, and with a sob, I wrap my arms around him and cry into his neck.

He holds me, murmuring into my ear until the doorbell rings.

Brock and Eddie arrive together just as the deli people leave, and the charcuterie board covers every inch of Sheppard's table. I didn't get to clean up the other rooms, and I didn't have time to change. My denim shorts and pink blouse will have to do, and I carry a grey hoodie downstairs. The evenings tend to cool down; the breeze off the ocean dropping to a temperature that leaves even me shivering.

"Olivia," Brock says, pulling me in for a surprising hug.

Eddie follows suit, his grip tight, smacking a kiss onto my cheek.

"Hands off," Sheppard says, tugging me against his chest and wrapping his arms around me.

Brock and Eddie are shrewd, their eyes narrowing at Sheppard's embrace.

My heart skitters. Sheppard may not have cared if his mother didn't like Melody, but I don't think he'd take Eddie's and Brock's opinions that lightly if they chose to dislike me.

Eddie grins and laughs. "Is that how it is?"

Sheppard nods sharply, his chin brushing the top of my head. "That's how it is."

Brock chuckles. "We thought maybe you two had something after seeing that photo online, but we didn't want to assume anything. We're happy for you."

Sheppard relaxes. "Thanks. Will you help me haul wood to the beach for the fire?"

"Yeah, sure," Brock says, and with a wink, he and Eddie follow Sheppard out the sliding glass doors, Scout running after them.

While they're outside, I fold throw blankets and do a few odds and ends I didn't get to, and I'm making a pot of coffee for anyone who doesn't want sparkling water or booze when, without knocking, Dalton steps into the kitchen. He startles me, and I let out a shaky laugh. "Mr. West," I say out of professional courtesy.

He chuckles. "I think we're on a more informal footing by now, don't you think? Call me Dalton if I can call you Olivia."

"That works. Eddie, Brock, and Sheppard are outside setting up the fire." I pause. "Can I talk to you a minute while we're alone?"

He sits at the breakfast bar, and though it's seven-thirty in the evening, I pour him a cup of coffee. "Sure. You and Shep, huh? That picture floating around oozes sexual chemistry. I'm happy he can move on after his divorce, though when I hired you, I never would have suspected this to happen."

"I didn't either." I stand opposite him and twist my fingers together. "Because of the way our relationship's evolved, I wouldn't feel right accepting payment after the summer's over."

He nods thoughtfully and lifts the mug to his mouth. "You're turning down a very lucrative salary for these three months."

"I know, but things are complicated enough as it is, and I don't want him to ever accuse me of staying here for the money."

"I don't think Shep would feel that way."

"Maybe not, but I wanted it off the table, regardless. He's more than a client to me, and I would never charge someone I lo—I would never charge someone I care about for my help."

Dalton sets the mug down, and it clinks against the marble counter. My impression of him remains the same: a kind and sensitive gentleman who's concerned about his best friend. He's handsome, if not a little worn around the edges like the others. Derrick's death affected everyone, and worrying about Sheppard and the fate of the band has rubbed him raw.

"So, then what? The contract is void?" he asks. "Do you want something new drawn up, though at this point, I don't know what it would entail. Are you two a couple? Dating? Engaged, perhaps?" He lifts an eyebrow.

"We haven't labeled it. I promised him I would stay through the summer. You have my absolute word on that, and if you want me to sign something, I will. Nothing else has changed but the payment. Even if you sent me a check, I wouldn't cash it." I will never accept money for helping Sheppard. I love him too much to be paid, and I love him too much not to follow through with what I've promised him I would do.

"Through the summer," he echoes. "You still plan to go back to Minnesota."

"I don't see why I would need to stay. Sheppard called his mom today, and every day that goes by, he's stronger than the day before. He'll be ready to give you what you want by the time September comes around, maybe sooner, and I don't have to see the evidence to know he won't have room for me when that happens."

Dalton frowns and thrums his fingers against the marble. "Have you spoken with him about his plans for the band?"

I pour my own mug of coffee, reluctant to go into details that are none of my business. Sheppard wants to put Derrick's death behind him before deciding what to do with Ghost Town, but that's for Sheppard to share with his friends, not me. "Not really. I don't press him to open up, and there are a few things he needs to work out first."

"Then I don't think you should assume what he will or will not have time for. If he wants you in his life, he'll make time. Over the past few years, Shep may have felt like a prisoner on a runaway train, but it slammed into a brick wall going two hundred miles an hour. He's not the same person he was last year."

I bite the inside of my cheek to keep from crying. Isn't that the whole point of me being here? To help him find the person he was before Derrick's death? I put on a brave face, lift my chin, and change the subject. "While you have a minute, can you skim my blogpost? After that photo came out, there have been so many rumors. I needed to defend myself and what I have going on with Sheppard, but I didn't want to step on any toes or break our NDA. Sheppard said I can write what I need to write, but I would feel better if you took a look before I pushed it out into the world."

"I appreciate that. Thank you."

I round the breakfast bar and head toward the den to retrieve my laptop.

Dalton's gaze bores into my back, but he doesn't stop me to say anything else.

Sheppard finds me with Dalton going over my post. He agrees with most, pointing out two or three sentences I could reword. I do and save it. I'm not ready to hit Publish yet. I want to be alone with Sheppard with his arms around me. My life will change when that goes live, and I'm not ready for that tonight.

His arms circle me from behind, and Dalton's eyes crinkle in amusement. "I had no idea what I was starting."

Sheppard buries his face in my hair. When he comes up for air, he says, "I'll never be able to repay you." The gratitude in his voice is apparent, and I stare at the floor.

Dalton clears his throat. "That's not necessary. We've never kept score. Are the guys outside? It's been a while since we've had a fire. I'm looking forward to it."

"Yeah. They unloaded coolers out of Eddie's truck, and they have beer, if you want something stronger than coffee. They brought their guitars, and we'll do a little jam session later."

"Good deal." Dalton lets himself out onto the patio, the bonfire's flame flickering through the glass.

"Liv," Sheppard says, his arms still around me.

"Yeah?"

"Kiss me."

I twist and reach onto my toes. I do all the work as he stands motionless, and I press my lips to his, holding his face between my hands, my palms tingling against his scruff. I nudge him with the tip of my tongue, and he opens his mouth. Finally, he hugs me to him and takes over, ravaging me in that way he does so well.

He releases me and says, "Are you okay?"

I press my fingers to my lips and look anywhere but him. "Yeah. Why?"

"I don't know. Did Dalt say anything to you?"

I meet his gaze and shake my head. "No."

Searching my face, he says, "I don't believe you."

I hold my features steady. I know how to lie like the best of them. "Why would he say anything? He's happy for us."

Sheppard nods, not entirely convinced, but he doesn't need to know what Dalton said confirmed my worst fears: that Sheppard and I only have the summer.

"Can you do something for me tonight, Liv?" he asks, brushing the bangs out of my eyes.

"Whatever you need. You know that."

"Can you not go too far? This will be the first time I play with the guys without Derrick and I—" His voice cracks. With all the progress he's made since I've been here, sometimes I forget he's still struggling.

"I'll stay glued to your side all night. You won't even be able to go to the bathroom without me."

He smiles like I hoped he would, but his eyes are wet. "Thanks."

"You're welcome. Let's go outside. I want to meet more of your neighbors, and I need to check on Scout. She might be thirsty or want to come in. She gets overstimulated by too many people."

"Like me," Sheppard says, leading me toward the door.

"If you need an out, let me know. I have no problem telling everyone you're done."

"We'll see how it goes."

Like Sheppard said would happen, the area in front of his house is crowded, people drawn to the fire like moths. They wave and shout hello, excited to see Sheppard in a social setting after Derrick's death, some unfolding canvas chairs, some dragging coolers heavy with their own drinks. Brock and Eddie are sitting in the sand with Dalton by the fire, sipping on bottles of beer, and I'm relieved Scout is okay lying near Eddie, his hand resting on the top of her head. I smile at him and mouth, "Thank you." He nods in acknowledgement.

Sheppard introduces me to everyone, but names go in one ear and out the other. The amount of accumulated wealth on this little stretch of beach is staggering, and the number of CEOs, music producers, movie directors, and the random model thrown in blows my mind. Sheppard takes it all in stride, inviting people into the house for snacks and fizzy water if they want something to eat or drink. Several do, and the board will be picked over quickly.

With his arm around my waist, we move from group to group, and he relaxes, catching up with people he hasn't seen for the past year. They're friendly, I'll give them that. Not a snotty person in the group, and they talk to me like I'm one of them. A few people know who I am, and they did before news came out I was helping Sheppard. A makeup artist who works on movie sets tells me she bought my book and asks me to sign it for her. I agree, but she'll have to find me and ask again because I have no idea who she is or where she lives.

Sheppard grows quiet, and when he stops participating in conversation, I tug on his hand. "Will you sit with me by the fire?" I ask, raising my voice. I want other people to understand it's me asking, not Sheppard hiding at his own party.

"That sounds good."

We sit off to the side away from the group but still a part of it. He cradles my body between his legs and I sit sideways, hooking the back of my knees over one of his thighs. His body heat is welcome—I don't have my hoodie with me. Holding me like a baby, he covers my mouth with his, pressing a hand to my neck, his thumb grazing my jaw. He wasn't kidding when he said he would touch me however he wanted without caring what anyone thought. The deep French kiss that's stealing the air from my lungs won't be mistaken for anything less than possession.

Either Eddie or Brock catcalls to us, and Sheppard breaks the kiss, chuckling, his warm breath whispering over my skin. He holds me tightly as people gravitate toward us, wanting to be in his space. Even simply sitting by the fire, he exudes a charm and charisma people can't ignore. Jeffrey and Gina sit across from us, and she briefly meets my eyes over the flames licking at the firewood. He looks angry and she looks tired, and I wish I could help them but I can't. They want different things, and I don't blame Gina for her impatience. She's lived how Jeffrey has wanted for a long time, and if he doesn't want to give her what she needs to be happy, there's no point in staying together.

Time drifts, and Sheppard and I sit while conversation hums around the fire.

After a while, Eddie shuffles through the sand and plops down next to us. "You wanna play in a bit?" he asks, and several people look our way in anticipation. That's what they came here for. They were hoping to hear the guys sing.

Sheppard stiffens, but he drags in a deep breath. "Sure. My guitar's inside."

I rise to my knees and wrap my arms around him. "I'll go get it," I mumble into his ear. "I should bring Scout into the house and I have to go to the bathroom. Will you be okay?"

He twists his fingers in my hair and lightly brushes a kiss over my cheek. What he says breaks my heart. "Yeah, I'll be fine."

I don't want him dependent on me, but it hurts and it shouldn't. That he's okay with his friends means I'm doing my job. He's healing and one day he can live without me. I force a smile and lean away. "Okay."

He grabs my hand and kisses my palm.

Scout knows where I'm headed and eagerly bounds to her feet. Tired and hungry, she follows me up the stairs and across the patio full of people. I haven't been to a party in a long time, and more people in the kitchen set my nerves on edge. Sheppard opened his house, and it'll be a while before it will be empty again. Scout tries to have a quick bite, but one man she's not sure of kneels to pet her, ruining her dinner. She glances at me, and I gesture for her to follow me. No one has gone upstairs, thank goodness, and my bedroom is empty and quiet. Scout hops onto the bed and settles into the comforter. I use more than my allotted time to enjoy the quiet, rubbing between her eyes hoping to soothe. I don't leave until she's sleeping, and I shut the door behind me, hoping people respect our boundaries, stay out, and leave her be.

Sheppard closed the wall to his secret living room, and I sneak in unnoticed and grab his guitar that's leaning against the couch. I don't know how to handle it; I've never held one before, and I don't want to damage it in any way. I hold it away from my body and try not to hit anything with it. He's had this guitar for forty years and while I'm disappointed he didn't come inside with me, I'm honored he trusted me with such an important task.

I snag my hoodie on the way through the kitchen, and people perk up when they see me carrying Sheppard's guitar. Everyone wants to hear Sheppard, Brock, and Eddie play, and they follow me onto the sand. Brock and Eddie are strumming their own guitars they must have unloaded from Eddie's truck, and Sheppard's sweating, waiting for his own instrument. They look good sitting together in their jeans and t-shirts, tattoos and messy hair, their faces covered in scruff. Dalton sits off to the side, watching, a bottle of beer dangling from his fingers, proud and pleased. He shoots me a thumbs up that Sheppard doesn't see, and I tilt my head. I can't take the credit for all of this. Some. It's Sheppard's strength that made the most difference. I can only work with what's already there. He wanted to change his life, and that's what made his progress possible.

A woman I don't know waves me over to sit next to her. I don't want to snub her and since she's close to Gina and Jeffrey, reluctantly, I do. Sheppard doesn't notice, strumming his guitar, familiarizing himself with notes and chords foreign but not forgotten.

They mumble among themselves, deciding on which song to start with, and a moment later, this stretch of beach is transported into a dreamy world of broken hearts and longing. They play seamlessly, harmonizing in only a way singers can when they aren't accompanied by anything but acoustic guitars, each other's voices, and years of friendship.

Sheppard's body quavers in the flame's heat, but the bonfire isn't why I'm sweating. I'm watching a momentous event, a piece of history—Ghost Town back together after a horrible tragedy. After tonight, Dalton will talk to Sheppard, pressure him to record another album. Sheppard and the rest of the band are ready, and Dalton won't want to waste any more time.

"They sound amazing," the woman next to me murmurs, and I don't disagree. Sheppard may not have played, may not have sung, for the past year, but it did nothing but rest his voice and refill his creative well. Rich and strong, the lyrics flow from his mouth, Eddie and Brock filling in with their own lush vocals.

The songs blend effortlessly into one another, years of material at their disposal, and they play for over an hour without stopping.

As the last chord fades over the sand, Jeffrey shouts, "What the hell is wrong with you?"

Gina jumps to her feet, tears already streaking her cheeks. "Nothing. Nothing you care about."

Jeffrey stands too, his bare feet sinking into the sand. "Don't run away from me. We're having this out right now." With his hands to her shoulders, he shakes her, and one man says a threatening, "Hey," that Jeffrey ignores.

"You're hurting me," Gina cries, but I know it's not his hands on her she's referring to.

Jeffrey knows it too and doesn't release her. "Tell me what to do."

Everyone sitting around the fire is still, even Sheppard doesn't move, his hands frozen on his guitar strings.

She staggers in the sand, swiping at her face. "All I ever wanted was for you to love me."

He steps toward her, but she backs away. "I do, Jesus Christ, you know I do."

Gina shakes her head, her kinky waves blowing in the breeze. "Then why does it feel like I'm waiting for you to find someone else?"

"This is about getting married." His tone is flat, and his body stiffens.

The fire crackles, and there isn't a sound from the group.

Lifting her chin in defiance, she says, "You will, one day."

He approaches her cautiously, and when she doesn't move, he holds her face between his hands. "I will love only you until the day I die. What can I do, Gina? Do you want to get married that badly? We'll get married."

Her tears glimmer in the bonfire's glow. She searches his eyes for a moment before launching herself against his chest, crying into his shoulder. He holds her and rubs her back, not paying us one bit of attention as she sobs.

They might have gotten things out into the open, but they didn't resolve anything. She didn't want him to propose to her like that, forced to get married against his will. She wanted him to want her, need her so desperately he would do anything to keep her, and all she'll feel like she did was issue an ultimatum that will shove even more distance between them.

That's one thing I'll learn from Jeffrey and Gina. I need to weigh my relationship with Sheppard very carefully and listen to all my intuition in the coming weeks. Because it will be very important to my heart to leave before Sheppard tells me to go.

Chapter Twenty-Two

Sheppard

"Well, that was something," Eddie says and chuckles uneasily.

I search for Liv, and she's still sitting in the sand, her eyes on Jeff and Gina as they walk toward their house. I want to get up and shake her just as roughly as Jeff did to Gina when he was begging her to talk to him. Liv knows I need her, yet she left me to play alone. When I fucking needed her most, she sat across the bonfire from me, and it doesn't matter I could see her, *fucking see her,* she's still too far away. I clench my jaw, finding control. I know why she did it. She knew I could handle singing without her beside me, and I did.

Brock studies me out of the corner of his eyes. "Are you okay?"

"Yeah, yeah. I needed the break anyway. I'm going to bring this inside and grab a bite to eat. You?" I ask, standing and brushing sand off my jeans. I catch Liv's gaze over the fire and jerk my head toward the house letting her know my intentions. She smiles, a bit tired, sad for Gina, maybe, and nods.

"I'm good. Eddie and I will store our guitars and hang out for a little longer if that's cool."

"Sure. I'll be back out in a minute. Liv made coffee, if there's any left."

"Perfect," he says. "I could use a caffeine fix later."

Dalt follows me up the stairs, and when I reach the patio, lights flicker on in Jeff and Gina's house. She paces the living room, her arms wrapped around herself, and Jeff glares, hands on his hips. They didn't resolve anything tonight, and I won't be surprised if Gina leaves him. After this, I don't know how Jeff could prove to her he wants to get married because he loves her. I feel sorry for him; he waited too long to fix things, and now he can't. Gina won't accept less.

"Women, huh?" Dalt says, stepping through the glass doors and into the kitchen.

"It works both ways," I say, defending Gina. Jeff should have cut her loose a long time ago if he didn't want to give her what she needed to feel secure in their relationship.

"Yeah, it does, if you know what they want," Dalt says, pulling a dripping bottle of Clearly Canadian from a decorative metal washtub full of melting ice.

The charcuterie board is half empty, and Dalt stands over it, finally choosing an olive and popping it into his mouth.

"It's your fault if you don't. Come to the back with me. I want to ask you something."

He thinks nothing of it, only tucks the bottle under his arm and fills a small appetizer plate with crackers, meat, cheese, and more olives. He follows me into the den, and I set my guitar on top of the piano.

"You sounded good," he says, milling around a room he hasn't been invited to for the past year. "You could hear it, though, the missing parts."

"Yeah, I know." I'm not ready to talk about that with him. I need to mull it over, bounce some ideas off Liv first, ask her what she thinks. I know she'll say to do whatever will make me the most comfortable, but that's choosing the lesser of the two evils because there is nothing about this that *will* be comfortable. "Can I ask you a question?"

"Shoot," Dalt says, studying a picture sitting on the mantle over the electric fireplace of the five of us.

"I've been digging around the night Derrick died, trying to get a handle on where everyone was. I talked to a couple of people a few days ago, and one of the stagehands said he saw you with lipstick on your neck. Are you seeing someone? *Were* you seeing someone?"

He jerks a shoulder and shoves a cracker with a piece of cheese on top of it into his mouth. He chews thoughtfully and swallows before he says, "I was in an empty office with a girl who worked the concessions. She was snooping around, hoping for an autograph. She didn't know who I was, but I talked her out of her panties quick enough. I've tried not to think about it because while I was fucking around, Derrick needed me. I knew he started drinking the second he walked off the stage, and I should have kept an eye on him. You will never know how sorry I am, Shep, that I let him climb the scaffolding that night." He sags and drops his plate and bottle of water onto the coffee table. He sinks onto the couch that Liv and I have turned into our sanctuary and pushes his thumbs into his eyes.

"We all share that blame, not just you. The constant recording and the touring has taken its toll on everyone, and if you're that lonely you resorted to a quick lay in an empty office with a stranger, you should have said something. If we'd slowed down, maybe Clarissa wouldn't have been so unhappy. Maybe Brock's and Eddie's kids wouldn't be strangers. Maybe Melody and I would have . . ."

"Would have what?" Dalt asks, an edge to his voice.

"I don't know, and I don't want to think of it because we did and I met Liv. I would never, ever, change that."

He relaxes and pokes at his plate. "You really love her."

"Since the day I met her, I think, but it's fucked up right now. Why she's here in the first place, why she would stay. I'm a client, but I need her to see I'm more than that."

"If you're sleeping with her, she probably does see that." He huffs in amusement.

"I don't think so."

"Have you told her any of this?"

"Not really. I don't want to scare her off. I'm twisted up, too. I need her, but I don't want to need her that way. Why she's here, but I do. Does that make any fucking sense?"

"Yeah. It does."

"You're always good for it. Got any advice?" I perch on the couch's armrest. I'll need to find Liv soon and check up on her. I don't want Jeff and Gina's fight to have shaken her.

"I think the best thing you could do for yourself is when the summer's over, let her go home."

"What the—" I explode, furious. I will never let Liv leave, unless she says she doesn't love me and wants to go back to Minnesota.

"Look," he says over me. "You just said you don't want to need her for the exact reason she's here. If that's the case, let her go home, and you both fucking breathe. Get a handle on how you would live without her, and let her do the same. If you're more than a client, she'll need less than twenty-four hours in Minnesota to see that. Her job here will be done, but her feelings for you won't be. Live without her for a few days. How will you feel waking up alone? Will you be steady, will she have taught you what you need to know to live without diving into a bottle or trying to drown yourself? If you can, why she's here now will be a moot point. Then you can tell her you love her, and she'll believe it comes from a place of security, not anxiety and self-doubt." He winces. "I'm sorry, I didn't mean to bring up your depression. That's a whole different thing."

I sigh. It's not, though, and something I forgot about. She might not want to try with another man who has depression, and if she doesn't, I have to respect that. I've been feeling okay, and my first appointment with Royce is in a couple of days. If I can just figure out what happened to Derrick and if I can't, at least *know* I can't so I can put it away, that will help, but that doesn't mean Liv wants to risk her heart again. "It's fine, just another fucked up thing I have to deal with."

"You okay with that? You haven't been drinking."

"Can't."

Dalt shoots me a puzzled look. "What do you mean?"

I tilt my head toward the bar, and he walks to the cabinet and opens one of the doors. He pulls out a bottle of scotch. "Did you drink it all?"

"No. Liv emptied it."

He laughs. "All of it?"

"Yeah. The one in the living room, too."

"Does she know she poured thousands of dollars of booze down the drain?"

"When it comes to me, I don't think she cares." And I'm a lucky son of a bitch to be able to say it.

"She probably doesn't. She's a pro. If you really want my advice," he says, closing the cabinet, "go slow. It's not even July yet. Enjoy her, let her help you. You still have plenty of decisions to make, and they're decisions you shouldn't make in a hurry. Talk to Eddie and Brock, find out what they think. We have enough money. It used to be a motivator, but it's not anymore. Honestly, Shep, I don't care what you decide for the band as long as you promise we'll always be friends. That's what started Ghost Town, and that's what will end it."

For the past three weeks, it's been one emotional landslide after another, and I choke up. I hold out my hand and he clasps it, turning our handshake into a hug. "Yeah. I can do that."

"I'm happy for you. I really am. It doesn't matter how you met Olivia. When it comes right down to it, you can't control love. Remember that, will you?" he asks urgently, gripping my hand too tightly.

"Yeah, sure," I say, but I don't know what he's talking about.

"Let's go outside. I want to sit with the guys for a bit and then I need to head home. I haven't been sleeping well and I want to hit the sack early."

"That sounds good to me," I say, walking out of the den with him and carefully closing the wall to keep unwanted guests from the room.

"Yeah, except I'm going to bed alone," Dalt says with a twist to his mouth.

"I can help with that," teases a woman who lives a few houses down. We all know she's happily married to a movie producer who just released the biggest blockbuster of the summer.

"That's one nice thing," I say, eager to find Liv. "I haven't slept this well in a long time."

"Yep, rub it in," Dalt mutters.

Eddie and a couple of my neighbors are sipping beer by the bonfire, and I scan the beach for Liv. I don't see her among the people still mingling and drinking, replaying the videos they filmed of us singing, and my heart starts to beat heavily against my ribs. I want her to like it here, Christ, you have no idea how much I want her to like it here, and I picture her curled into a miserable ball in her bedroom waiting for everyone to leave.

Sweat slicks my skin, and I bound up the stairs. I knock on the door before I push it open, but her room is empty, her cell laying on top of the comforter. I try to calm down. Her clothes are here, and she wouldn't go anywhere without her phone. Now I'm worried where she could be and I trot down the stairs, double check the den, and rush into the kitchen. "Have you seen Liv?" I ask Brock who's measuring grounds into the coffeemaker to brew a fresh pot.

"Yeah, actually, she brought Scout outside to the driveway. She said it would be quieter out there."

My throat tightens. "For her or the dog?"

"Maybe both? People have been talking Olivia's ear off all night. You'd think she's the superstar around here—after this party, my ego might be a little bruised up. I think she needed a break. It's okay, Shep."

No, it's not, and I hurry through the garage and burst through the door. Only two vehicles are in the driveway—Eddie's truck and Dalt's convertible. I don't see Liv, and I have to swallow the ball of unexplained and out of control anxiety that is going to turn into a major panic attack any second.

I see her behind Jeff and Gina's house, Scout sniffing along a flowerbed Gina planted years ago that borders their driveway. I clear the few hundred feet in seconds, and she barely has time to turn toward me before I lift her into my arms, crushing her, my hand shaking so terribly the only thing that stops it is grabbing a fistful of her hair and hanging on. She wraps her arms around me without a word, and a sob escapes my throat as I press my face into her neck.

I hold her captive for a long time, her feet dangling above the ground, Scout waiting patiently for me to release her mistress. Liv gives me all the time in the world, not saying a word, not wiggling to be put down. She lets me have what I need, always, and when I set her to her feet, I'm calmer and a little embarrassed.

She rests her cheek against my chest. "What happened? Was it the singing? You looked like you were doing okay."

"It wasn't that. I couldn't find you and I thought you got tired of m—this."

She tips her head up at me, and her eyes sparkle with humor in the light shining from above Jeff and Gina's garage. It's late, the sun setting a while ago, but the sky is still dusky with pink and purple. "You remember what I do, right? I'm fine, but I think you've reached your limit."

"Liv . . ." I want to try to explain what happened, what was going through my head. Fuck Dalt for suggesting Liv go home in the fall for even twenty-four hours.

"Sheppard, I will always be here when you need me. Scout had to pee, and the beach is too crowded. Everyone wanted to pet her, and she got overwhelmed. She's fine. I'm fine. Kiss me."

Her definition of need and mine are very different, but I accept it for now and cover her lips with mine. A hum vibrates from the back of her throat, and it reminds me we haven't made love since this morning because of how busy we've been. I'm instantly hard and press her hand to my cock. I nudge her mouth open with my tongue and devour her, cupping one of her breasts in my hand. Need is only a shadow of an emotion compared to how desperately I want Liv.

She rubs my cock through my jeans, and if she does it a minute longer, I'm going to have to change my briefs. Reluctantly, I tear my mouth from hers, and she sucks in air.

"We better get back to the party, and I'll let everyone know it's time to wrap it up. Let's not push, okay? Please?" she asks, and she has a point. Anyone would say I did well for my first time out since Derrick's death, and I should call it a night before the evening goes south.

"Okay." I link our fingers and walk her back to the house, Scout at our heels. I open the door for us, and the second she's inside, she races up the stairs to Liv's room.

The kitchen's empty except for a tipsy woman I don't know

who stumbles out of the bathroom and fumbles with the glass door, giggling, before letting herself outside. I look to Liv, worried all over again, but she only smiles in amusement and pours a mug of the coffee Brock started earlier.

Carrying the mug with her, we join the crowd on the sand, and in low tones, I ask Brock and Eddie to start circulating the word we're going to pack it in. Someone suggests moving the party a few houses away, and everyone besides my friends slowly disperse. Liv was right, and with the silence, I relax.

She sits between my legs like before and we watch the fire snap and pop. Brock, Eddie, and Dalt eventually join us after saying their own goodbyes to friends they haven't seen for the past year. I miss Derrick, and his absence is a physical ache. I struggle with the loss, but it's easier holding Liv. She wouldn't like it, and I won't tell her. I can't replace Derrick's friendship with my relationship with her, and I know that, but having her here eases the pain. She and the guys murmur back and forth, and she tells Dalt to prepare for some social media activity in the morning when her blogpost goes live. They talk PR for a bit, what it means for the band she and I are together, what it will mean for her, and I cuddle her to me, grateful she and the guys like each other. Whether we decide to record another album or not, go on another tour or not, they'll always be my friends and in some way, no matter how small, they'll always be a part of my life.

"This was good," Dalt says and guzzles the last of a beer he picked up from somewhere, "and it was needed. Thanks for the invite, but I gotta head back."

Eddie and Brock take the hint, and we kill the fire, filling buckets of water with the hose attached to the house. It doesn't need much as it was already burning down, and it hisses in displeasure.

Olivia busies herself straightening the kitchen while I say

goodbye to the guys in the driveway. Dalt's taillights fade from view, but Brock and Eddie linger. "Are you still looking into Derrick's fall?" Brock asks, kicking at one of the truck's tires, uncomfortable mentioning Derrick when the evening has gone so well.

"Yeah, but I'm not going to find anything. I was hoping for a call back from a stagehand, but he's on the circuit with Viola Young. I doubt he'll have time and probably forgot about me by now. I haven't spoken with the detective on the Chicago PD, either, but what am I going to do the cops can't? I promised Liv I would put it away, and I will." I pause. "We need to talk about the band. Not only what I want, but what you want, too. We'll decide together, yeah?"

Brock sighs, and I know all that sigh encompasses. An end of an era, and the start of a life they're unsure of. They don't have Liv in their corner, a future with a woman they love. Divorced and single, they've been drifting since Derrick's death, the band the only thing anchoring them to the ground. If Ghost Town falls apart, they'll have nothing.

"Yeah. Take it easy," Eddie says, sliding behind the wheel.

"Will do. You do the same," I say as Brock lifts himself into the passenger's seat.

"Yep. Say goodbye to Olivia for us. You struck lucky with her, Shep." Brock slams the door, and Eddie backs into the street. I stand in the driveway until I can't see his truck anymore, and sounds of the party still going strong a few houses away carry in the air. I listen for the siren, and she's faint. I don't expect her to ever disappear; her song is a part of my blood, like Ghost Town. Her lyrics have shaped who I am, but I wouldn't miss her if she completely faded away.

Scout's mowing her way through a bowl of kibble when I step into the house, and Liv's wiping down the sink. She's quick, and the whole kitchen is clean, even the coffeemaker sparkles, waiting for us to put on a pot in the morning. A rush of love and gratitude hit me so hard I almost fall to my knees. This is what I want. Not Liv in the kitchen, per se, but picturing her pregnant with my baby is an image I don't bat away. She wants children as much as I do, and I'll be the one to give them to her.

She looks over her shoulder at me and smiles. "Was it difficult to say goodbye?"

"It's not so bad when you have no reason to think you won't see them again."

Her smile turns into sympathy, but that's not where I want her thoughts. I tug on her hand and lead her up the stairs. I don't say anything and push her toward her room. I leave the door cracked in case Scout decides to sleep with us later.

"What?" she asks, confused. "Are you tired?"

"No." I slide her t-shirt over her head and reveal her satin bra. I know what her lingerie looks like—I watched her dress this morning.

"Is this where your mind is?" she asks as I unbutton her jean shorts.

"Hmmm. I seem to recall offering you some reciprocation earlier. I'm going to cash in."

"*You're* going to?" She lifts one leg and then the other. I toss her shorts aside and rake my gaze up and down her body. She's perfect; there's not one thing about her I would change. "If it's mine, I should decide when I want it."

"That's not how it works." Gripping her ass, I nose her cleft and inhale her sweet scent. I lick at her through the cotton, and she moans, shoving her fingers through my hair, urging me closer. I gladly accept and scrape my teeth over her delicate skin. Even with the cotton layer between us, she reacts to my touch, and my cock stiffens and presses uncomfortably against the zipper of my jeans.

"How does it work?" she mumbles, and Christ, is she sexy.

I can't wait another minute and unhook her bra, letting the straps slide down her arms. The scrap of satin drops to the floor. Slowly, torturously, I tug her panties over her hips and down her slim thighs. She lifts her feet, and they join her shorts in a pile of denim and lace.

"I'll give it to you when I want to give it to you," I say, pressing her backward until she falls onto the bed. Staying on my knees, I push her legs open, and with only the light in the hallway to see by, I lower my head.

"Sheppard," she whispers. "Are you sure?"

I skim her folds and gently push a finger inside her. Her stomach quivers, her greedy muscles clenching around me. She whimpers, and I need all my control not to strip, slide into her, and fuck her until neither of us can see straight. "I'm very sure. Now shh, in two seconds my mouth is going to be too full to talk."

Adding a second finger, I cover her with my mouth, and she cries out, her hips lifting off the bed.

She's so sweet, her clit growing under my tongue. She doesn't need long, and I know her body. I hold my fingers inside her as deeply as I can, bruising her, maybe, and she comes with a sob, her pussy pressed against my mouth. I twist my fingers and lick until she does nothing but lie there, a sweaty mess, shaking.

Tenderly, I pull my fingers from inside her and her breath hitches. As does mine. I never, ever want to hurt her. "I'm sorry," I murmur, yanking my t-shirt over my head.

"For what?" she asks, wiping tears from her eyes.

"Hurting you."

She laughs and lifts her head. "If that's what you think you did, more of that, please."

I chuckle, relieved. "Scoot up," I say, unbuttoning my jeans and releasing my cock. I wish I could go bare, and it's right there to ask if I can. She'd say yes, I know she would, but I always want to do whatever I can to keep her safe and knocking her up on accident isn't it. Reluctantly, I retrieve a condom from the nightstand, and she licks her lips. I offer it to her, and she sits up and rips the package open.

She lowers her head and sucks the tip of my cock. I drag in a breath, torn between letting her keep going and needing to be inside her.

"That's not where I was going with this. You had your fun this morning."

"I don't think you can complain. I swallowed your fun," she says, but she rolls the condom onto my cock.

"And I loved watching you do it." Her fingertips skim my sensitive skin, and my cock jerks under her touch. "I need you now."

She meets my eyes, and her irises shimmer with want, need, love, and fear. I swear to God I have never seen anything more heartbreaking. "I'm all yours."

I cover her body and sink into her, and there's nothing that has ever felt more right. Not when we're standing on stage, thousands of people screaming at us, not when I come up with the perfect lyrics to the perfect music. Not even, God help me, when I looked into Melody's eyes when we said our vows. Nothing, *nothing*, will ever compare to how I feel when I'm as close to Liv as one man can be to a woman. She is my entire life, and this, right here, is what I'll live for now.

I try to hold off for as long as possible, but I only need a couple of seconds to come. She holds me so tightly, I don't know how I'm not crushing her.

There are so many things I could say, the words right there on the tip of my tongue, but I hold off. I try to show her instead, and my kisses are long and unhurried, soft and delicate, but strong, like my love is for her. Nothing will ever break us, and I will always be there to catch her if she falls.

Gently, I pull out of her. "I'm going to clean up. Is there anything you needed to do before we go to bed?"

"Just brush my teeth. Dalton looked at my post and said it's good to go, but I'll do that in the morning. Is that okay?"

"I wouldn't want you to do that without me."

She smiles, but she's tired and still a little sad. "Thanks."

"I'm going to the bathroom. I'll be right back."

"Okay."

She's lying in bed when I'm done, and I crawl in beside her and waste approximately no seconds curling my body around hers. She rolls over and props her head on my chest with her hands. "I'm proud of you. You did a lot of hard things today."

Brushing my hand down her hair, I say, "I'm proud of you, too. Thank you for being with me tonight. I think everyone had a good time."

She rubs her lips over my chest. "Yeah. Brock and Eddie, though. What's going on with them?"

"I don't know. I haven't kept up, and I'll do better. They're both lonely, like I was before I met you. We haven't talked about the band and what we're going to do. I think their lives would be better if we slowed down, stopped completely, even, but what would they do to fill that time?"

"What would *you* do?" Liv asks, always reversing the tables.

I want to ask her what her plans are, if she's thinking she could live here, share my life, but I can't turn all of her into all of me. I need to have plans, a goal, to work toward that doesn't include her because her coaching won't include me.

"I don't know yet. I need something, and I would like Ghost Town to be a part of it, somehow. We're under contract to do another album. Maybe that wouldn't hurt so much now that the worst is over, but that's only delaying the inevitable. We *will* retire, at some point, and I'll still need something to fill my time when we do."

She slides off my chest and rolls onto her side away from me. I upset her, and I don't know what I said. I thought she wanted me to record another album. When I step into that recording studio, she'll have done her job. Another success story she can share on her blog.

"You said you're in good voice, and I heard that for myself tonight," she says to the bedroom door. "You can record and tour for a long time yet."

"Yeah, I guess I could." I spoon her, my hand splayed over her belly. One day I'll feel my son or daughter kicking, and that will mean more to me than any album. "But I don't want to. I want more, and I want it with you."

She rolls over and searches my face. "Really?"

"Liv, where do you think we're heading? What do you think we're doing? You haven't been here a month, and Christ, I know how fast we're going. Stop thinking about the end of the summer before it's here. Can you give me time, please?"

"I'm sorry. I don't want to keep you from doing anything you want to do."

"My only focus right now is you. Anything else is second. Let me show you. Let me show you, baby."

I know it's wrong, but I don't care. I slide into her bareback, and she doesn't say one fucking thing. When I come, I pray, and for the first time in my life, I'll let God decide.

Chapter Twenty-Three

Olivia

I wake to Sheppard kissing my belly, his scruff scraping my skin, and I wonder what he's thinking while his lips graze over exactly where our baby would grow. The summer will be long over before I start to show if what we did created something he'll regret, and he'll never need to know.

My cell chimes on the nightstand, and Scout lifts her head from her place at the foot of the bed. It's easy to pretend Sheppard and I are married, that this is our life, how we would wake every morning, and Gina's text is a welcome distraction. *Are you busy? Can you come over in an hour?*

"It better be an emergency," Sheppard murmurs, his hands roaming over my thighs, nudging my legs apart.

"It's Gina. She's asking me to stop by in a little bit."

"How little is a little bit?"

"An hour."

His lips travel from my belly, across my ribs, and stops at my breast. He flicks my nipple with the tip of his tongue, and it hardens in an instant. "We have time for this, yeah?" he asks, positioning himself between my legs.

I'm wet, and already my hips are lifting in anticipation. "Sheppard, last night—"

He pauses. "I know. It was wrong."

I scrub my fingers through his whiskers. "There are consequences. I don't know what you want."

"Uh-huh. For once, this isn't on me. It's on you. You didn't stop me. What do *you* want?"

I want to tell him I want it all, but you don't tell the hottest rockstar on the planet that you want him, that you want to get married, that you want his babies. Even Melody didn't tell him all of that, and I'm torn. I want to get pregnant, and you don't have to tell me how irresponsible that is. I can raise a baby on my own. I don't need Sheppard or his money. But I have to think very carefully if that's something I want to sign up for. To look into my baby's eyes and see Sheppard every day for the rest of my life and having to explain when he or she is older that Sheppard Carpenter of Ghost Town had a choice between us and music and he chose music.

"Liv?" he asks, kneeling between my legs, waiting for me to decide.

I take the coward's way out. "I want what you want."

He settles on top of me and pushes inside me, his lips fused to mine. "You're all I want."

All I want is to believe that's true.

After Sheppard and I make love that I'm sure I'll go to hell for, I wrap the top sheet around my breasts and send a text to Gina telling her I can be there in forty-five minutes. I hope she's okay. Jeffrey was furious, and after they went inside, everyone could hear his and Gina's angry shouting over the beach.

"Are you going over there?" Sheppard asks, standing in my doorway wearing shorts and a muscle t-shirt. Scout's waiting for him to let her outside and I need to shower and dress. I don't know if this is a casual visit, or if she wants to finish my interviews before she moves out.

I ask her what she wants me to wear and press Send. "Yeah. I want to check on her. Do you mind? Will you be okay?"

"Yeah, it's fine. Jeff didn't say anything about running, and if Gina asked you to stop by, he might be at a meeting or he's pissed and doesn't want to be at the house."

"Are you sure? What are you going to do?"

"I'll go for a run with Scout and shower after. Put some laundry in. I'll clean up what you didn't get to last night. You're not my maid, and I appreciate you cleaning the kitchen, but I'll do the rest of the house. Dalt brought a plate of meat and cheese to the den that he didn't take with him when we were done talking, and I'm sure there's other garbage to throw away. I'll look around the beach, too. After that, you need to get your blog online, and maybe, after that, we'll just hang out. Okay?"

We made a lot of progress yesterday, and sitting around sounds good.

Gina answers me: *Casual is fine. I'm not filming you today.*

"Okay," I say reluctantly.

He kisses my cheek and trots downstairs with an excited Scout on his heels. They're gone by the time I'm done showering and dressing.

Hesitantly, I walk across the sand, unsure of what I'm going to find, but Gina's waiting for me, dressed in khaki shorts and a blue tank top, and miraculously, a smile on her lips.

"Come in! Thanks for meeting me on such short notice. I

didn't interrupt anything, did I?" she asks, gesturing me into the kitchen. There's coffee, and I gratefully accept her offer.

I twist my lips. "He was still able to fit it in." My cheeks darken. "That's not what I meant."

Gina laughs. "You look great together, and Shep's a different man around you. You're so good for him, Olivia."

As she usually does, Gina has pastries set out with the coffee carafe, but this time, along with breakfast, there's a notebook sitting next to her plate. I sit across from her. "But what about you? We were all worried about you two."

Her eyes twinkle. Something good must have happened last night. "Everyone thought they heard Jeff yelling at me because he was angry, but he's always had that reaction when deep down, he's scared. He was afraid I was cheating on him and getting ready to leave him."

"You were, though. Not the cheating part, but you were going to move out."

"I was, and he knew it. He wasn't angry I wanted to get married, he was scared of losing me. A long time ago, we talked about getting married, and he said he'd prefer it if we didn't. I always thought it was because he was waiting for something better to come along, but last night he explained he didn't want to ruin what we had. I'll be right back." She darts off her chair and hurries down the hallway. She comes back a few seconds later with a small box in her hands. She flips the lid and sets it on the table near my mug.

Picking up the velvet box, I say, "This is gorgeous. Did he propose?" The large diamond sits on a platinum band. It would look perfect on Gina's finger.

"Not . . . really. He saved the receipt. Look at the date." She pushes a worn strip of paper at me. The ink is faded, and I need a moment to locate the date and time at the bottom.

"2015?" I ask, surprised. Eight years ago. He bought it a year after they met.

"He said he was going to ask, but things were perfect and he didn't want to risk it. We both grew up in LA, both come from Hollywood families. We've seen marriages fall apart over and over again, and he was trying to avoid the same fate."

"What are you going to do? We heard him tell you he would marry you if that's what you wanted."

She tucks the receipt inside the box and closes the lid. "He did, and you probably know I would never accept a proposal like that. Coercion isn't the best way to begin a marriage."

"No, it's not," I murmur.

"We talk a lot about compromise. Give and take. Not just women in marriage, but women in any kind of relationship. We tend to give more than we take because we're raised to be nurturers and to make sacrifices even if who we're sacrificing for doesn't need it or doesn't appreciate it. It would be easy to say that in our relationship I've done my share, but Jeff and I talked until late. He truly feels what we have will suffer if we get married, and knowing that, I'm happy how we are. I didn't know that's how he felt, and I didn't know he bought this ring. That he was thinking about it when we met is enough."

"I'm happy for you. When I heard you fighting last night, I didn't know what would happen."

She blows out a sigh and stares at her notebook. "If he wouldn't have had this tucked away in his sock drawer, I'm not sure what I would have done. I was convinced I was only a placeholder until something better came along. No amount of groveling on his part would have changed my mind. Actions are so powerful, and his saved our relationship. Not to mention, he hasn't loved on me like that in a long time. I'm sore in places I haven't been in years." She laughs and pours herself a cup of coffee. "We'll be okay now. How about you and Sheppard?"

"What about us? He's talking about the band and recording another album. He's on track."

"And you think that track is a dead end for your relationship."

She doesn't turn it into a question because she knows that's how I feel. "Of course it is. He won't have time for me once he starts writing songs and recording. They'll do another tour, and it will start back up again." I sound like a broken record, pardon the pun, or a song's chorus. He won't have time for me, he won't have time for me, he won't have time for me.

"He might have the same fears about you. What are you going to do, Olivia?"

"I don't know what you mean. How can you compare what I do with Sheppard's stardom? With how popular Ghost Town is?"

Gina's eyes widen. "Jeff said you guys were too busy kissing to check into the real world and he wasn't kidding. Do you *know* what's happening online? Have you checked your *phone?* Your interview with Oprah is viewed thousands of times a day. Your book is number one in self-help on all the bookseller's websites right now, and in several places, the print edition is out of stock. Everyone is writing about you, and if you haven't put up your blogpost or issued some kind of press release, you need to do that *now*. Oprah isn't going to call you to guest on one of her talk shows . . . she's going to ask you to host your own on her network."

"What?" I whisper. "My book is five years old."

"Nobody cares. Do you have an agent? I'm surprised she's not ordering you to open your laptop and write another one ASAP. Your publisher would offer you hundreds of thousands in an advance. Olivia, you need to wake up and crawl out of Shep's bed."

I rest my forehead on my arm. "Oh, God." I'm not praying, either.

"That's why I asked you over. You're staying in LA, aren't you?"

Rubbing my belly, I say, "I don't know. Sheppard and I don't talk about things like that. I have obligations and family in Minnesota."

"And a career, I imagine, but what you have going on now is bigger than what you had. I'm sure Sheppard's taking his time because you met only a few weeks ago, but a couple doesn't need long to know if it's going to work or not. The moment I met Jeff, I knew he was it for me, and I bet if you asked Sheppard, he would say he feels the same about you."

"He hasn't started recording yet."

"And you haven't delved into what your self-help career could be like if you embraced everything helping Shep is going to give you." She pauses. "What if I wanted you to work with me?"

I sip my coffee to wet my mouth. I didn't think taking Sheppard on as a client would kick me out of retirement, and I didn't consider how fast my own star would rise or if I wanted it to. "Doing what?"

"Doing what you're doing, but on a bigger scale. You missed the lunch I had with the other women—"

"I'm sorry. I've been focused on Sheppard."

"I know, and I'm not asking you to apologize, but the point is, there are thousands of women out there who need a helping hand—guidance after something traumatizing happens to them. Rape, assault, domestic violence, loss of a loved one, anything can derail you at any moment, like what happened with you and Michael's death. What if we started an organization that helped women get back onto their feet? Counseling, job assistance. But I don't want to simply be an employment agency, I want to do what you're doing—focus on making positive adjustments in someone's life. Changing mindset. Reaching goals. Classes, not educational ones like what you'd find at a university, but on how to grow emotionally, spiritually, if that's something you're comfortable with," she says, nodding at my necklace. "Women's empowerment. I know you had several male clients, and I don't want to discount what men need, but it's not a secret that women lack support. You can write another book, a series, perhaps, and I want to start a podcast. I know that can't compete with having your own talk show, and I may have sounded glib before, but Sheppard isn't simply opening a door, he's blowing it off its hinges. You can have whatever you want."

"What if that's Sheppard?" I ask, but there's no hope in my voice.

"With the way he had his hands all over you last night, you already have him, but you need to talk. He'll be busy if they record another album—people have careers and you can't get away from that. Michael was busy teaching and grading papers, perhaps writing for literary journals and magazines. Maybe he was writing the next bestselling thriller. Why are you turning what Sheppard does into something more than it is? I admit, if you two pushed it all the way, yeah, he'd never have time for you, but you wouldn't have time for him, either. Hosting your own talk show is no joke. You'd live on set. Your relationship doesn't only depend on what Sheppard wants, it depends on what you want, too. Shep's already had his fifteen minutes, and he's tired. But you haven't. Do you think he wants to be the one to ask you to give up those things?"

"That's why you were talking about compromise."

"Yeah. Because I want that compromise to be working with me."

I bite my lip. "Starting an organization like that would take a lot of work."

"Maybe, maybe not. You already have a foundation of what we'd need. You must have developed a basic program and adapted it to your individual clients. I have networking for fundraising in place, and Clarissa used to manage a bar. She did all their books, marketing, and human resources. She had a baby a few months ago, and she's not working right now. She has time to help us."

"Clarissa?" The name is familiar, but I can't place it.

"Derrick's wife. She didn't find out she was pregnant until the band had been on the road for several weeks. Mason's ten months old now."

"That's sad. Sheppard didn't say anything."

"No one knows. She was barely showing when they had Derrick's funeral, and she's been keeping to herself." She pours more coffee into our mugs.

"Then how do you know?"

"I ran into her at Whole Foods in Brentwood. She tried to dodge me—Mason was having a meltdown—but I'm not so easily dissuaded."

"She'll want to work with us? I'm assuming our organization will be a nonprofit. Can she afford to work for free?"

Gina shoots me an incredulous look. Of course Clarissa can. Derrick was a multi-millionaire when he died. I cover my face with my hands.

"It won't be unpaid forever. After a while, we'll look for sponsors for the podcast, and most of the courses we'll offer will have a small fee. We can charge for webinars, and you'll have another book. You have savings, don't you? And Shep will support you while we get this off the ground. Trust me, there's no money in indie documentaries. I pay myself a small wage for being a director, but Jeff pays all our bills."

My eyes flit around her house. "You're doing so terribly, too."

She laughs. "Will you at least think about it?"

I wilt. This sounds impossible. "Gina . . ."

"Olivia, he doesn't have to say it for it to be true."

"It's presumptuous." Presumptuous to think that maybe, maybe, Sheppard is in love with me.

She tips her head. "Fair. I have no idea what he's thinking. But, I do know how popular you are, and how popular you will be once Shep and the guys record another album. Shep's honest and he'll give you all the credit. This will be nothing compared to what will happen once he does that, and I wanted to toss my hat into the ring before you decided anything."

"Okay. I'll keep it in mind on the off chance Oprah calls. You've been thinking about this . . . what would we have to do first?"

She brightens and flips the notebook open. "We'd need office space . . ."

Chapter Twenty-Four

Sheppard

I could very much get used to this. Have fantastic morning sex then shoo Olivia out the door to a job down the street while I . . .

The run alone gives me time to think. I need to talk to Liv about the band. She's going to publish her blogpost when she comes back from Gina's, and while we're in that frame of mind, I'll ask her what she thinks. I miss making music, and I've shirked on plenty of promises and responsibilities. I don't want Ghost Town to end with a broken contract. It wouldn't feel right, a bad omen to start off my life with Liv. We'd meet in the middle. Record here at the house and tell Dalt a US tour only. Fifteen to twenty cities to say goodbye. Liv and I will get married, and if she can carve out some time, I'd like to have a baby. I don't know how she'd feel about that when her comeback would be front and center, but I'm hoping we can work something out. We might have already done something, in which case, we're getting married the minute that second line turns pink.

I shower, missing Liv and her lavender body wash. I use her bathroom, just so I can hold her loofah to my nose. Yeah, I got it bad. Scout naps on my bed while I dress, and she swaps the bed for the couch while I clean up the living room. There's an errant empty bottle of beer hiding here and there that Liv didn't find last night, and Dalt's plate is still sitting where he left it in the den on the coffee table. I clean up all that, run the vacuum, and backtrack upstairs and strip the bed Liv and I have been sharing and start a load of sheets.

I don't know when Liv will be back from Gina's and I'm sharing cheese and crackers with Scout when she slides the glass door open and steps into the kitchen. I scan her face, searching for anything wrong. She always comes back a little worse for wear, Gina shoving her through the wringer talking about Michael, but she looks steady, gorgeous, in fact, wearing a dark green blouse and denim shorts. She must have packed bottomless suitcases. I haven't seen her repeat an outfit once.

"How's Gina?" I ask as she retrieves one of the leftover bottles of sparkling water out of the fridge.

"Good." She leans against the breakfast bar and snags one of my crackers. While she nibbles, she explains Jeff purchased Gina a ring years ago that should have gone with a proposal but never came, and while I like Jeff and respect him, I think it's bullshit after all these years he never asked Gina to marry him. If Gina's happy, I can't take umbrage on her behalf, but when I buy Liv a ring, she's going to fucking wear it. "Things are blowing up online. Agatha and Tammy must be keeping a lot of it from me because I haven't heard anything except what Gina told me earlier."

"Is it bad?" I ask, offering her another cracker.

"Actually, no. My book sales are taking off again and my interview on YouTube is still getting thousands of hits. Gina seems to think someone is going to reach out about doing my own talk show."

"You'll be Dr. Phil yet," I force myself to tease, but it's anything but funny. She won't want me, won't want a baby, if her career explodes, and I push back a panic attack.

"Yeah, well, be careful what you wish for and all that," she says. "But I need to publish that post now. Will you sit with me?"

"You don't have to ask me something like that. I'll always be here for you, you know that, right?" I ask, linking our fingers near the cracker and cheese plate on the counter.

"Sure," she whispers, but she's not looking at me, or our hands, she's staring at the floor, clearly not believing me.

I lead her into the den, and pulling her into my lap, we settle on the couch. Her laptop is sitting on the coffee table, and she drags it onto her thighs. She lifts the lid, and the backend of her website is still there, the post Dalt looked over waiting to be sent out into the world. With a shaking hand, she uses the touchpad and clicks Publish. It's not that simple, and her website asks if she wants to publish now or schedule for later and she clicks Now. It congratulates her for posting success-fully and reroutes to a stats page where already in just that five seconds between publishing and the refresh ten people have viewed her blogpost.

She slams the lid shut and all but throws her laptop onto the coffee table. She presses her face against my chest, and I wrap my arms tightly around her. This is all going to hell in a handbasket. I can feel it, I can taste it, and the siren's grip is back, stronger than it ever was before, around my ankle.

With a finger under her chin, I ask Liv to look at me, and her bluish-green eyes sheen with tears. "I'm scared, Liv," I say, putting it all out there. It's time to tell her how I feel, how I don't want to live without her. The timing isn't right, but I can't wait any longer.

Lightly, she brushes her fingers over my cheek. "Of what?"

"Living without you. I need you. I know you hate hearing it, but I need you with me, always. Stay here, even after the summer. We'll figure it out."

"What are you going to do with Ghost Town?"

This is where it gets sticky, and I have to force the words out. "We'll do another album. It's not right to break a contract. Then a short farewell tour to end it. That's it. The tour wouldn't be for a while—a touring company will book venues a couple years out, and we'll need that long to write and record the songs and do promo for the album anyway. Then I'll be done."

"What about Derrick?" she whispers.

I rub her leg. "I've done all I can. It's time to put it away."

"Sheppard—"

I can feel her slipping through my fingers, and I try desperately to hold on. "You can write your book, and I'll write lyrics. The talk show thing—if that happens, there's no better place to live than in California, right? Drew Barrymore, Kelly Clarkson, Dr. Phil—" I try to smile around a ball of anxiety "—they all film right here in LA. It's perfect."

"Yeah, it's perfect," she says, a slight smile full of sadness on her mouth.

I trace her lips, wishing I could give her what she wants, but I don't know what that is. I should record another album, and Liv didn't tell me that's not what she wanted. I asked her to spend the rest of her life with me, and that wasn't enough. I don't know what is. God, I don't know what is.

"Make love to me, Sheppard," she says, brushing her lips over mine.

I carry her up to bed, the words she didn't say a fading note between us.

One last time.

I wear a condom when I ravage her, and after I clean up, I wrap my body around hers praying to any entity that will listen to give me what I need to keep Liv in my life. She didn't say she was leaving, but I know the next time I have to go anywhere, when I come back, she'll be gone. Maybe she'll wait to tell me goodbye, her professionalism winning over a quick escape, but I won't have her for the rest of the summer, much less the rest of my life.

Liv's still sleeping when I get up, dress, and let Scout outside. My cell phone buzzes in the pocket of my shorts, and an unfamiliar number glows on my screen. Not many people have my cell number, and if they have it, they're meant to. "This is Sheppard," I answer as Scout sniffs around the sand. I sit on a lounger, and she bounds up the stairs and lies on the one next to mine.

"Shep, this is Josh Johnson, ah, JJ. Taylor said you wanted to talk to me."

I blink in surprise. "I didn't think you'd call me back."

He coughs, a smoker's hack. "Christ, you know how it is. Years ago, my grandpa took me to see George Strait. All he did was stand on stage for two and a half hours, play his guitar, and sing. No one does that anymore, you know? Fuck. Fireworks and aerial choreography. It's ridiculous. I got a few minutes. What's up?"

"I wanted to ask you if you saw anything the night Derrick fell. I wasn't at the arena anymore."

JJ quiets, and between Scout's snores and the water, I think maybe the call dropped. I rub her neck, and she rouses long enough to follow me into the house. I quickly walk through the living room and into the den, the faithful dog never far behind.

Liv's laptop sits on the coffee table, a sad reminder her future won't include me.

JJ draws in a breath. "Yeah, yeah, I did, and I've been hoping this day wouldn't come."

"What?" I ask, my mouth dry.

"I'd just finished hitting the head. I ate a burger from one of the concessions, and it didn't sit well with me. I was gone longer than I should have and was hurrying back before Hicks kicked my ass for wasting time. I took a wrong turn, and I heard shouting from one of the back offices. It sounded like Dalton, and I wanted to see if he needed help. A drunk fan, a pissed off groupie, something. The door was wide open. Dalton was standing there, his pants around his knees, and Melody was with him. Derrick had walked in on them. He was drunk and pissed, screaming he was going to tell you that Melody was a cheating bitch. I'm sorry, Shep."

I sit down hard on the piano bench, and Scout whines, a paw to my leg. I was right after all. Melody *had* been cheating on me, but it was with the last person I ever expected. No wonder she wanted to go on tour with us. She didn't want Dalt on the road without her. "What makes you think Dalt had anything to do with Derrick's death?"

He hacks, the sound muffled. "I don't. You asked if I saw anything that night, and that's what I saw. Derrick threatened to tell you. Did you know?"

"No. I had suspicions she was cheating, but I never would have guessed with who."

"If Dalton was afraid Derrick was going to tell you . . ." JJ lets the implication hang in the air. It's not such a farfetched idea, but I can't leap from them arguing to murder.

"Did you tell the police when they questioned everyone?"

"No—they didn't get to me. I had to run back to the bathroom, and I was in the men's locker room all night. I ended up going to a twenty-four hour walk-in clinic. There was no way I would have lasted ten seconds on a bus. I had food poisoning. To tell you the truth, man, I was glad. I didn't want to be the one to say anything. Could be no one would have believed me anyway. My word against Dalton's, and I like this job."

"I got that. Are you sure that's what they were doing?"

"Yeah. Sorry, man. I must have rounded the corner just a second after Derrick pushed the door open. Melody was sitting on a desk . . . her skirt was up around her waist. I already told you what Dalton looked like. He didn't deny it, just said he didn't want you to know."

I pause. "You know I can't keep this to myself."

"Figured. I'd appreciate you putting in a good word for me, though. Derrick was a good guy. I didn't mean to hurt anyone."

"No harm in looking after yourself, and I don't blame you. I'll do what I can. Thanks for your help."

"Yep."

The line disconnects, JJ probably thinking his job's on the chopping block. I'm not an attorney, don't know if JJ could be in trouble for keeping this from the cops. If it comes to that, I'll pay if he needs to lawyer up, but for now there's only one thing I can do. Confront Dalt. I'll know if he's lying. The man plays a mean hand of poker, but even he won't be able to hide the truth if he killed one of our best friends.

Liv's still lying in bed, and I sit on the edge of the mattress and smooth the hair away from her face. "Hey, I need to run an errand. Will you be okay?"

She knows me so well, and she sits up, gripping my arm. "What's wrong?"

"The stagehand I was waiting for called me back. He said he saw something, and I need to talk to Dalt."

Her shoulders sag. "Sheppard."

"We don't know the whole story yet."

"What can I do?"

"Be here when I get back."

She opens her mouth in denial but presses her lips closed. She might know me, but I know her, too. "Okay."

"Thank you." I kiss her forehead and lurch wearily off the bed. I motion for Scout to stay with Liv, and with a heavy heart, drive to Dalt's. I trust Olivia. She'll be there when I'm done talking to Dalt, but I don't know for how long. I can't keep her in California. I can't keep her with me, but I would do anything if she didn't go.

Dalton lives in the Hollywood Hills in a house made of glass that overlooks LA. Five bedrooms and seven bathrooms, it's too large for a single man, but it's everything the manager of Ghost Town would be expected to live in. Pool, hot tub, sauna, top of the line kitchen and sound system, it offers every luxury, but it wasn't enough for him to keep his hands off my wife. He looked me in the eye, maybe for years, and never once had the guts to tell me he was sleeping with her.

I punch in the code to his alarm system and let myself into his garage. The car he uses when he doesn't order a limo is parked there; I know he's here. The door connected to the mudroom is unlocked and I close the door quietly behind me. The cloying scent of Melody's perfume hangs in the air. Now I know why I smelled it in Dalt's office the day I tore into him for asking her to be at that meeting. That also makes sense. She would want to know every detail of everything that even remotely concerned her.

I follow Melody's laugh up the stairs and to the master bedroom. I'm familiar with the house—Dalt's lived here a long time. I push the door open, letting in the light from the hallway. He drew the blinds, and in the darkness, they both sit up, surprised to be interrupted. Her eyes meet mine, and in alarm, she covers herself. I catch her baby bump before she hides it under the comforter.

"Don't bother, sweetheart," I drawl, hurting. "I've seen it all before."

Dalt clears his throat. "Shep. What are you doing here? I can explain."

"I hope you can because I have a lot of questions." I leave him to get dressed, and I'm sipping on a bottle of lemon Perrier and spinning the cap on the marble counter when he shuffles into the kitchen wearing jeans and a black button down shirt.

"We didn't want to upset you," he says, his arms crossed against his chest. I bet Liv can read body language a mile away and even I know it's a classic defensive gesture.

I laugh. "You know what? I don't give a fuck if she was cheating on me with you. It explains some things, yeah, but I honestly don't give a shit. As far as I can tell, you deserve each other."

He frowns. "Someone told you I'm sleeping with her. If you don't care, why are you here?"

"Because that someone told me he saw you and Derrick fighting over it. Derrick caught you fucking Melody's brains out in Chicago, and he wanted to tell me. *What did you do?*"

Dalt pales, and his shoulders start shaking. "It was an accident. I swear to God, Shep, it was an accident. We wanted to tell you ourselves. I love her. I love her so much."

That might have softened me some if he hadn't kept it from me, if he'd been man enough to tell me he and Melody had fallen in love and wanted to be together. She could have owned it, asked me for a divorce long before Chicago. Maybe none of this would have happened.

"She's pregnant, and we're getting married. I know it's too much to ask that you be happy for us."

"Are you fucking crazy? I didn't come here for that." I slam the bottle onto the marble countertop, and Dalt jerks. "*What* was an accident? You and Derrick fought, and you followed him up the scaffolding, didn't you?"

He's sweating, and a bead of perspiration drips down his temple. With an agitated swipe, he wipes it from his skin with the back of his hand. "I shouldn't have. I should have waited until he was sober, but he was always drunk. I only wanted to ask him to wait. We were going to tell you ourselves. He would have found you right then, but you'd already gone back to the hotel."

"Jesus. That's why I couldn't find her. Because she was fucking you. Did you push him?"

"No!" Dalt bursts out, and he staggers toward me, his eyes wild. "No. I only wanted to talk some sense into him, and I grabbed his arm. He was smashed. Couldn't walk a straight line if his life depended on it—" He pales. In this instance, Derrick's life *had* depended on it. "He lost his balance. I tried to stop him, but it was all over so quickly. I watched him fall and hit the stage. No one saw me go after him, and no one saw me climb down. I pretended to hear the news like everyone else. I am so sorry, Shep. You don't know how guilty I've felt this past year."

"Is that why you hired Olivia? To make up for what you did?" My stomach curdles. Dalt didn't care about me, didn't care about my mourning Derrick's death. All he cared about was how my grieving affected him and the band.

"Not entirely. I was worried about you. I didn't know Derrick's death triggered your depression. I didn't know how bad off you were until the paparazzi took pictures of you standing in the water, and I didn't want to be the cause of another friend's death. I did the only thing I could. I found someone who could be with you twenty-four/seven to keep an eye on you, and it worked."

I feel like I could throw up. "Does Olivia know why you hired her? Was she in on this?" Nothing about our relationship was real. Her holding me in the water, her letting me sleep with her. "Make love to me, Sheppard" she'd whisper, and I fell for all of it.

"No. She didn't know anything except you needed help. Not the why. She didn't know about Derrick or the part I played in his death. She wouldn't have taken you on as a client if I hadn't begged. Last night, she told me because of how she felt about you she wouldn't let me pay her. She's innocent in all this. If you don't believe anything else, believe that."

It's a small consolation. She might be innocent, but that doesn't mean our relationship is real. Dalt wouldn't have needed to hire her at all if he wasn't a conniving asshole. I fell in love under false pretenses.

"I won't let you get away with this. You *will* pay for what you did to Derrick. It might have been an accident and his autopsy proved he was drunk, but you shouldn't have hidden the truth. Maybe you won't go to prison, but that's not up to me. Lawyer up, and don't ever call me again." To make my point clear, I throw my Perrier bottle against the wall. The bottle doesn't do me the courtesy of shattering, only bounces onto the floor, the remainder of the water fizzing across the tile.

Calmly, I walk out of his house, climb into my car, and drive away.

I stop at the first bar I see, a swanky nightclub that's just opening for the day. I'm the only one in the place, black leather and neon pink tracking. The stage is empty, and while it's not our type of club, it reminds me of the days when we would sing at the bars and summer street fairs. Those were simpler times, when Derrick was sober and Dalt kept track of our gigs on a secondhand laptop and accepted a fistful of crumpled bills for payment. When we didn't have assistants and stage-hands and makeup artists. We only had each other, and that was enough.

"What can I get you?" the bartender asks, a trendy guy wearing a black dress shirt and hot pink tie, a crisp black vest buttoned over his flat stomach. He pays his rent with tips the women give him along with their phone numbers, but his wedding ring glints a rose gold in the pink light, his wife a cock-tail waitress hoping to strike it rich on the silver screen.

"Whiskey, neat."

"Gotcha."

He sets the lowball on a napkin stamped with the club's logo, and I circle my fingertip over the rim of the glass. Liv's disappointed face flickers in the amber liquid, but how can I trust what's real? Dalt killed Derrick because Derrick caught him fucking my wife and he threatened to tell me. Were the three weeks Olivia spent with me all lies? The day she cried when she told me about Michael, that day was real, and I know it's true because of the nasty things people said about her online. The first time we made love. That was real. The way she cried while I held her, buried so deep inside her I never wanted to let her go. That was real. But the rest? All the talk-ing, and her pretending to care. I was only a job, and now that I know the truth about Derrick, her job is done.

"Gonna drink that?" the bartender asks, drying a clean glass.

It would be easy to down it, order another, and another. Walk out of here shitfaced.

Derrick's memory deserves more.

And maybe, after all this time, I do, too.

I nod at his wedding ring. "How do you know?"

He rubs his ring between his fingers and scoffs. "If you have to ask, she ain't it."

I pull a twenty out of my wallet and place it next to my glass. "Thanks."

After sitting in the dark, the sunlight is blinding, and I slide behind the wheel wanting to see Liv with a desperation unmatched by anything I have ever felt before, and a reluctance so great, I want to rush back into the bar and guzzle a whole bottle of whatever I can get my hands on.

The drive is excruciating, but I will never forget the pain that pierced through me when I stepped into the house. Her suitcases are packed and waiting, and she's staring out the glass door wearing the same dress she wore the day I met her. She turns around when I throw my keys onto the breakfast bar, tears running down her cheeks.

"Dalton called. He told me to hope for the best but be prepared for the worst. I already know what the worst is, so you don't have to explain."

"Did he tell you all of it?"

She nods and rubs her palms over her dress. "Yeah, I mean, I think so. I'm sorry about Derrick. Dalton's going to turn himself in. He said you think I was a part of it, and I'm sorry you believe that, but it saves me, you know, from having to do it."

I frown. "Do what?"

"Break it off. I'm going home. From the second I started having feelings for you, I knew it wouldn't work. I'm a little hick girl from Minnesota. Why would I have a chance with the great Sheppard Carpenter? It's better this way, so don't be sorry. You'll be so busy recording and touring, I know you won't have time for me. I ordered a car when I heard you park. It will be here any minute."

I walk around her suitcases and into the kitchen. I open a

cabinet and in a box of tea I never drink, I pull out her ring. "Here. You should have this back."

Her hand trembles so violently she needs more than a few moments to take it from me without dropping it.

She breaks my heart when she slides it onto the ring finger of her left hand. "Thanks. I shouldn't have taken it off. It's what you get for wanting things you can't have." She steps toward her suitcases, her heels clicking against the floor.

"What will you do?" I ask, needing one more minute with her.

"Go back to my little life. Live in my little house in my little town. Start up my coaching again, maybe write another book. I called Gina and told her goodbye. She said we can finish what she needs for her documentary over Zoom, so you don't have to worry about seeing me again." She pauses. "Here, I want you to have this." She yanks her necklace from her throat, breaking the clasp. She presses the cross into the palm of my hand as her cell chimes with a text. "Take care of yourself, Sheppard. I think now that the truth is out, you'll be okay."

I fold my fingers around it, and the points dig into my skin.

Scout whines, torn between staying with me and going with Liv, and when she opens the door, Scout sits, whimpering. She kneels and presses a kiss to her dog's nose. "It's okay, sweetie," she whispers, rubbing Scout's neck. "Look after him for me. I love him very much." She stands, her eyes never leaving the floor, opens the door, and carries her suitcases into the garage. With one last quick wave to Scout, she shuts the door, and a few moments later, through the silence, I hear the car drive away. Scout walks over the hardwood, her nails scratching, and she headbutts me, her soft brown eyes sad, already missing Liv.

I sink to the floor, the necklace Liv gave me falling out of my hand, unnoticed.

To my utter amazement, the siren is quiet, and there's

nothing but the sound of my heart as it cracks into a million pieces only a waif from Minnesota can put back together.

I walk out onto the beach, the ocean blending into the grey sky. Scout sits on the sand far enough away the waves won't touch her. I can't breathe, and the urge to walk into the water and not come out is stronger than it ever was, but I think of Liv and who would feed her dog. Scout saved her life every day. Now that she left Scout here with me, who will do that for her?

I stand frozen, not sure what to do.

"Olivia went home, huh?" Jeff says behind me.

"Yeah."

"Do you have a minute? I want to show you something."

I'm numb, and unable to think for myself, Scout and I follow him across the sand and into the house.

He trots up the stairs and down the hallway to Gina's office, and her video recorder is hooked up to a monitor on her desk. "She was editing bits of Olivia's interview. I want you to listen to it." Jeff closes the curtains and starts the video.

There's my Liv, sitting on the loveseat behind me. She's wearing the dress I peeled off her body the first time we made love.

The interview is sad, like I knew it would be, but I'm nearly knocked onto my knees when Gina asks, ""Do you have survivor's guilt, Olivia? Do you feel guilty he's gone but you're still here?" And Liv answers, "Every day."

Scout whines and lifts a paw when she hears Liv's voice.

Off camera, Gina pauses. "Do you think it should have been you?"

Her face is passive, revealing nothing when she says, "Yes."

"Oh, Liv," I murmur. Maybe I never understood how much

pain Michael caused her. I knew she blamed herself, but to say she wished she'd been the one instead of him . . . How close had she been to doing the same thing her fiancé did? To wish she would never wake up.

Scout saved her life every day and she left her dog with me.

"She'll be okay," I say aloud, praying it will be true.

Jeff doesn't answer, and he lets the interview play out.

"I wasn't enough," Liv whispers, her face pasty white and her eyes flat.

Gina's voice is low and sad. "Olivia, honey, a woman by herself never is."

The screen fades to black, and a ball of fire fills my throat.

"Last night, I stood in the hallway and listened to Gina say those words. You don't know how ashamed I am that for nine years, I taught her that. This morning, I asked her to marry me, and it took me a long time to convince her I was serious. I was scared if I changed the dynamic of our relationship, it would ruin what we had, but all I was doing was telling her she wasn't good enough to marry when I believed the complete opposite. She's too good to lose. Why did you let Olivia go home?"

"I was her job," I say, but that doesn't have the same weight behind it as it once did. "Dalt hired her to ease his own guilt. He and Derrick fought on that scaffolding. That's why he fell."

"And you think the way she felt about you wasn't real? Because of the way you met?"

"Yeah, maybe. No. That the way *I* felt about *her* wasn't real because of the way we met."

"Then you did the right thing. She already had one relationship that wasn't what she thought it was. She can go home, know she did right by you, and pick up the pieces. Maybe she'll meet someone who can convince her that two failed relationships weren't her fault. Maybe. I think she'll always blame herself for not seeing Michael's depression, and you. Well. She wasn't enough for you, right? Who cares how you met? Every couple meets by chance. I met Gina at a fundraiser I didn't want to go to. I could very easily have skipped it. Maybe Dalton did hire Olivia out of guilt, but he also cares about you. He didn't have to hire her. Hell, you lying there drunk off your ass all day would have guaranteed you never would have found out what he did. Olivia sobered you up, and the first thing you did was look into Derrick's death. You think Dalton wouldn't have thought of that? I hope you told her it wasn't her. That you were choosing the band over a relationship with her."

"She knew." *You'll be so busy recording and touring, I know you won't have time for me.*

"So, what's next?" he asks, stepping out of the room.

I follow him, but I want to stay and watch her interview again. I need to see her face.

"I don't know." I can't think beyond where she is right now. Checking her luggage? Walking through security? Is she on the plane waiting for it to taxi down the runway? I'll never see her again because I was her job and I told her we were over.

"Gina's heartbroken, you know. They were going to start up some kind of women's empowerment organization."

I stop in the middle of his living room. "What?"

Jeff chuckles. "Yeah. Gina watched Olivia's career explode online, and when she was here earlier, Gina asked her before all the big offers started rolling in. Olivia accepted—on the condition she would have time to start a family with you. She said all she wanted was to keep her career small and be with you. You did her a favor. Now she can do whatever she wants."

I swallow. That's why she wasn't excited when we talked about filming her own show. She didn't care about that. She was waiting for me to give her what she really wanted—my love. I told her I wanted to keep her forever, but I didn't tell her the words and didn't ask her to marry me. Instead, I gave her

Michael's ring back, and she wasted no time slipping it onto her finger. Resuming her position in a dead man's life she no doubt felt she deserved.

"If you let her go home, she'll never risk coming back here, you know that, don't you?" Jeff asks.

I do know that. If I want to prove I love her, the next time she goes to Minnesota, I'll have to go with her. I want to meet her mom and her sister. I want to see the house where she and Michael lived. I can't give her the kind of life she was going to have in Minnesota, but maybe I can give her something better.

"Do you want a ride to the airport?" he presses.

"Yeah. But we need to make a stop first."

Chapter Twenty-Five

Olivia

I don't cry, and I'm pretty proud of myself for that. Instead, I call Agatha and tell her I'm on the way to the airport and give her my flight information. I ask her to pick me up at the airport and hint that I wouldn't mind staying at her place tonight, and tomorrow night, and the night after that. I'll need a friend.

When Dalton called and told me what he'd done and that Sheppard accused me of knowing about it, I knew Sheppard would dump me. We were already on shaky ground, and a lot of that was my fault. I held myself back because I didn't want to lose too much of myself in a rockstar who would kick me to the curb the second he wanted to record more music, and that's exactly what happened. He needed me until he didn't, and that's what I'd been afraid of all along. It's good; I did my job. I don't want him to be with me because he needs me to stay stable, to keep his depression at a tolerable level, to hold his hand while he writes new music and sings without Derrick. I want him to need me because he can't live without me, and that obviously didn't happen.

It's good.

I already miss Scout, but I knew that was inevitable too, and I'll adopt another dog as soon as I'm home. I'll put my house on the market and find something closer to my mom and sister. If she adopts all those kids, I want to be there to help her. I'll be an aunt, and maybe I can turn that into something just as fulfilling as being a mother. There's no way I'll put myself out there for another man. Twice I gave my heart away, and twice a man broke it in the most unimaginable way possible.

The driver lets me off at the terminal, and he unloads my suitcases from the trunk. After Dalton called me, the first thing I did when he disconnected was book a flight. There wasn't much to go with on such short notice, and I bought one of the last tickets on a flight leaving at 10 PM. It worked out since Sheppard must have stopped somewhere between Dalton's and driving to his beach house, and I wanted to say goodbye. It's just as well. I never would have thought to ask for Michael's ring. I don't know what I'll do with it. It doesn't feel right to wear it, but I don't know who I am without it. I'm more comfortable being the widow of a college professor than I am the discarded girlfriend of a rockstar.

The line to check baggage is long, snaking its way around the gleaming tiled floor. There are no amenities before security like there is in the Minneapolis/St. Paul airport, and I stand in line empty-handed. It would be nice to sip on a cup of coffee, but maybe I shouldn't put anything in my stomach. I'm in shock, and I hope I'm in a safe place at Agatha's when I come out of it. Once I truly realize Sheppard doesn't want me, it's going to hurt, and it's going to hurt bad.

The line moves at a snail's pace, but my travel anxiety doesn't surface. I have more than enough time to check my bags and wait through the security line. I didn't pack a carry-on, but

I won't need anything to keep me occupied. I have three weeks of memories to sort through and put away.

Me and Sheppard Carpenter. What had I been thinking?

I'm nearer to the baggage check-in when a current travels through the air. I try to ignore it. More than likely it's a reality star not famous enough for the VIP terminal. I'm lucky tonight; if anyone knows who I am, they've left me alone. I'm not in the mood to sign books or take selfies or dispense off-the-cuff advice. I'm not in the mood to answer the questions, "Why are you leaving? Aren't you and Sheppard Carpenter a thing?"

Yeah, we were something all right.

I sigh, push back tears, and nudge my suitcases up another half an inch. I just want to go home, wherever that may be.

"Olivia Bloom!"

My name trips down my spine like I imagine Sheppard's fingers trailing over his piano keys, and I freeze. His voice quiets the entire terminal.

I don't turn around or call attention to myself in any way. Maybe he'll give up and leave. I don't want to hear what he has to say. That he doesn't want to keep the necklace I gave him, and I don't know why I did that either, except I wanted him to think about me sometimes, but that was dumb. Maybe he doesn't want to keep Scout, and if that's really true, I should know so I can take her home. I would have to book a different flight—I didn't purchase two seats.

The businessman waiting in front of me frowns. "Isn't that you?"

I stare him down. "No."

He laughs. "My wife made me read your book, by the way." He sticks his fingers into his mouth and blasts the shrillest whistle I have ever heard. "She's over here!"

"And now you're paying me back for it," I mumble, my heart thumping madly against my ribs.

The crowd parts for Sheppard like the Red Sea parted for Moses, and he's here, standing in front of me wearing what I saw him in last—shorts and a muscle t-shirt and holding a huge bouquet of pink roses.

There isn't one person in the entire terminal who isn't staring at us, and you could hear a pin drop when he falls to his knees.

Chapter Twenty-Six

Sheppard

I didn't think I would make it in time. When Jeff asked me what terminal she was flying out of, I had no fucking clue. She didn't tell me when she left, and why would she have? She's not the type to let something like that slip in hopes I would come for her. Nope, Liv's as real as it gets, and when she knew I was telling her we were over, that was it for her and in her mind, we were done.

There's only one person whom I would think Olivia would tell, and that's her friend, Agatha.

I don't know Agatha's last name, but how many literary agents named Agatha are in the Minneapolis/St. Paul area? Turns out, only one, but she doesn't work in her office on a Sunday evening. Finding her home number after grabbing her full name on her literary agency's website is easy enough, and I scramble to connect as Jeff navigates through traffic heading toward LAX.

"Who is this?" she asks instead of a regular hello.

Christ.

"Agatha, this is Sheppard Carpenter. I need to know the flight Liv's on."

She scoffs, and I picture a tornado of a woman ready to tear me to shreds for hurting her friend. "I'm not telling you. You hurt her, and like fuck I'll give you another chance."

"I made a mistake. Did she tell you everything?"

"She told me enough."

"Then you know I had a reason to fuck up, but I'm trying to fix it. I love her, Agatha. Come on."

Jeff flicks me a glance while we pause at a red light. We're getting closer, the buses that carry passengers to and from the car rental places starting to clog the road.

A florist's shop is up ahead, and I point.

Agatha's quiet, debating. She wants what's best for Liv, and she's not sure that's me. I let her think on it, and Jeff double parks in front of the shop.

"I need five seconds." I climb out of his car, Agatha's agitated breathing in my ear.

"Agatha," I say, prompting her. "I need to catch her before she boards."

I'm wearing her down, and I wait. Inside the florist's shop, I gesture to an older woman behind a counter. "I need twenty-four pink long-stemmed roses wrapped up. No vase."

"Sheppard," Agatha says, the last three years of Liv's life in those two syllables.

"I know. She told me."

"If you make me regret this, I will hunt you down in your pretty little beach house, kill you, and dump you off a pier. Do you understand me?"

She sounds younger than me by ten years or so, but I still say, "Yes, ma'am."

"Jesus Christ on a bicycle," she mutters, and I smile. I think I'm going to like this woman. "Terminal six. If she makes it through security before you get there, her gate is 65B. Her flight number is 5791, American Airlines, to Dallas/Fort Worth. She has a two hour layover."

"Thank you. I appreciate it."

"Liv's my best friend, and she hasn't deserved all the shit. The last three years have been a living hell, and if you don't think you can't die of a broken heart, then you never saw her the year after Michael passed away. When she told me you dumped her, I have never been so scared for someone. She's not strong enough, Sheppard. Not after Michael."

The florist lays the bouquet on the counter, and with my cell tucked between my chin and shoulder, I swipe my debit card. I don't wait for a receipt or for her to tell me to have a nice day, or good luck for that matter, and I'll need a lot of it. I shove the card into my wallet, push it into my pocket, and I'm out the door with the bouquet. Jeff's pissing people off, double parked on the narrow street, and I climb in, the cellophane crinkling.

"She doesn't have to be, not anymore. I've got her. Thanks, Agatha." I hang up and tell Jeff, "Terminal six, American Airlines."

Jeff stomps on the gas, cutting off a sedan behind us, and the driver lays on the horn as well as his brakes. The traffic around the airport is thick and it crawls, and a ball of anxiety gathers in my chest. I can't lose her because I was stupid and blinded by what Dalt did to Derrick.

"You'll make it. The lines in the airport are as slow as the traffic out here, and if she by chance happens to get through security, buy a ticket and go after her. Chase her all the way to Minnesota if you have to," Jeff says in an attempt to calm me down.

It doesn't work. Nothing will until Liv is in my arms.

I didn't ask Agatha when her flight leaves, but I don't risk calling her back. I pull my phone out of my pocket and look up her flight number as Jeff lurches through the crush. "Her flight leaves at ten."

"And you know those things are always late. You have plenty of time, Shep."

"I hope so."

Fifteen minutes later, Jeff drops me in front of terminal six's American Airlines desk. "I'll find a place to park. Text me when you two need a ride home."

I jerk my head in a terse nod. "Thanks."

Desperately, I clutch at the bouquet and all the promises the flowers hold with them, and my heart drops when I step into the terminal. It's packed, and the line to check baggage is a mile long. I'll never find Liv in all these people, and that's only if she hasn't checked her suitcases and is in the corridor waiting to go through security.

I do the only thing I can do. I may not be yelling into a microphone, but I'm not an old man yet. "Olivia Bloom!"

The entire terminal quiets, my voice filling the entire space. This may be the one and only time I'll ever appreciate what my stage presence can do. I might not look like a rockstar in my grubby shorts and worn out t-shirt, but I've always known how to hold an audience in my hand, and I do it now, hoping against hope it will earn me more than millions of dollars. Liv's love is priceless.

Everyone knows who she is, and they look around, hoping to spot her. A few seconds later a whistle from the right pierces the air. "She's over here!"

I don't waste any time heading toward the voice, and people scramble out of my way, creating a path that leads straight to her.

Liv stares, her eyes dry, but her face is pinched with pain. She's pale, and her hands shake, the fluorescent lights catching the diamond ring I should never have let her put on her hand. It doesn't belong there anymore.

I drop to my knees on the tile, and a woman standing in line gasps and grapples for her phone. We're on full display, and everything Liv and I say or do now will be recorded forever, splashed on social media for the world to see.

I didn't practice what I would say. She doesn't think she's enough for me, doesn't think that I would make room in my life for her while the band and I record one last album. I can make promises, but at this point, all I can do is hope she trusts me enough not to break them. That's a lot to ask considering I've already broken her heart.

"When we met, I was in bad shape," I start, and she licks her lips. At least she's listening. "I'd lost my wife, my best friend. I'd lost my love of music, didn't care about anything but my next drink to forget about all of it. You know the siren sang to me every day, every second her song seeped into my veins until my blood was nothing but sludge and booze. What Dalt did, calling you, he said it wasn't to ease his guilty conscience, and maybe it wasn't. Maybe he did want to help me, I don't know, and more than likely, I'll never know his true intentions. What you were afraid of, Liv, it happened, and you were right to be scared of it. Why you were with me, what my feelings for you turned into. I was only your client, but since the first time I held you, you were always more to me than a life coach. You were a lifeline, and that scared me too."

"Sheppard—"

"Don't tell me your job is finished, I know it is."

Her eyes fill with tears, but that's not how I meant it and I forge on.

"After I confronted Dalt and he confessed, I drove to the

first bar I saw. I ordered a whiskey, and I wanted with all my heart to down it and order another and another, but I thought of how disappointed you'd be, how disappointed I'd be in myself. I got up and walked away. I don't need you that way anymore. Someone told me it doesn't matter how we met, that I should be grateful we did, and I see the truth in that now."

The crowd is hanging on my every word, phones flash, recording me down on my knees, filming Liv and her reaction to what I'm saying. None of it matters but the energy, that last note hanging in the air, and this is the heartbeat I've been waiting for. The magic, the stardust, the timing I needed, but I just didn't know how to get here.

I shift uncomfortably on the hard floor and grip the bouquet with a sweaty hand. "You said love is a verb, and I'm showing you, right now, how much I do. I know you're scared I need you for the wrong reasons, but Liv, let me love you for the right ones. I'm asking you to marry me, and if you say yes, I'll buy you flowers whenever the fuck I want."

My knees ache like hell, and stiffly, I stand to my feet. Tears run down her cheeks, her eyes glued to the roses. We didn't talk about my depression, how she would cope with loving another man who suffers from it, but I will do whatever it takes to keep it under control.

"What do you say?" The magic is fading, the heartbeat in time I needed gone. She's going to tell me I hurt her too terribly to try again, and I'll deserve it. None of this was her fault, and I blamed her for all of it. "Give this old rockstar another chance to make you happy? I won't mess up this time. I promise."

"Will you tell me again?" she asks, her voice a whisper.

"I love you, Olivia. I'll support whatever you want to do with your career. I'd love for us to have a couple of kids and maybe adopt another dog. I will always have time for you, sweetheart. It doesn't matter if I'm writing music or recording. When we go on tour, we'll space out the dates and explore every city. I've never done that before, and I think it might be fun. What do you think?"

The crowd is growing agitated, wanting her answer, but not as much as I do. The rest of my life depends on this woman standing in front of me.

Finally, she smiles and wipes her cheeks. "Yes, I'll marry you," she says and rushes into my arms.

I hug her to me, and everyone in the terminal claps and cheers. I bury my face in the elegant curve of her neck while I inhale the lavender scent I've grown so much to depend on. Liv is my safe place, and if she's by my side, I'll be able to get through anything. With Dalt and the band, there will be a lot.

After too many minutes but not enough, I set her to the floor and offer her the bouquet.

Tentatively, she reaches for it, understanding the promise behind it. She sniffs at one of the flowers, and when she lifts her head, her eyes are clear. "Thank you."

"Thank you for giving me another chance."

"Since you asked me a question, can I ask you one?"

I brush the bangs out of her eyes. "Yeah."

"Will you kiss me?"

The crowd looks on, some of them filming, some of them too enthralled with the live show to record it, and I wrap my arms around her.

I lower my head, and she drops the flowers onto the floor to pull me closer.

I think every single person claps as I seal my lips over hers, but there will be no encores in the airport. I'm done living in the spotlight.

For the past two years, my life has been nothing but twisted alibis, but those days were done the morning I found Liv in my kitchen. I can't leave the past behind, but the future is steady and full of opportunities and from now on, when the siren sings, I'll sing with her.

Chapter Twenty-Seven

Eddie

I wish to hell Dalt didn't need to tell Shep about Melody.

Now I'm fucked.

I whip my drumstick across the room, and it bounces off the wall with a sharp *crack*. I should be practicing. Shep hasn't laid it all out there, but now that he's happy and settled with Olivia, we'll do another album. It's not like him to break contracts, and Ghost Town won't split up on a bad note, pardon the terrible pun. Shep might decide to do the bare minimum, nine songs instead of twelve, but he's eager to knock Olivia up and I can't say I blame him at all. One of my greatest joys was when I held Abby after she was born, and my biggest regret is letting her slip out of my life.

The evening is empty time, and I sigh.

My phone rings, a welcome distraction, but it's heaven and hell when I see who's calling.

"What is it?" I ask, not wanting to sound like an asshole, but I can't help it.

"He's fussy again, and you're the only one who can calm him down. Will you come over?"

She's exhausted, and I bite back a groan. I want to help, but I'm the last person she should be asking.

"Hire a nanny," I snap.

She sucks in a breath. "Forget it. I'm sorry I called."

Fuck.

"No, I'm sorry. I'm not taking the news very well. I'll be there in ten minutes."

"Thank you."

Her voice is nothing but a whisper, and if my phone wouldn't have beeped indicating she disconnected, I could have imagined she hadn't called at all.

I leave, anticipation and dread twisting my stomach. For hours I'm going to hold a baby that's not mine, in a house that doesn't belong to me, with a woman I can't have.

No matter how much I love her.

That's a lesson Dalt taught us.

You can't want another bandmate's wife.

Even if he's dead.

Eddie and Clarissa's story in *Twisted Lullabies* will be available September, 2023, on Kindle, in Kindle Unlimited, and paperback.

For news, cover reveals, bonus content, and more, sign up for my newsletter at www.vmrheault.com/subscribe. As a thank you, you'll be able to download a free full-length ugly-duckling billionaire novel, *My Biggest Mistake.*

VM Rheault writes billionaire romance and contemporary romance under Vania Rheault.

She lives in Minnesota with two children. When she's not writing, she's working her day job, sleeping, or enjoying the four seasons with a hot cup of coffee in hand.

Find her at vmrheault.com.